VARMINTS

ANDY HIRSCH

Color by Hilary Sycamore

First Second

NEW YORK

For my family,
and in memory of
Ridley

CHAPTER ONE

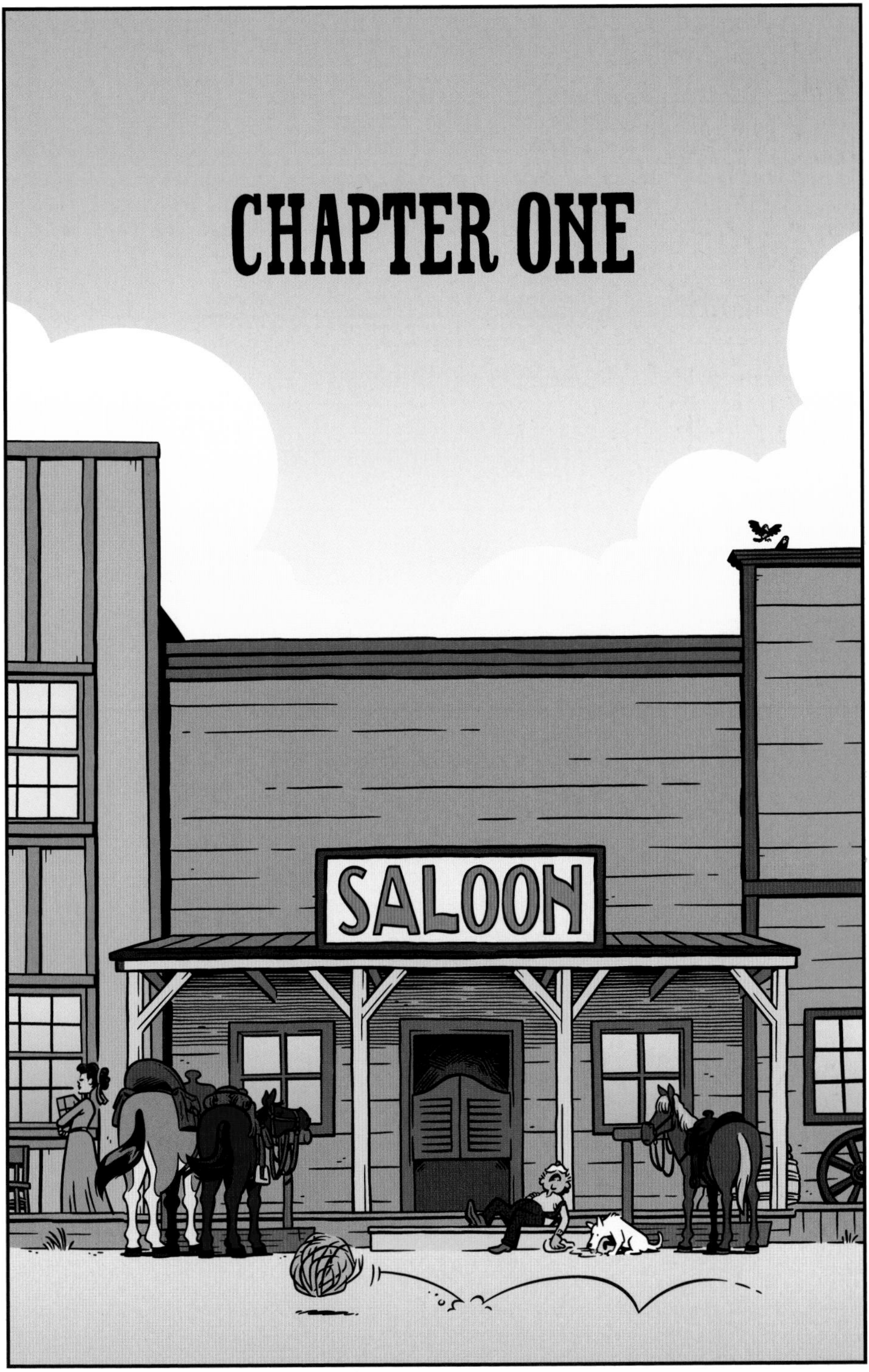
SALOON

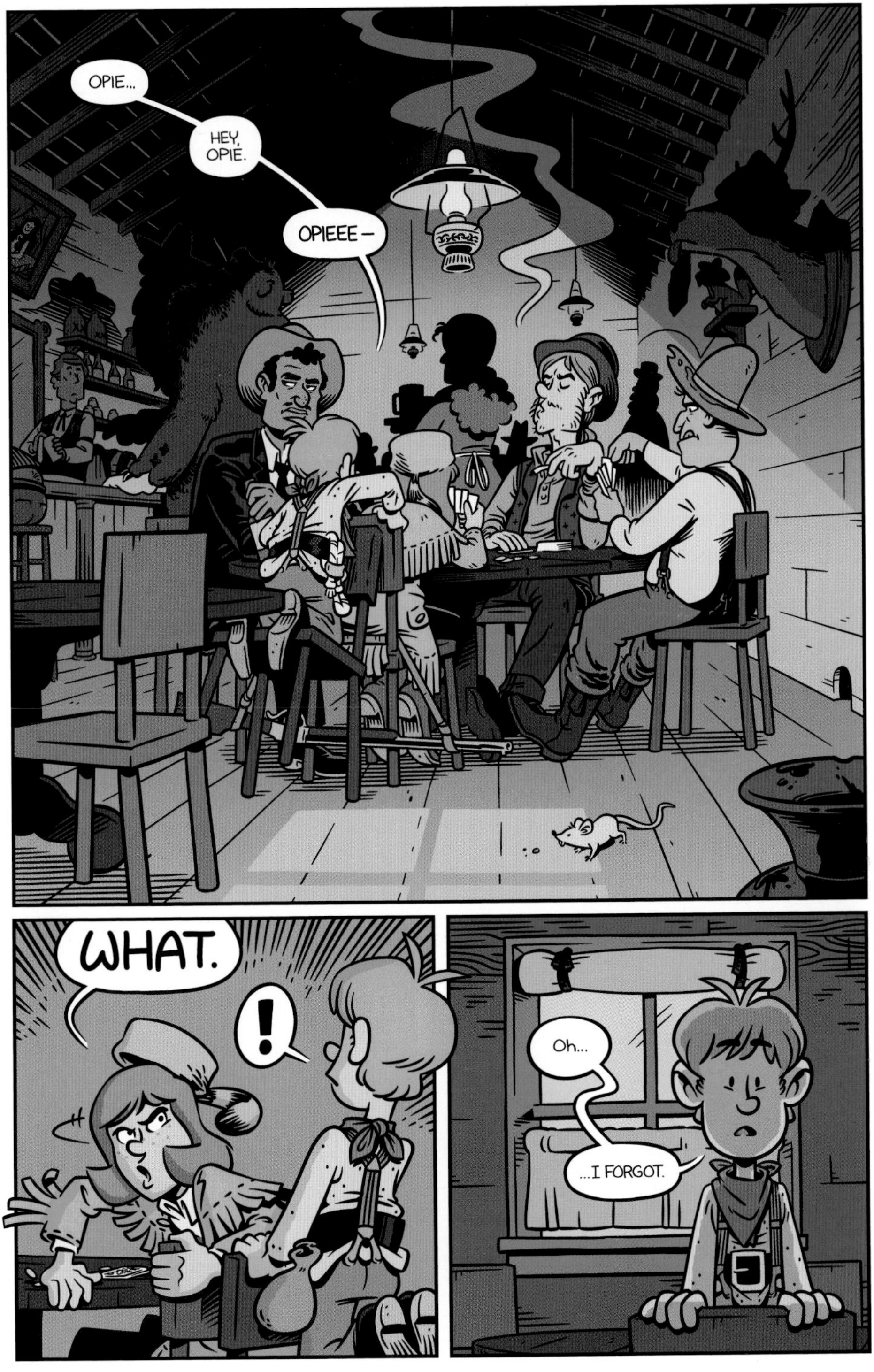
OPIE...
HEY, OPIE.
OPIEEE—
WHAT.
!
Oh...
...I FORGOT.

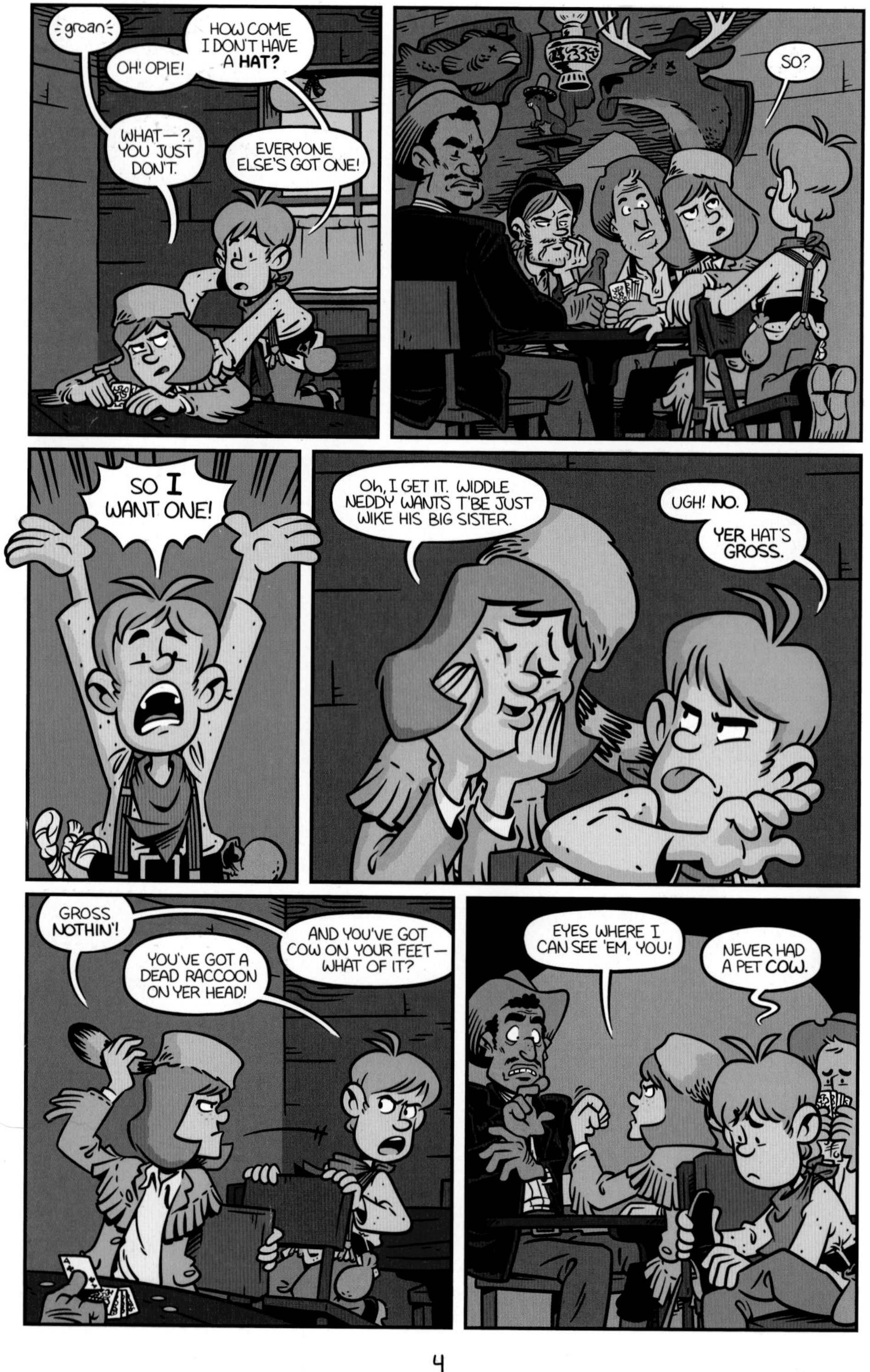

groan
OH! OPIE!
HOW COME I DON'T HAVE A **HAT?**
WHAT—? YOU JUST DON'T.
EVERYONE ELSE'S GOT ONE!
SO?
SO **I** WANT ONE!
Oh, I GET IT. WIDDLE NEDDY WANTS T'BE JUST WIKE HIS BIG SISTER.
UGH! **NO.**
YER HAT'S GROSS.
GROSS **NOTHIN'!**
YOU'VE GOT A DEAD RACCOON ON YER HEAD!
AND YOU'VE GOT COW ON YOUR FEET— WHAT OF IT?
EYES WHERE I CAN SEE 'EM, YOU!
NEVER HAD A PET **COW.**

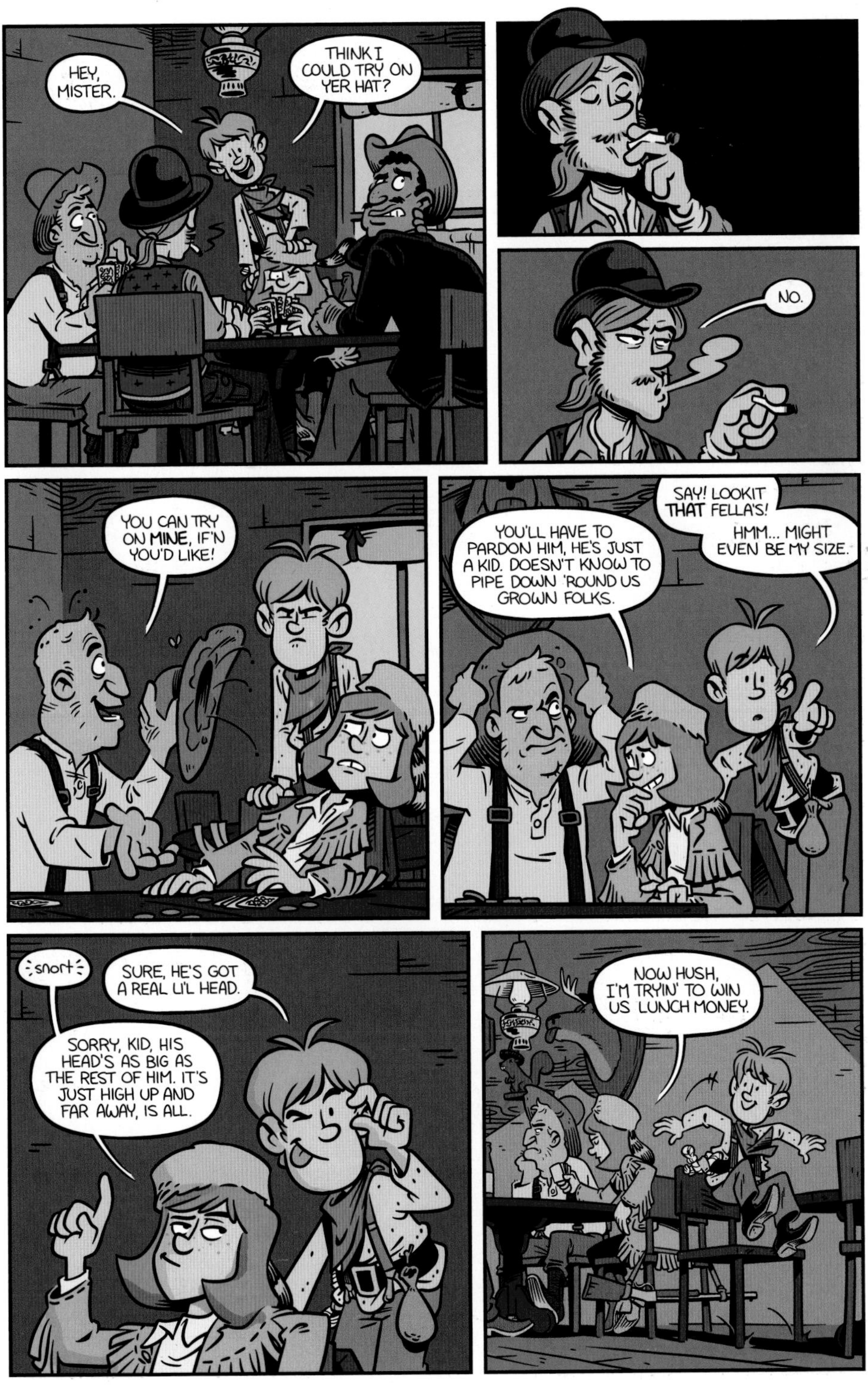
HEY, MISTER.
THINK I COULD TRY ON YER HAT?
NO.
YOU CAN TRY ON MINE, IF'N YOU'D LIKE!
YOU'LL HAVE TO PARDON HIM, HE'S JUST A KID. DOESN'T KNOW TO PIPE DOWN 'ROUND US GROWN FOLKS.
SAY! LOOKIT THAT FELLA'S!
HMM... MIGHT EVEN BE MY SIZE.
snort
SORRY, KID, HIS HEAD'S AS BIG AS THE REST OF HIM. IT'S JUST HIGH UP AND FAR AWAY, IS ALL.
SURE, HE'S GOT A REAL LI'L HEAD.
NOW HUSH, I'M TRYIN' TO WIN US LUNCH MONEY.

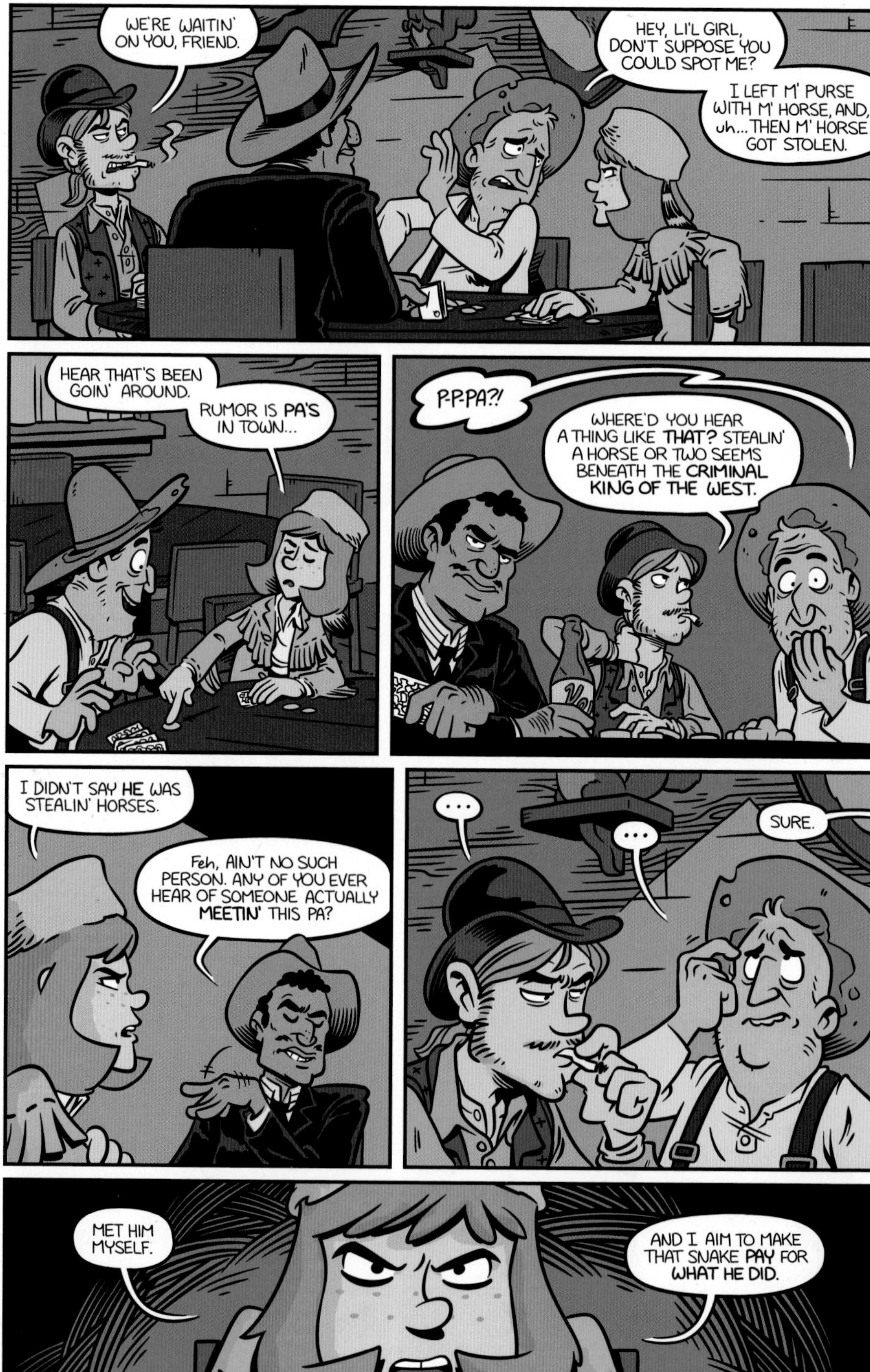
WE'RE WAITIN' ON YOU, FRIEND.
HEY, LI'L GIRL, DON'T SUPPOSE YOU COULD SPOT ME?
I LEFT M' PURSE WITH M' HORSE, AND, uh... THEN M' HORSE GOT STOLEN.
HEAR THAT'S BEEN GOIN' AROUND.
RUMOR IS PA'S IN TOWN...
P-P-PA?!
WHERE'D YOU HEAR A THING LIKE THAT? STEALIN' A HORSE OR TWO SEEMS BENEATH THE CRIMINAL KING OF THE WEST.
I DIDN'T SAY HE WAS STEALIN' HORSES.
Feh, AIN'T NO SUCH PERSON. ANY OF YOU EVER HEAR OF SOMEONE ACTUALLY MEETIN' THIS PA?
...
...
SURE.
MET HIM MYSELF.
AND I AIM TO MAKE THAT SNAKE PAY FOR WHAT HE DID.

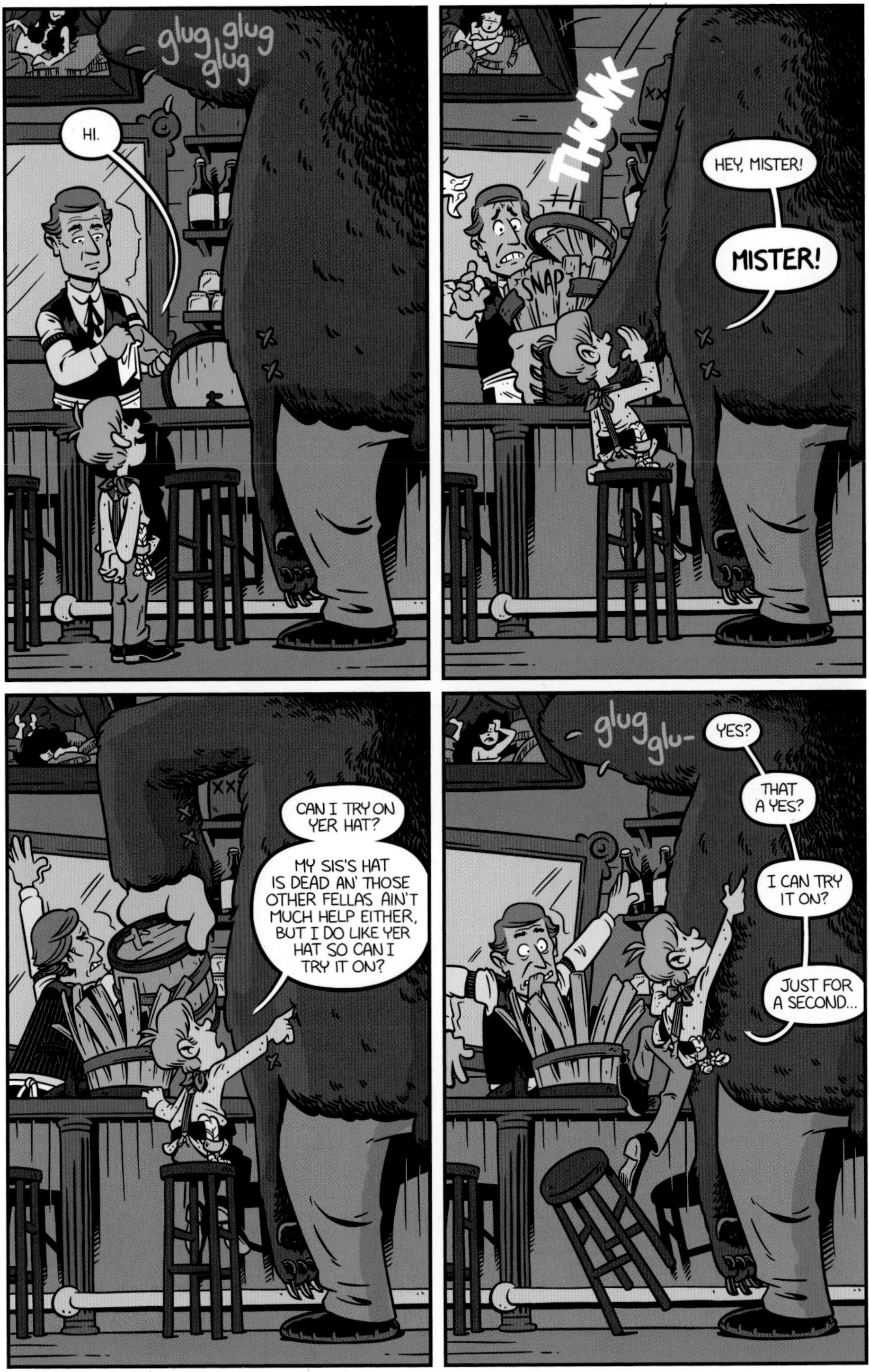
glug glug glug
HI.
THUNK
SNAP
HEY, MISTER!
MISTER!
CAN I TRY ON YER HAT?
MY SIS'S HAT IS DEAD AN' THOSE OTHER FELLAS AIN'T MUCH HELP EITHER, BUT I DO LIKE YER HAT SO CAN I TRY IT ON?
glug glu-
YES?
THAT A YES?
I CAN TRY IT ON?
JUST FOR A SECOND...

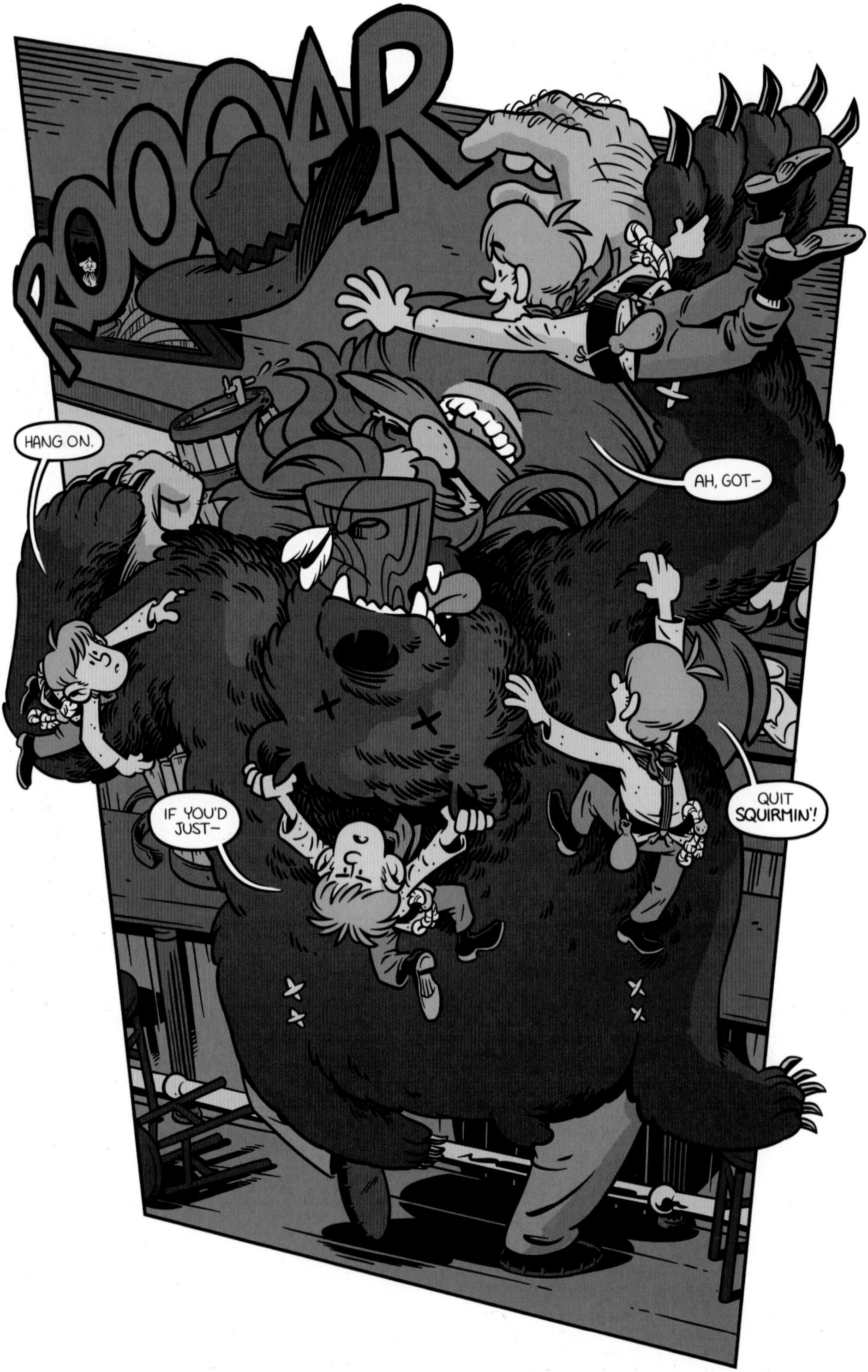
ROOOAR
HANG ON.
AH, GOT-
IF YOU'D JUST-
QUIT SQUIRMIN'!

SWAT!

Oof!

Aw... I'M RUNNIN' OUTTA THESE.

roll roll roll

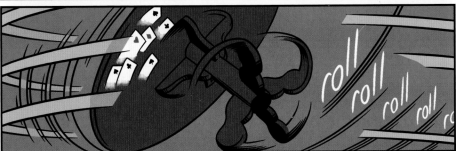

roll roll roll roll

LOTTA ACES STUCK DOWN THERE, BOYS AN' GIRL...

roll roll roll roll

WHAT'RE YOU LOOKIN' AT ME FOR?!

roll roll roll

Keep on rollin'... Keeeep on rollin'...

roll roll

!

NOW WAIT JUST A—

9

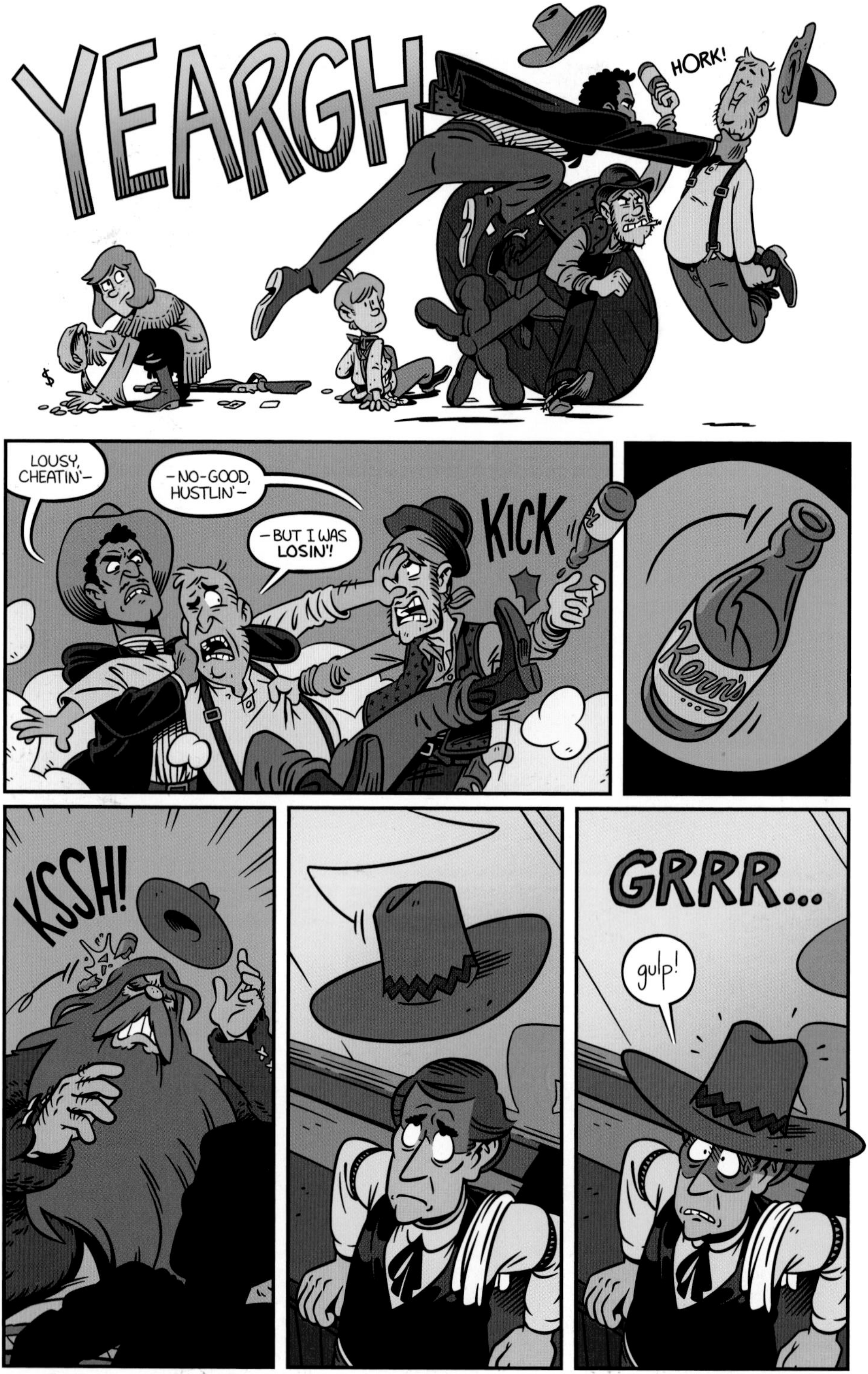
YEARGH
HORK!
LOUSY, CHEATIN'—
—NO-GOOD, HUSTLIN'—
—BUT I WAS LOSIN'!
KICK
Kern's
KSSH!
GRRR...
gulp!

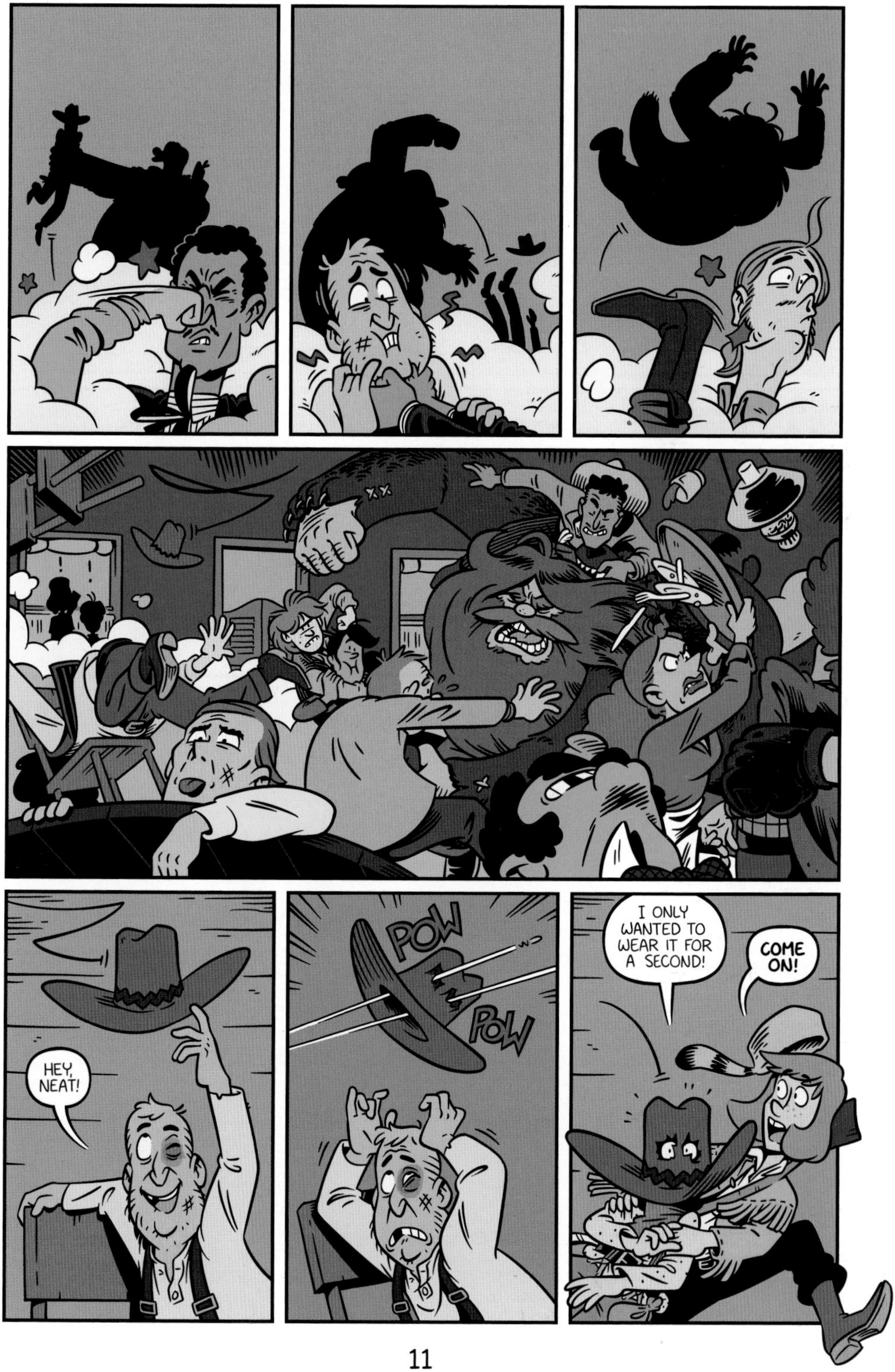
HEY, NEAT!
POW
POW
I ONLY WANTED TO WEAR IT FOR A SECOND!
COME ON!

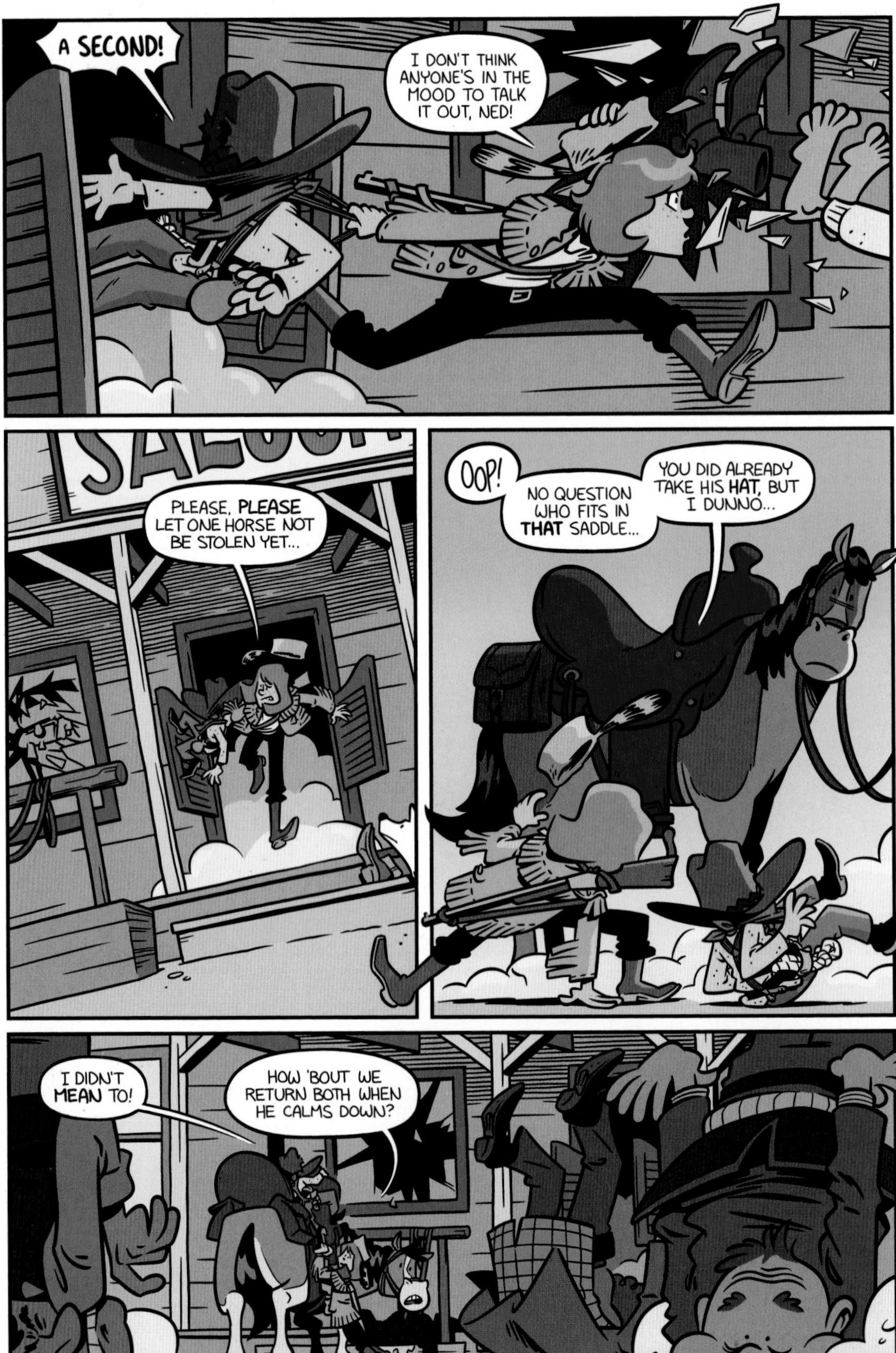
A SECOND!
I DON'T THINK ANYONE'S IN THE MOOD TO TALK IT OUT, NED!
SALOON
PLEASE, **PLEASE** LET ONE HORSE NOT BE STOLEN YET...
OOP!
NO QUESTION WHO FITS IN **THAT** SADDLE...
YOU DID ALREADY TAKE HIS **HAT**, BUT I DUNNO...
I DIDN'T **MEAN** TO!
HOW 'BOUT WE RETURN BOTH WHEN HE CALMS DOWN?

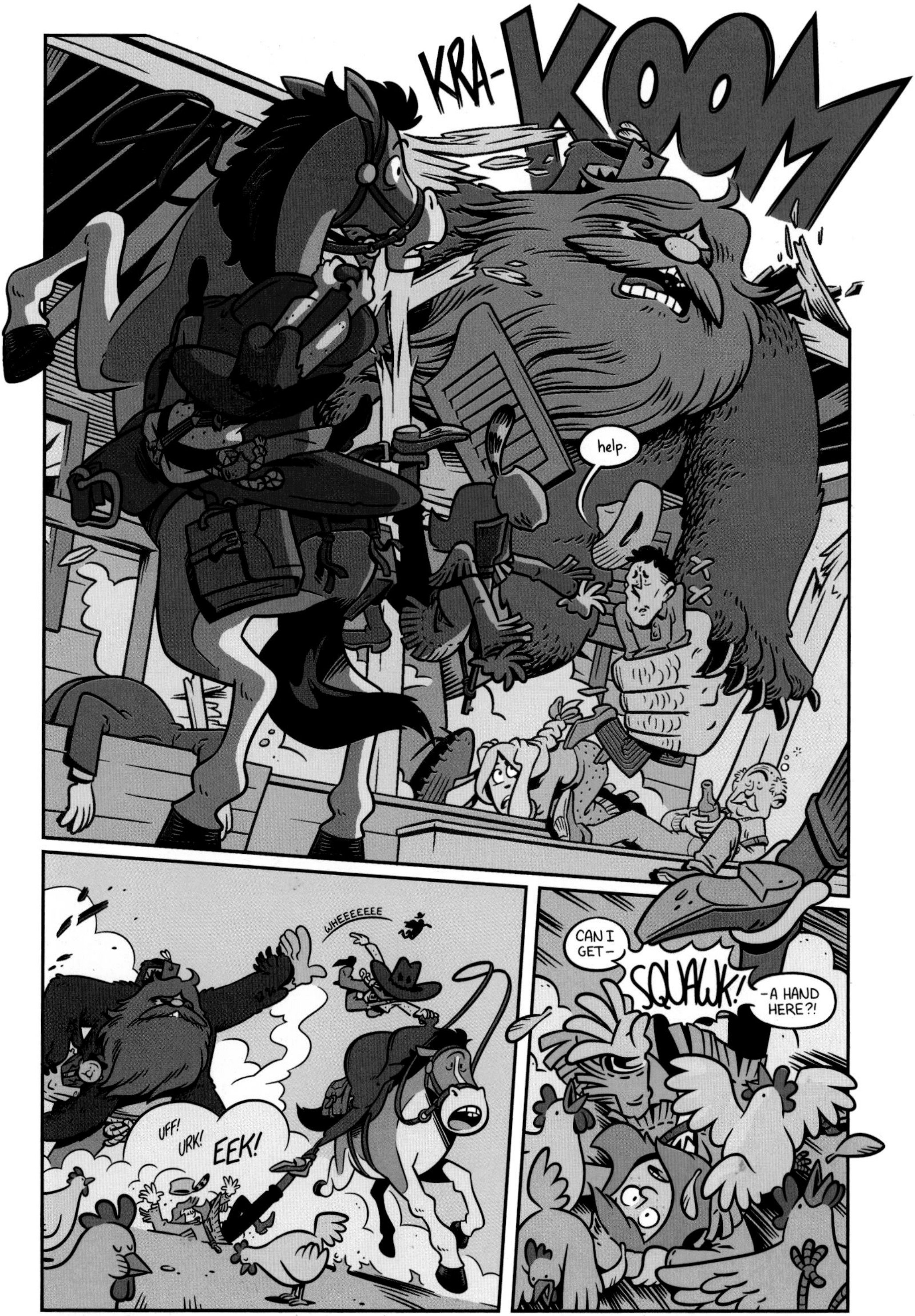
KRA-KOOM
help.
WHEEEEEEE
UFF!
URK!
EEK!
CAN I GET—
SQUAWK!
—A HAND HERE?!

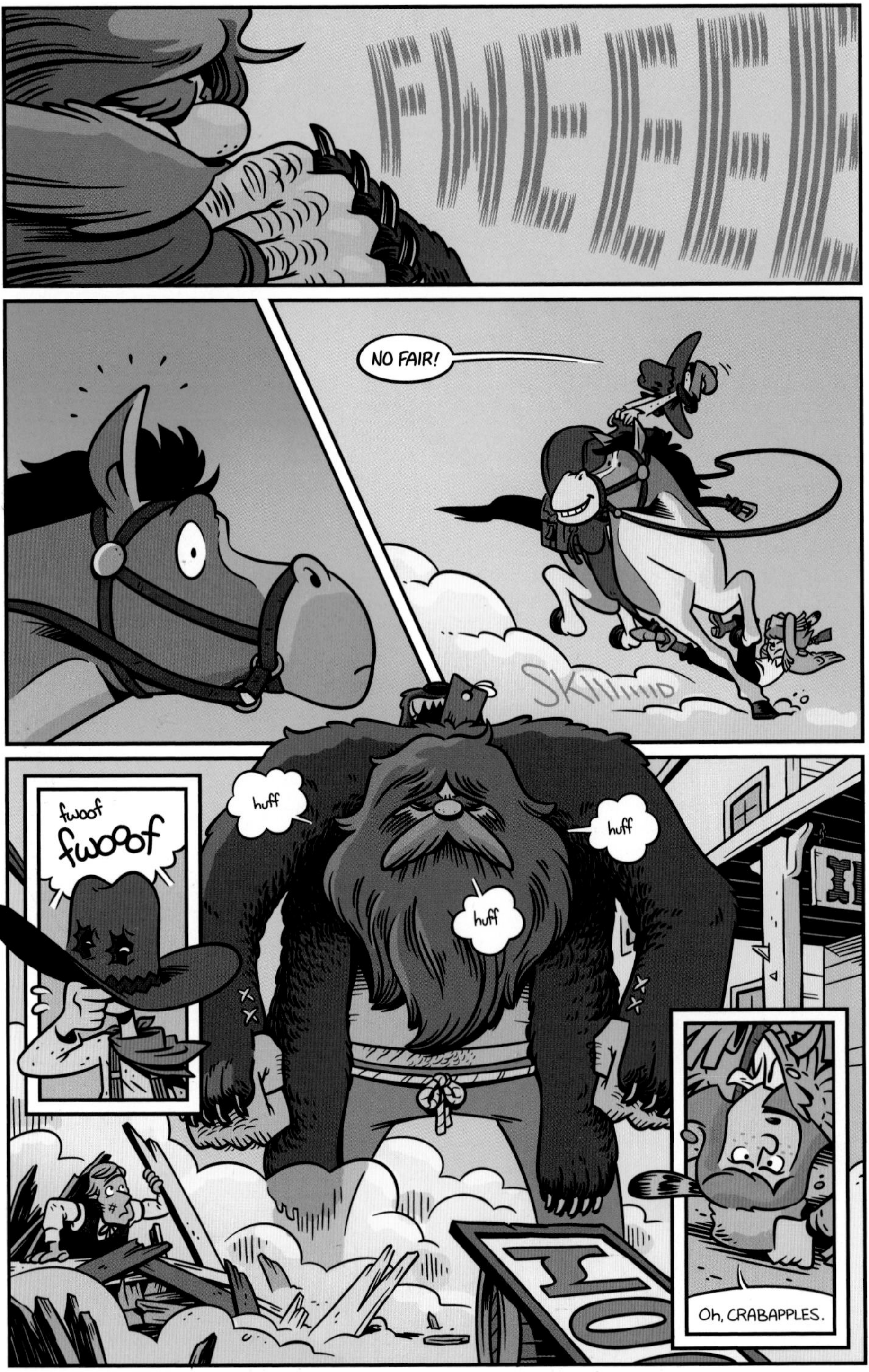
FWEEEE
NO FAIR!
SKIIIIIID
fwoof
fwooof
huff
huff
huff
Oh, CRABAPPLES.

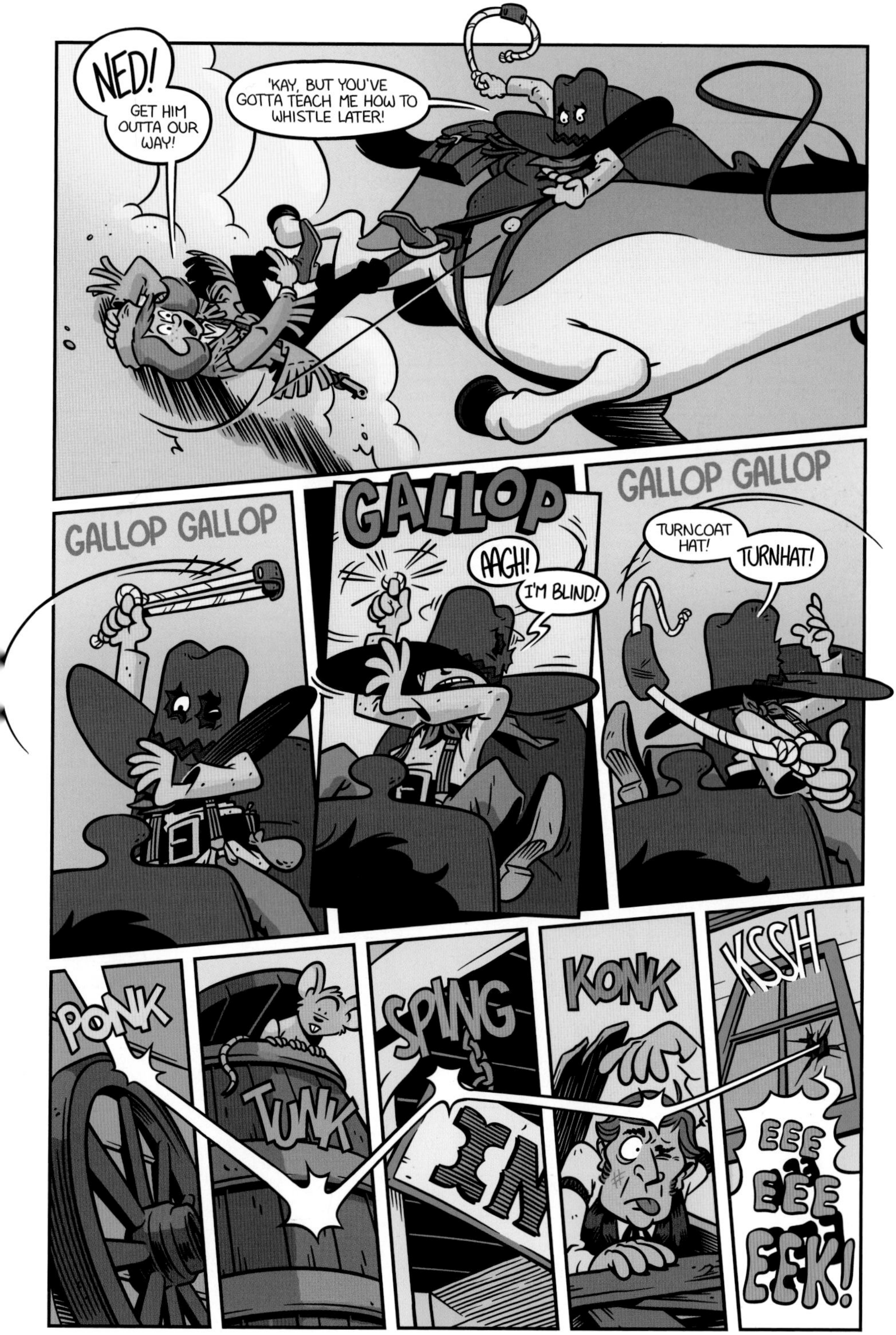
NED! GET HIM OUTTA OUR WAY!
'KAY, BUT YOU'VE GOTTA TEACH ME HOW TO WHISTLE LATER!
GALLOP GALLOP
GALLOP
AAGH!
I'M BLIND!
GALLOP GALLOP
TURNCOAT HAT!
TURNHAT!
PONK
TUNK
SPING
KONK
KSSH
EEE EEE EEK!

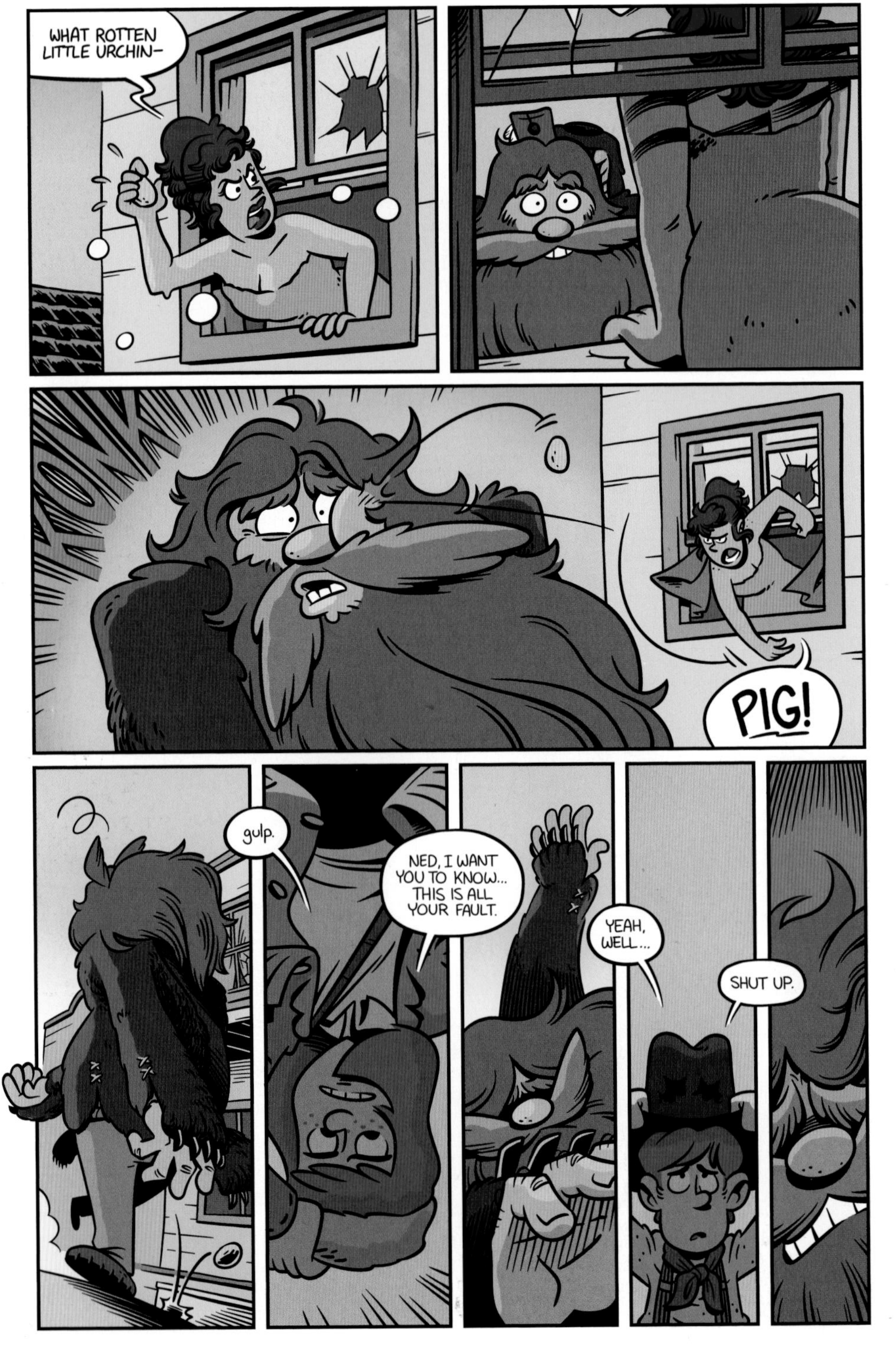
WHAT ROTTEN LITTLE URCHIN–
PIG!
gulp.
NED, I WANT YOU TO KNOW... THIS IS ALL YOUR FAULT.
YEAH, WELL...
SHUT UP.

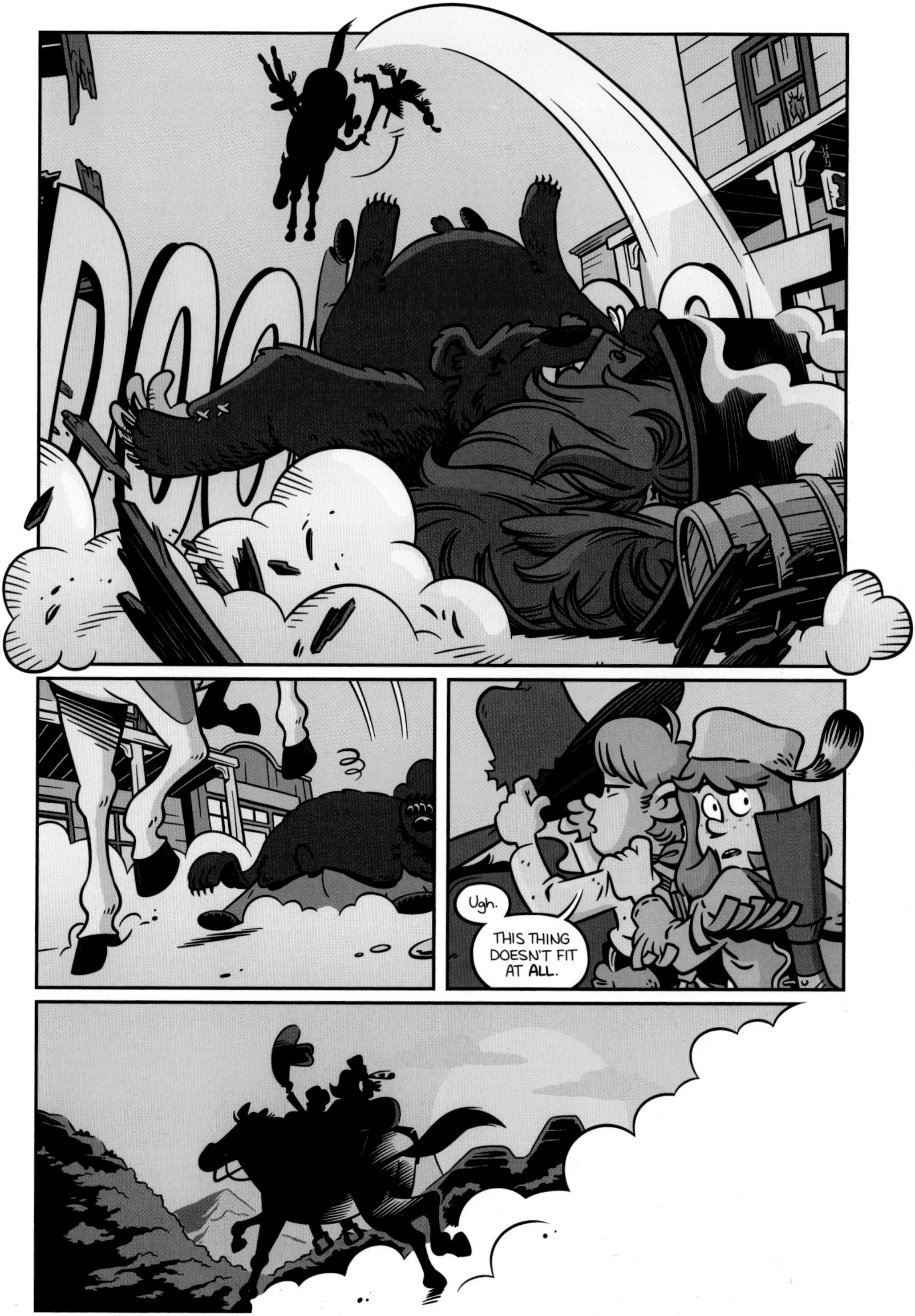
Ugh.
THIS THING DOESN'T FIT AT ALL.

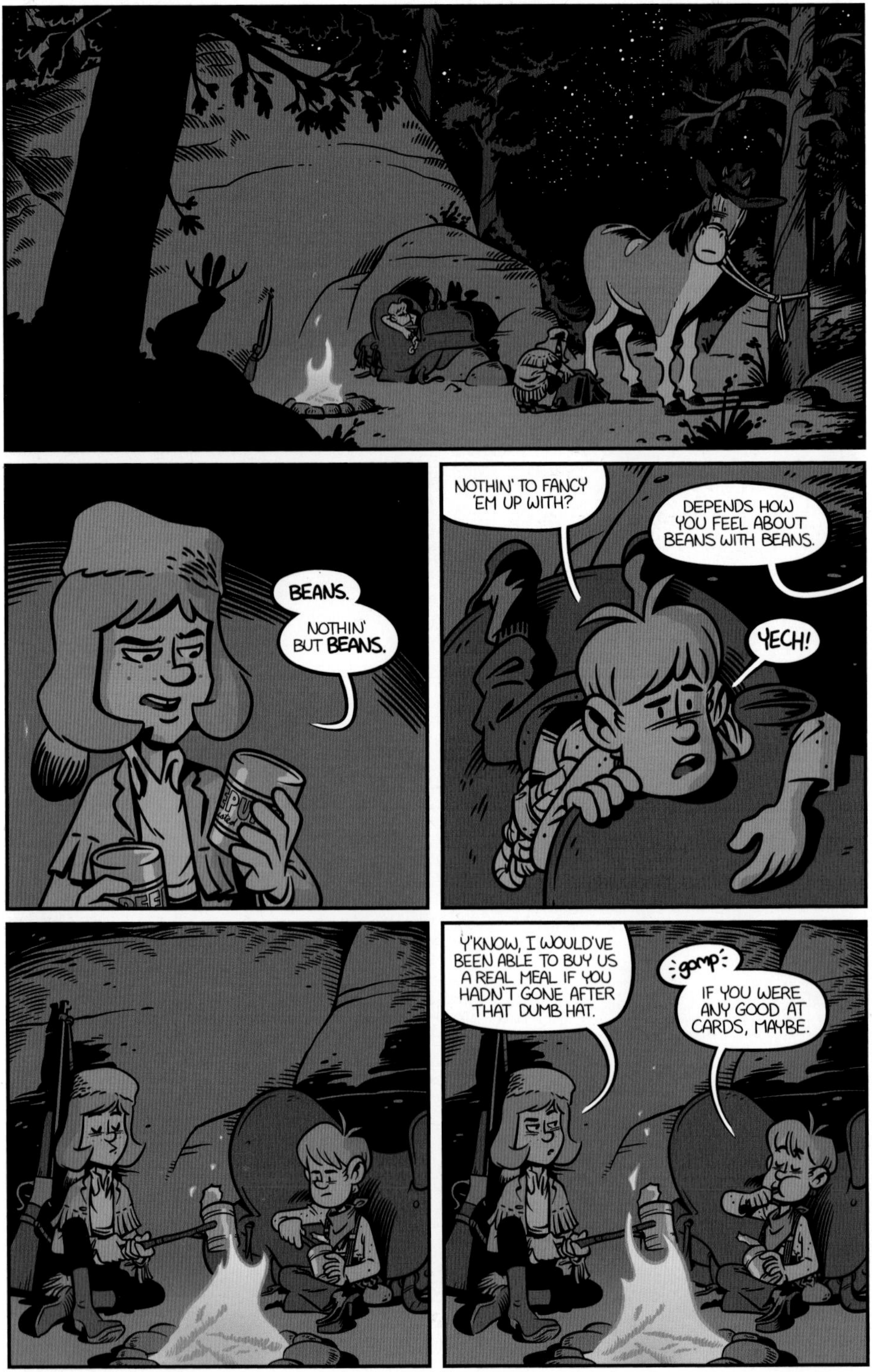
BEANS.
NOTHIN' BUT BEANS.
NOTHIN' TO FANCY 'EM UP WITH?
DEPENDS HOW YOU FEEL ABOUT BEANS WITH BEANS.
YECH!
Y'KNOW, I WOULD'VE BEEN ABLE TO BUY US A REAL MEAL IF YOU HADN'T GONE AFTER THAT DUMB HAT.
gomp
IF YOU WERE ANY GOOD AT CARDS, MAYBE.

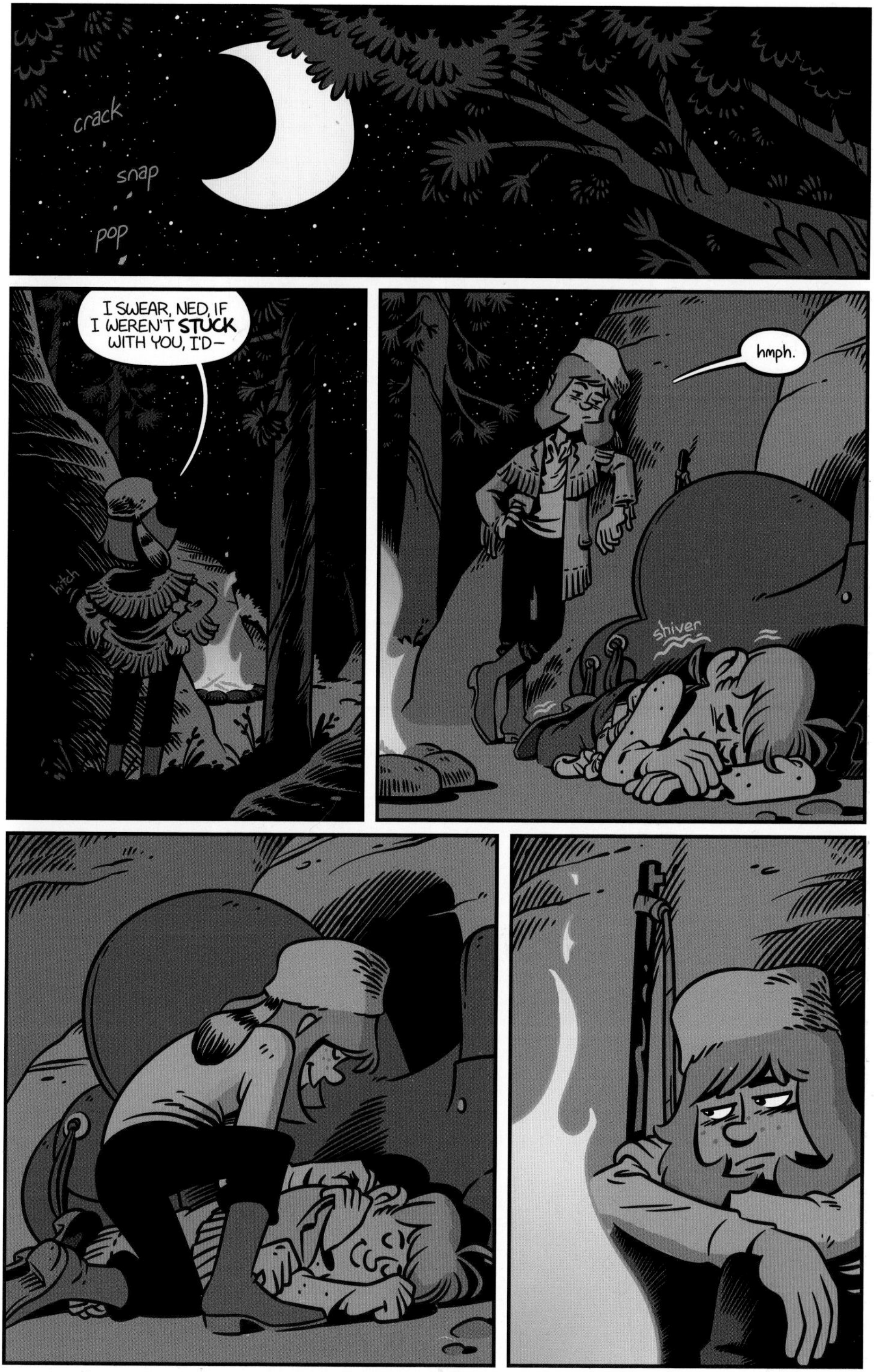
crack
snap
pop
I SWEAR, NED, IF I WEREN'T **STUCK** WITH YOU, I'D—
hitch
hmph.
shiver

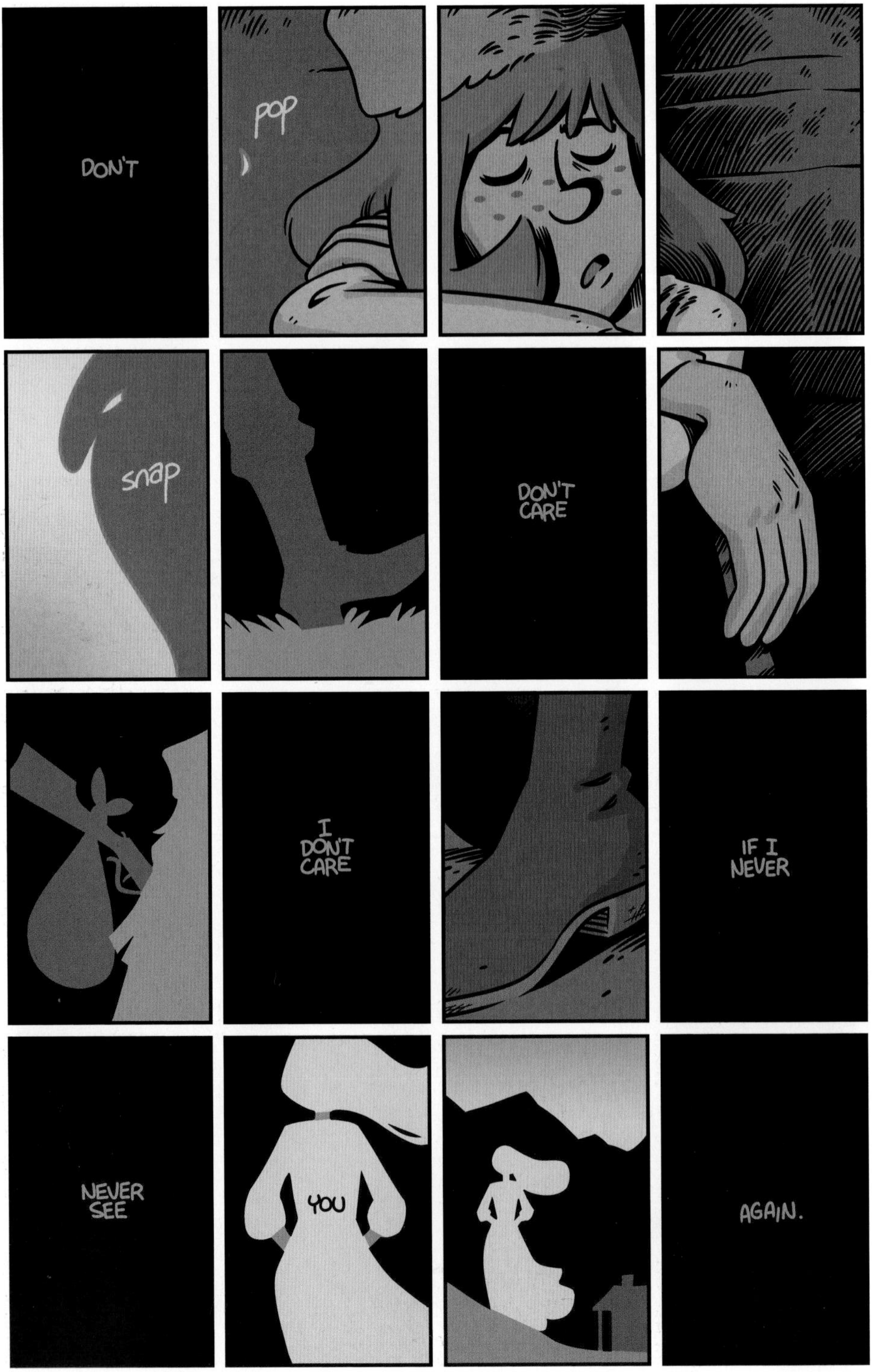
DON'T
pop
snap
DON'T CARE
I DON'T CARE
IF I NEVER
NEVER SEE
YOU
AGAIN.

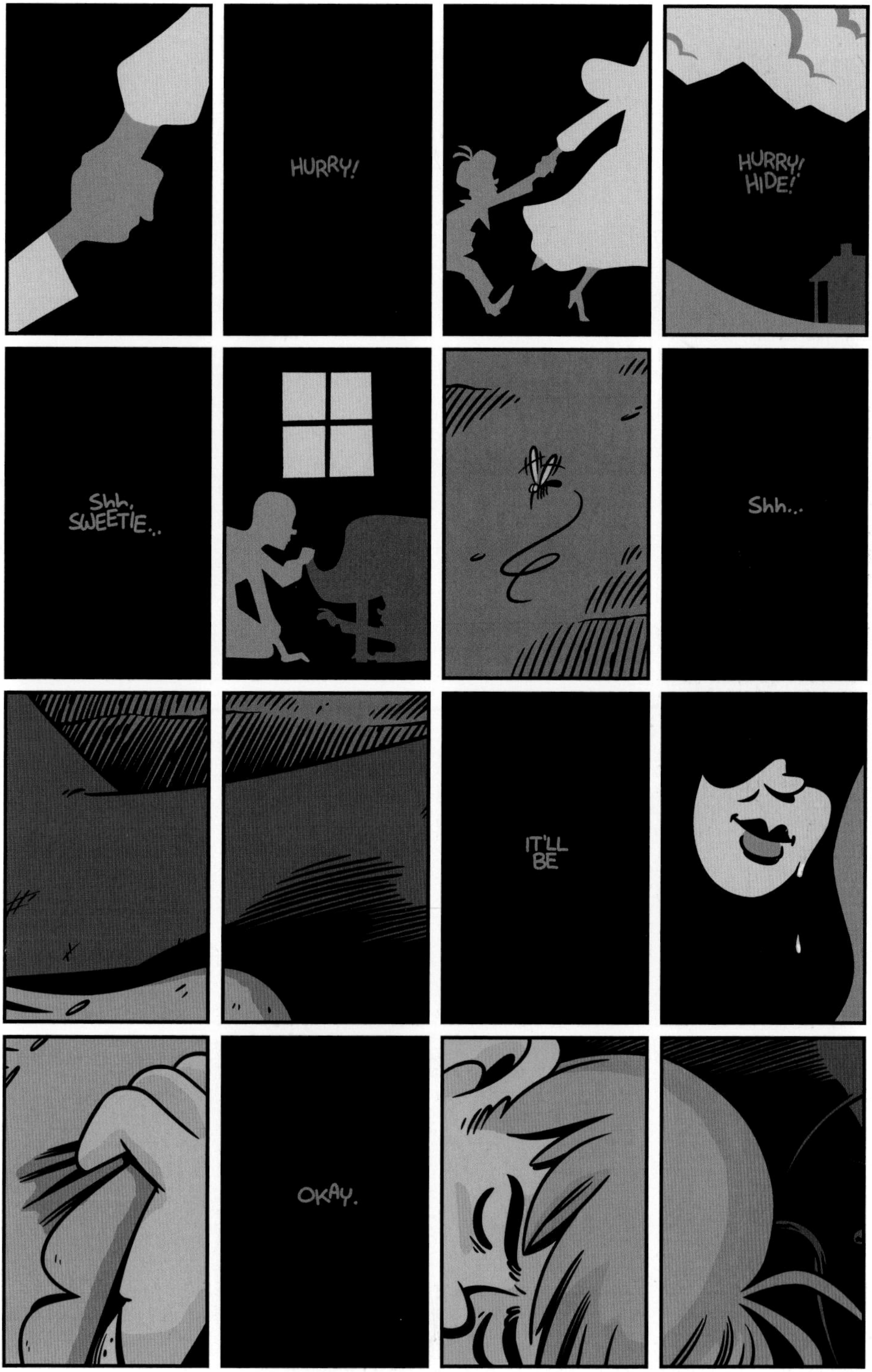
HURRY!
HURRY! HIDE!
Shh, SWEETIE...
Shh...
IT'LL BE
OKAY.

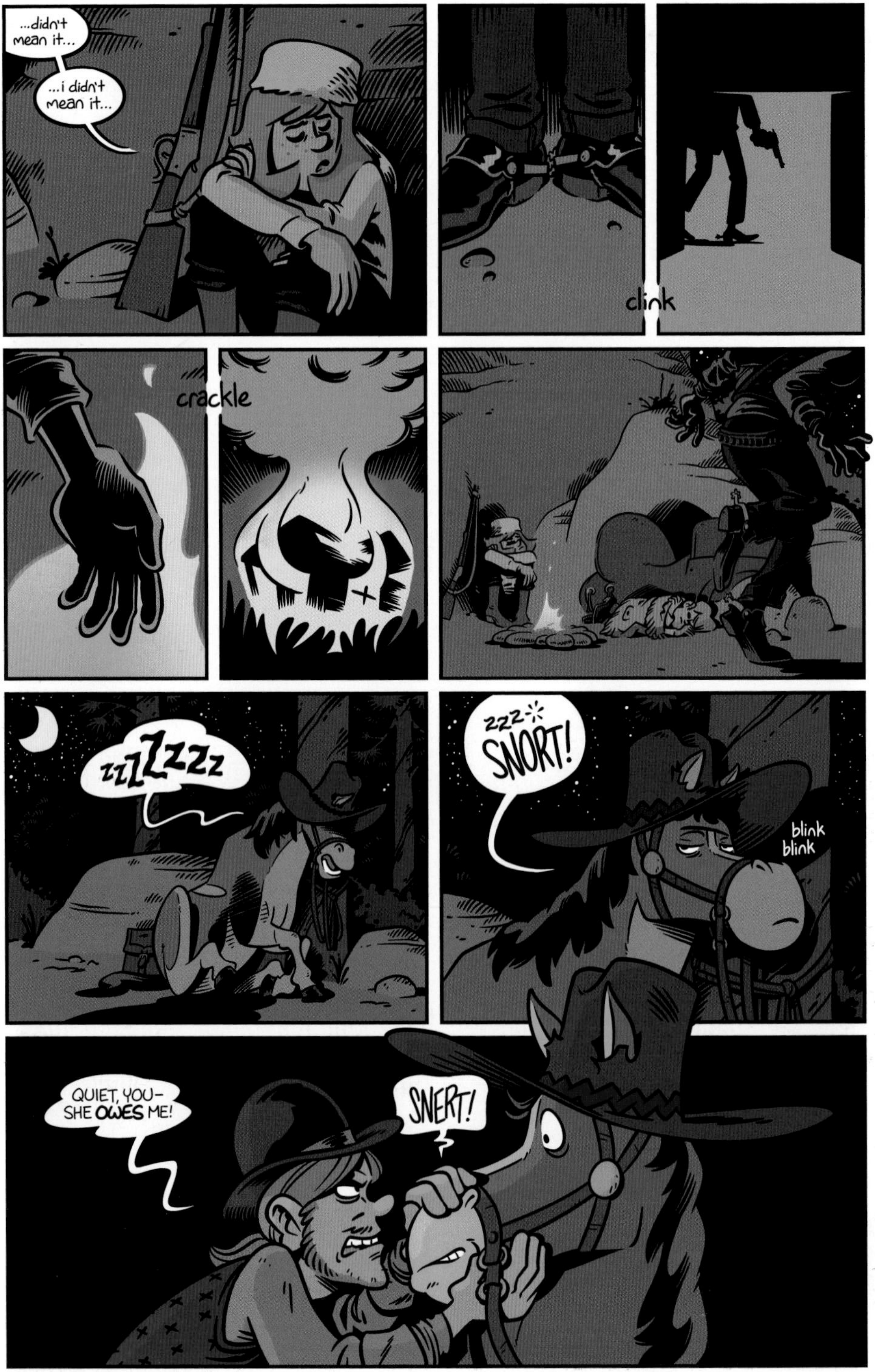

...didn't mean it...
...i didn't mean it...
clink
crackle
zzZZzzz
zzz SNORT!
blink blink
QUIET, YOU– SHE OWES ME!
SNERT!

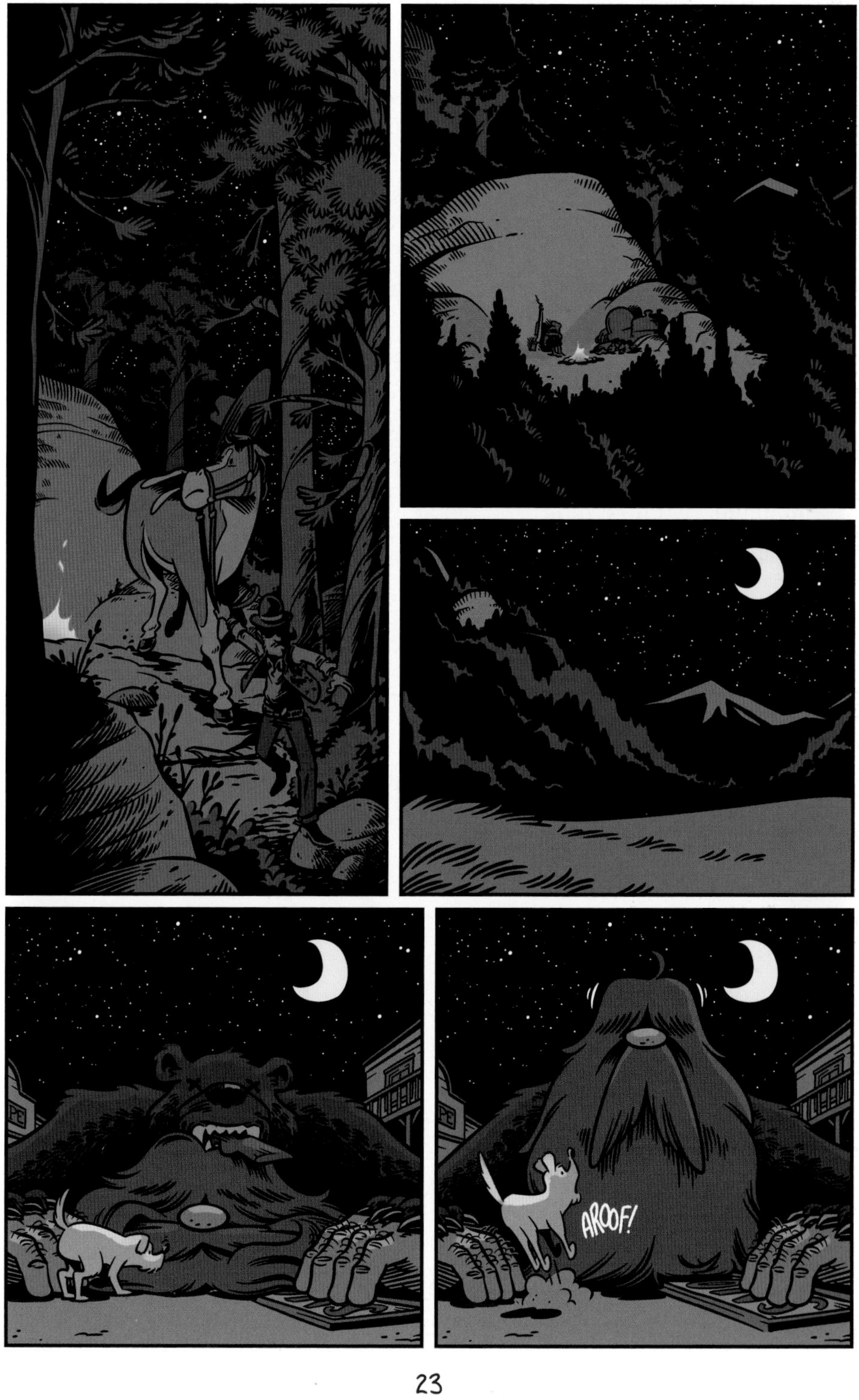
AROOF!

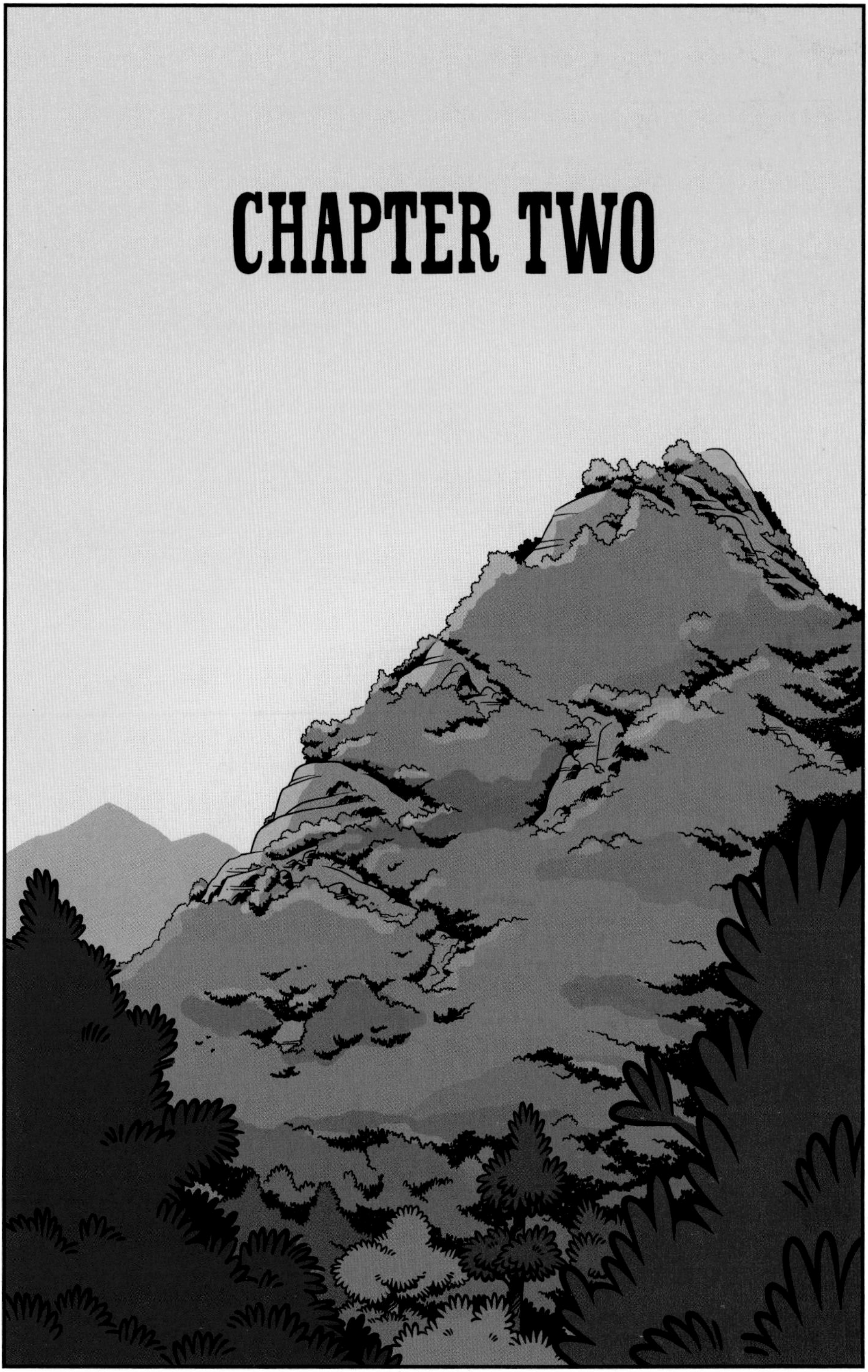
CHAPTER TWO

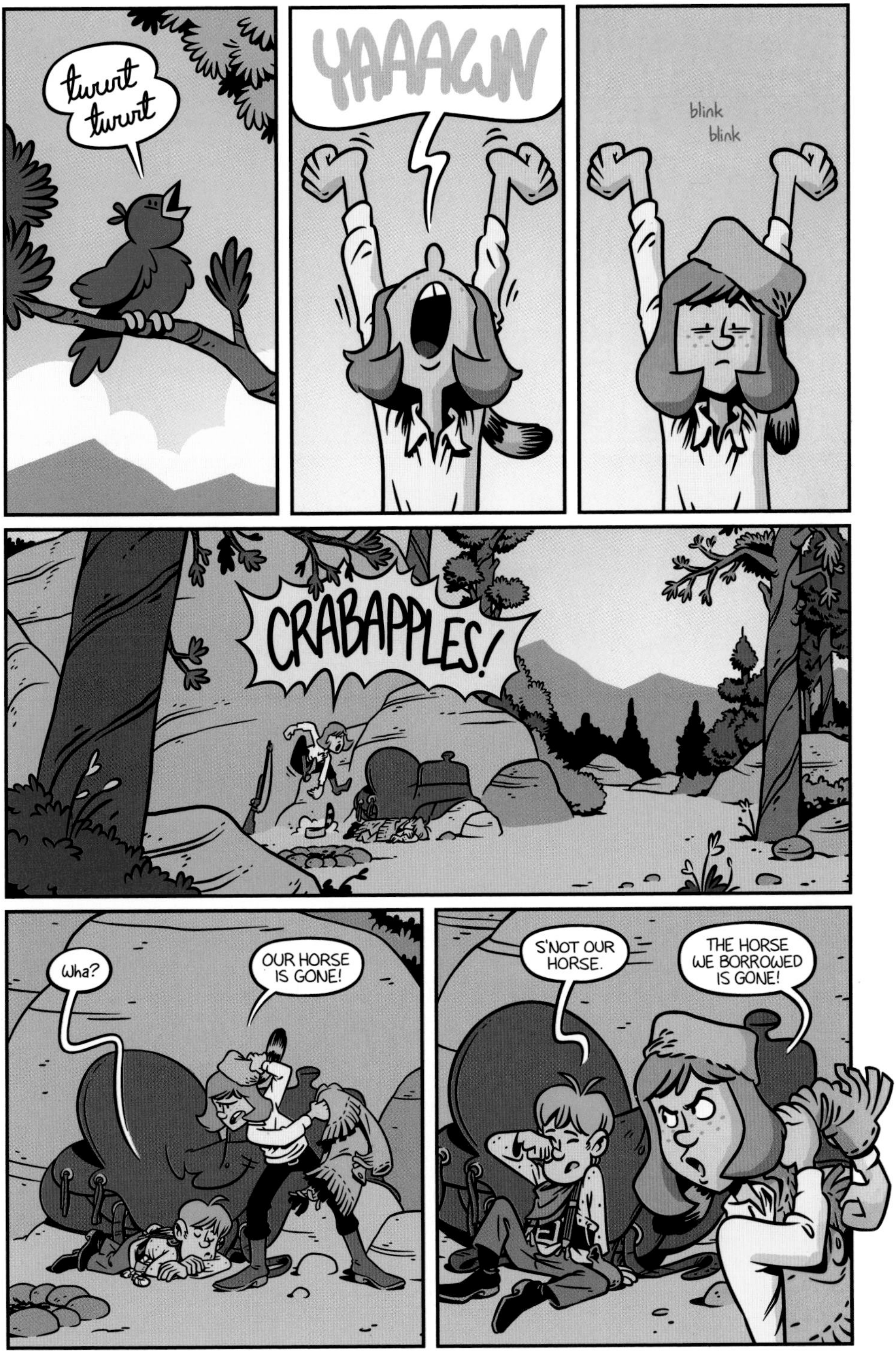
twurt twurt
YAAAWN
blink
blink
CRABAPPLES!
Wha?
OUR HORSE IS GONE!
S'NOT OUR HORSE.
THE HORSE WE BORROWED IS GONE!

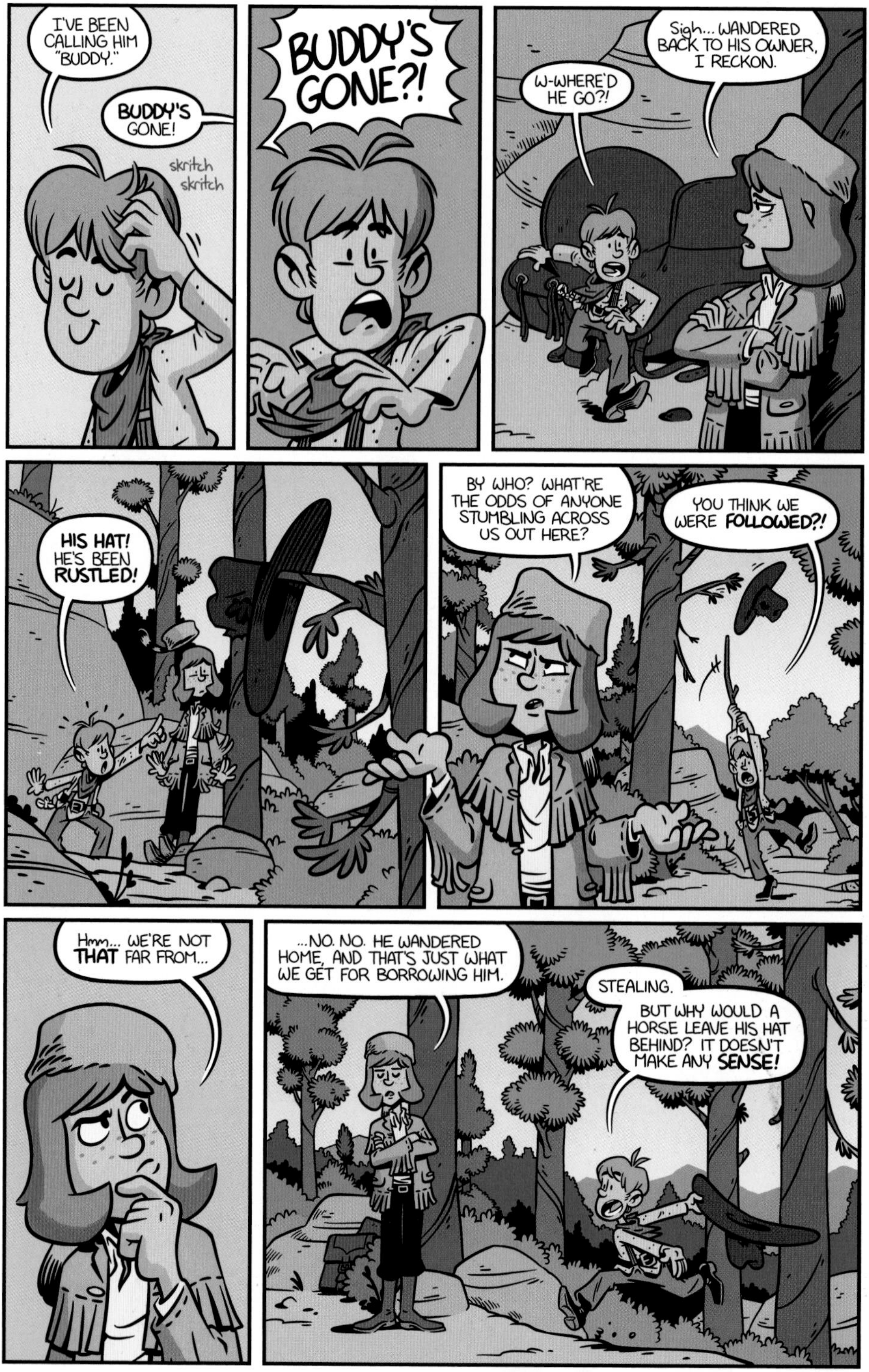
I'VE BEEN CALLING HIM "BUDDY."
BUDDY'S GONE!
skritch skritch
BUDDY'S GONE?!
W-WHERE'D HE GO?!
Sigh... WANDERED BACK TO HIS OWNER, I RECKON.
HIS HAT! HE'S BEEN RUSTLED!
BY WHO? WHAT'RE THE ODDS OF ANYONE STUMBLING ACROSS US OUT HERE?
YOU THINK WE WERE FOLLOWED?!
Hmm... WE'RE NOT THAT FAR FROM...
...NO. NO. HE WANDERED HOME, AND THAT'S JUST WHAT WE GET FOR BORROWING HIM.
STEALING.
BUT WHY WOULD A HORSE LEAVE HIS HAT BEHIND? IT DOESN'T MAKE ANY SENSE!

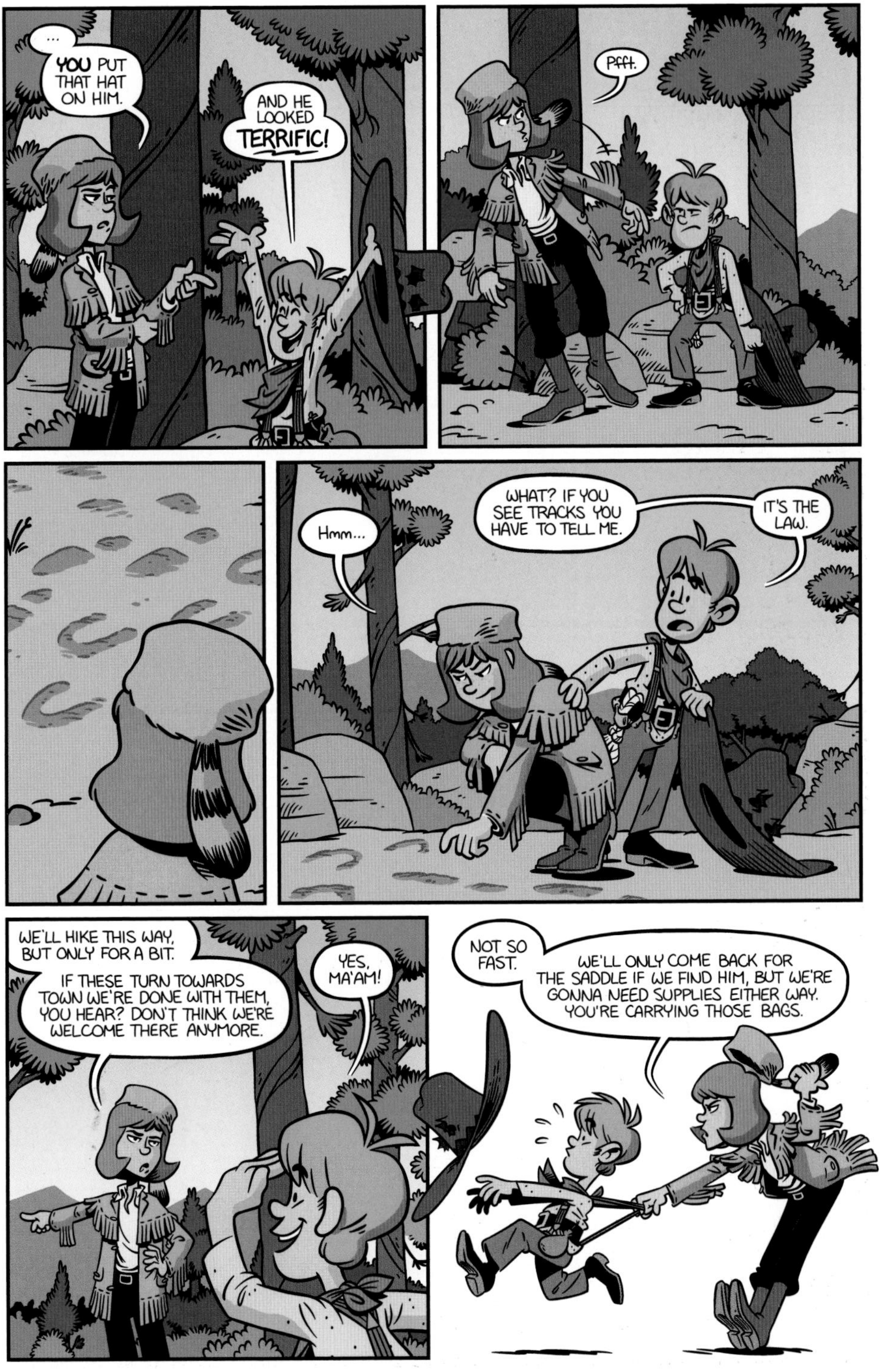
...
YOU PUT THAT HAT ON HIM.
AND HE LOOKED TERRIFIC!
Pfft.
Hmm...
WHAT? IF YOU SEE TRACKS YOU HAVE TO TELL ME.
IT'S THE LAW.
WE'LL HIKE THIS WAY, BUT ONLY FOR A BIT.
IF THESE TURN TOWARDS TOWN WE'RE DONE WITH THEM, YOU HEAR? DON'T THINK WE'RE WELCOME THERE ANYMORE.
YES, MA'AM!
NOT SO FAST.
WE'LL ONLY COME BACK FOR THE SADDLE IF WE FIND HIM, BUT WE'RE GONNA NEED SUPPLIES EITHER WAY. YOU'RE CARRYING THOSE BAGS.

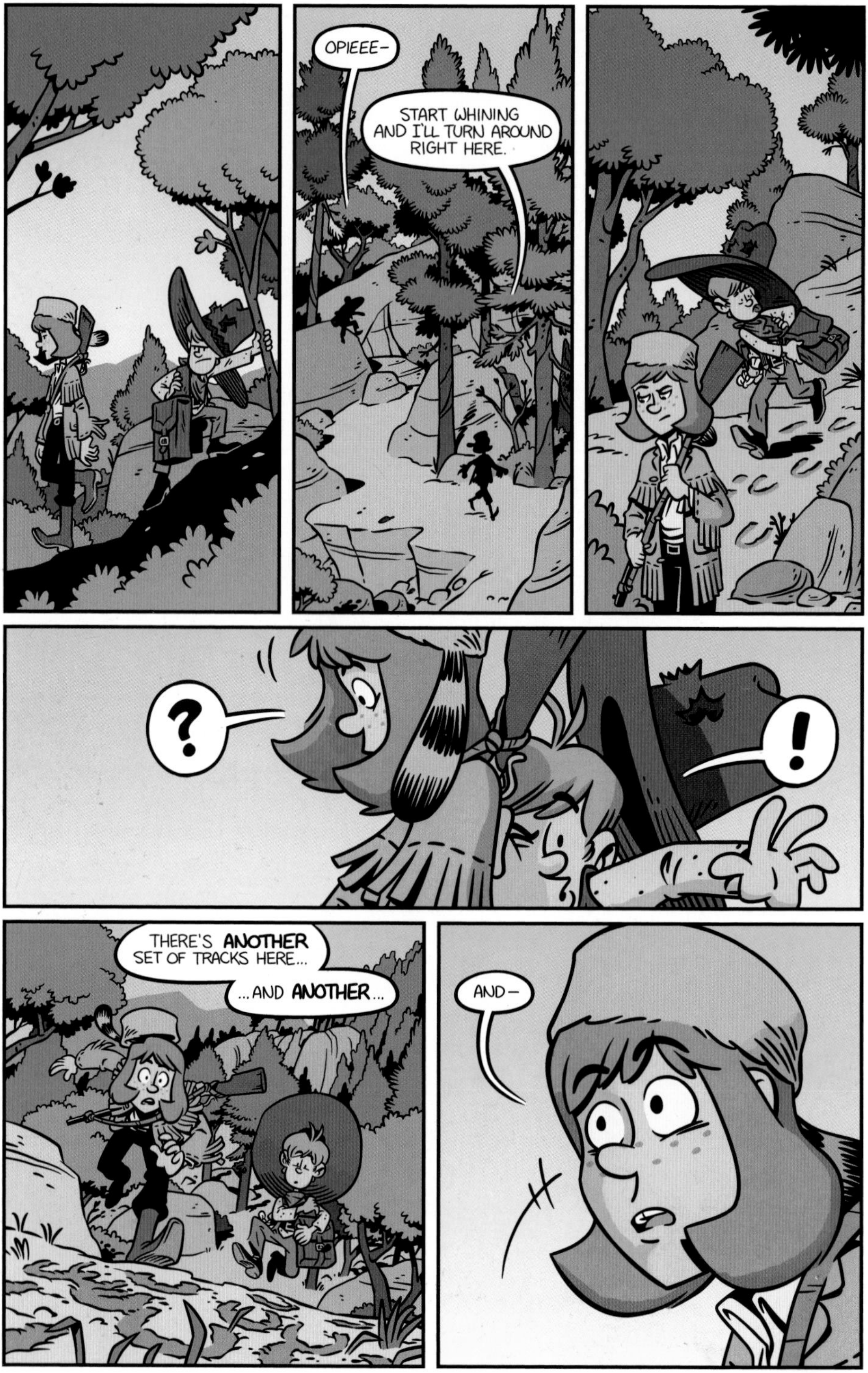
OPIEEE–
START WHINING AND I'LL TURN AROUND RIGHT HERE.
?
!
THERE'S **ANOTHER** SET OF TRACKS HERE...
...AND **ANOTHER**...
AND–

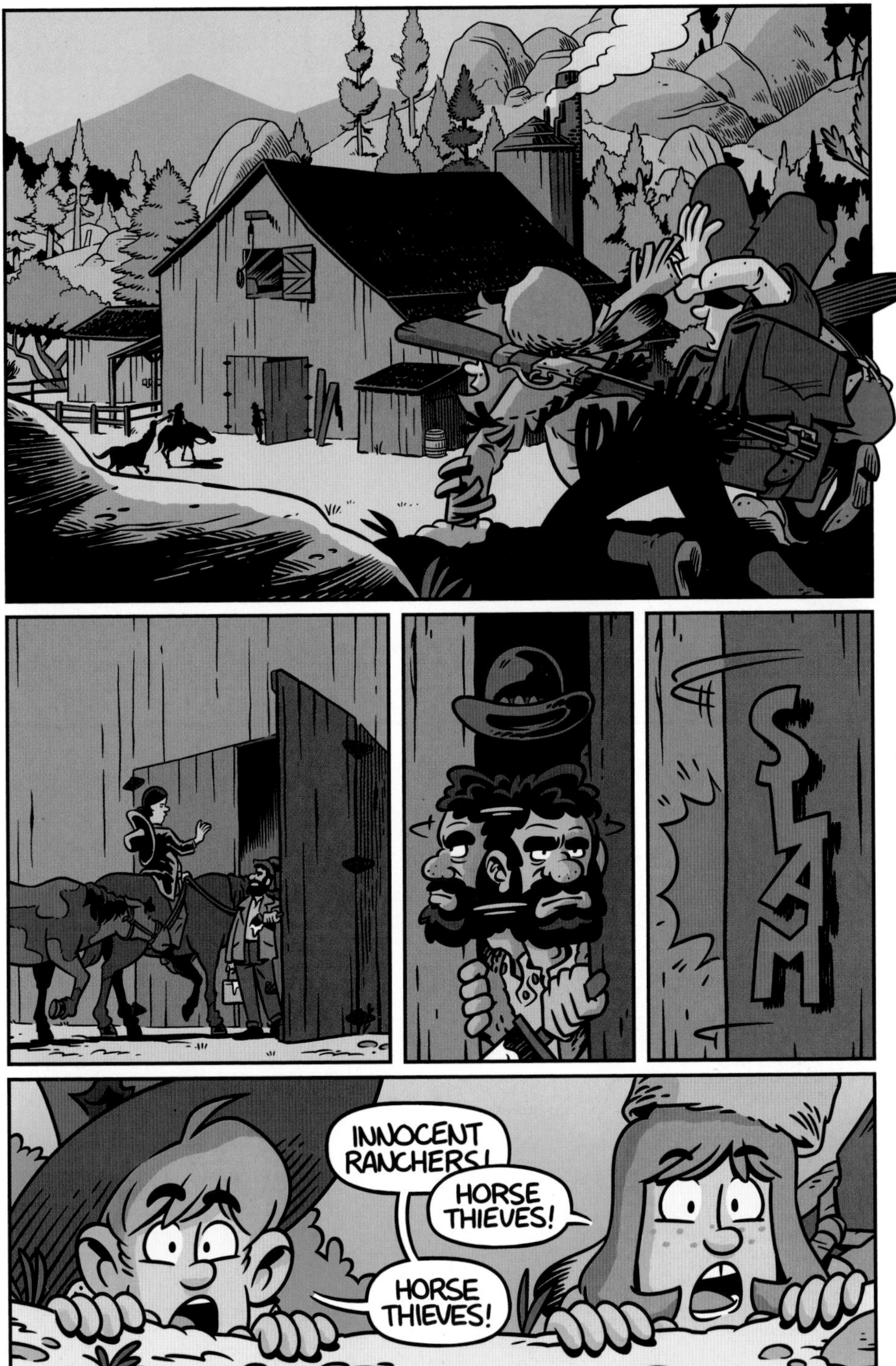
SLAM
INNOCENT RANCHERS!
HORSE THIEVES!
HORSE THIEVES!

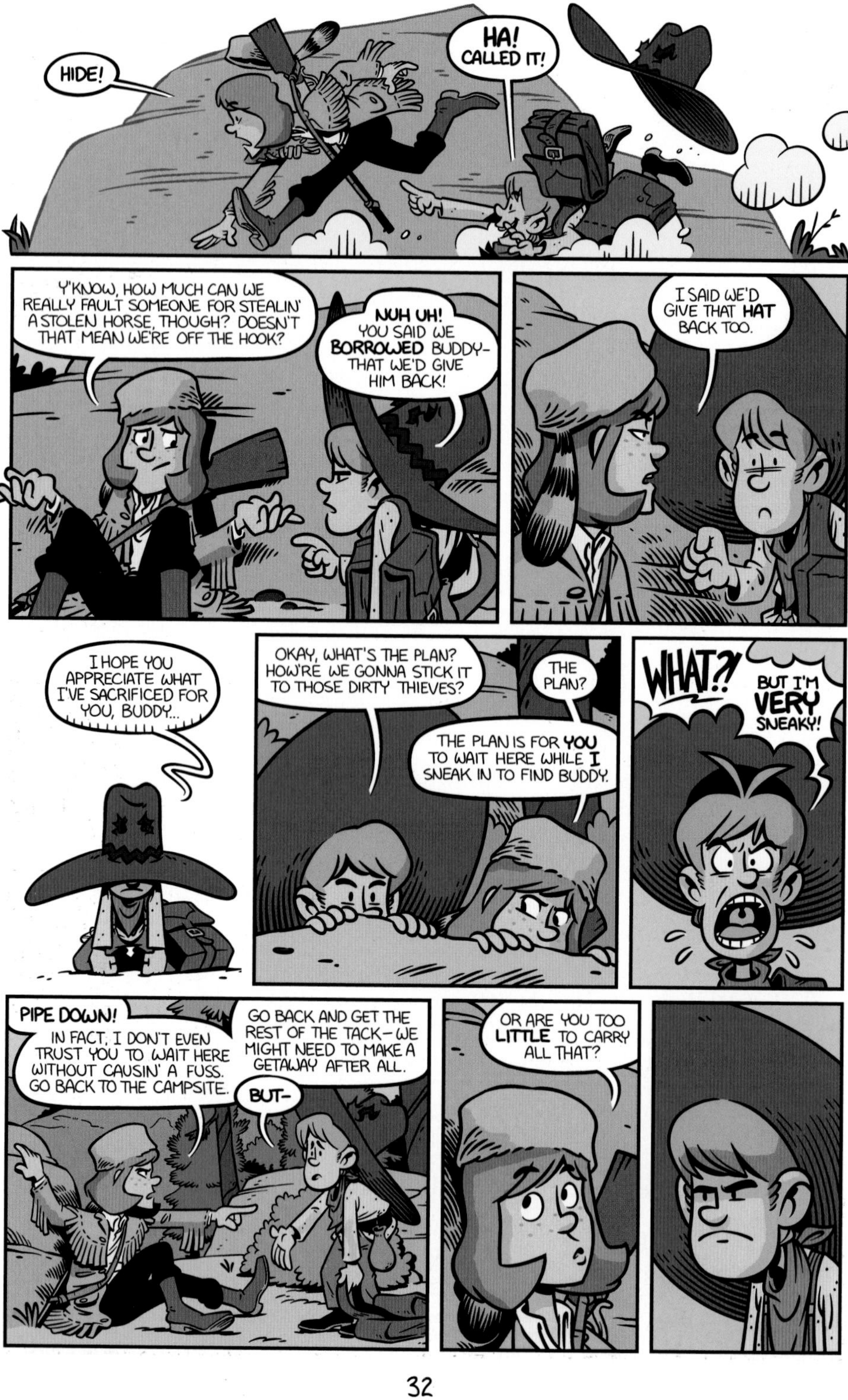
HIDE!
HA! CALLED IT!
Y'KNOW, HOW MUCH CAN WE REALLY FAULT SOMEONE FOR STEALIN' A STOLEN HORSE, THOUGH? DOESN'T THAT MEAN WE'RE OFF THE HOOK?
NUH UH! YOU SAID WE BORROWED BUDDY— THAT WE'D GIVE HIM BACK!
I SAID WE'D GIVE THAT HAT BACK TOO.
I HOPE YOU APPRECIATE WHAT I'VE SACRIFICED FOR YOU, BUDDY...
OKAY, WHAT'S THE PLAN? HOW'RE WE GONNA STICK IT TO THOSE DIRTY THIEVES?
THE PLAN?
THE PLAN IS FOR YOU TO WAIT HERE WHILE I SNEAK IN TO FIND BUDDY.
WHAT?!
BUT I'M VERY SNEAKY!
PIPE DOWN!
IN FACT, I DON'T EVEN TRUST YOU TO WAIT HERE WITHOUT CAUSIN' A FUSS. GO BACK TO THE CAMPSITE.
GO BACK AND GET THE REST OF THE TACK— WE MIGHT NEED TO MAKE A GETAWAY AFTER ALL.
BUT—
OR ARE YOU TOO LITTLE TO CARRY ALL THAT?

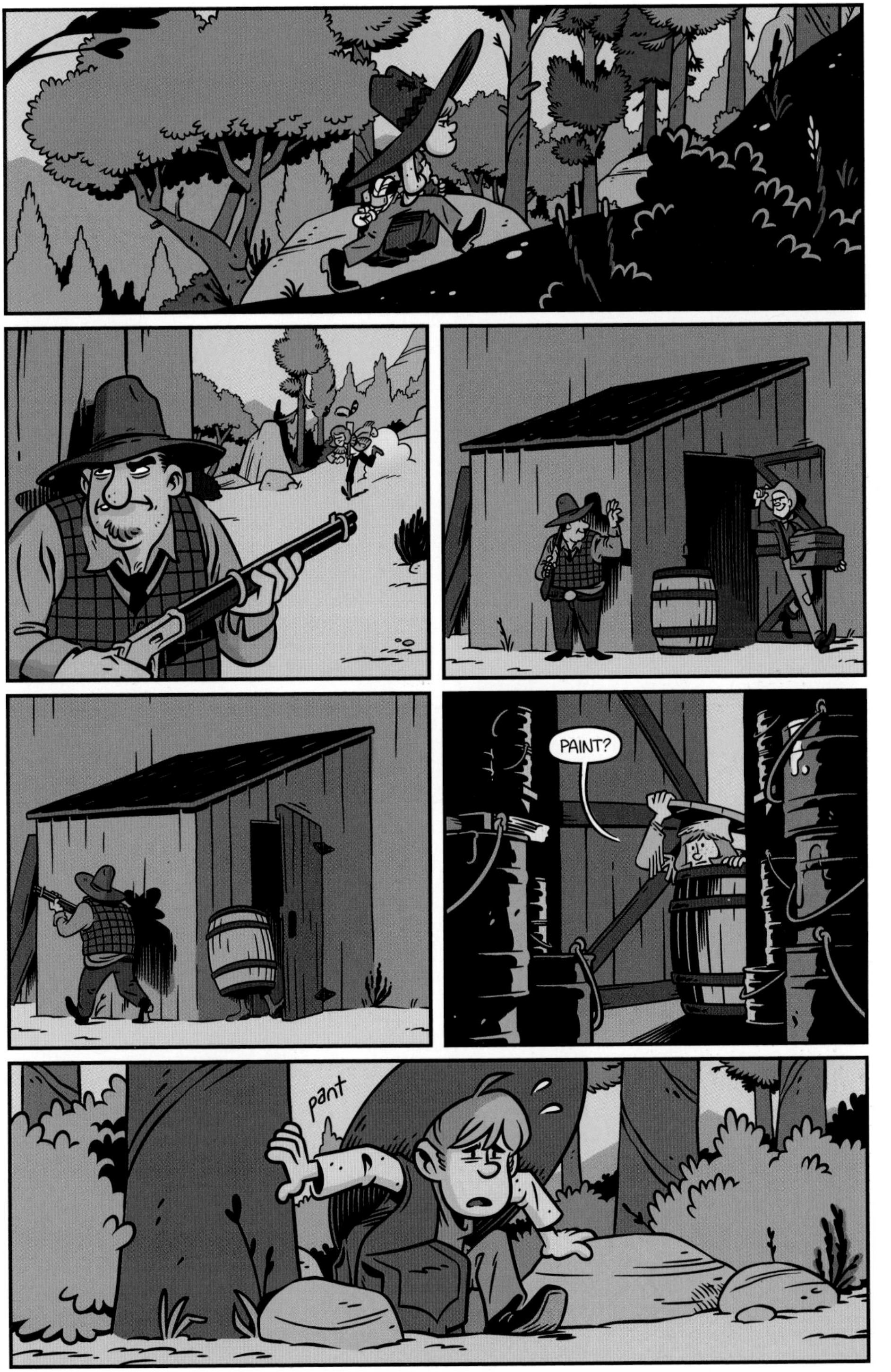
PAINT?
pant

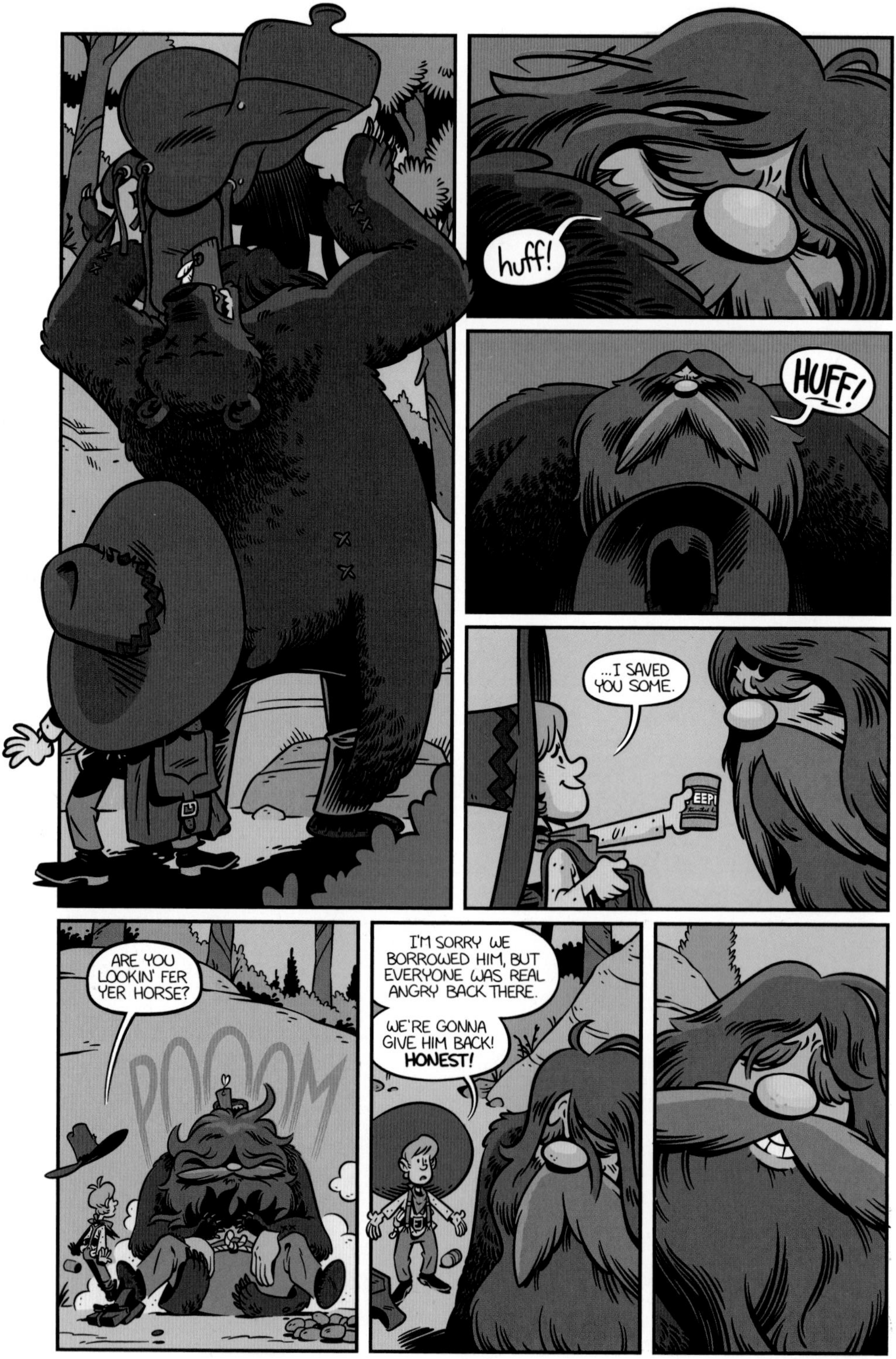

huff!
HUFF!
...I SAVED YOU SOME.
ARE YOU LOOKIN' FER YER HORSE?
POOOM
I'M SORRY WE BORROWED HIM, BUT EVERYONE WAS REAL ANGRY BACK THERE.
WE'RE GONNA GIVE HIM BACK! **HONEST!**

Oh, um... NOT RIGHT **NOW**.

WE...WE LOST 'IM.

BUT WE'RE LOOKIN' REAL HARD!

I CAN SHOW YOU WHERE WE THINK HE IS!

I HELD ONTO YOUR HAT FOR YOU.

IT'S...GOT SOME HOLES, BUT BUDDY CAN WEAR IT NOW. HIS EARS STICK THROUGH REAL CUTE.

?

HAR!

Oh... GUESS THAT'S PROB'LY NOT HIS NAME, HUH?

scrawl scrawl

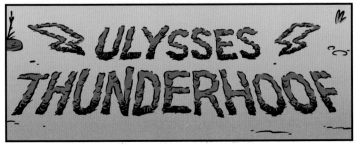

ULYSSES THUNDERHOOF

GASP!

35

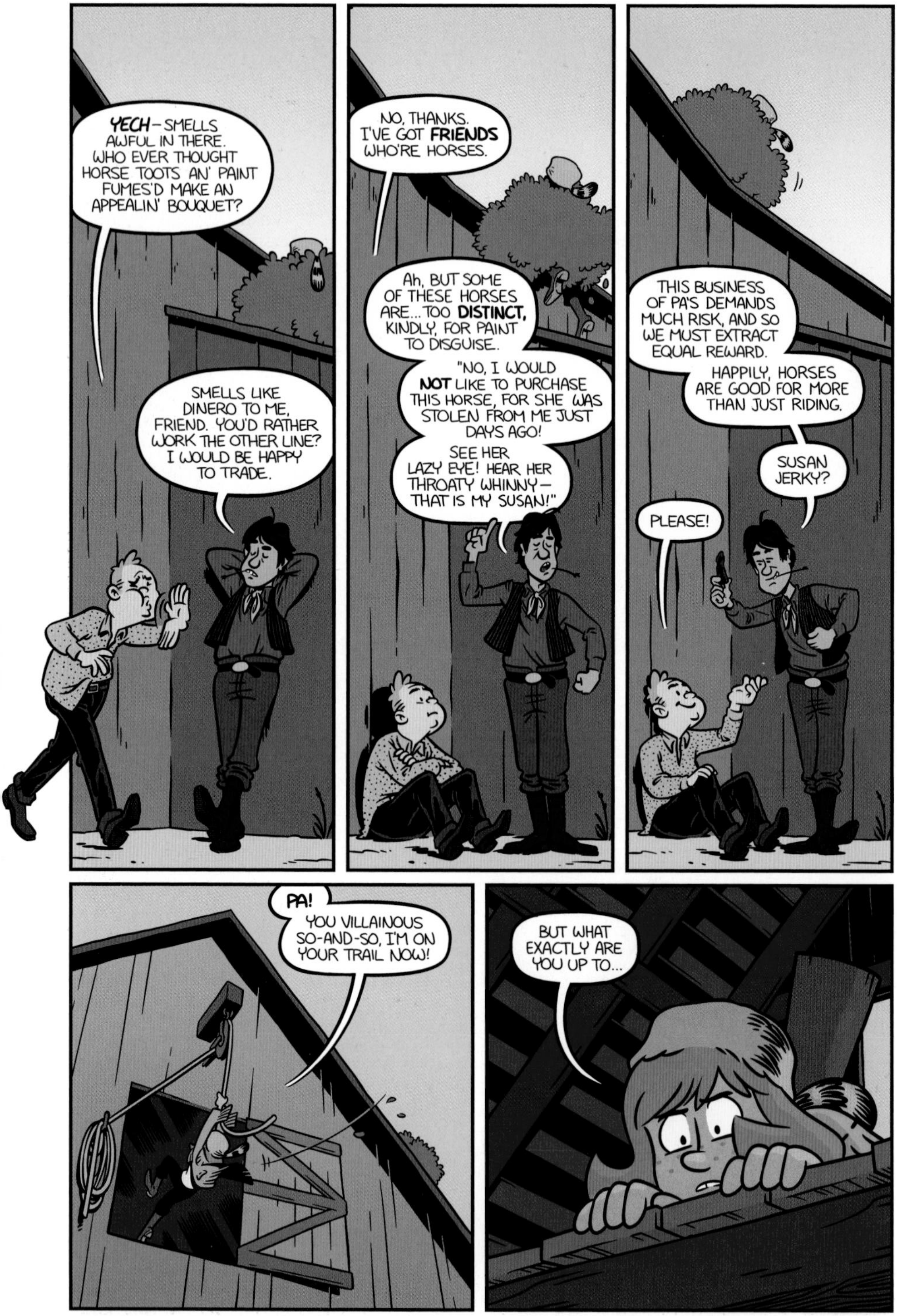
YECH—SMELLS AWFUL IN THERE. WHO EVER THOUGHT HORSE TOOTS AN' PAINT FUMES'D MAKE AN APPEALIN' BOUQUET?
SMELLS LIKE DINERO TO ME, FRIEND. YOU'D RATHER WORK THE OTHER LINE? I WOULD BE HAPPY TO TRADE.
NO, THANKS. I'VE GOT FRIENDS WHO'RE HORSES.
Ah, BUT SOME OF THESE HORSES ARE... TOO DISTINCT, KINDLY, FOR PAINT TO DISGUISE.
"NO, I WOULD NOT LIKE TO PURCHASE THIS HORSE, FOR SHE WAS STOLEN FROM ME JUST DAYS AGO!
SEE HER LAZY EYE! HEAR HER THROATY WHINNY—THAT IS MY SUSAN!"
THIS BUSINESS OF PA'S DEMANDS MUCH RISK, AND SO WE MUST EXTRACT EQUAL REWARD.
HAPPILY, HORSES ARE GOOD FOR MORE THAN JUST RIDING.
SUSAN JERKY?
PLEASE!
PA!
YOU VILLAINOUS SO-AND-SO, I'M ON YOUR TRAIL NOW!
BUT WHAT EXACTLY ARE YOU UP TO...

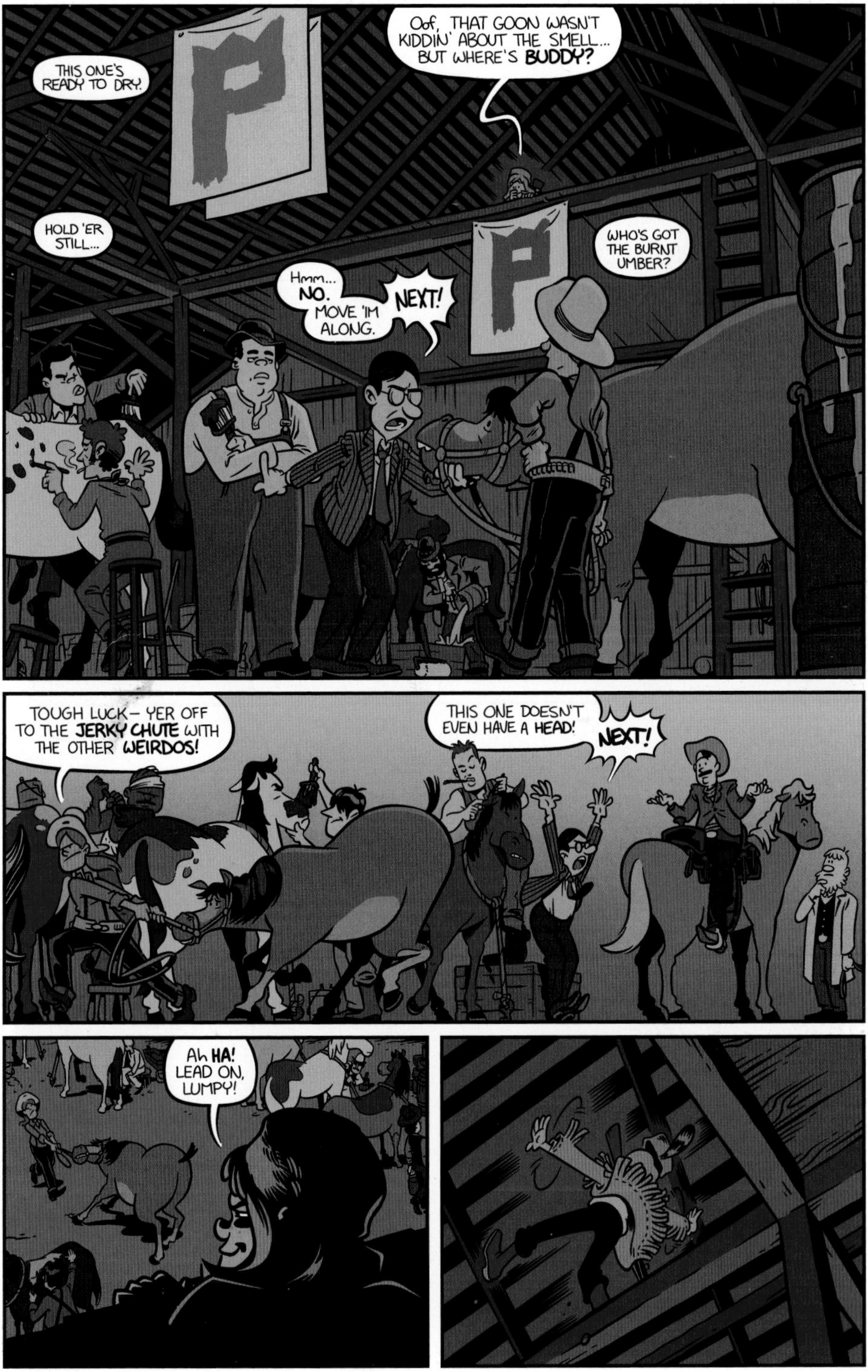
THIS ONE'S READY TO DRY.
Oof, THAT GOON WASN'T KIDDIN' ABOUT THE SMELL... BUT WHERE'S BUDDY?
HOLD 'ER STILL...
Hmm... NO. MOVE 'IM ALONG.
NEXT!
WHO'S GOT THE BURNT UMBER?
TOUGH LUCK– YER OFF TO THE JERKY CHUTE WITH THE OTHER WEIRDOS!
THIS ONE DOESN'T EVEN HAVE A HEAD!
NEXT!
Ah HA! LEAD ON, LUMPY!

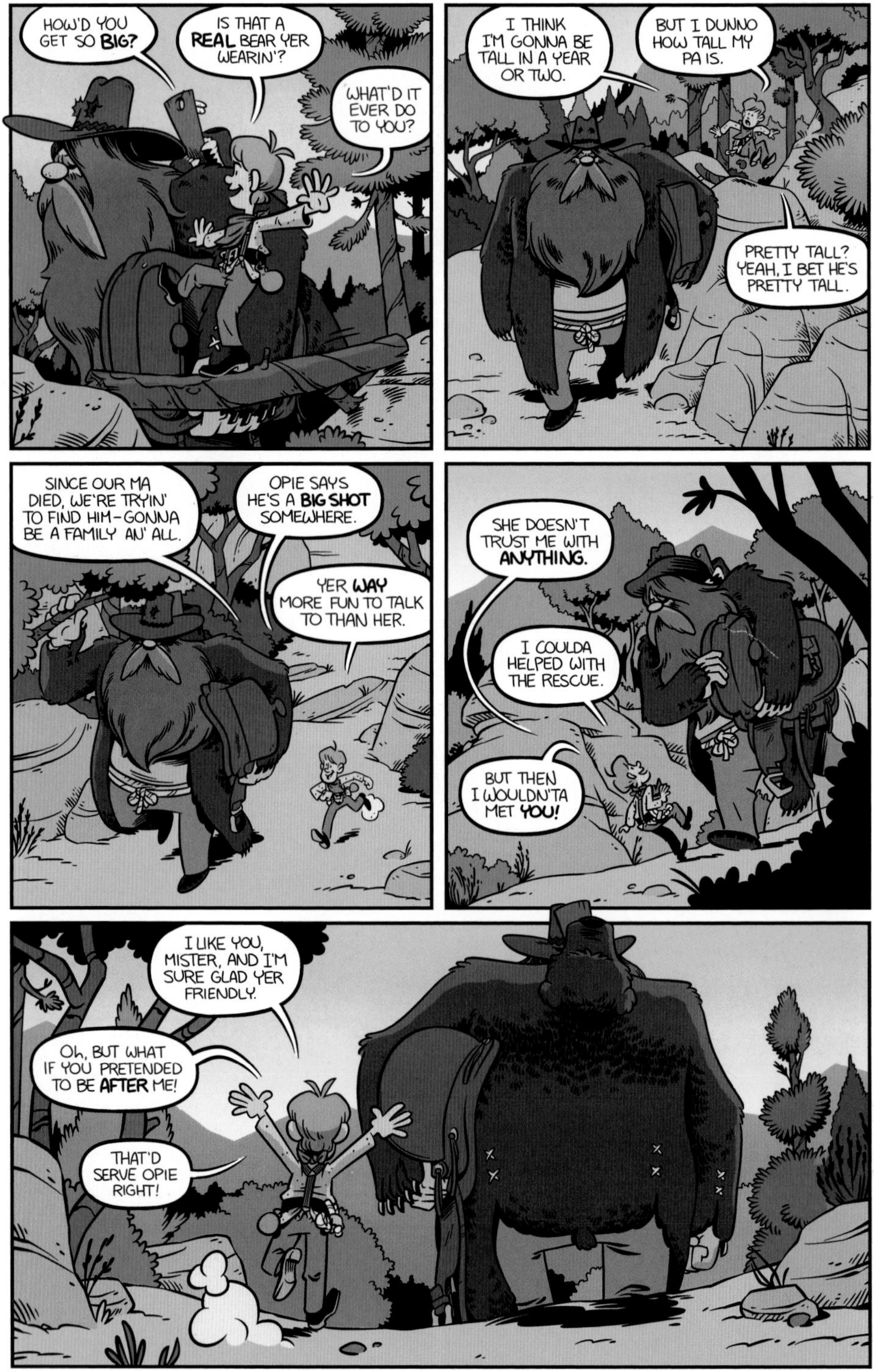
HOW'D YOU GET SO BIG?
IS THAT A REAL BEAR YER WEARIN'?
WHAT'D IT EVER DO TO YOU?
I THINK I'M GONNA BE TALL IN A YEAR OR TWO.
BUT I DUNNO HOW TALL MY PA IS.
PRETTY TALL? YEAH, I BET HE'S PRETTY TALL.
SINCE OUR MA DIED, WE'RE TRYIN' TO FIND HIM-GONNA BE A FAMILY AN' ALL.
OPIE SAYS HE'S A BIG SHOT SOMEWHERE.
YER WAY MORE FUN TO TALK TO THAN HER.
SHE DOESN'T TRUST ME WITH ANYTHING.
I COULDA HELPED WITH THE RESCUE.
BUT THEN I WOULDN'TA MET YOU!
I LIKE YOU, MISTER, AND I'M SURE GLAD YER FRIENDLY.
Oh, BUT WHAT IF YOU PRETENDED TO BE AFTER ME!
THAT'D SERVE OPIE RIGHT!

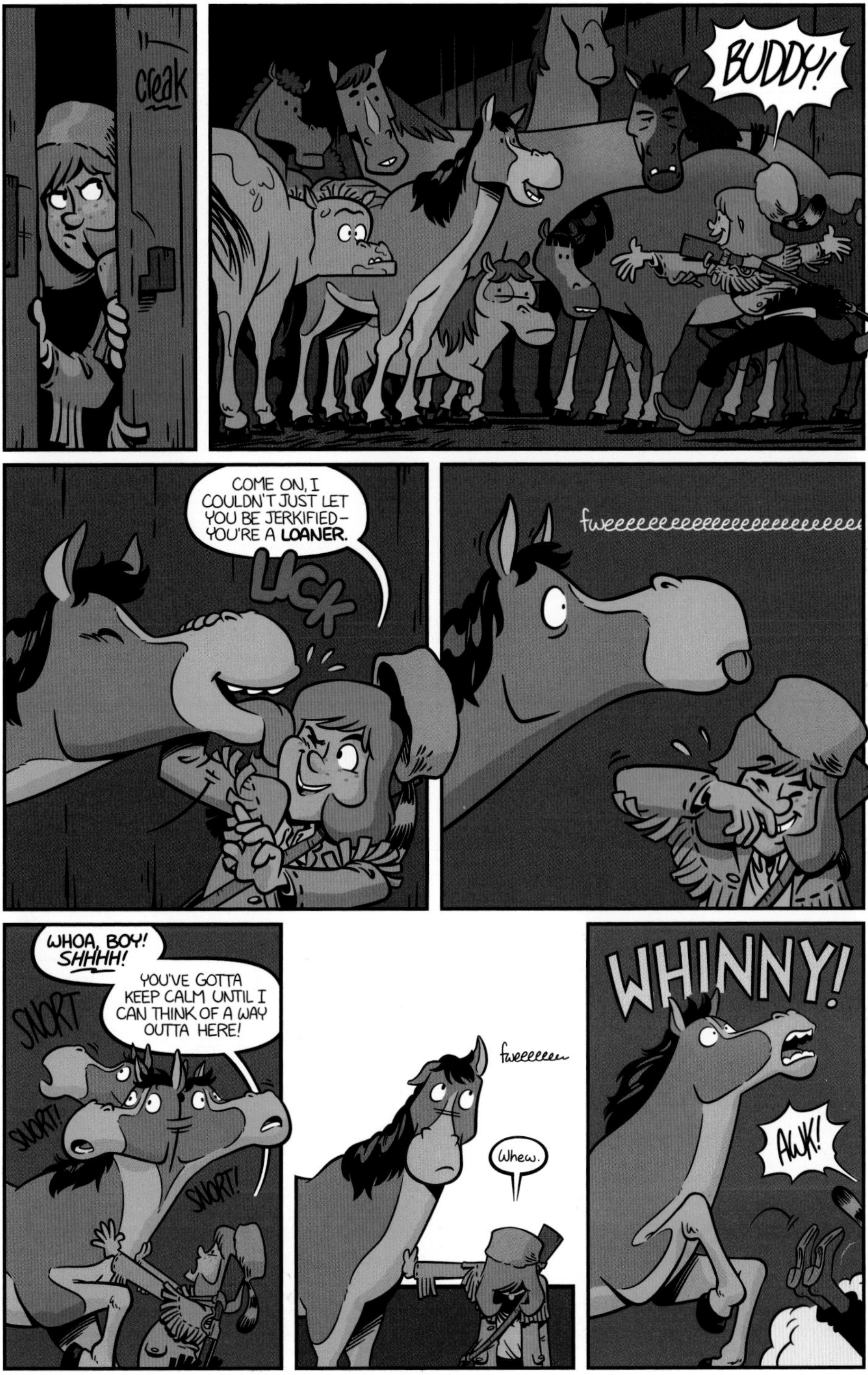
creak
BUDDY!
COME ON, I COULDN'T JUST LET YOU BE JERKIFIED— YOU'RE A **LOANER**.
LICK
fweeeeeeeeeeeeeeeeeeeeeeee
WHOA, BOY! SHHHH!
YOU'VE GOTTA KEEP CALM UNTIL I CAN THINK OF A WAY OUTTA HERE!
SNORT
SNORT!
SNORT!
fweeeeeee
Whew.
WHINNY!
AWK!

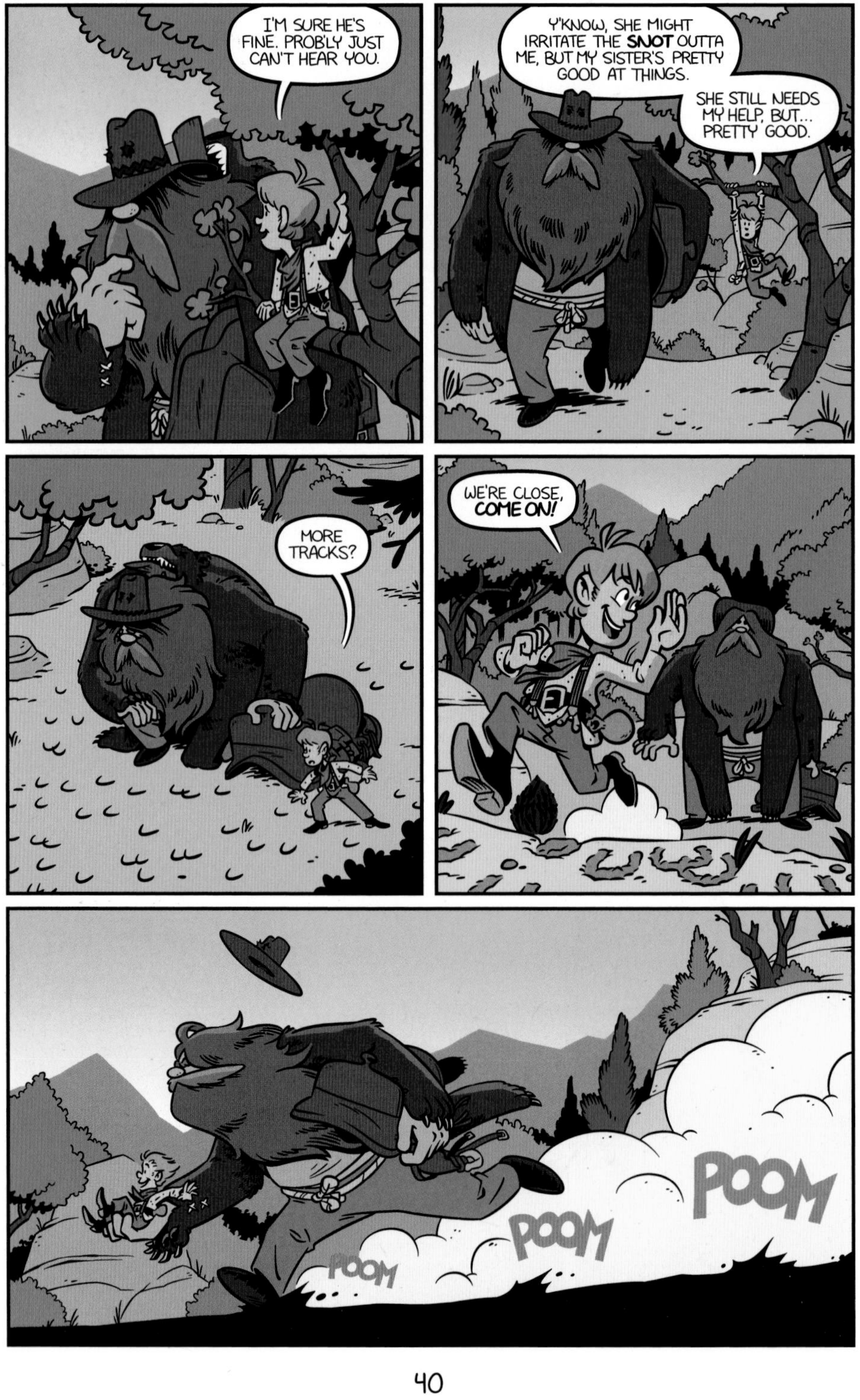
I'M SURE HE'S FINE. PROB'LY JUST CAN'T HEAR YOU.
Y'KNOW, SHE MIGHT IRRITATE THE **SNOT** OUTTA ME, BUT MY SISTER'S PRETTY GOOD AT THINGS.
SHE STILL NEEDS MY HELP, BUT... PRETTY GOOD.
MORE TRACKS?
WE'RE CLOSE, **COME ON!**
POOM
POOM
POOM

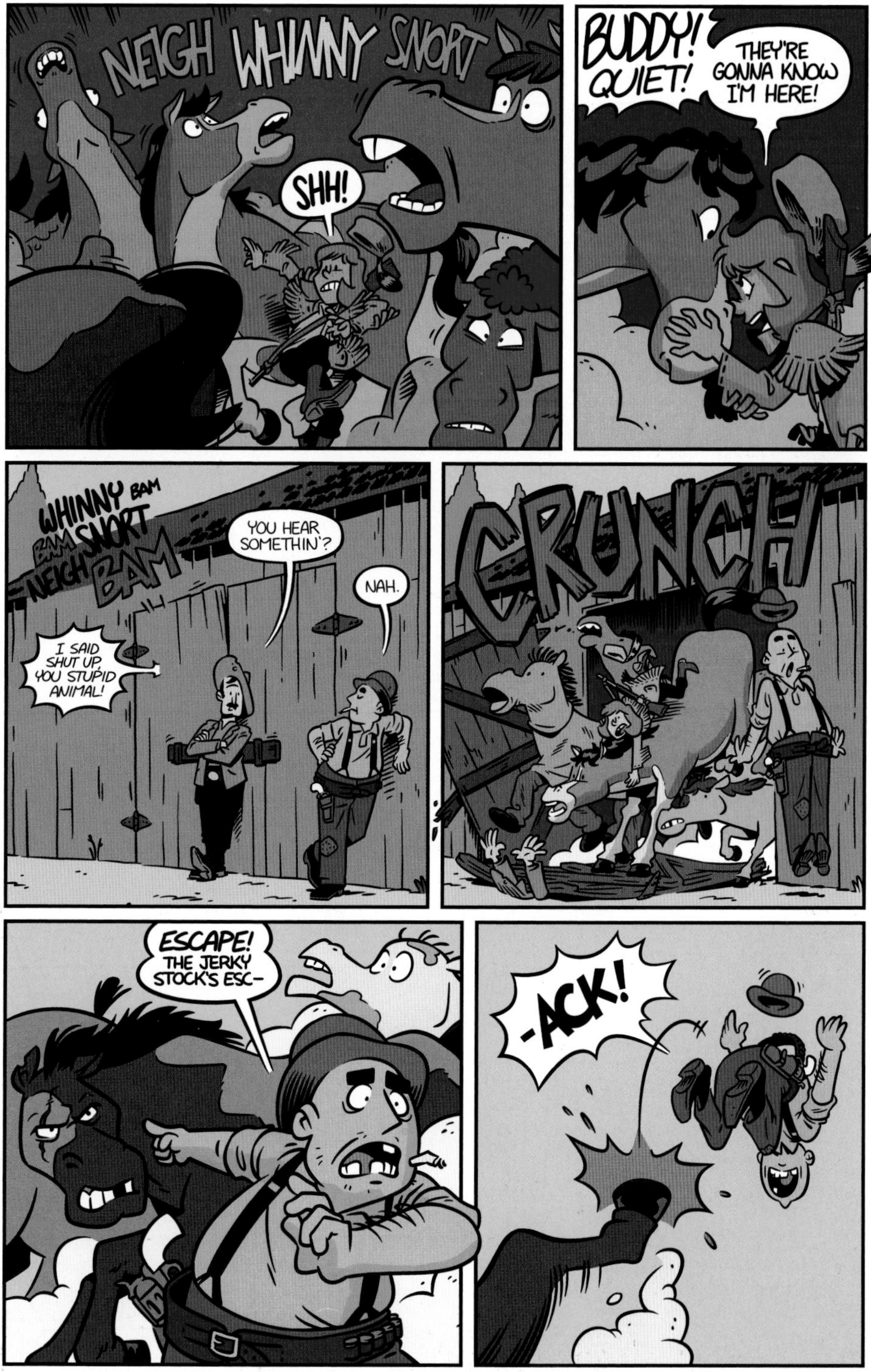
NEIGH WHINNY SNORT
SHH!
BUDDY! QUIET!
THEY'RE GONNA KNOW I'M HERE!
WHINNY BAM BAM SNORT NEIGH BAM
YOU HEAR SOMETHIN'?
NAH.
I SAID SHUT UP, YOU STUPID ANIMAL!
CRUNCH
ESCAPE! THE JERKY STOCK'S ESC-
-ACK!

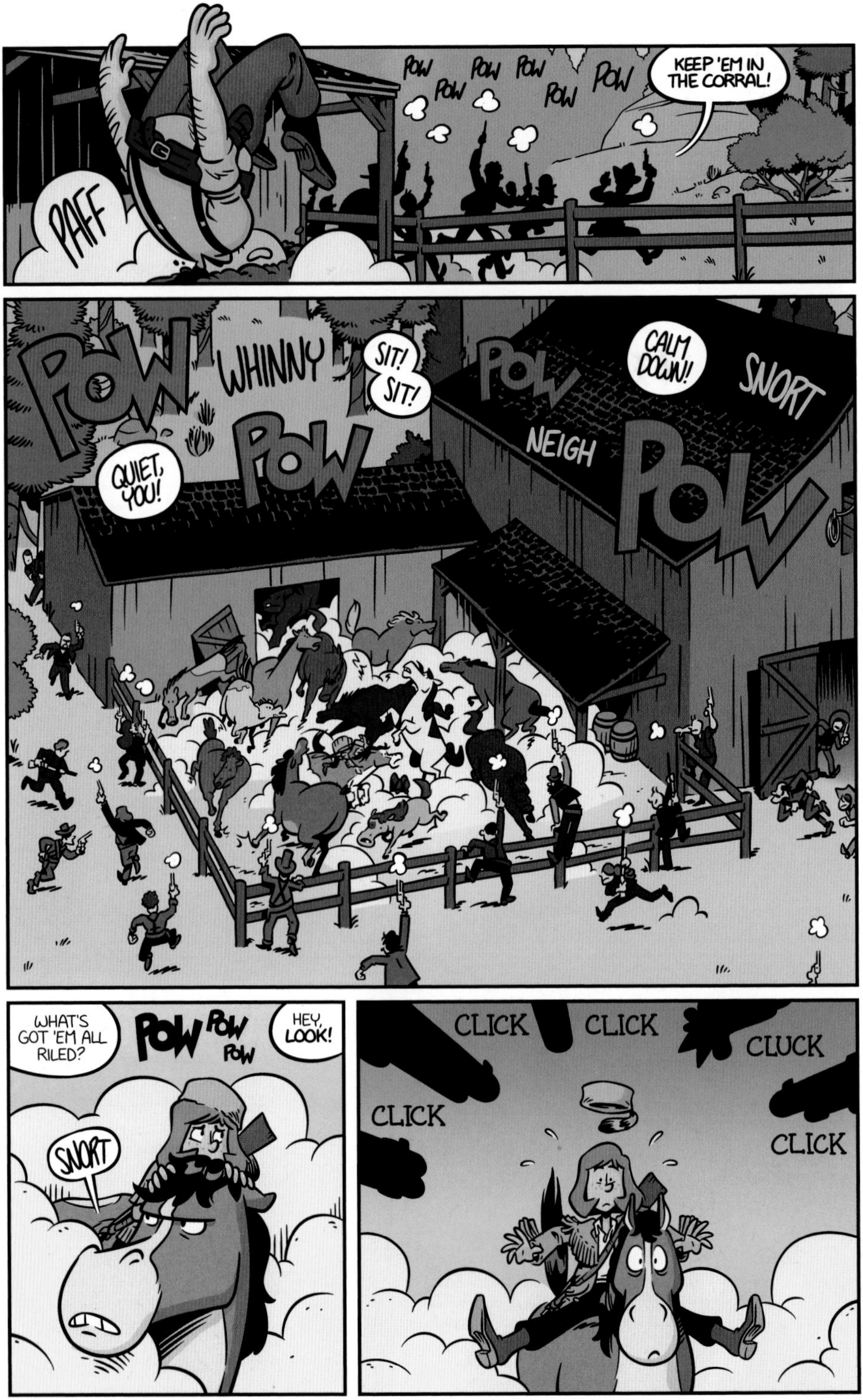
PAFF
POW POW POW POW POW POW
KEEP 'EM IN THE CORRAL!
POW
WHINNY
SIT! SIT!
POW
CALM DOWN!
SNORT
QUIET, YOU!
POW
NEIGH
POW
WHAT'S GOT 'EM ALL RILED?
POW POW POW
HEY, LOOK!
SNORT
CLICK
CLICK
CLUCK
CLICK
CLICK

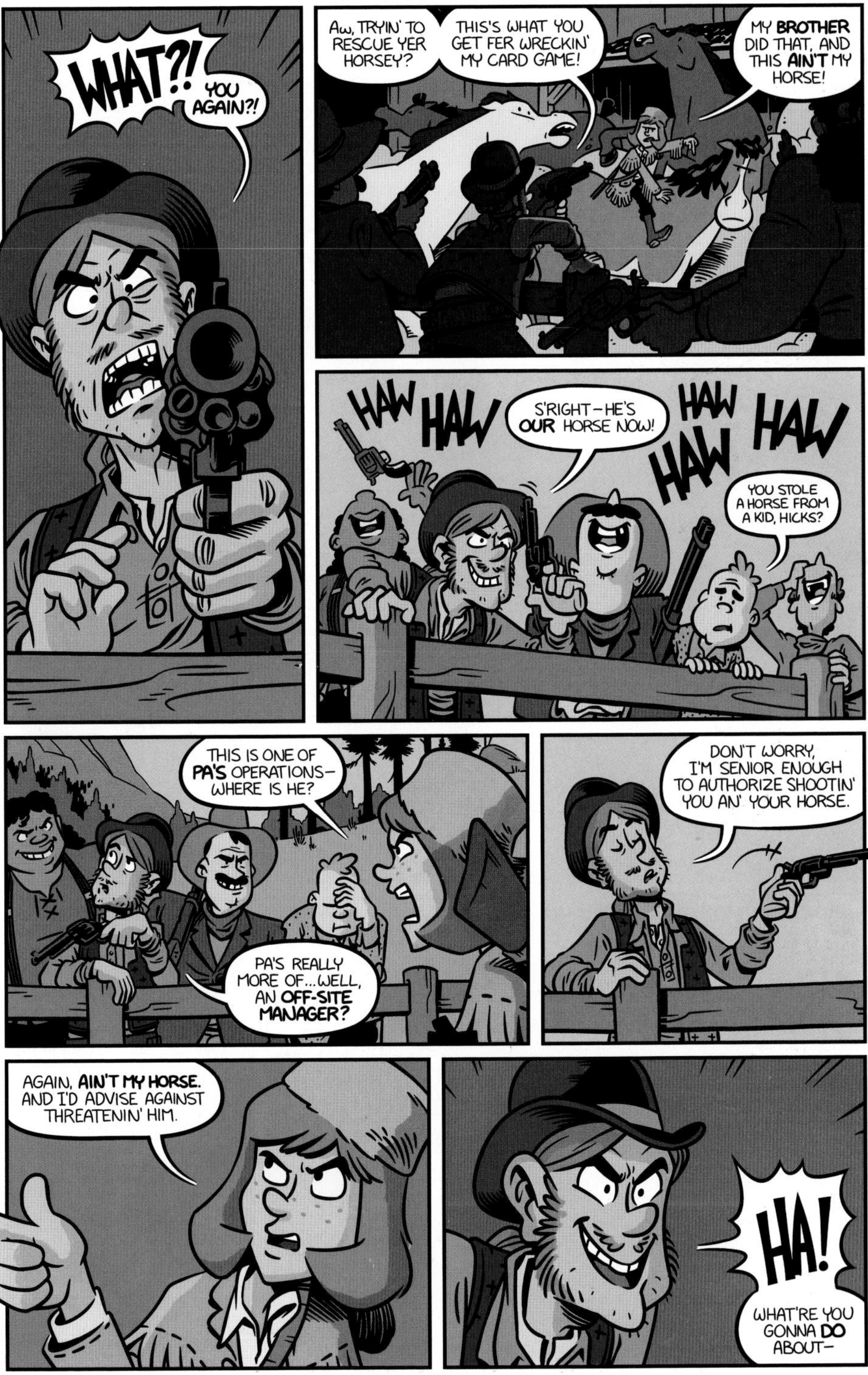
WHAT?!
YOU AGAIN?!
Aw, TRYIN' TO RESCUE YER HORSEY?
THIS'S WHAT YOU GET FER WRECKIN' MY CARD GAME!
MY BROTHER DID THAT, AND THIS AIN'T MY HORSE!
HAW HAW
S'RIGHT—HE'S OUR HORSE NOW!
HAW HAW HAW
YOU STOLE A HORSE FROM A KID, HICKS?
THIS IS ONE OF PA'S OPERATIONS—WHERE IS HE?
PA'S REALLY MORE OF...WELL, AN OFF-SITE MANAGER?
DON'T WORRY, I'M SENIOR ENOUGH TO AUTHORIZE SHOOTIN' YOU AN' YOUR HORSE.
AGAIN, AIN'T MY HORSE. AND I'D ADVISE AGAINST THREATENIN' HIM.
HA!
WHAT'RE YOU GONNA DO ABOUT—

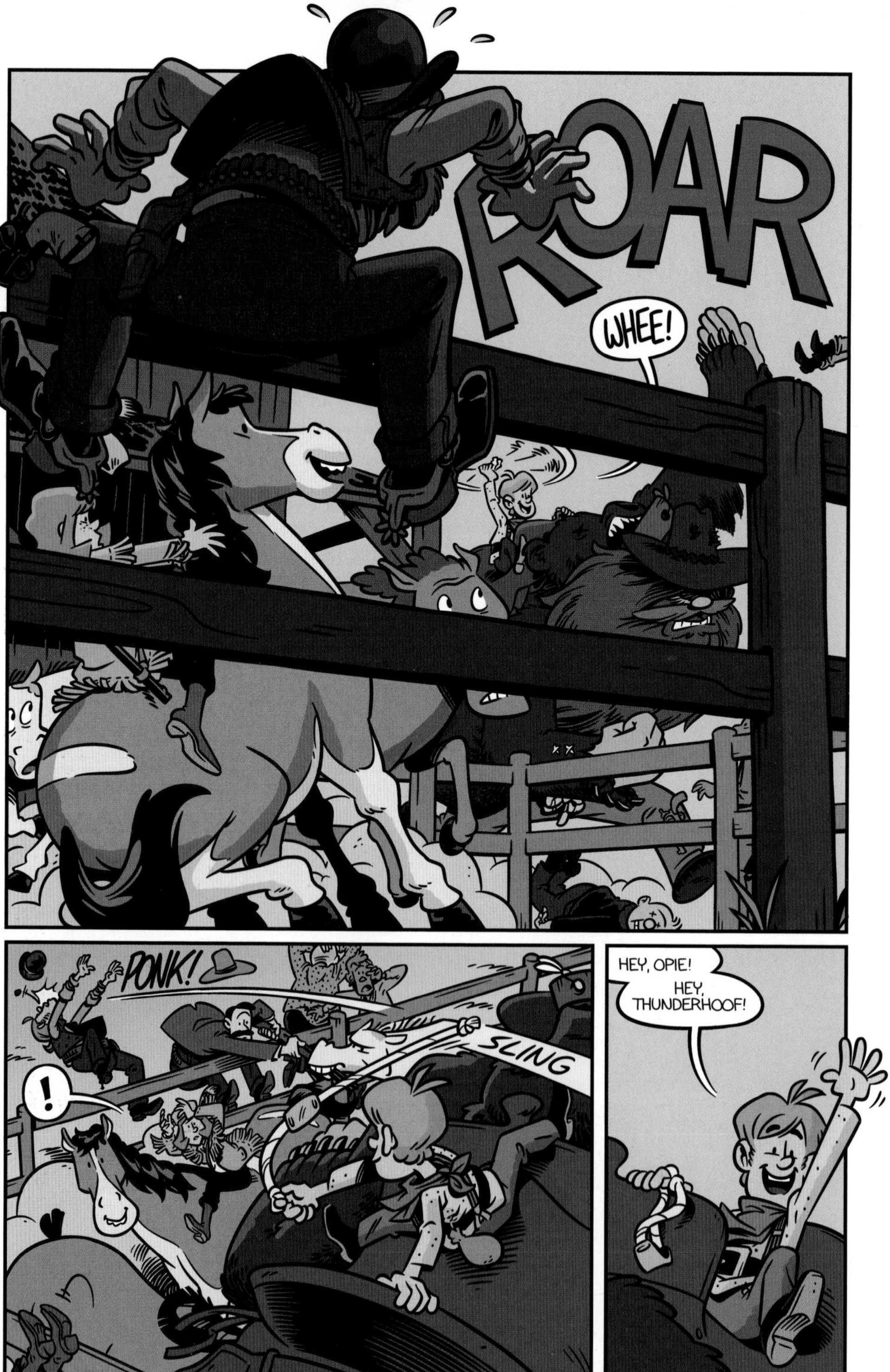
ROAR
WHEE!
PONK!
SLING
!
HEY, OPIE!
HEY, THUNDERHOOF!

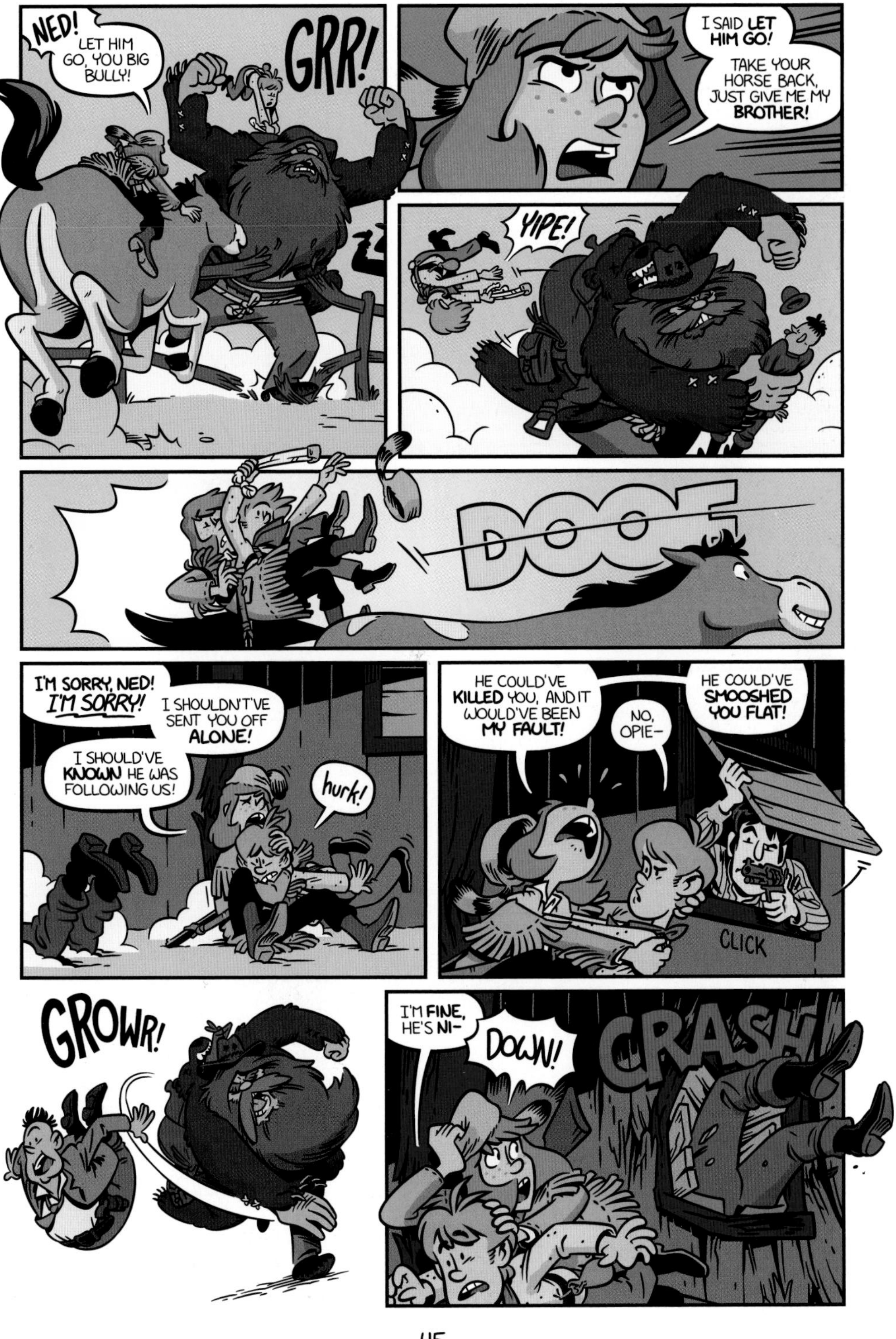
NED!
LET HIM GO, YOU BIG BULLY!
GRR!
I SAID LET HIM GO!
TAKE YOUR HORSE BACK, JUST GIVE ME MY BROTHER!
YIPE!
DOOF
I'M SORRY, NED! I'M SORRY!
I SHOULDN'T'VE SENT YOU OFF ALONE!
I SHOULD'VE KNOWN HE WAS FOLLOWING US!
hurk!
HE COULD'VE KILLED YOU, AND IT WOULD'VE BEEN MY FAULT!
NO, OPIE-
HE COULD'VE SMOOSHED YOU FLAT!
CLICK
GROWR!
I'M FINE, HE'S NI-
DOWN!
CRASH

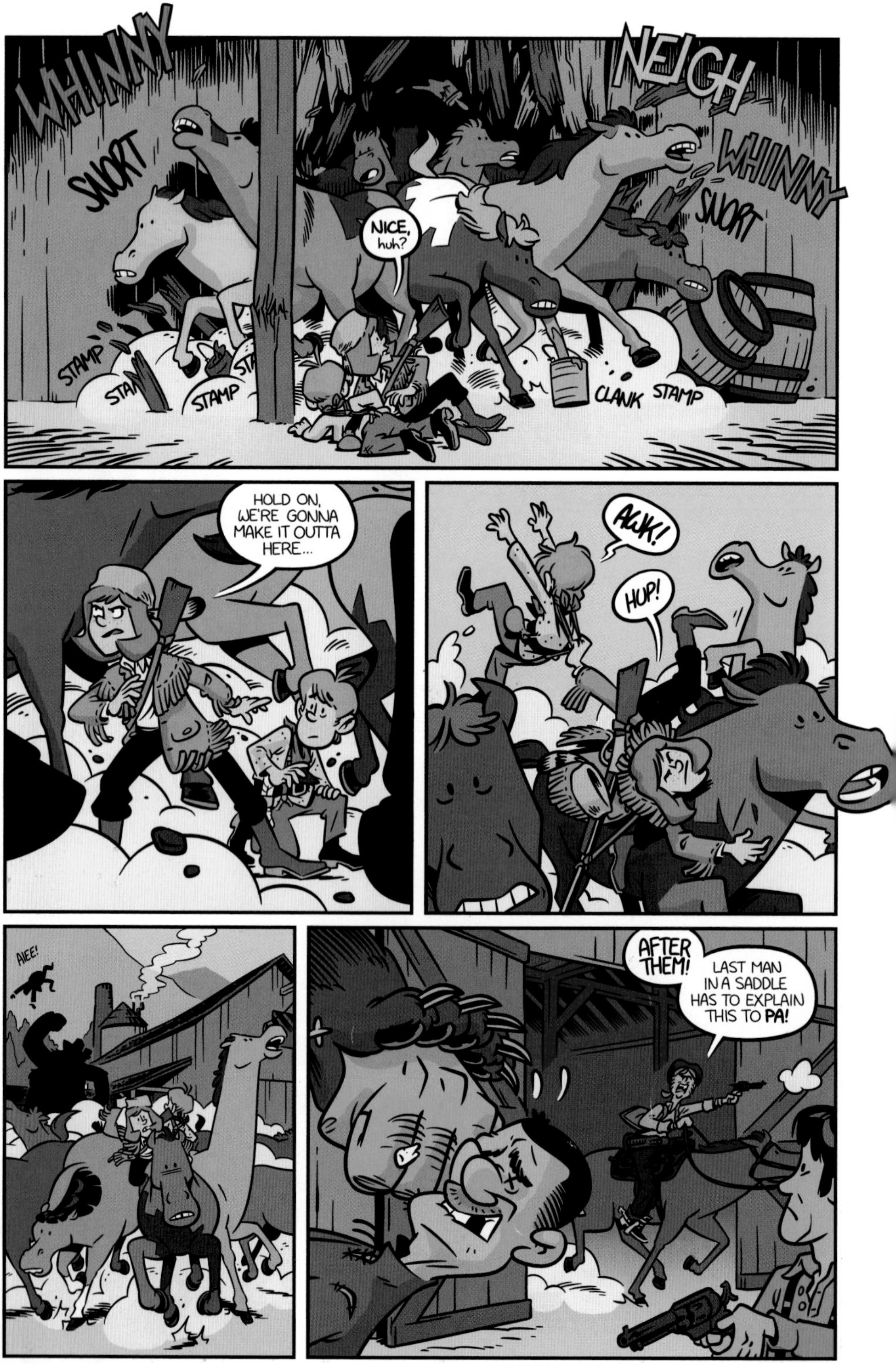
WHINNY
NEIGH
SNORT
NICE, huh?
WHINNY
SNORT
STAMP
STAMP
STAMP
CLANK
STAMP
HOLD ON, WE'RE GONNA MAKE IT OUTTA HERE...
AWK!
HUP!
AIEE!
AFTER THEM!
LAST MAN IN A SADDLE HAS TO EXPLAIN THIS TO PA!

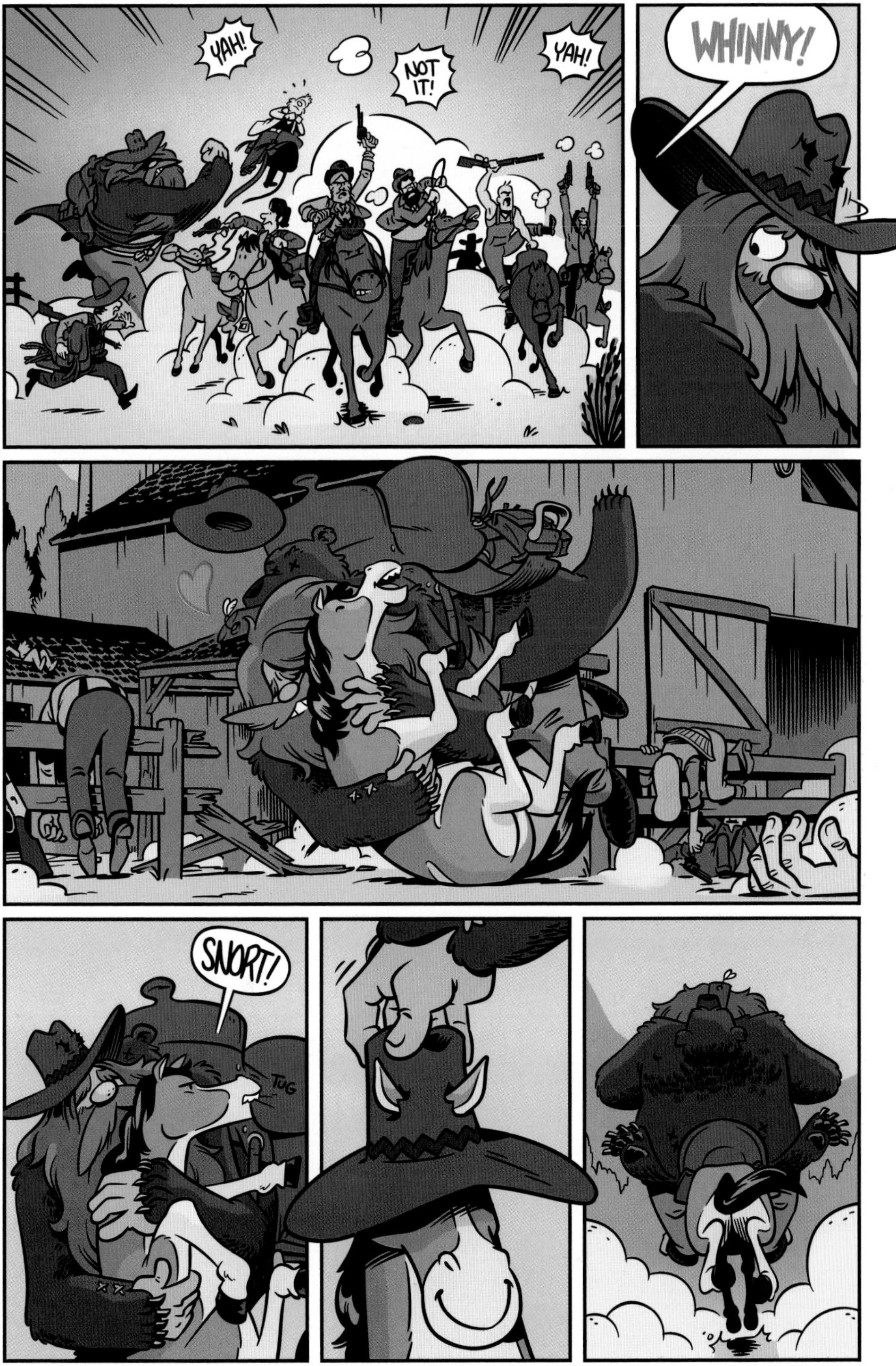
YAH!
NOT IT!
YAH!
WHINNY!
SNORT!
TUG

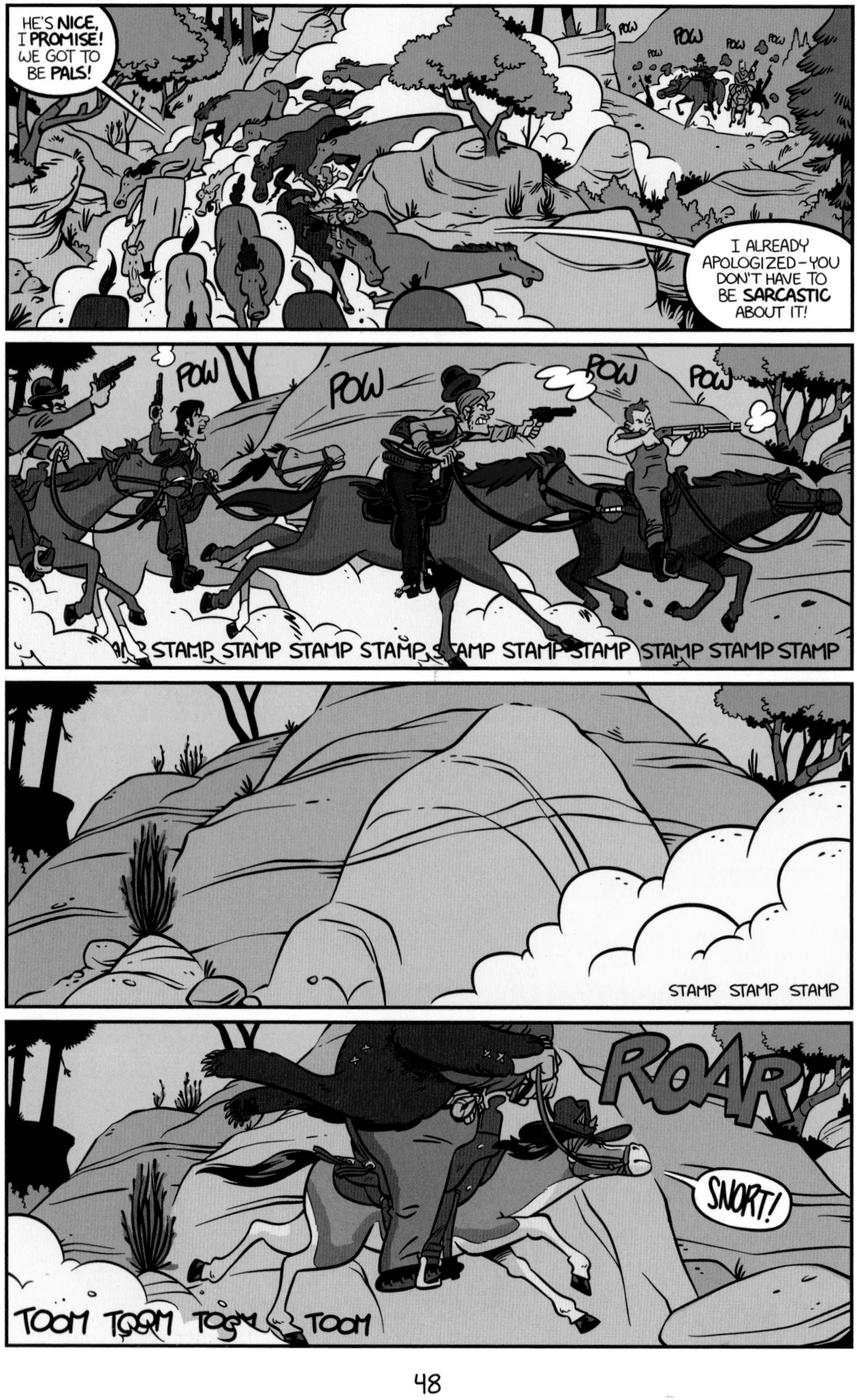
HE'S NICE, I PROMISE! WE GOT TO BE PALS!
POW
I ALREADY APOLOGIZED–YOU DON'T HAVE TO BE SARCASTIC ABOUT IT!
POW
POW
POW
POW
STAMP STAMP STAMP STAMP STAMP STAMP STAMP STAMP STAMP
STAMP STAMP STAMP
ROAR
SNORT!
TOOM TOOM

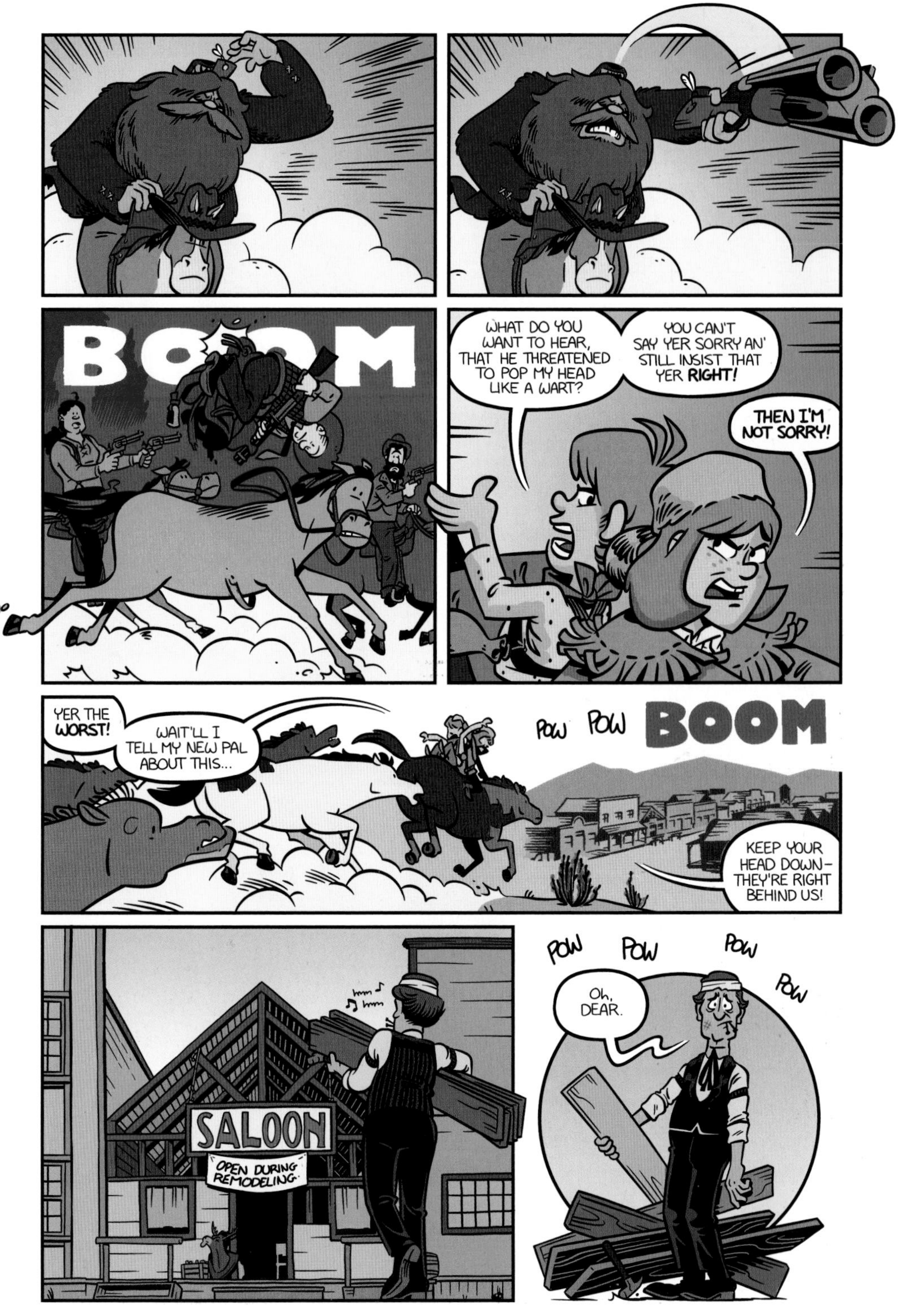
BOOM
WHAT DO YOU WANT TO HEAR, THAT HE THREATENED TO POP MY HEAD LIKE A WART?
YOU CAN'T SAY YER SORRY AN' STILL INSIST THAT YER **RIGHT!**
THEN I'M NOT SORRY!
YER THE **WORST!**
WAIT'LL I TELL MY NEW PAL ABOUT THIS...
POW POW BOOM
KEEP YOUR HEAD DOWN—THEY'RE RIGHT BEHIND US!
hmm hmm
SALOON
OPEN DURING REMODELING
POW POW POW POW
Oh, DEAR.

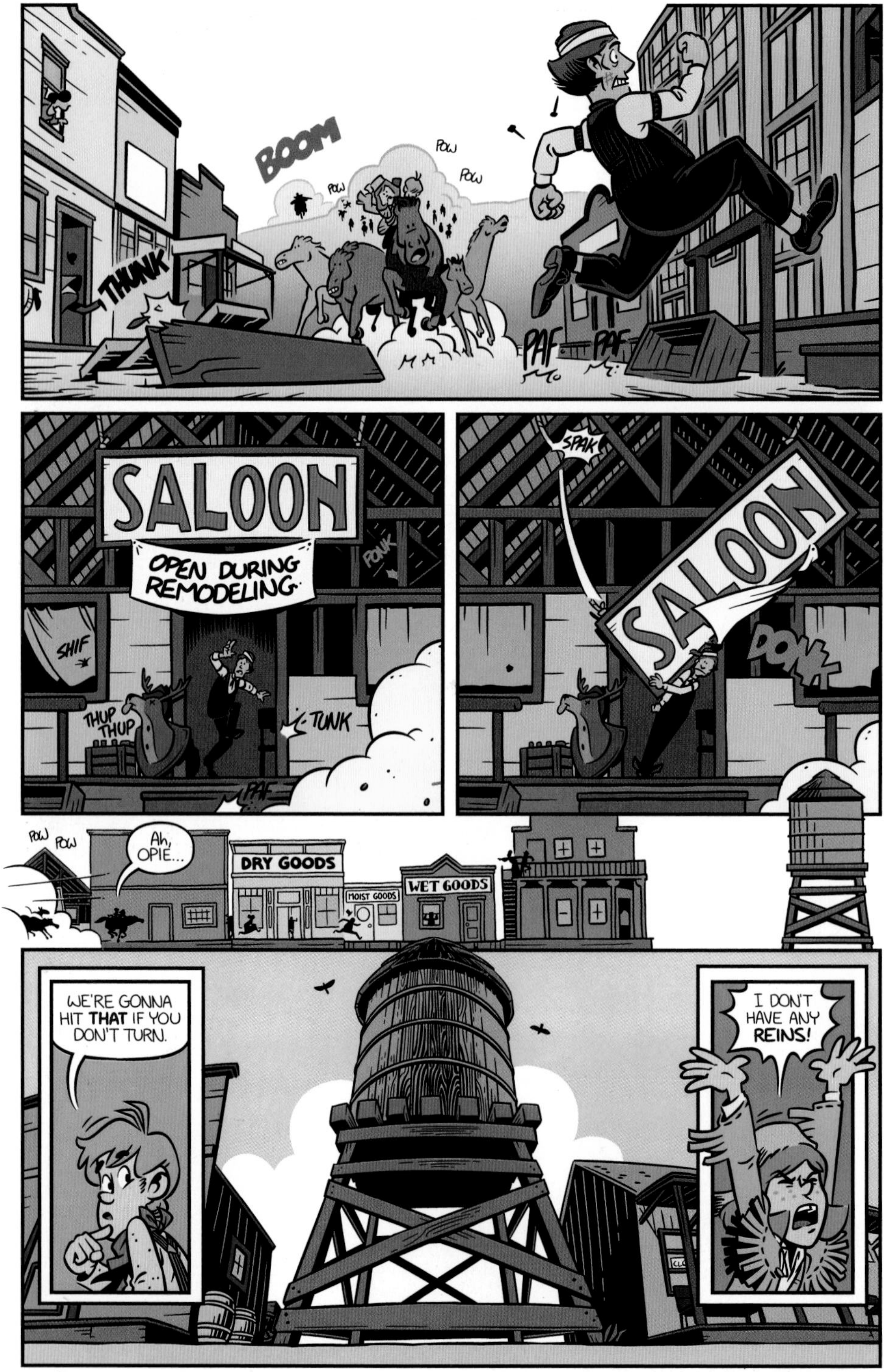
BOOM
POW
POW
POW
THUNK
PAF
PAF
SALOON
OPEN DURING REMODELING
PONK
SHIF
THUP THUP
TUNK
PAF
SPAK
SALOON
DONK
POW
POW
Ah, OPIE...
DRY GOODS
MOIST GOODS
WET GOODS
WE'RE GONNA HIT **THAT** IF YOU DON'T TURN.
I DON'T HAVE ANY **REINS!**

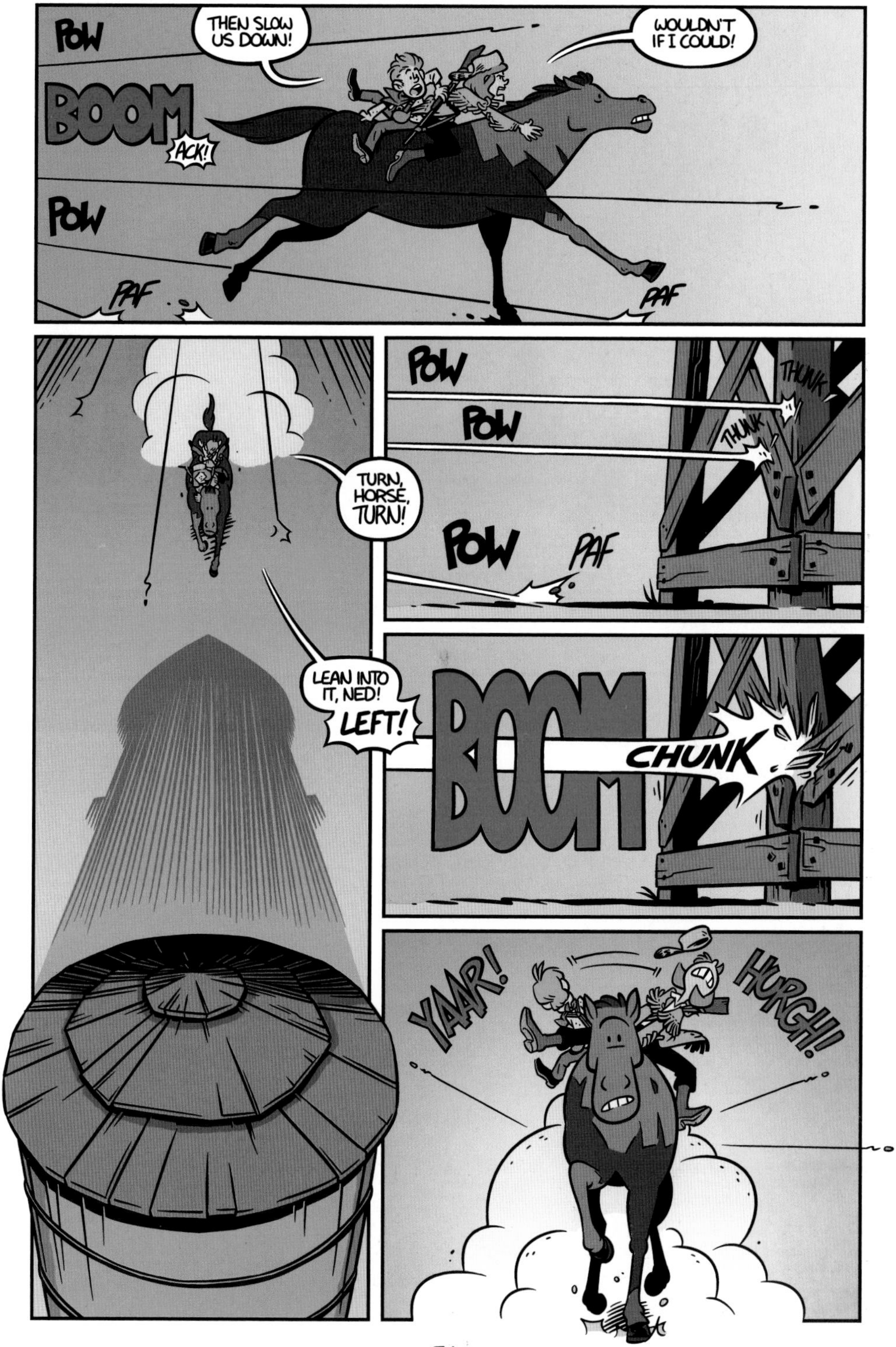
POW
THEN SLOW US DOWN!
WOULDN'T IF I COULD!
BOOM
ACK!
POW
PAF
PAF
TURN, HORSE, TURN!
LEAN INTO IT, NED! LEFT!
POW
THUNK
POW
THUNK
POW
PAF
BOOM
CHUNK
YAAR!
HURGH!

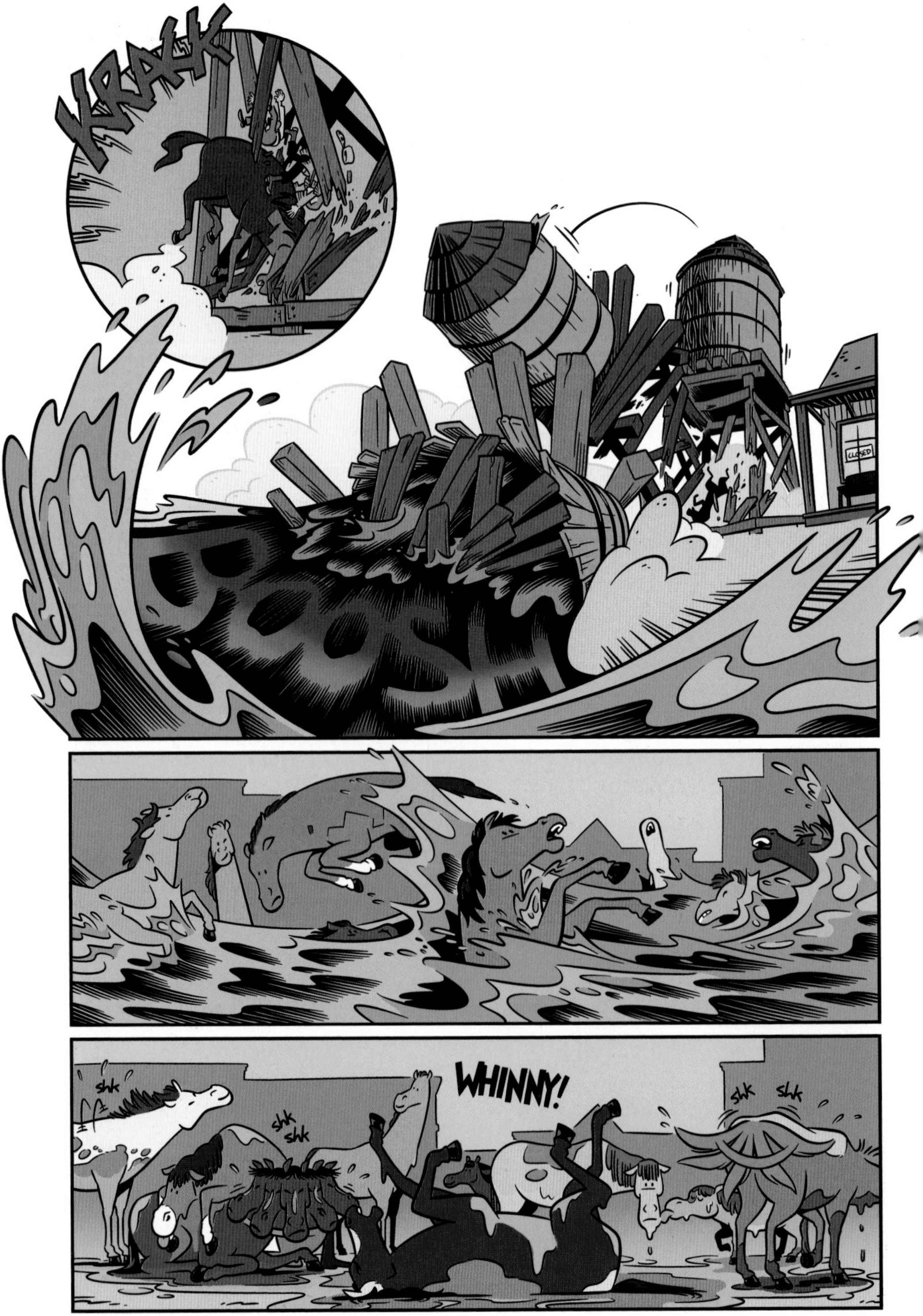
KRAKK
CLOSED
BOOSH
shk
shk
shk
WHINNY!
shk
shk

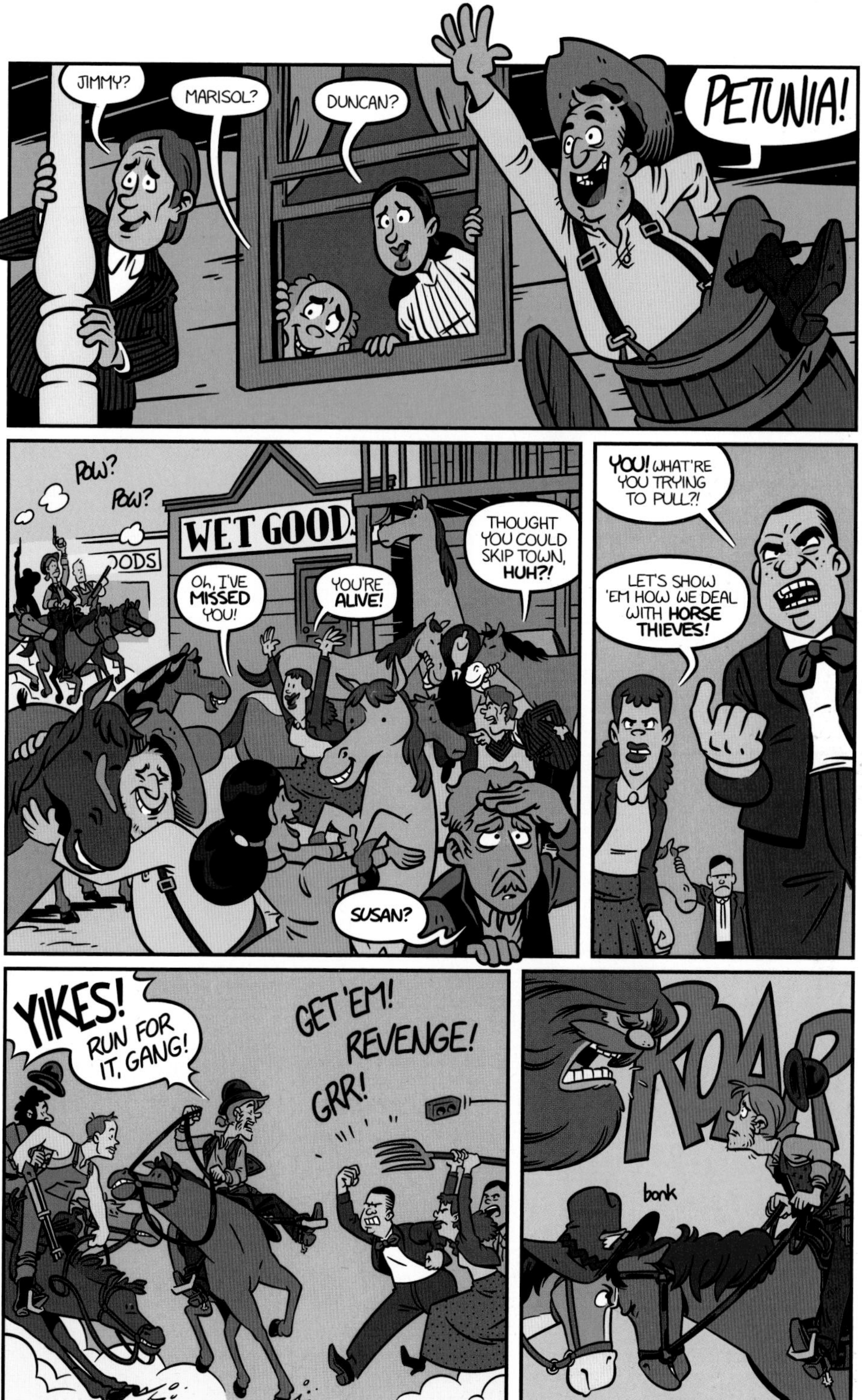

JIMMY?
MARISOL?
DUNCAN?
PETUNIA!
POW?
POW?
WET GOOD
OODS
Oh, I'VE MISSED YOU!
YOU'RE ALIVE!
THOUGHT YOU COULD SKIP TOWN, HUH?!
SUSAN?
YOU! WHAT'RE YOU TRYING TO PULL?!
LET'S SHOW 'EM HOW WE DEAL WITH HORSE THIEVES!
YIKES! RUN FOR IT, GANG!
GET 'EM!
REVENGE!
GRR!
ROAR
bonk

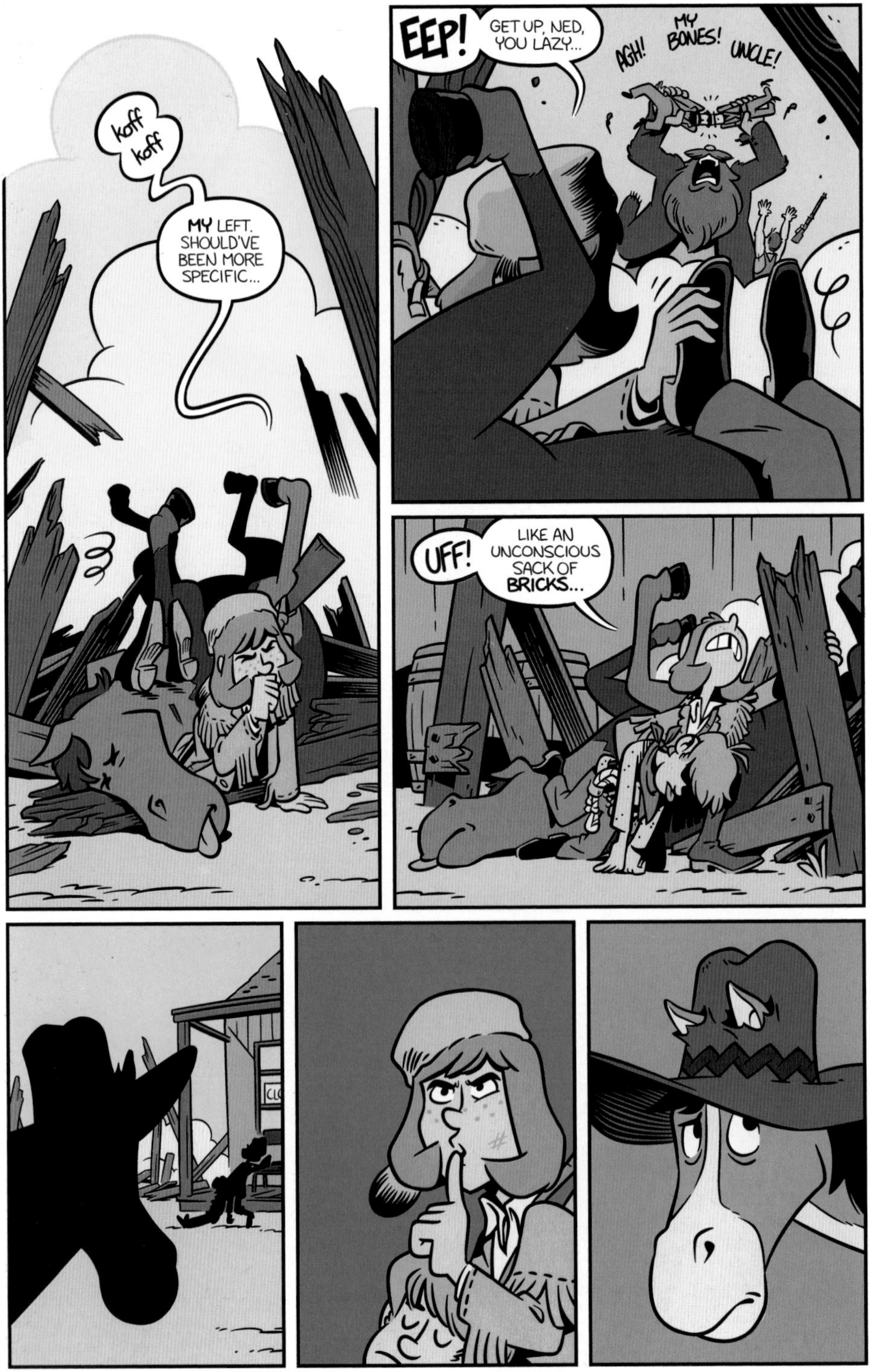
koff koff
MY LEFT. SHOULD'VE BEEN MORE SPECIFIC...
EEP!
GET UP, NED, YOU LAZY...
AGH!
MY BONES!
UNCLE!
UFF!
LIKE AN UNCONSCIOUS SACK OF BRICKS...

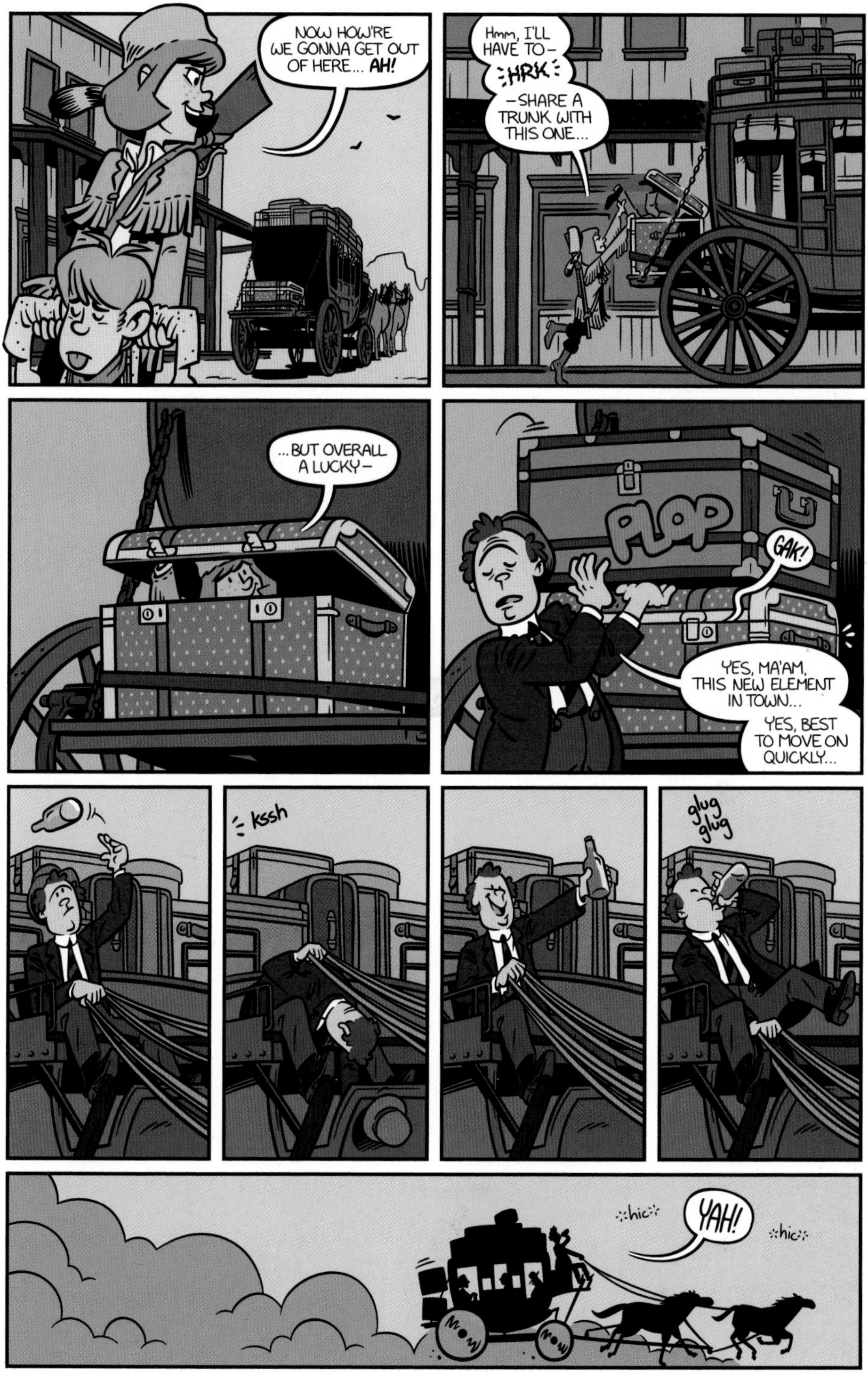
NOW HOW'RE WE GONNA GET OUT OF HERE... AH!
Hmm, I'LL HAVE TO–
HRK
–SHARE A TRUNK WITH THIS ONE...
...BUT OVERALL A LUCKY–
PLOP
GAK!
YES, MA'AM, THIS NEW ELEMENT IN TOWN...
YES, BEST TO MOVE ON QUICKLY...
kssh
glug glug
hic
YAH!
hic

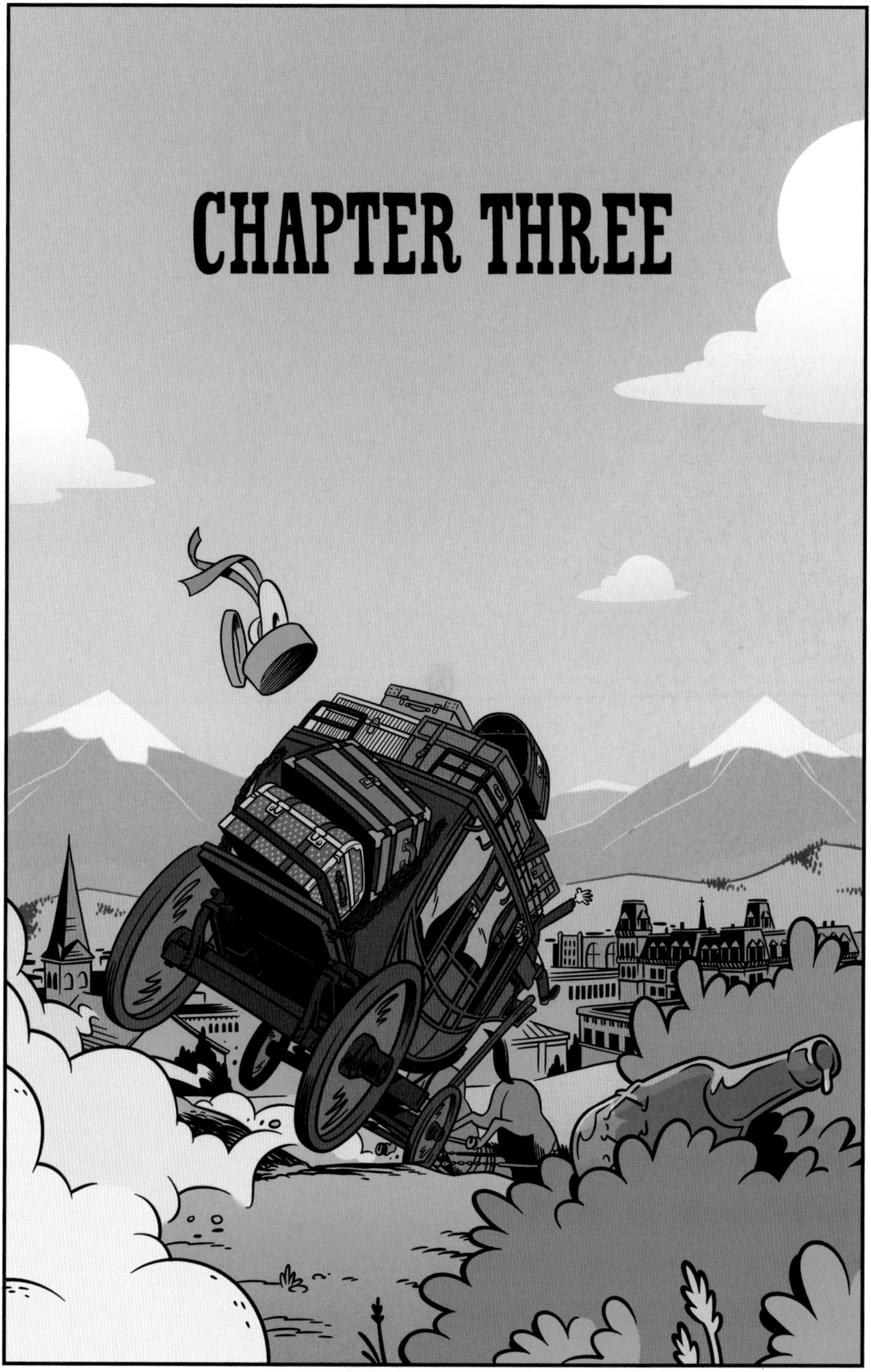
CHAPTER THREE

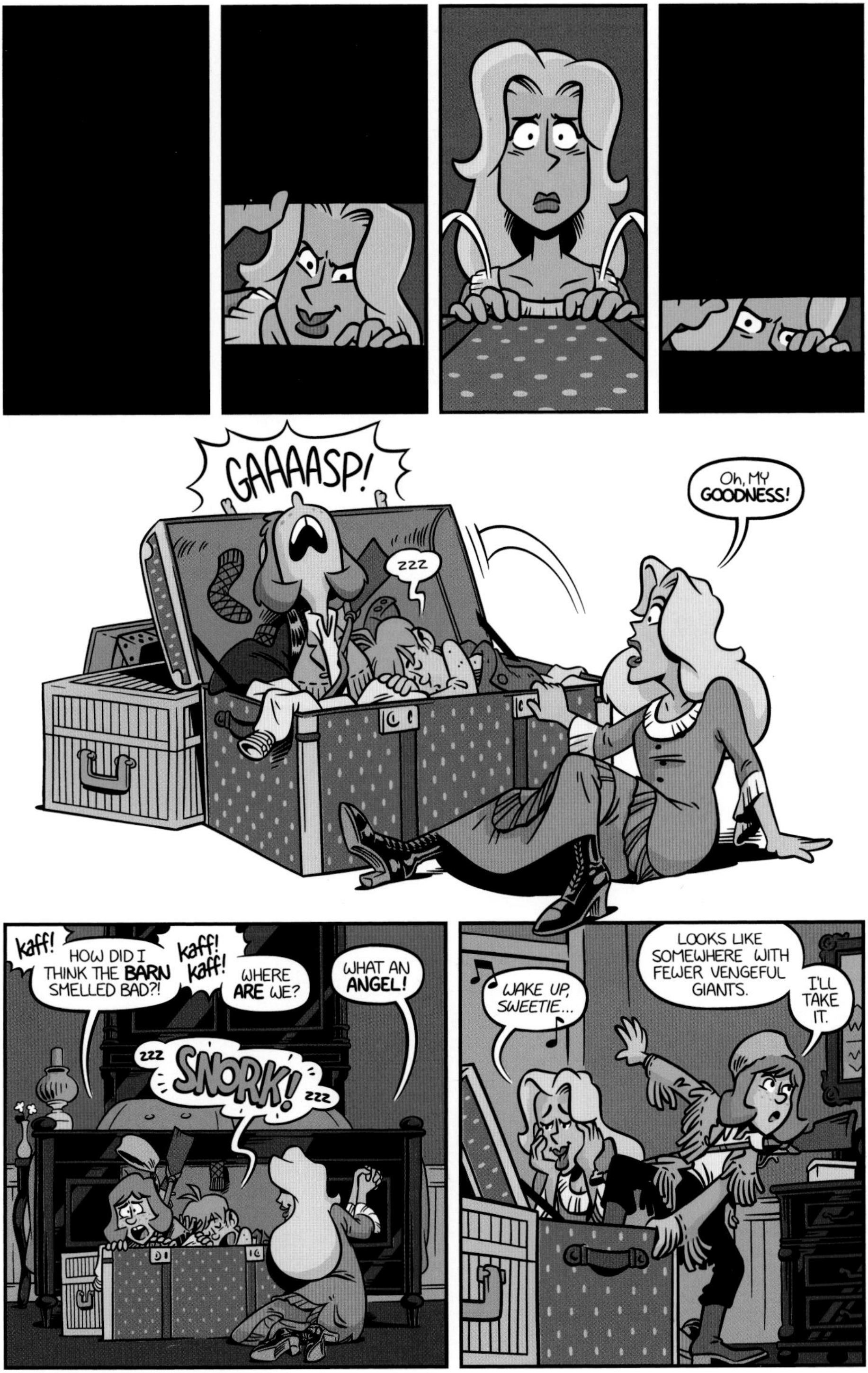
GAAAASP!
zzz
Oh, MY GOODNESS!
kaff!
HOW DID I THINK THE BARN SMELLED BAD?!
kaff! kaff!
WHERE ARE WE?
WHAT AN ANGEL!
zzz SNORK! zzz
WAKE UP, SWEETIE...
LOOKS LIKE SOMEWHERE WITH FEWER VENGEFUL GIANTS.
I'LL TAKE IT.

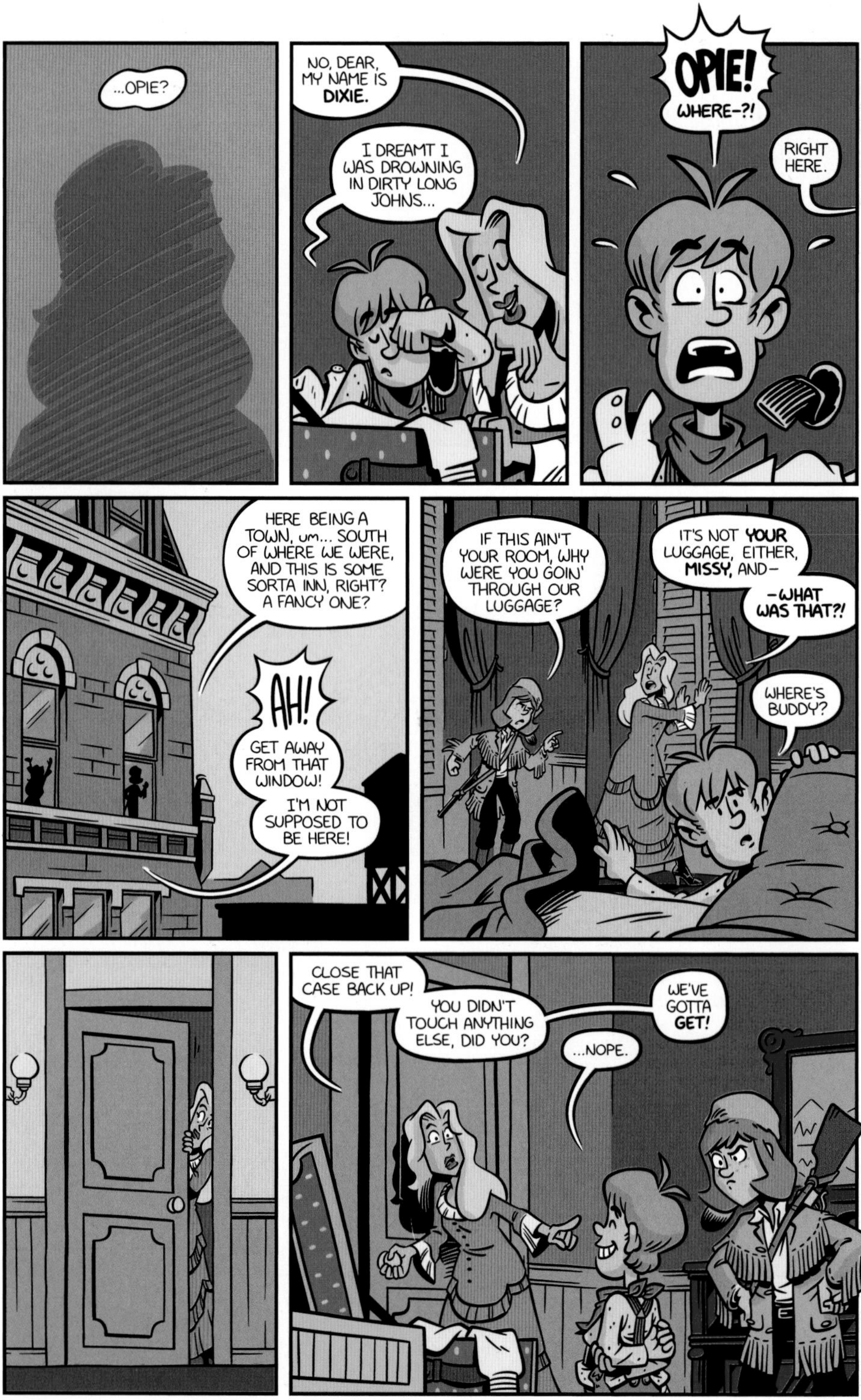
...OPIE?
NO, DEAR, MY NAME IS **DIXIE.**
I DREAMT I WAS DROWNING IN DIRTY LONG JOHNS...
OPIE!
WHERE-?!
RIGHT HERE.
HERE BEING A TOWN, um... SOUTH OF WHERE WE WERE, AND THIS IS SOME SORTA INN, RIGHT? A FANCY ONE?
AH!
GET AWAY FROM THAT WINDOW!
I'M NOT SUPPOSED TO BE HERE!
IF THIS AIN'T YOUR ROOM, WHY WERE YOU GOIN' THROUGH OUR LUGGAGE?
IT'S NOT **YOUR** LUGGAGE, EITHER, **MISSY,** AND–
–WHAT WAS THAT?!
WHERE'S BUDDY?
CLOSE THAT CASE BACK UP!
YOU DIDN'T TOUCH ANYTHING ELSE, DID YOU?
WE'VE GOTTA **GET!**
...NOPE.

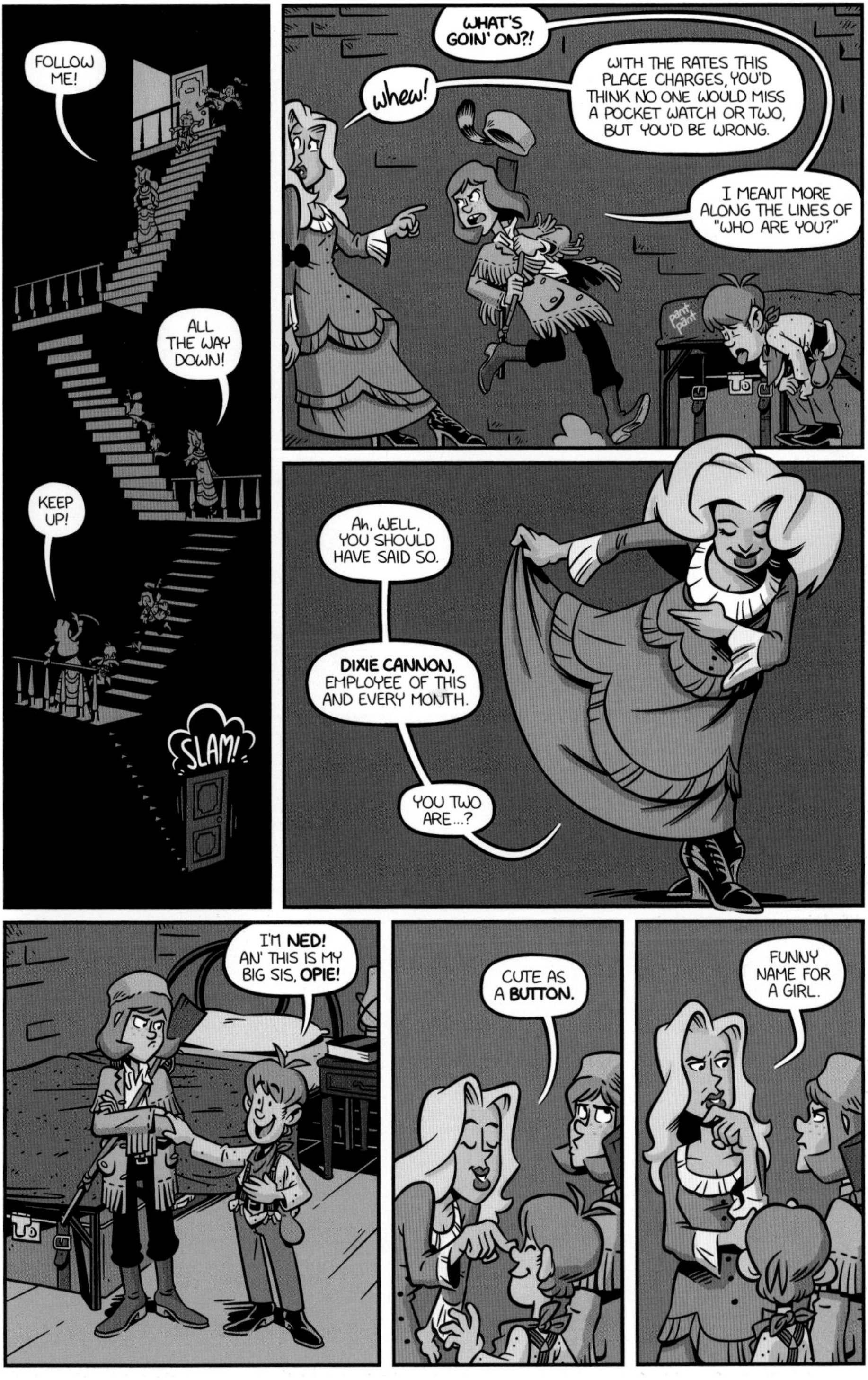
FOLLOW ME!
ALL THE WAY DOWN!
KEEP UP!
SLAM!
WHAT'S GOIN' ON?!
whew!
WITH THE RATES THIS PLACE CHARGES, YOU'D THINK NO ONE WOULD MISS A POCKET WATCH OR TWO, BUT YOU'D BE WRONG.
I MEANT MORE ALONG THE LINES OF "WHO ARE YOU?"
pant pant
Ah, WELL, YOU SHOULD HAVE SAID SO.
DIXIE CANNON, EMPLOYEE OF THIS AND EVERY MONTH.
YOU TWO ARE...?
I'M NED! AN' THIS IS MY BIG SIS, OPIE!
CUTE AS A BUTTON.
FUNNY NAME FOR A GIRL.

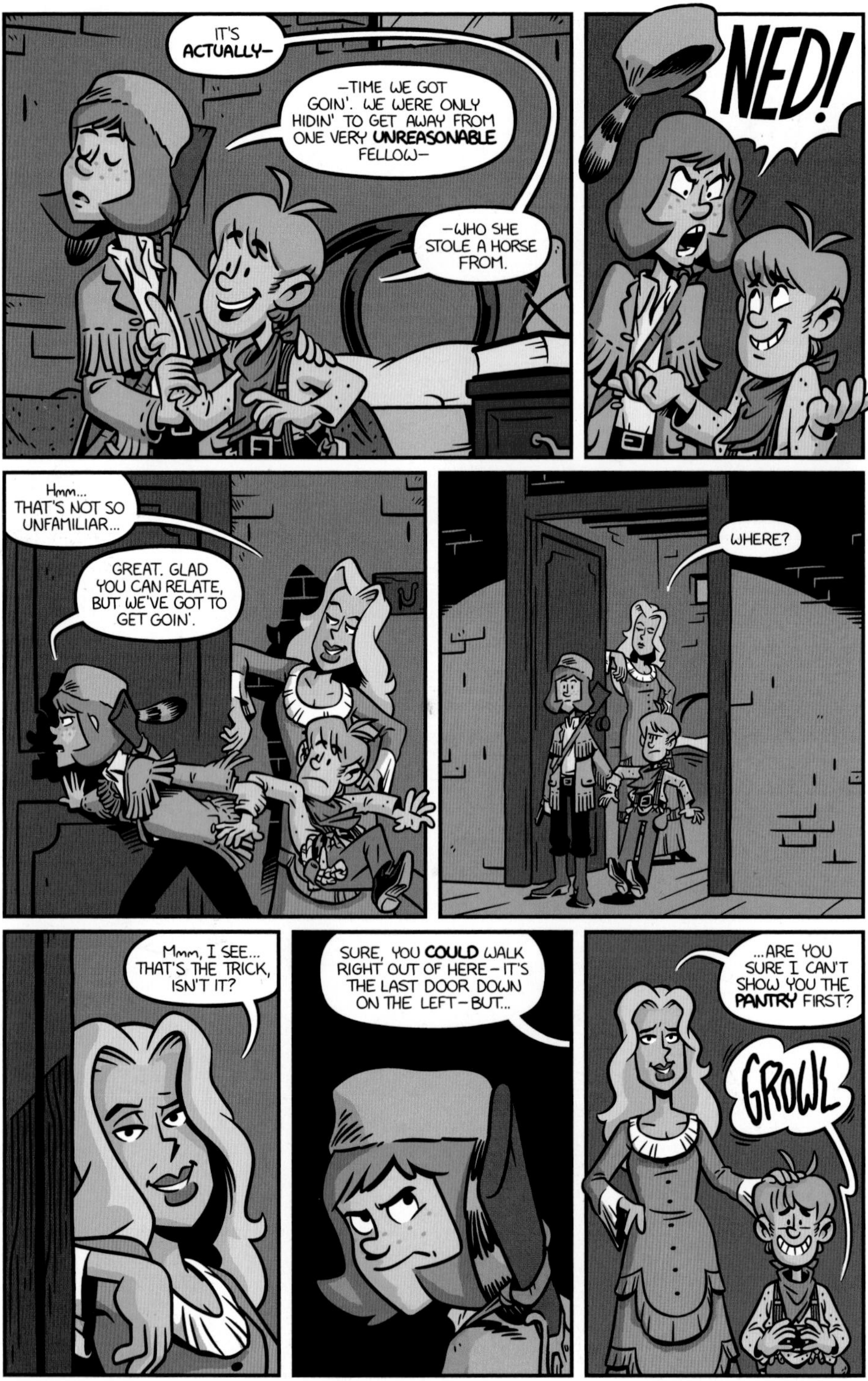
IT'S ACTUALLY—
—TIME WE GOT GOIN'. WE WERE ONLY HIDIN' TO GET AWAY FROM ONE VERY UNREASONABLE FELLOW—
—WHO SHE STOLE A HORSE FROM.
NED!
Hmm... THAT'S NOT SO UNFAMILIAR...
GREAT. GLAD YOU CAN RELATE, BUT WE'VE GOT TO GET GOIN'.
WHERE?
Mmm, I SEE... THAT'S THE TRICK, ISN'T IT?
SURE, YOU COULD WALK RIGHT OUT OF HERE—IT'S THE LAST DOOR DOWN ON THE LEFT—BUT...
...ARE YOU SURE I CAN'T SHOW YOU THE PANTRY FIRST?
GROWL

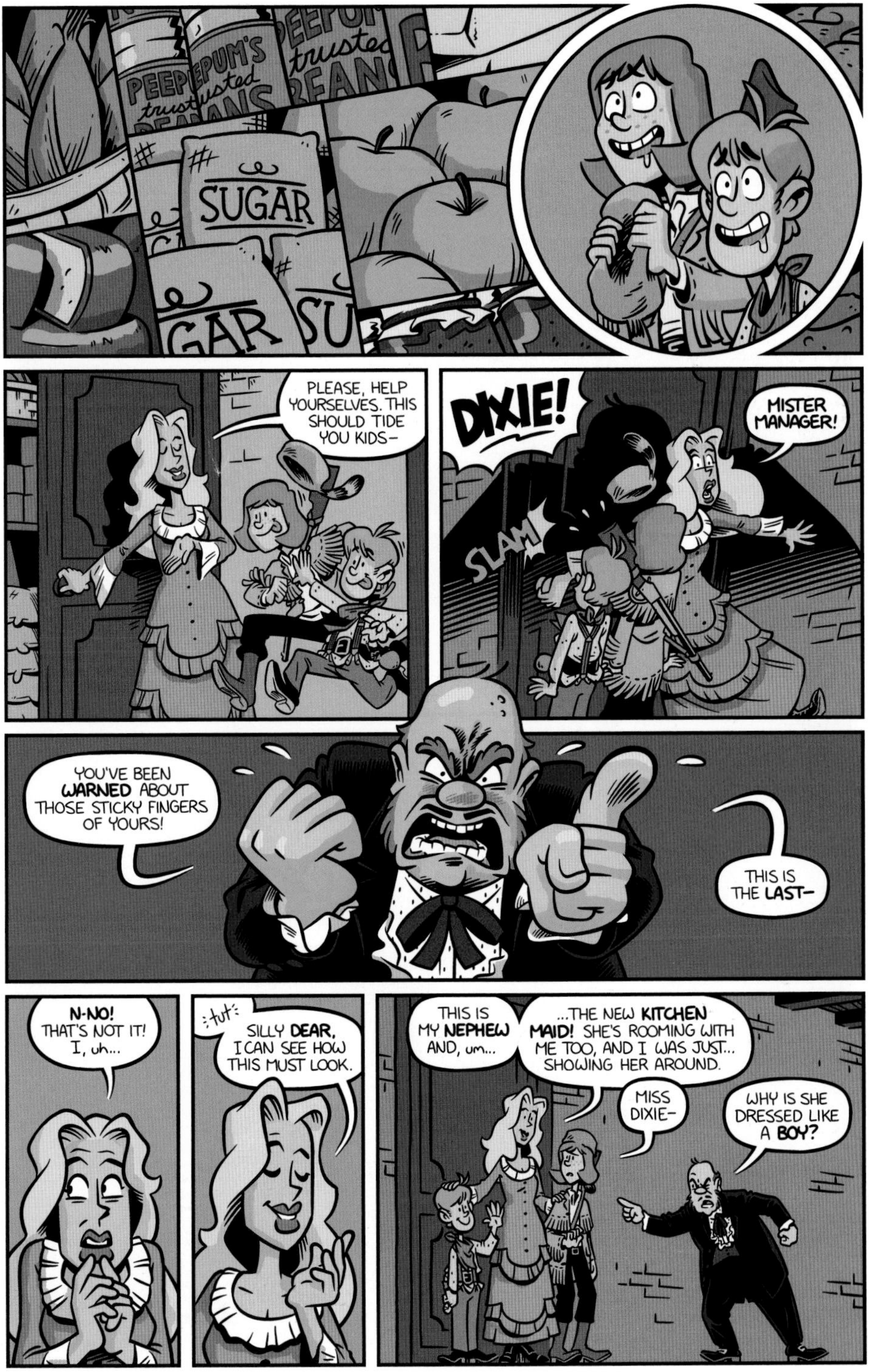
PEEPEPUM'S trusted BEANS
SUGAR
PLEASE, HELP YOURSELVES. THIS SHOULD TIDE YOU KIDS–
DIXIE!
MISTER MANAGER!
SLAM
YOU'VE BEEN WARNED ABOUT THOSE STICKY FINGERS OF YOURS!
THIS IS THE LAST–
N-NO! THAT'S NOT IT! I, uh...
tut
SILLY DEAR, I CAN SEE HOW THIS MUST LOOK.
THIS IS MY NEPHEW AND, um...
...THE NEW KITCHEN MAID! SHE'S ROOMING WITH ME TOO, AND I WAS JUST... SHOWING HER AROUND.
MISS DIXIE–
WHY IS SHE DRESSED LIKE A BOY?

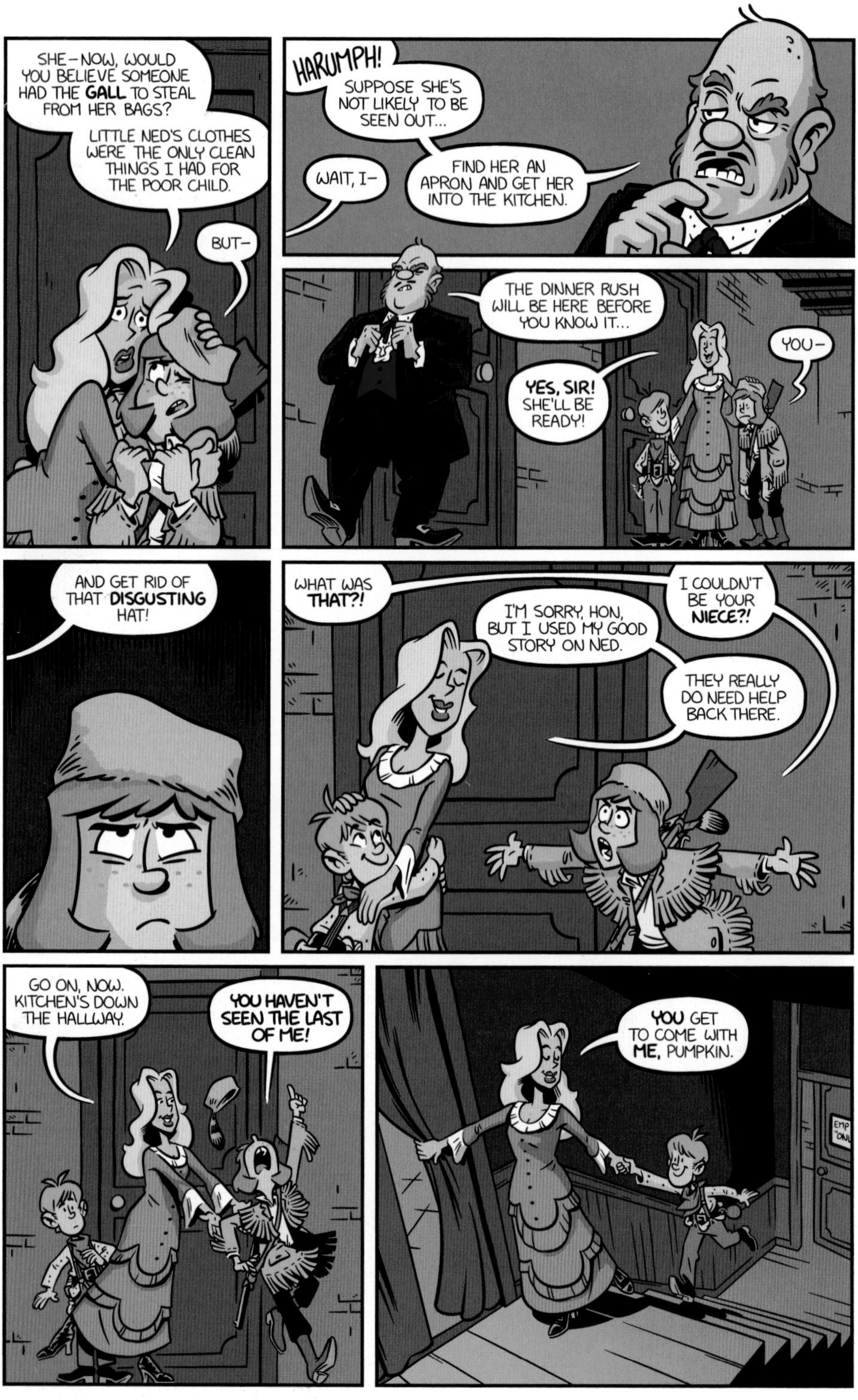
SHE—NOW, WOULD YOU BELIEVE SOMEONE HAD THE **GALL** TO STEAL FROM HER BAGS?
LITTLE NED'S CLOTHES WERE THE ONLY CLEAN THINGS I HAD FOR THE POOR CHILD.
BUT—
HARUMPH!
SUPPOSE SHE'S NOT LIKELY TO BE SEEN OUT...
WAIT, I—
FIND HER AN APRON AND GET HER INTO THE KITCHEN.
THE DINNER RUSH WILL BE HERE BEFORE YOU KNOW IT...
YES, SIR! SHE'LL BE READY!
YOU—
AND GET RID OF THAT **DISGUSTING** HAT!
WHAT WAS **THAT?!**
I COULDN'T BE YOUR **NIECE?!**
I'M SORRY, HON, BUT I USED MY GOOD STORY ON NED.
THEY REALLY DO NEED HELP BACK THERE.
GO ON, NOW. KITCHEN'S DOWN THE HALLWAY.
YOU HAVEN'T SEEN THE LAST OF ME!
YOU GET TO COME WITH **ME,** PUMPKIN.

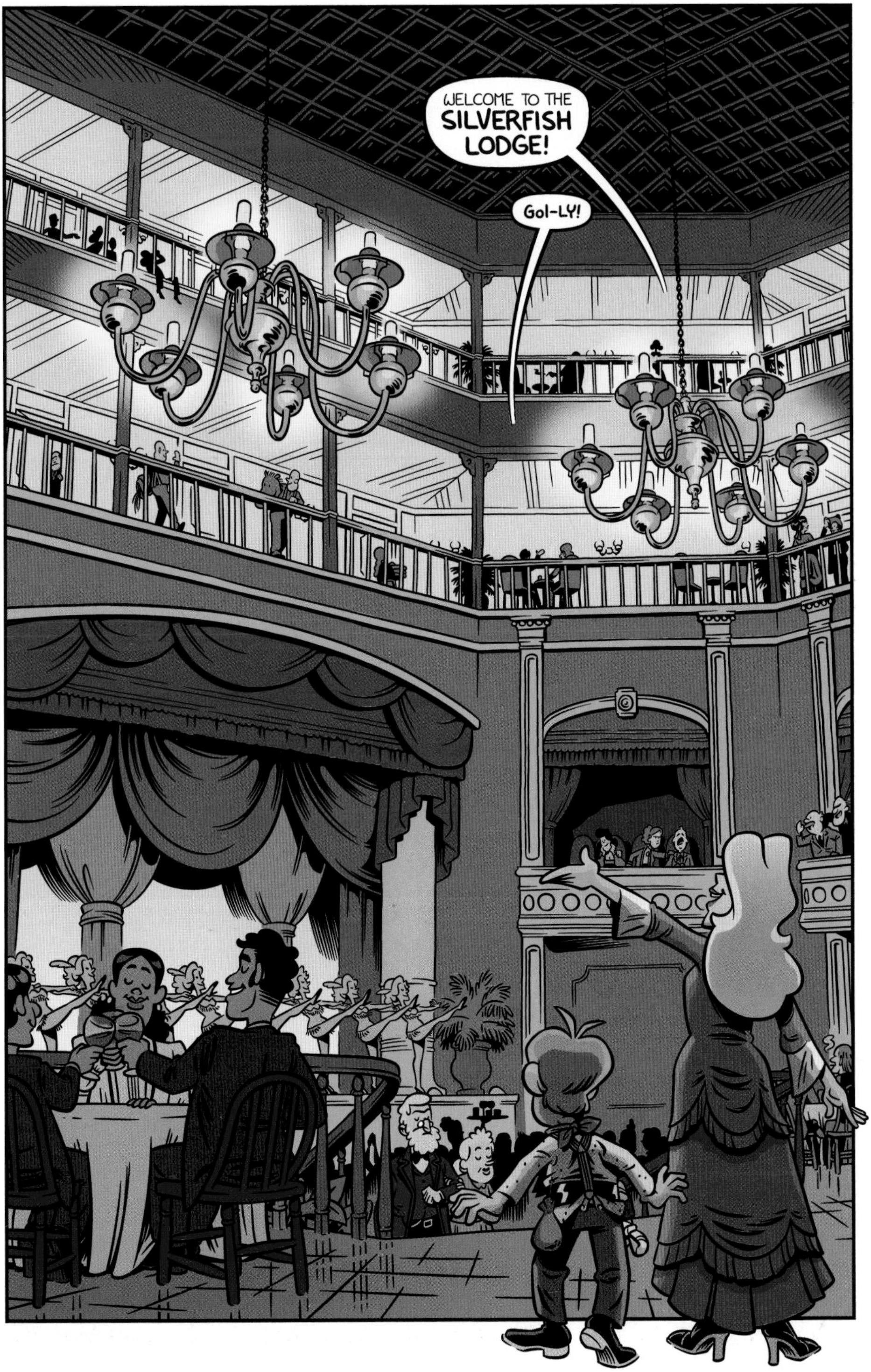
WELCOME TO THE SILVERFISH LODGE!
Gol-LY!

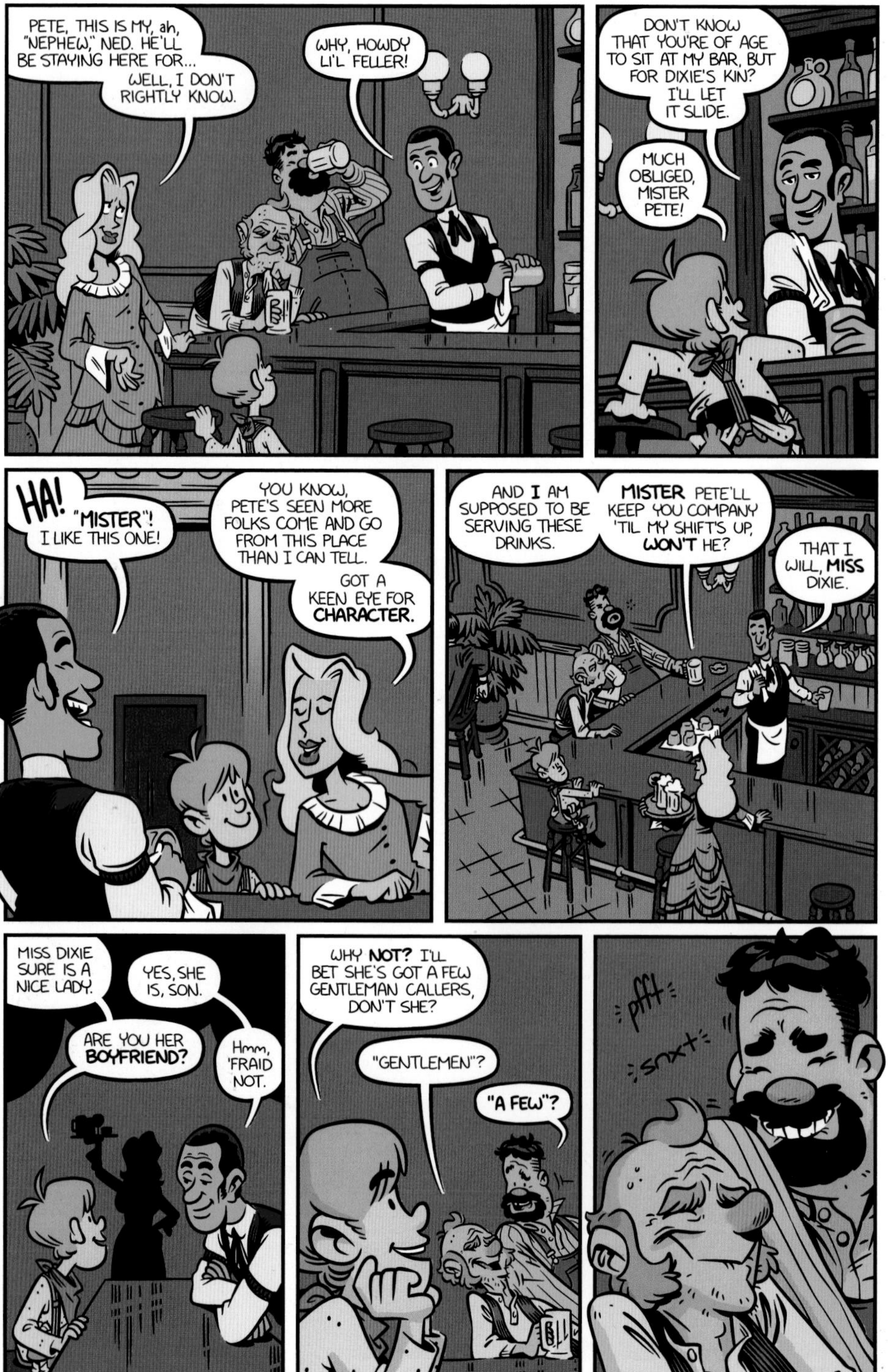
PETE, THIS IS MY, ah, "NEPHEW," NED. HE'LL BE STAYING HERE FOR...
WELL, I DON'T RIGHTLY KNOW.
WHY, HOWDY LI'L FELLER!
DON'T KNOW THAT YOU'RE OF AGE TO SIT AT MY BAR, BUT FOR DIXIE'S KIN? I'LL LET IT SLIDE.
MUCH OBLIGED, MISTER PETE!
HA! "MISTER"! I LIKE THIS ONE!
YOU KNOW, PETE'S SEEN MORE FOLKS COME AND GO FROM THIS PLACE THAN I CAN TELL.
GOT A KEEN EYE FOR CHARACTER.
AND I AM SUPPOSED TO BE SERVING THESE DRINKS.
MISTER PETE'LL KEEP YOU COMPANY 'TIL MY SHIFT'S UP, WON'T HE?
THAT I WILL, MISS DIXIE.
MISS DIXIE SURE IS A NICE LADY.
YES, SHE IS, SON.
ARE YOU HER BOYFRIEND?
Hmm, 'FRAID NOT.
WHY NOT? I'LL BET SHE'S GOT A FEW GENTLEMAN CALLERS, DON'T SHE?
"GENTLEMEN"?
"A FEW"?
pfft
snxt

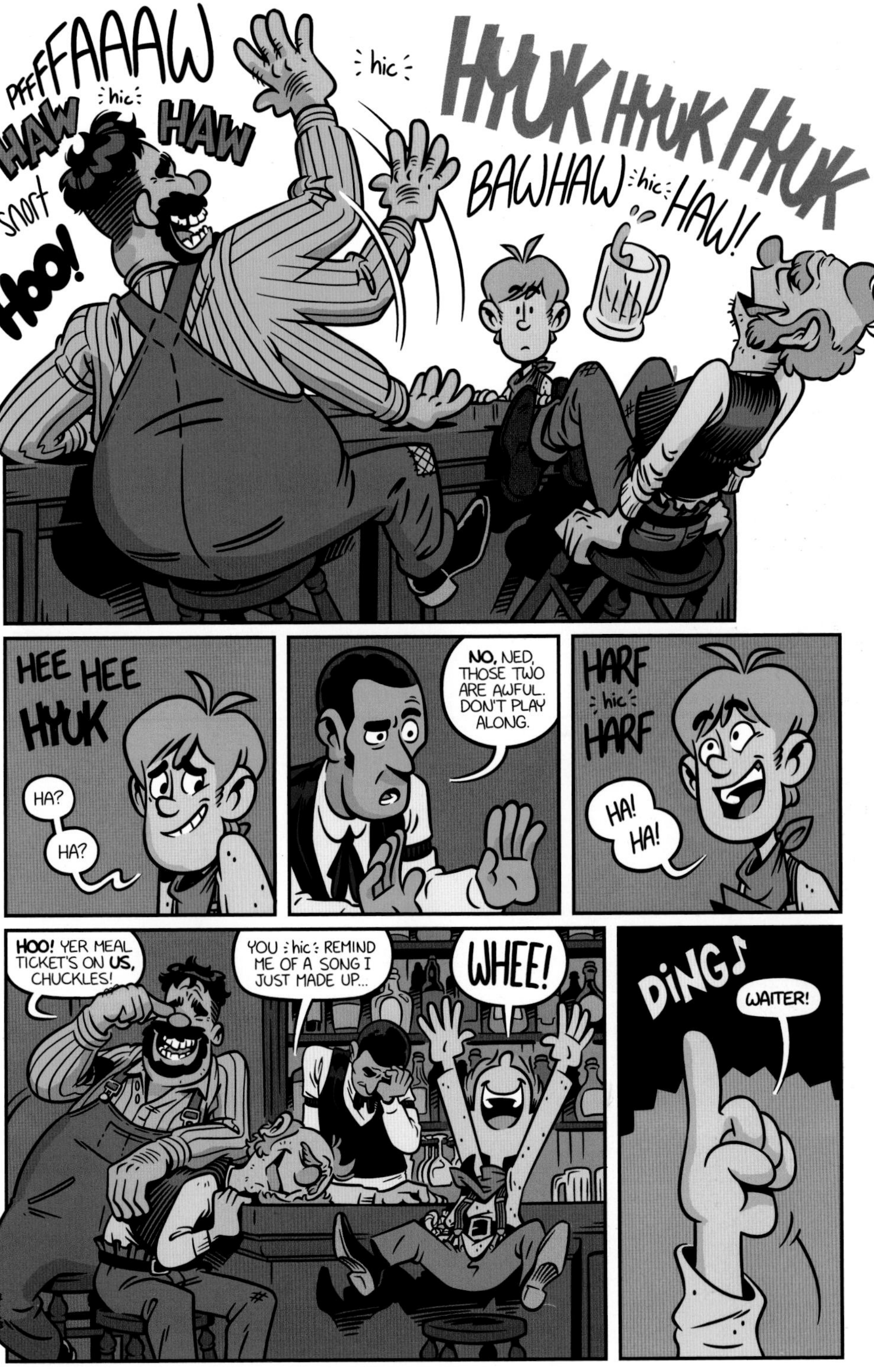
PFFFFAAAW
HAW hic HAW
snort
HOO!
hic
HYUK HYUK HYUK
BAWHAW hic HAW!
HEE HEE
HYUK
HA?
HA?
NO, NED, THOSE TWO ARE AWFUL. DON'T PLAY ALONG.
HARF hic HARF
HA! HA!
HOO! YER MEAL TICKET'S ON US, CHUCKLES!
YOU hic REMIND ME OF A SONG I JUST MADE UP...
WHEE!
DING♪
WAITER!

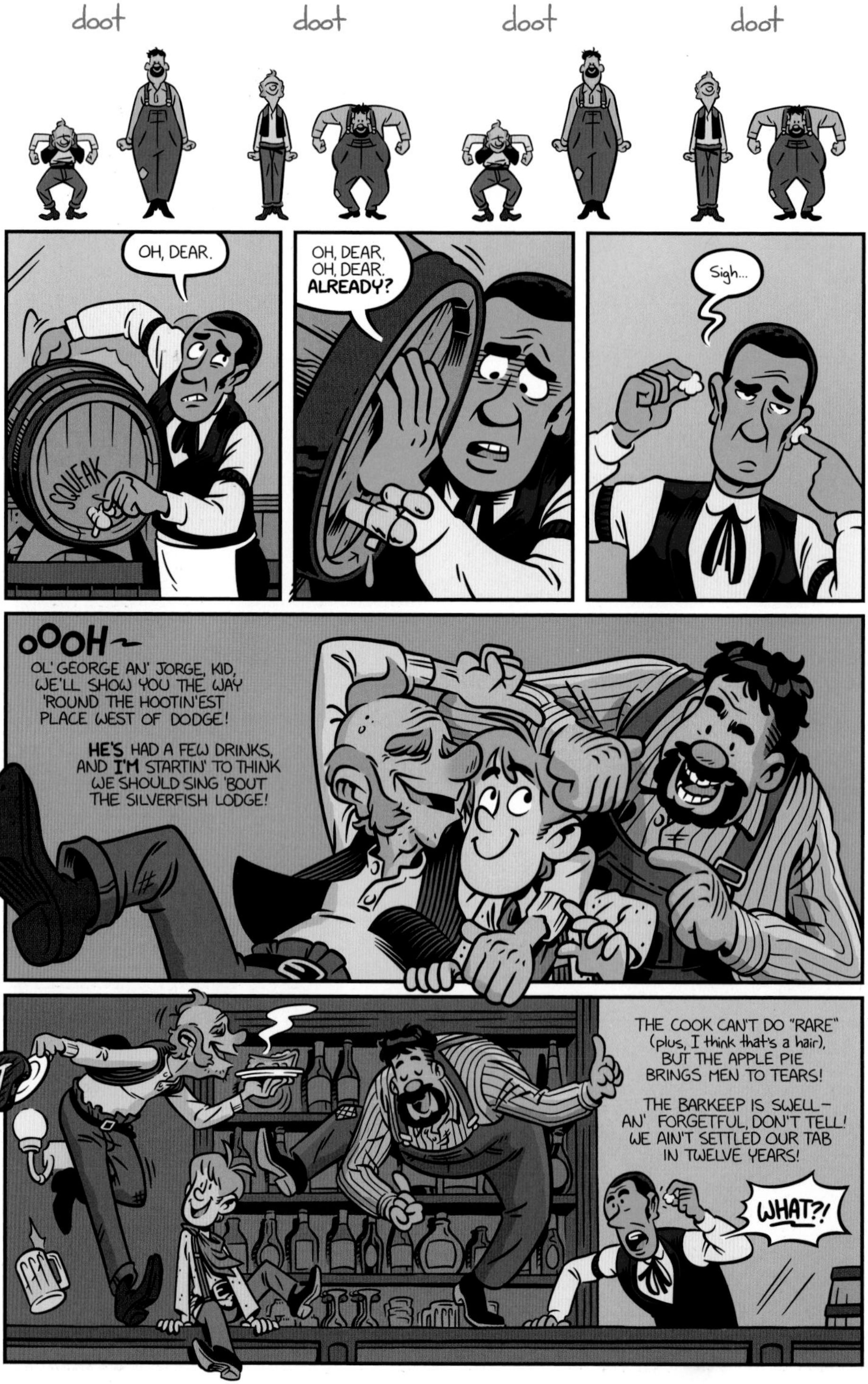
doot
doot
doot
doot
OH, DEAR.
SQUEAK
OH, DEAR, OH, DEAR. **ALREADY?**
Sigh...
OOOH~
OL' GEORGE AN' JORGE, KID, WE'LL SHOW YOU THE WAY 'ROUND THE HOOTIN'EST PLACE WEST OF DODGE!
HE'S HAD A FEW DRINKS, AND **I'M** STARTIN' TO THINK WE SHOULD SING 'BOUT THE SILVERFISH LODGE!
THE COOK CAN'T DO "RARE" (plus, I think that's a hair), BUT THE APPLE PIE BRINGS MEN TO TEARS!
THE BARKEEP IS SWELL— AN' FORGETFUL, DON'T TELL! WE AIN'T SETTLED OUR TAB IN TWELVE YEARS!
WHAT?!

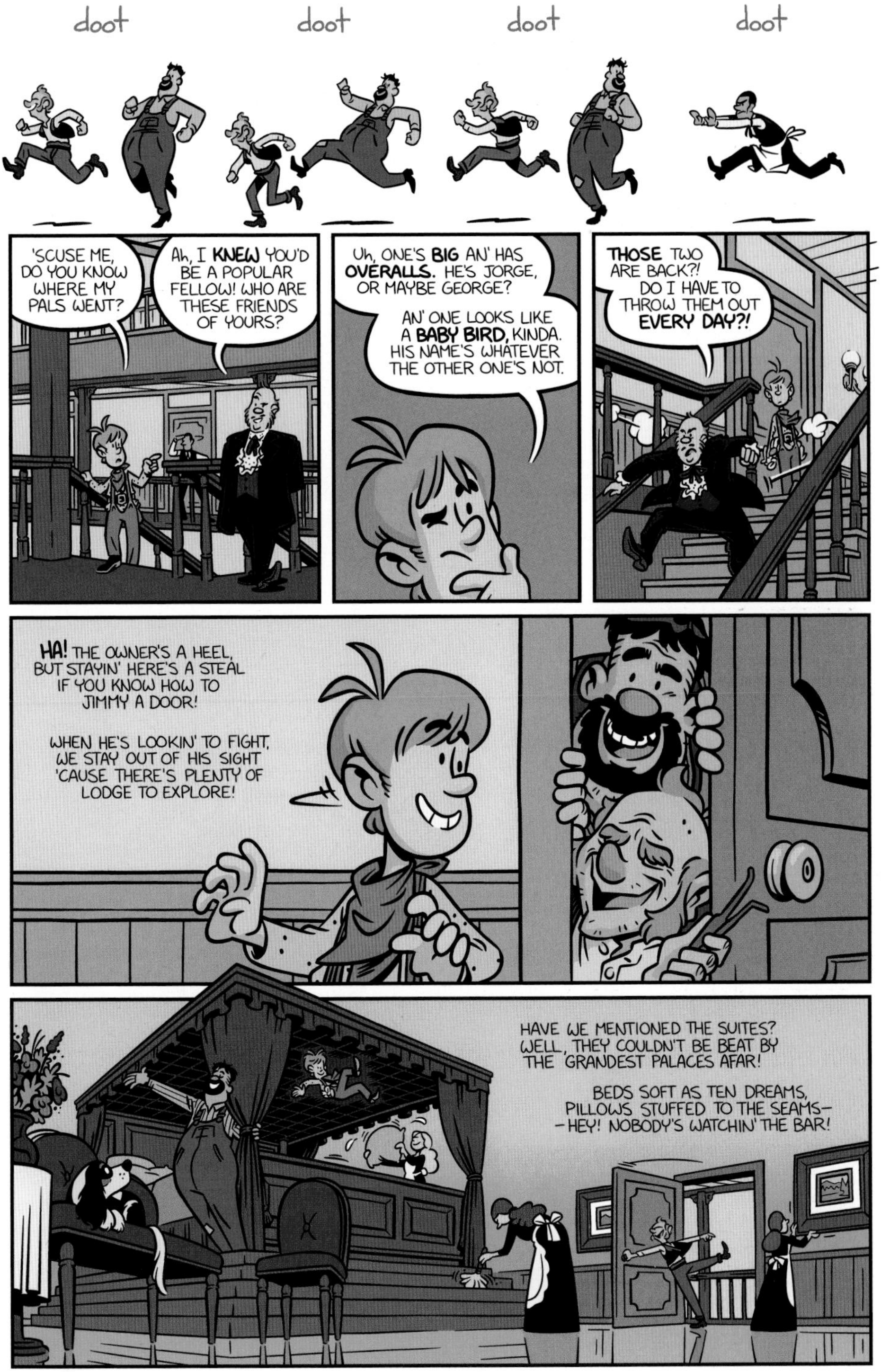
doot
doot
doot
doot
'SCUSE ME, DO YOU KNOW WHERE MY PALS WENT?
Ah, I KNEW YOU'D BE A POPULAR FELLOW! WHO ARE THESE FRIENDS OF YOURS?
Uh, ONE'S BIG AN' HAS OVERALLS. HE'S JORGE, OR MAYBE GEORGE?
AN' ONE LOOKS LIKE A BABY BIRD, KINDA. HIS NAME'S WHATEVER THE OTHER ONE'S NOT.
THOSE TWO ARE BACK?! DO I HAVE TO THROW THEM OUT EVERY DAY?!
HA! THE OWNER'S A HEEL, BUT STAYIN' HERE'S A STEAL IF YOU KNOW HOW TO JIMMY A DOOR!
WHEN HE'S LOOKIN' TO FIGHT, WE STAY OUT OF HIS SIGHT 'CAUSE THERE'S PLENTY OF LODGE TO EXPLORE!
HAVE WE MENTIONED THE SUITES? WELL, THEY COULDN'T BE BEAT BY THE GRANDEST PALACES AFAR!
BEDS SOFT AS TEN DREAMS, PILLOWS STUFFED TO THE SEAMS— —HEY! NOBODY'S WATCHIN' THE BAR!

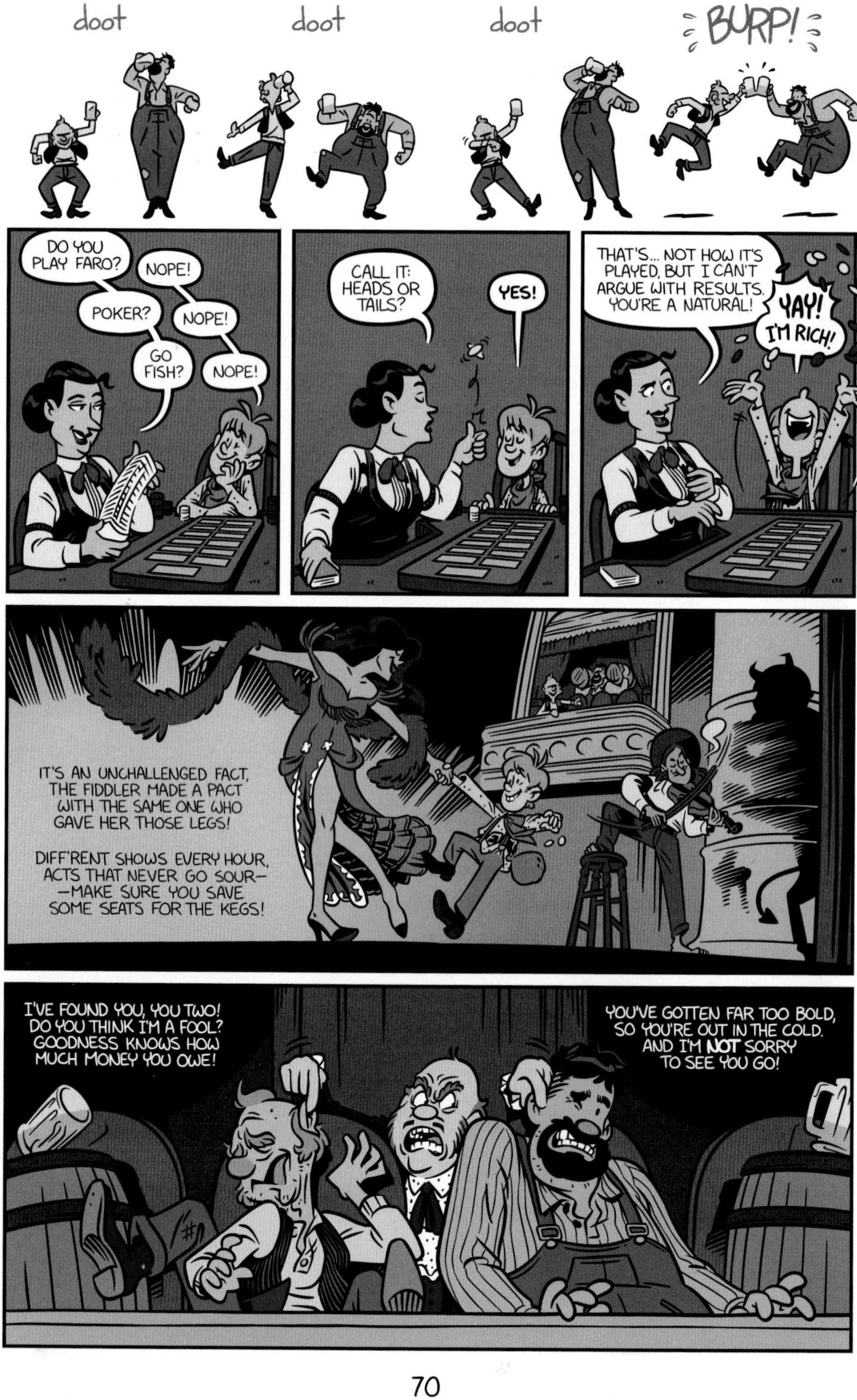

doot
doot
doot
BURP!
DO YOU PLAY FARO?
NOPE!
POKER?
NOPE!
GO FISH?
NOPE!
CALL IT: HEADS OR TAILS?
YES!
THAT'S... NOT HOW IT'S PLAYED, BUT I CAN'T ARGUE WITH RESULTS. YOU'RE A NATURAL!
YAY! I'M RICH!
IT'S AN UNCHALLENGED FACT, THE FIDDLER MADE A PACT WITH THE SAME ONE WHO GAVE HER THOSE LEGS!
DIFF'RENT SHOWS EVERY HOUR, ACTS THAT NEVER GO SOUR— —MAKE SURE YOU SAVE SOME SEATS FOR THE KEGS!
I'VE FOUND YOU, YOU TWO! DO YOU THINK I'M A FOOL? GOODNESS KNOWS HOW MUCH MONEY YOU OWE!
YOU'VE GOTTEN FAR TOO BOLD, SO YOU'RE OUT IN THE COLD. AND I'M **NOT** SORRY TO SEE YOU GO!

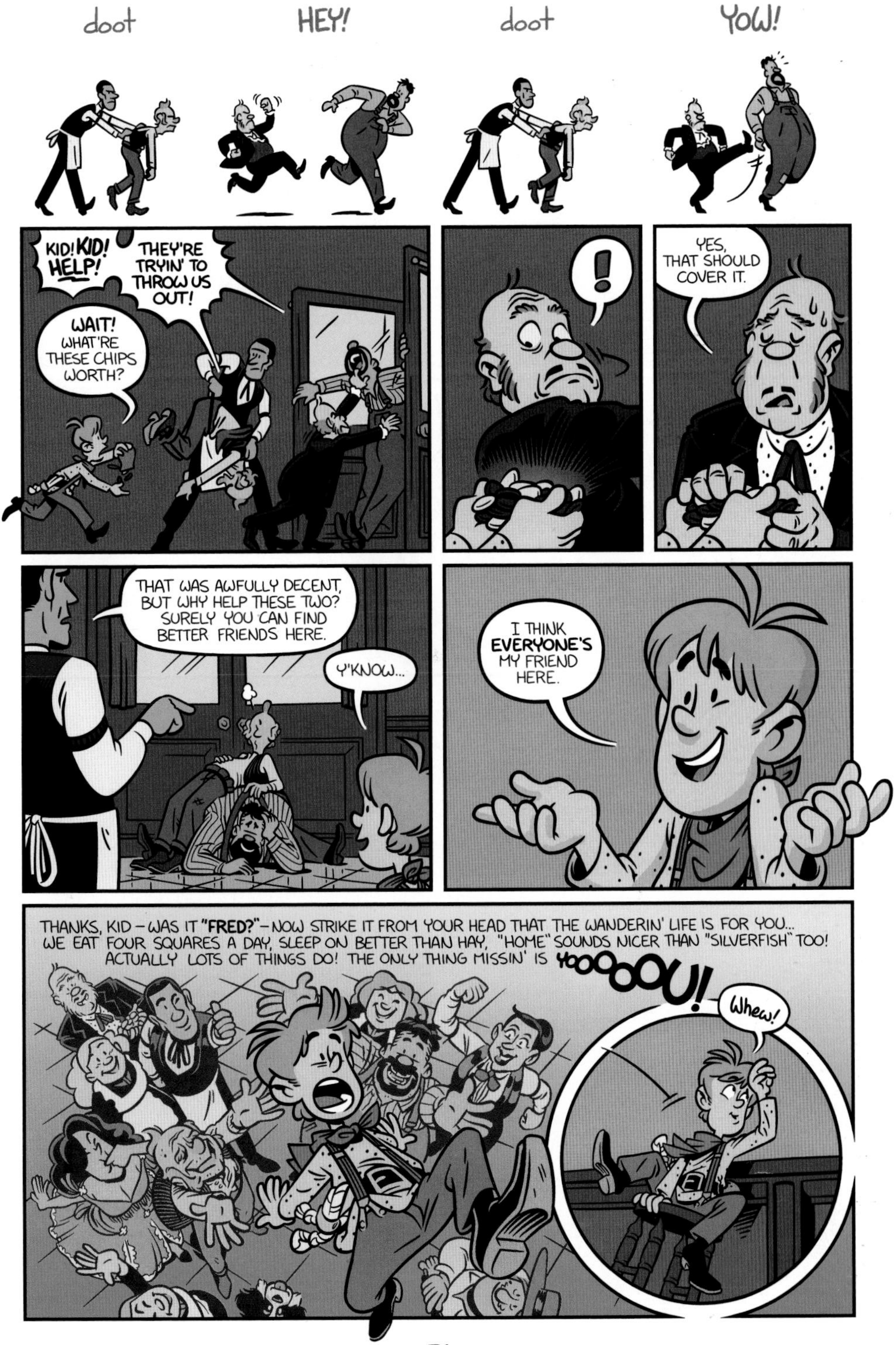
doot
HEY!
doot
YOW!
KID! KID! HELP!
THEY'RE TRYIN' TO THROW US OUT!
WAIT! WHAT'RE THESE CHIPS WORTH?
!
YES, THAT SHOULD COVER IT.
THAT WAS AWFULLY DECENT, BUT WHY HELP THESE TWO? SURELY YOU CAN FIND BETTER FRIENDS HERE.
Y'KNOW...
I THINK EVERYONE'S MY FRIEND HERE.
THANKS, KID—WAS IT "FRED?"—NOW STRIKE IT FROM YOUR HEAD THAT THE WANDERIN' LIFE IS FOR YOU...
WE EAT FOUR SQUARES A DAY, SLEEP ON BETTER THAN HAY, "HOME" SOUNDS NICER THAN "SILVERFISH" TOO!
ACTUALLY LOTS OF THINGS DO! THE ONLY THING MISSIN' IS YOOOOOU!
Whew!

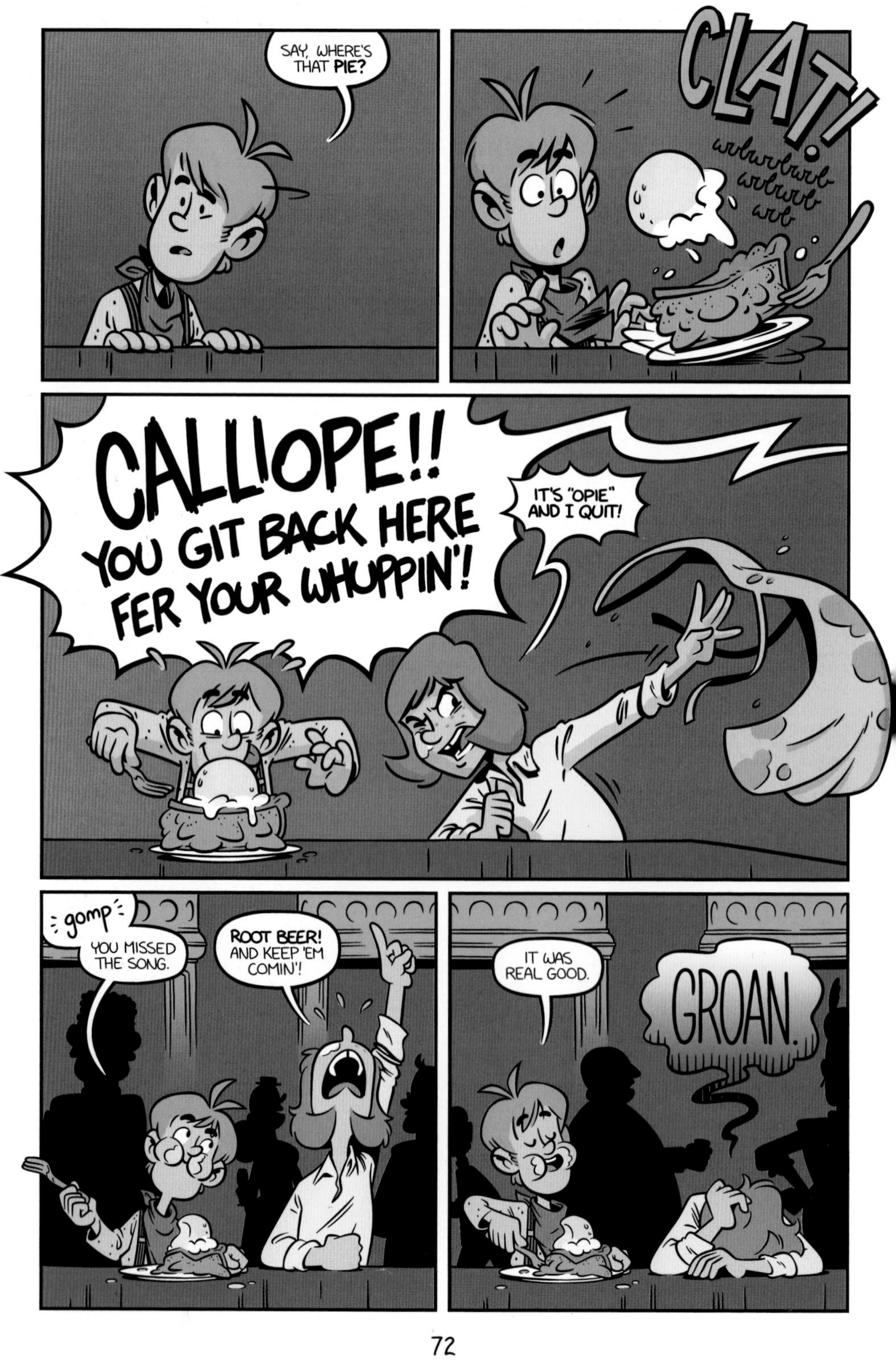
SAY, WHERE'S THAT PIE?
CLAT!
wrbwrbwrb wrbwrb wrb
CALLIOPE!! YOU GIT BACK HERE FER YOUR WHUPPIN'!
IT'S "OPIE" AND I QUIT!
gomp
YOU MISSED THE SONG.
ROOT BEER! AND KEEP 'EM COMIN'!
IT WAS REAL GOOD.
GROAN.

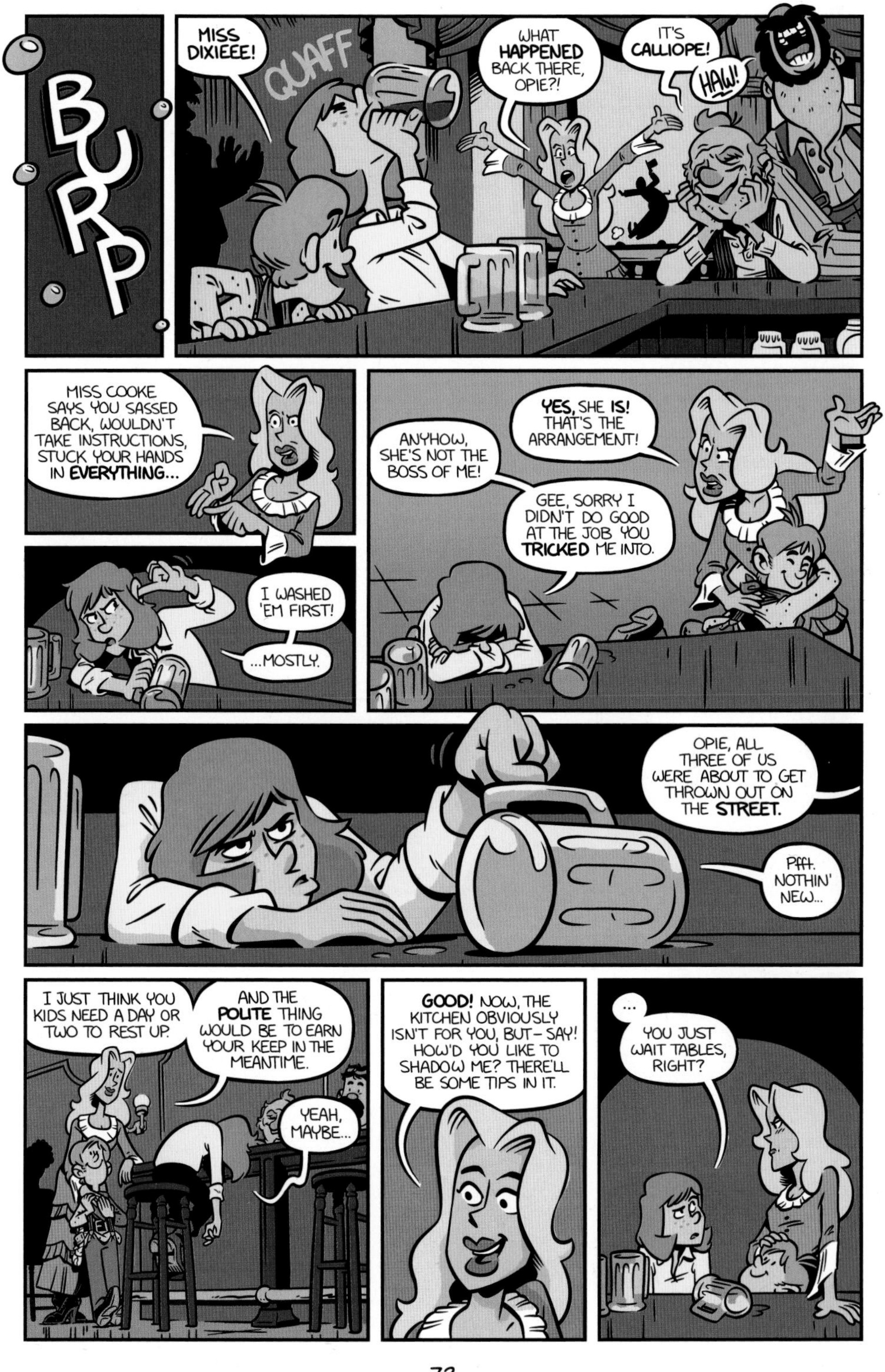

BURP
MISS DIXIEEE!
QUAFF
WHAT HAPPENED BACK THERE, OPIE?!
IT'S CALLIOPE!
HAW!
MISS COOKE SAYS YOU SASSED BACK, WOULDN'T TAKE INSTRUCTIONS, STUCK YOUR HANDS IN EVERYTHING...
I WASHED 'EM FIRST!
...MOSTLY.
ANYHOW, SHE'S NOT THE BOSS OF ME!
YES, SHE IS! THAT'S THE ARRANGEMENT!
GEE, SORRY I DIDN'T DO GOOD AT THE JOB YOU TRICKED ME INTO.
OPIE, ALL THREE OF US WERE ABOUT TO GET THROWN OUT ON THE STREET.
Pfft. NOTHIN' NEW...
I JUST THINK YOU KIDS NEED A DAY OR TWO TO REST UP.
AND THE POLITE THING WOULD BE TO EARN YOUR KEEP IN THE MEANTIME.
YEAH, MAYBE...
GOOD! NOW, THE KITCHEN OBVIOUSLY ISN'T FOR YOU, BUT– SAY! HOW'D YOU LIKE TO SHADOW ME? THERE'LL BE SOME TIPS IN IT.
...
YOU JUST WAIT TABLES, RIGHT?

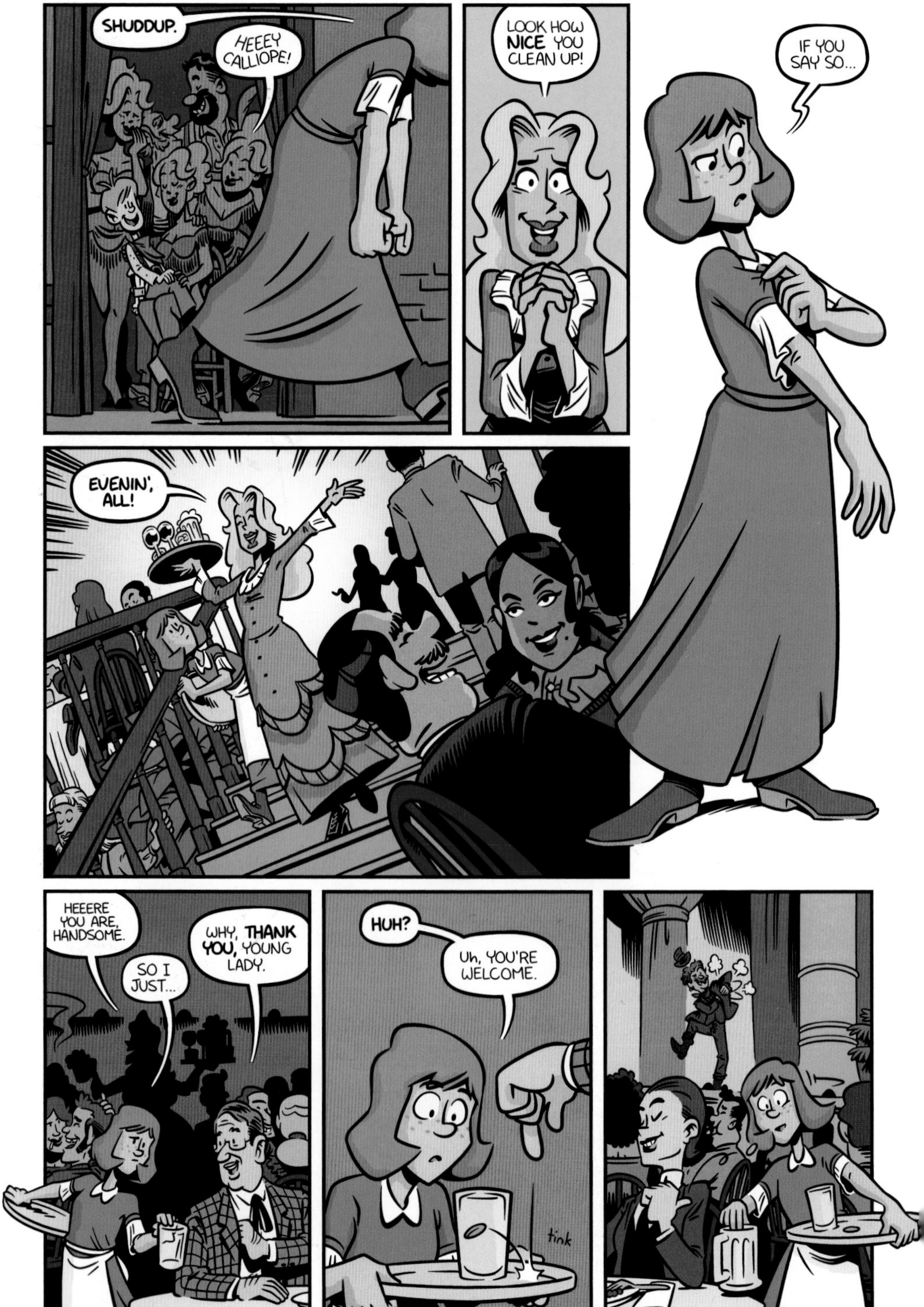
SHUDDUP.
HEEEY CALLIOPE!
LOOK HOW NICE YOU CLEAN UP!
IF YOU SAY SO...
EVENIN', ALL!
HEEERE YOU ARE, HANDSOME.
SO I JUST...
WHY, THANK YOU, YOUNG LADY.
HUH?
Uh, YOU'RE WELCOME.
tink

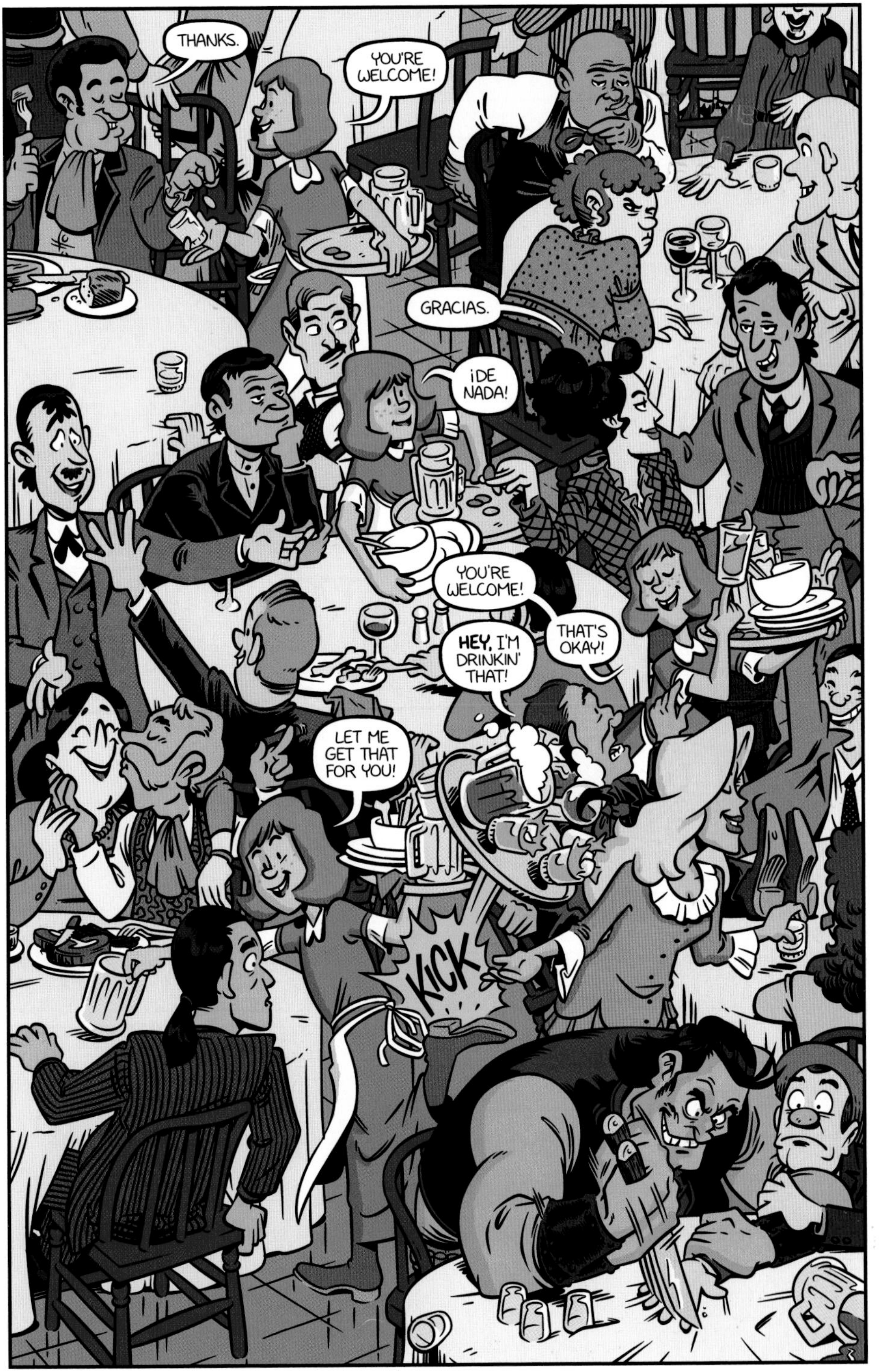
THANKS.
YOU'RE WELCOME!
GRACIAS.
¡DE NADA!
YOU'RE WELCOME!
THAT'S OKAY!
HEY, I'M DRINKIN' THAT!
LET ME GET THAT FOR YOU!
KICK

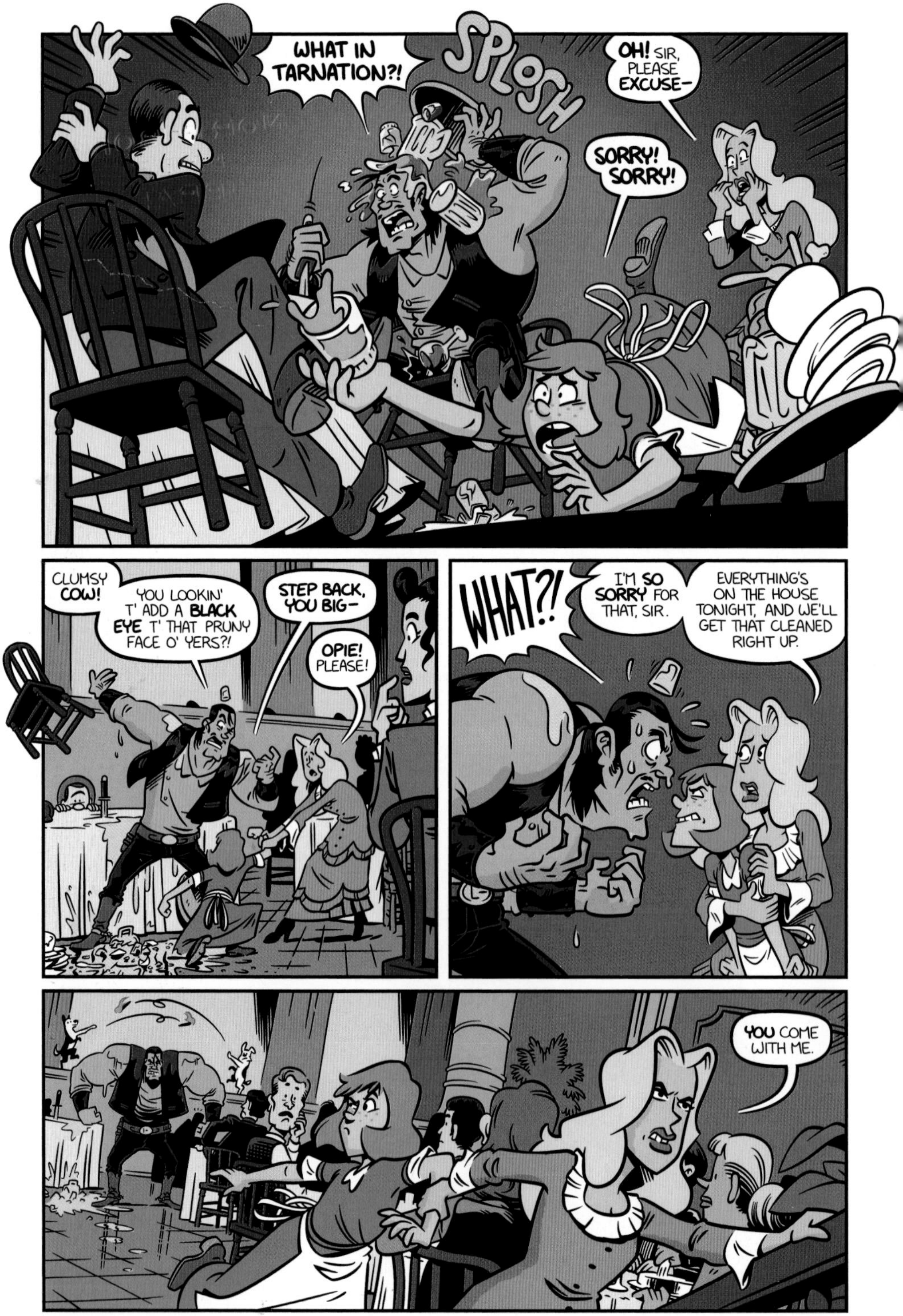
WHAT IN TARNATION?!
SPLOSH
OH! SIR, PLEASE EXCUSE-
SORRY! SORRY!
CLUMSY COW!
YOU LOOKIN' T' ADD A BLACK EYE T' THAT PRUNY FACE O' YERS?!
STEP BACK, YOU BIG-
OPIE! PLEASE!
WHAT?!
I'M SO SORRY FOR THAT, SIR.
EVERYTHING'S ON THE HOUSE TONIGHT, AND WE'LL GET THAT CLEANED RIGHT UP.
YOU COME WITH ME.

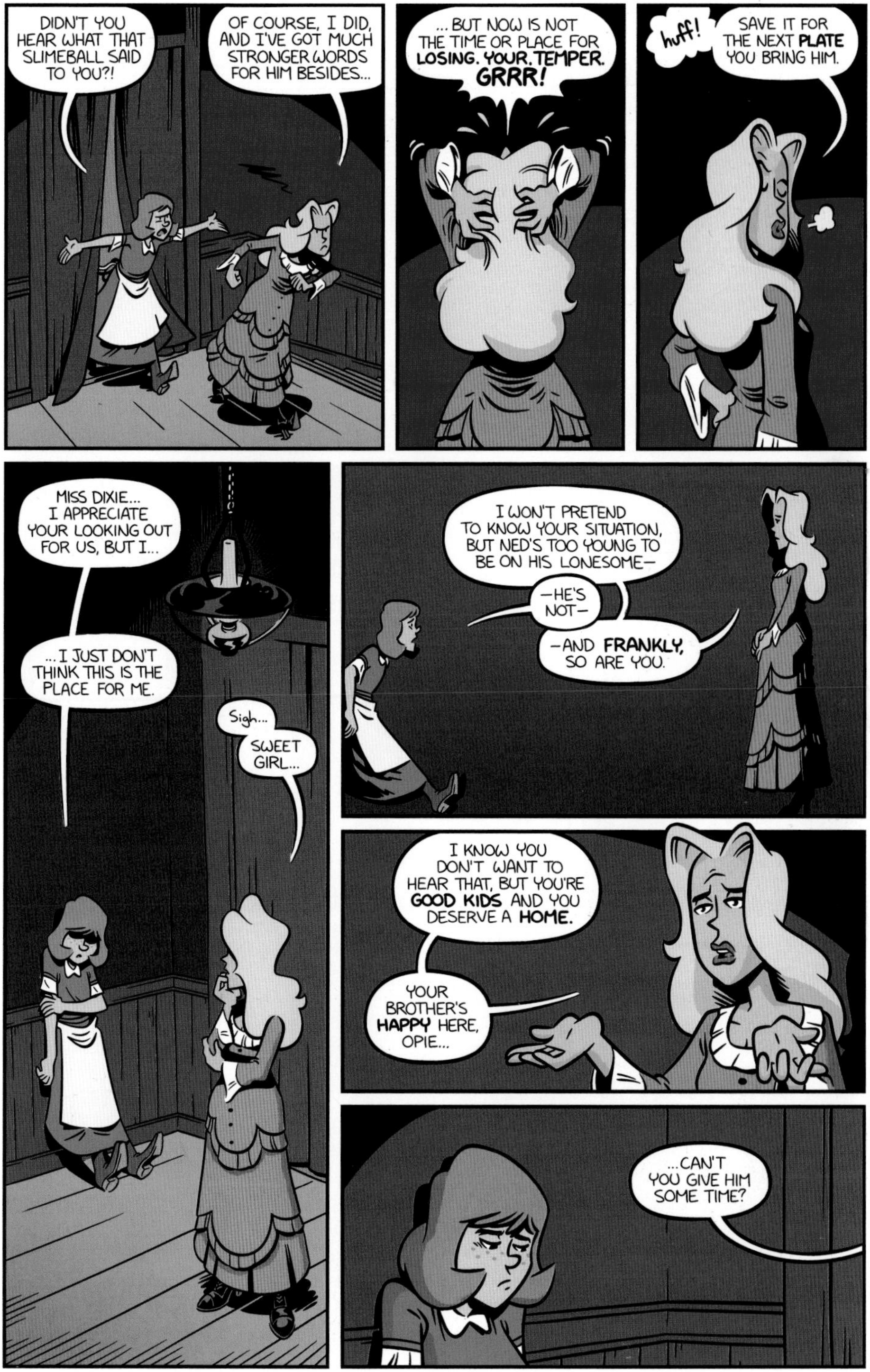
DIDN'T YOU HEAR WHAT THAT SLIMEBALL SAID TO YOU?!
OF COURSE, I DID, AND I'VE GOT MUCH STRONGER WORDS FOR HIM BESIDES...
... BUT NOW IS NOT THE TIME OR PLACE FOR LOSING. YOUR. TEMPER. GRRR!
huff!
SAVE IT FOR THE NEXT PLATE YOU BRING HIM.
MISS DIXIE... I APPRECIATE YOUR LOOKING OUT FOR US, BUT I...
... I JUST DON'T THINK THIS IS THE PLACE FOR ME.
Sigh...
SWEET GIRL...
I WON'T PRETEND TO KNOW YOUR SITUATION, BUT NED'S TOO YOUNG TO BE ON HIS LONESOME—
—HE'S NOT—
—AND FRANKLY, SO ARE YOU.
I KNOW YOU DON'T WANT TO HEAR THAT, BUT YOU'RE GOOD KIDS AND YOU DESERVE A HOME.
YOUR BROTHER'S HAPPY HERE, OPIE...
...CAN'T YOU GIVE HIM SOME TIME?

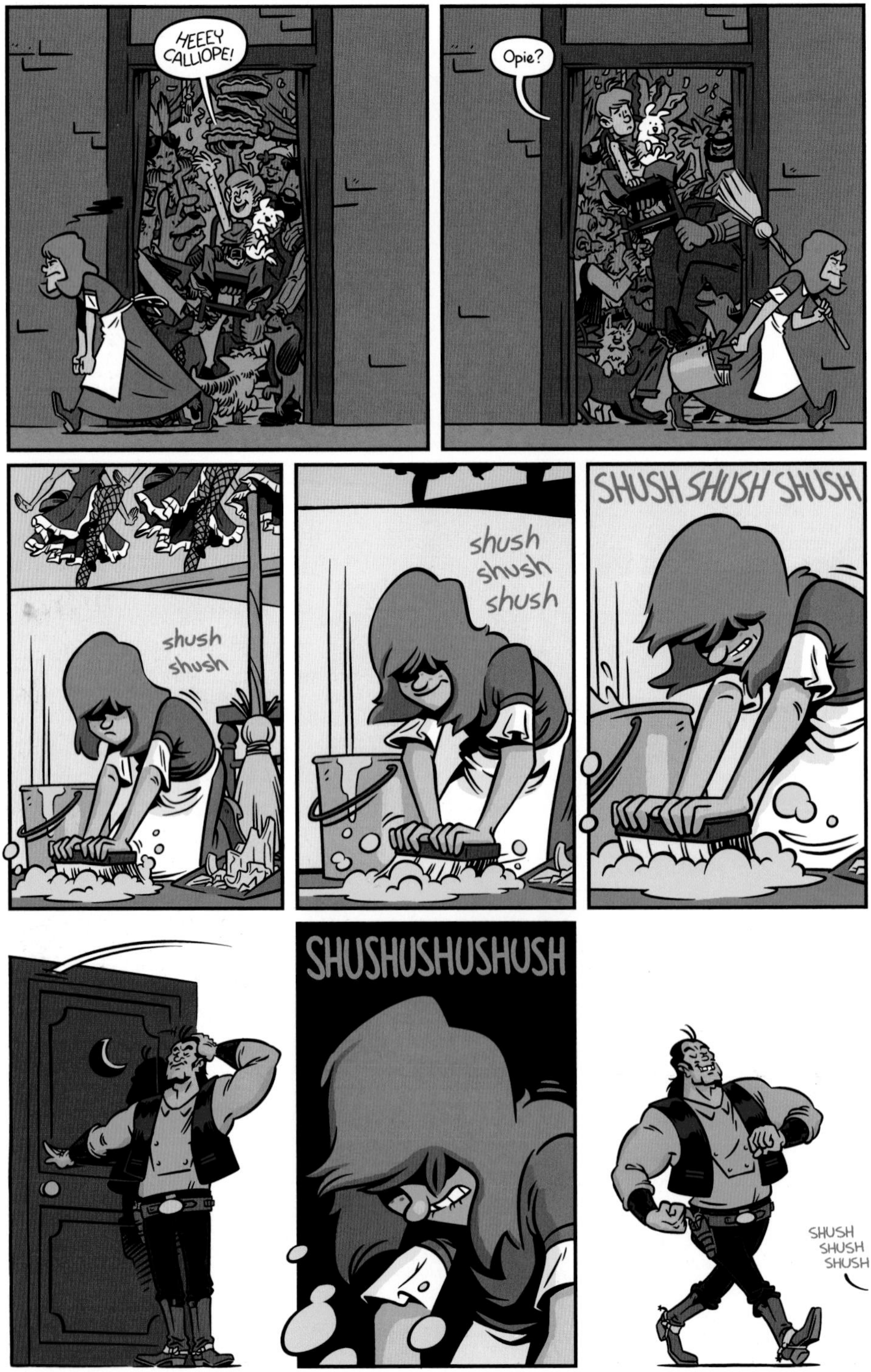
HEEEY CALLIOPE!
Opie?
shush
shush
shush
shush
shush
SHUSH SHUSH SHUSH
SHUSHUSHUSHUSH
SHUSH
SHUSH
SHUSH

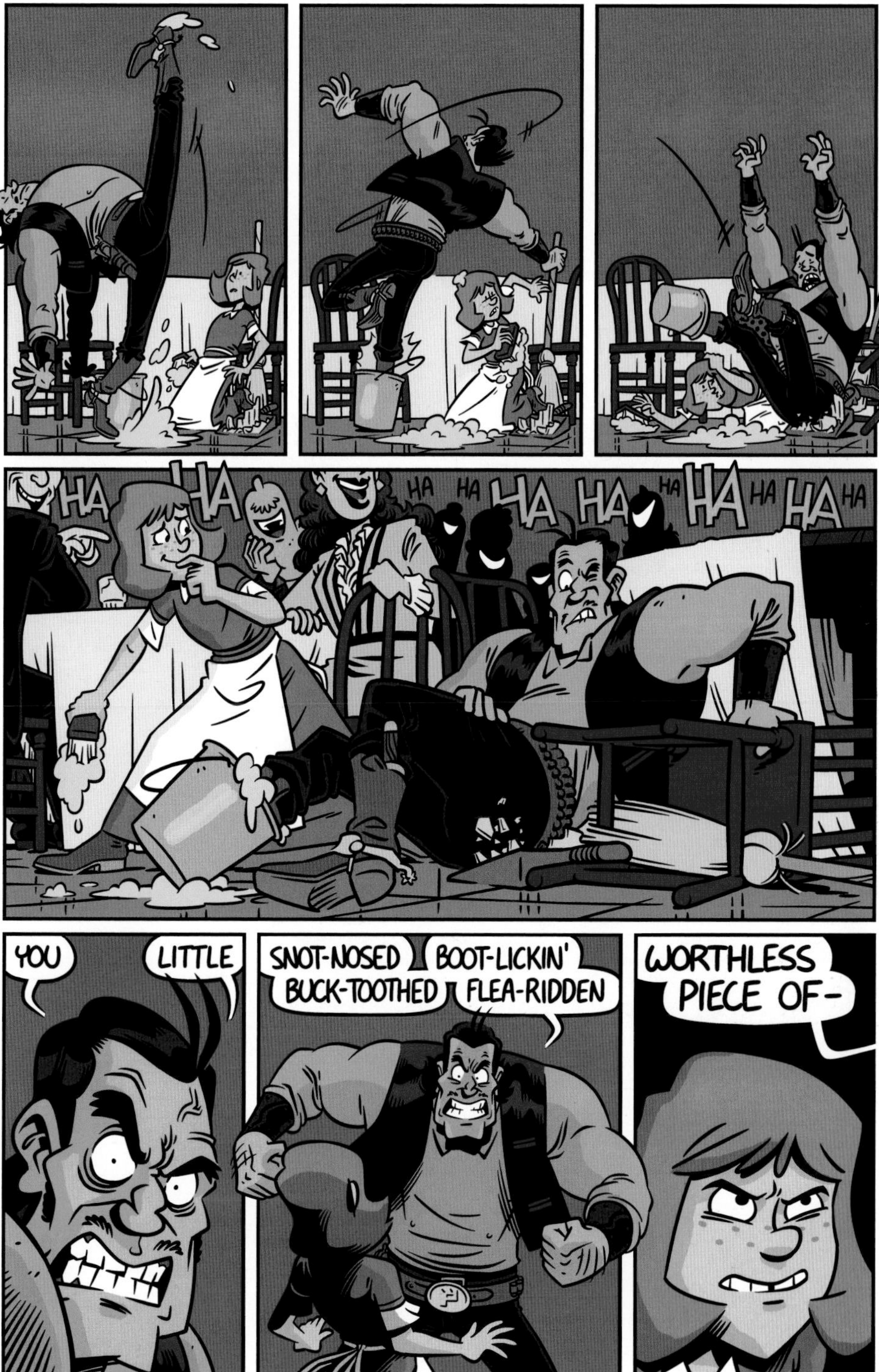
HA HA HA HA HA HA HA HA HA HA HA HA
YOU
LITTLE
SNOT-NOSED
BOOT-LICKIN'
BUCK-TOOTHED
FLEA-RIDDEN
WORTHLESS PIECE OF-

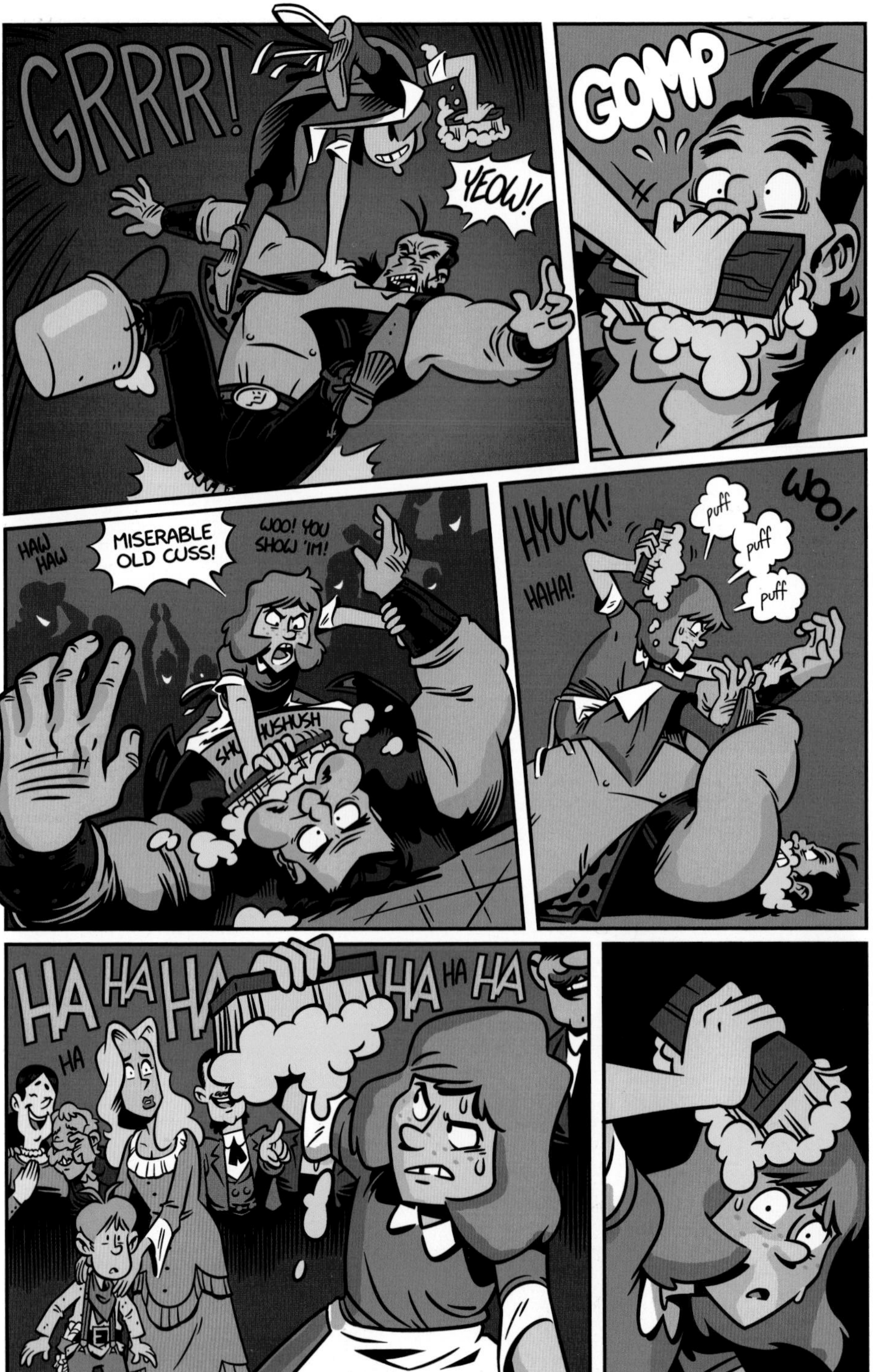
GRRRR!
YEOW!
GOMP
HAW HAW
MISERABLE OLD CUSS!
WOO! YOU SHOW 'IM!
SHUSHUSH
HYUCK!
WOO!
HAHA!
puff
puff
puff
HA HA HA HA
HA HA HA
HA

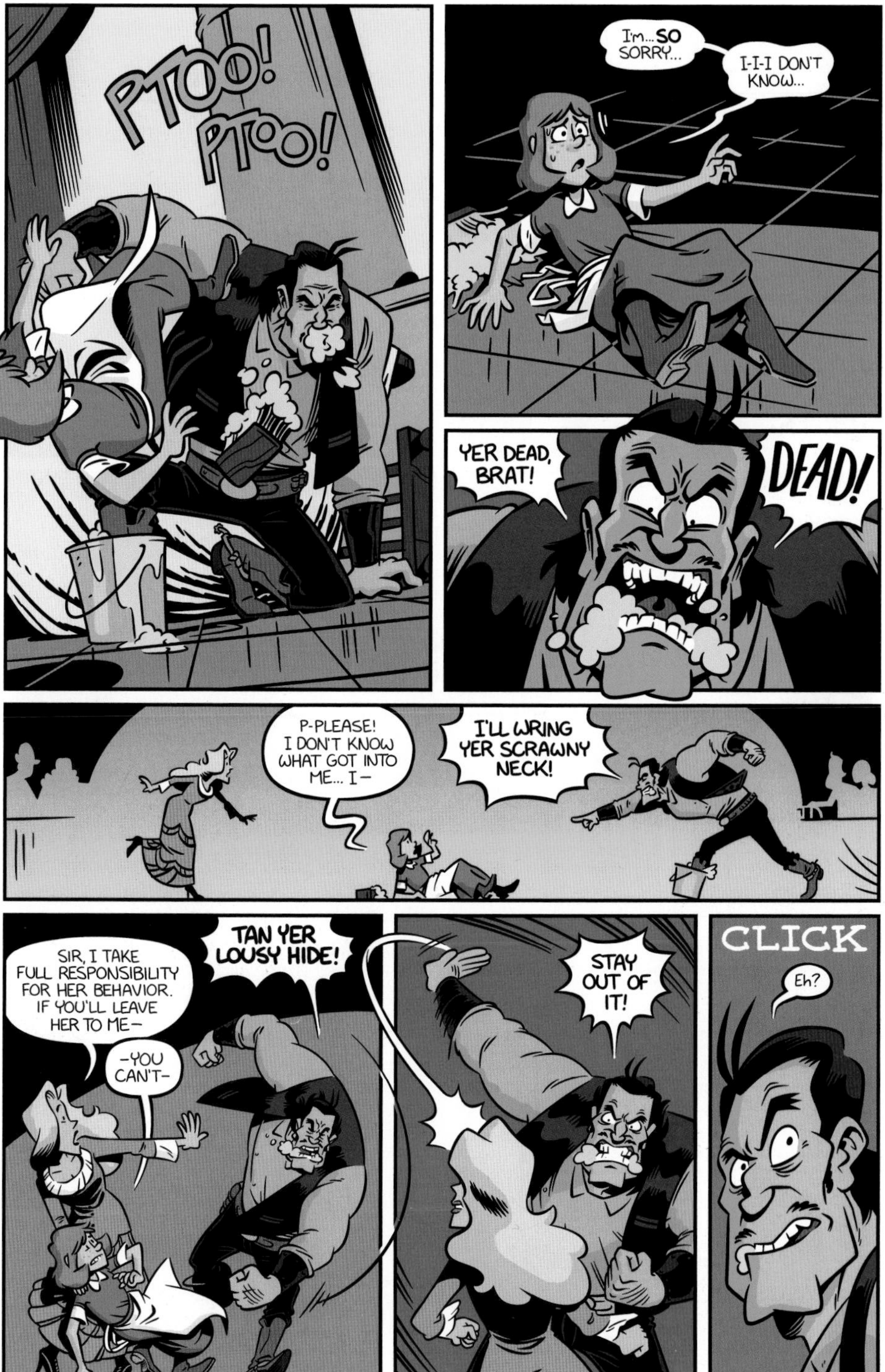
PTOO! PTOO!
I'm... SO SORRY...
I-I-I DON'T KNOW...
YER DEAD, BRAT!
DEAD!
P-PLEASE! I DON'T KNOW WHAT GOT INTO ME... I—
I'LL WRING YER SCRAWNY NECK!
SIR, I TAKE FULL RESPONSIBILITY FOR HER BEHAVIOR. IF YOU'LL LEAVE HER TO ME—
TAN YER LOUSY HIDE!
—YOU CAN'T—
STAY OUT OF IT!
CLICK
Eh?

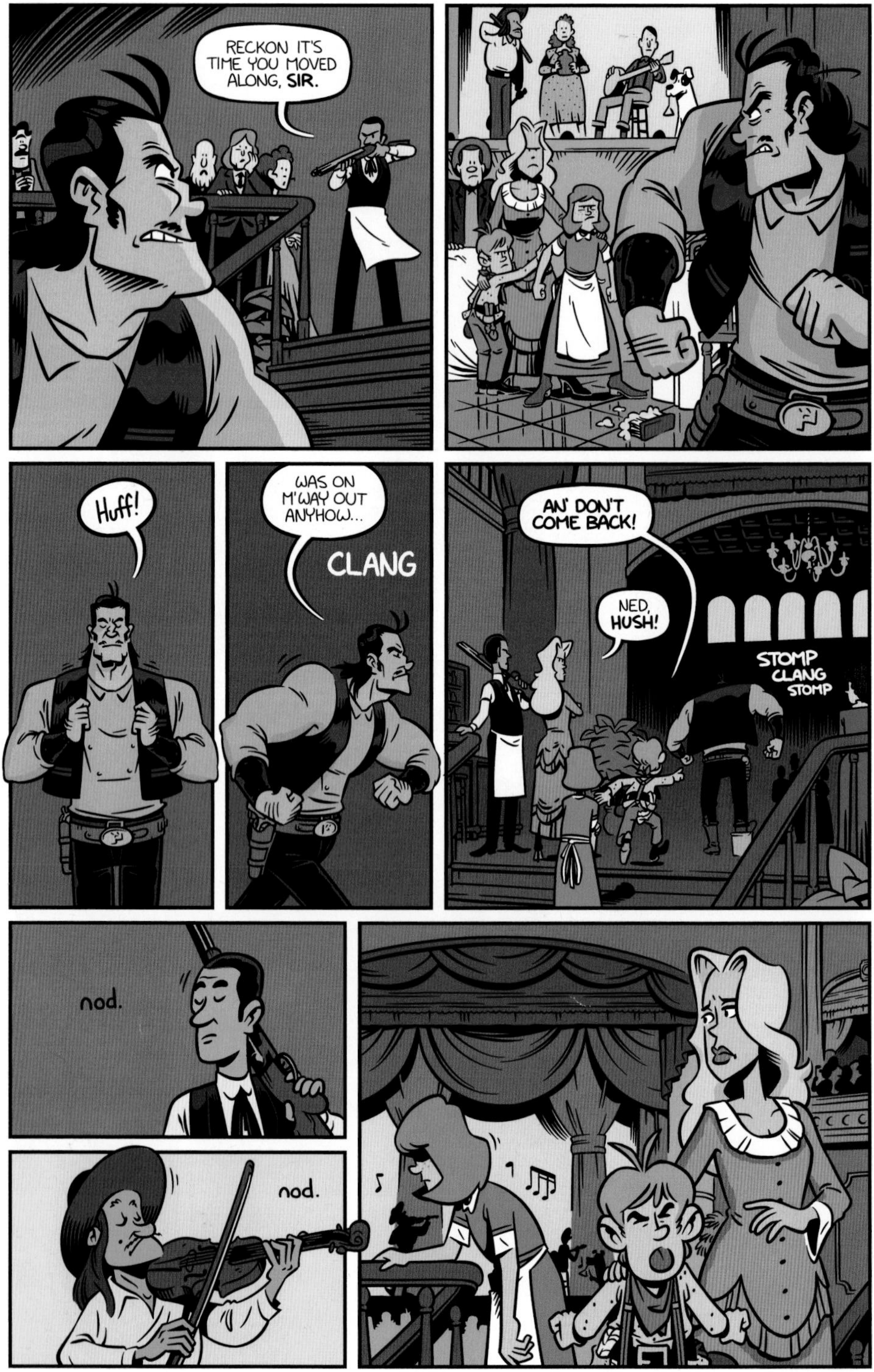
RECKON IT'S TIME YOU MOVED ALONG, **SIR.**
Huff!
WAS ON M'WAY OUT ANYHOW...
CLANG
AN' DON'T COME BACK!
NED, **HUSH!**
STOMP
CLANG
STOMP
nod.
nod.

knock knock

OPIE? CAN I COME IN?

≷ sniff ≷

Oh, HON, HON...

A-bluh huh huuuh! ≷SOB≷

Shh... shh, IT'S OKAY...

≷SNIFF≷ koff koff

NO, IT ISN'T... I CAN'T TAKE CARE OF HIM!

CAN'T EVEN TAKE CARE OF MYSELF...

COULDN'T TAKE CARE OF MA...

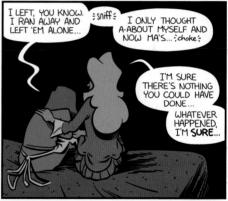
I LEFT, YOU KNOW. I RAN AWAY AND LEFT 'EM ALONE...

≷sniff≷

I ONLY THOUGHT A-ABOUT MYSELF AND NOW MA'S... ≷choke≷

I'M SURE THERE'S NOTHING YOU COULD HAVE DONE...

WHATEVER HAPPENED, I'M SURE...

BUT... BUT I THINK I LED HIM RIGHT TO HER...

sob

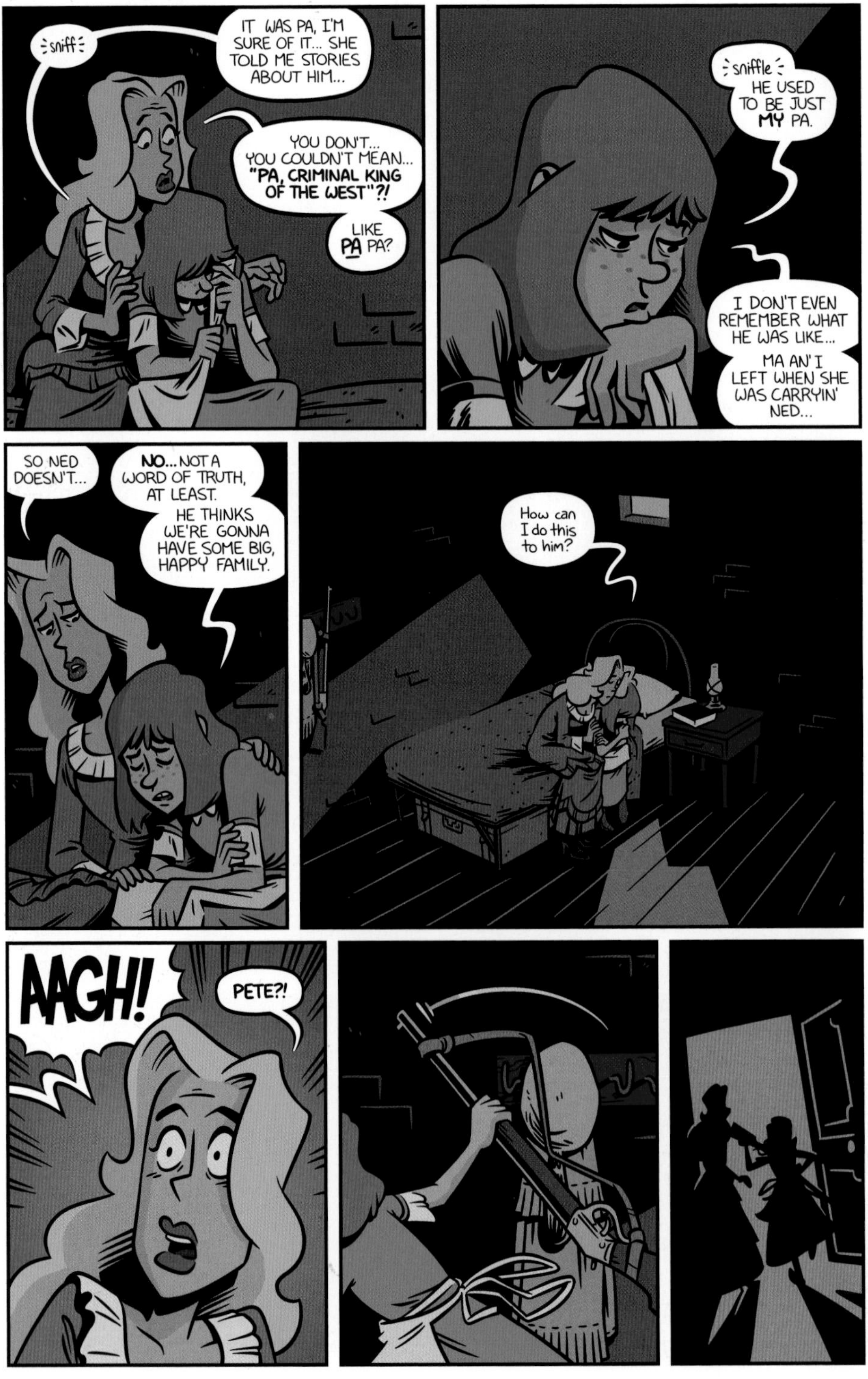
sniff
IT WAS PA, I'M SURE OF IT... SHE TOLD ME STORIES ABOUT HIM...
YOU DON'T... YOU COULDN'T MEAN... "PA, CRIMINAL KING OF THE WEST"?!
LIKE PA PA?
sniffle
HE USED TO BE JUST MY PA.
I DON'T EVEN REMEMBER WHAT HE WAS LIKE...
MA AN' I LEFT WHEN SHE WAS CARRYIN' NED...
SO NED DOESN'T...
NO... NOT A WORD OF TRUTH, AT LEAST.
HE THINKS WE'RE GONNA HAVE SOME BIG, HAPPY FAMILY.
How can I do this to him?
AAGH!
PETE?!

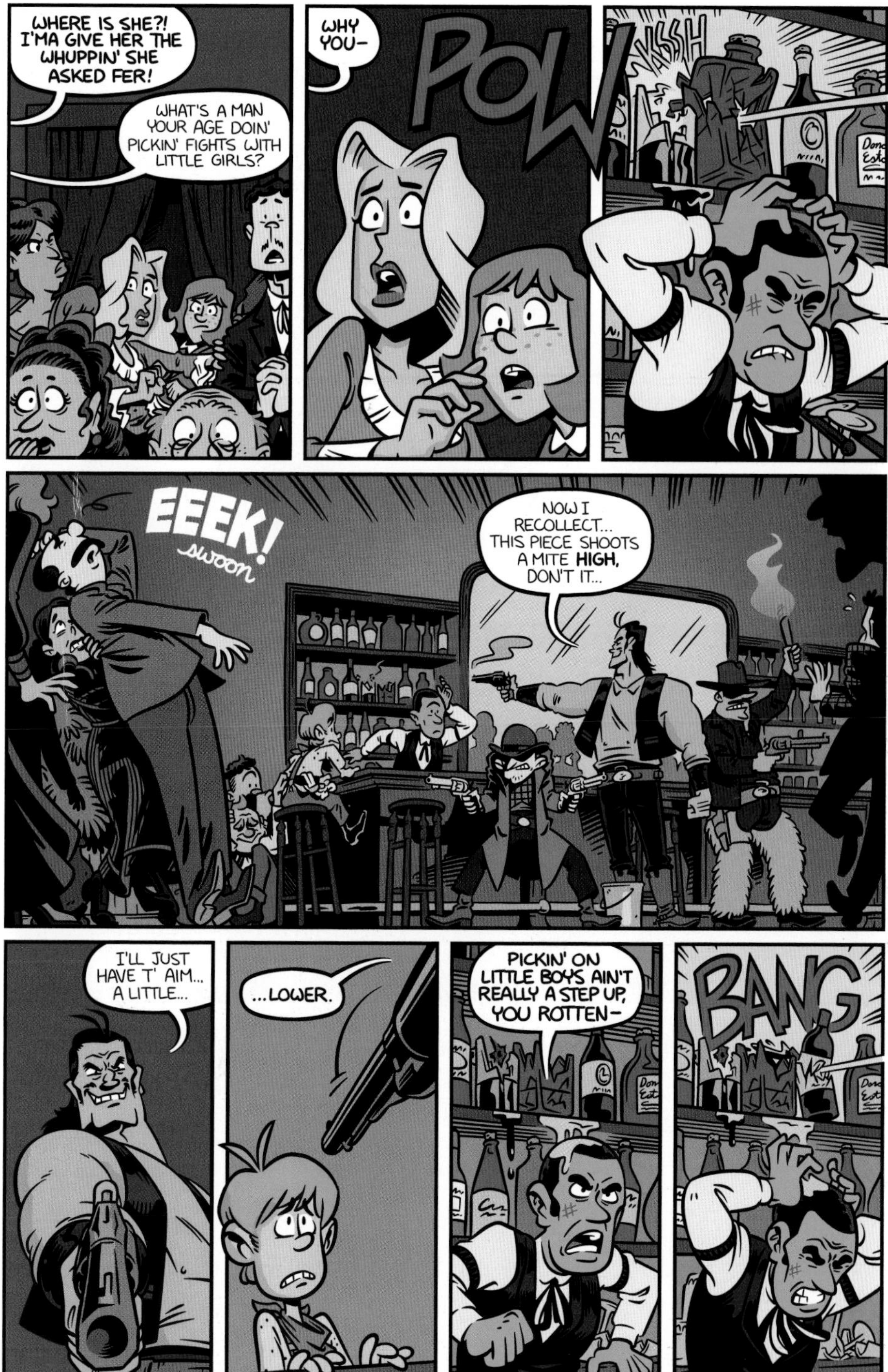
WHERE IS SHE?! I'MA GIVE HER THE WHUPPIN' SHE ASKED FER!
WHAT'S A MAN YOUR AGE DOIN' PICKIN' FIGHTS WITH LITTLE GIRLS?
WHY YOU—
POW
KSSH
EEEK!
swoon
NOW I RECOLLECT... THIS PIECE SHOOTS A MITE **HIGH,** DON'T IT...
I'LL JUST HAVE T' AIM... A LITTLE...
...LOWER.
PICKIN' ON LITTLE BOYS AIN'T REALLY A STEP UP, YOU ROTTEN—
BANG

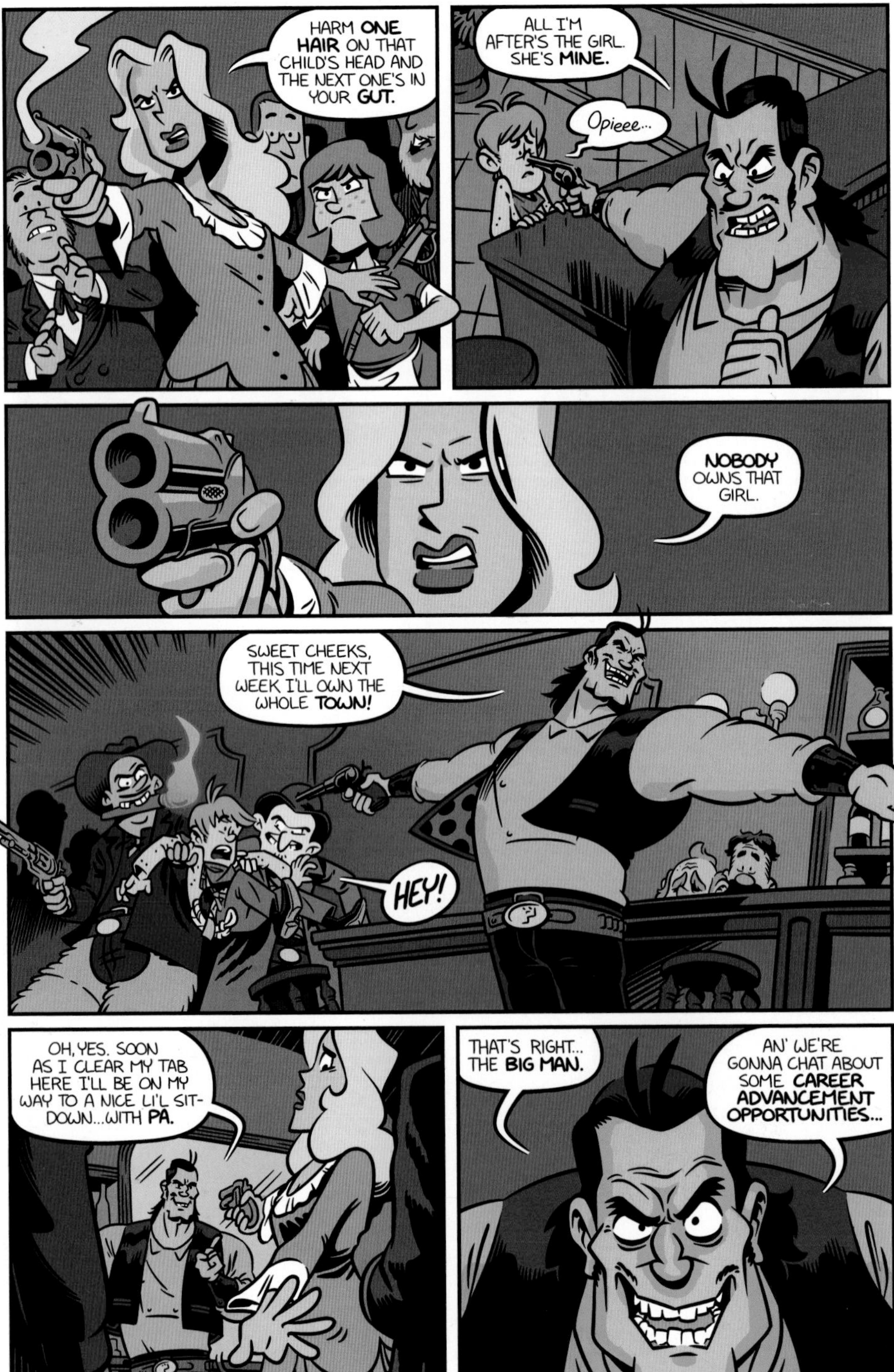
HARM **ONE HAIR** ON THAT CHILD'S HEAD AND THE NEXT ONE'S IN YOUR **GUT.**
ALL I'M AFTER'S THE GIRL. SHE'S **MINE.**
Opieee...
NOBODY OWNS THAT GIRL.
SWEET CHEEKS, THIS TIME NEXT WEEK I'LL OWN THE WHOLE **TOWN!**
HEY!
OH, YES. SOON AS I CLEAR MY TAB HERE I'LL BE ON MY WAY TO A NICE LI'L SIT-DOWN... WITH **PA.**
THAT'S RIGHT... THE **BIG MAN.**
AN' WE'RE GONNA CHAT ABOUT SOME **CAREER ADVANCEMENT OPPORTUNITIES...**

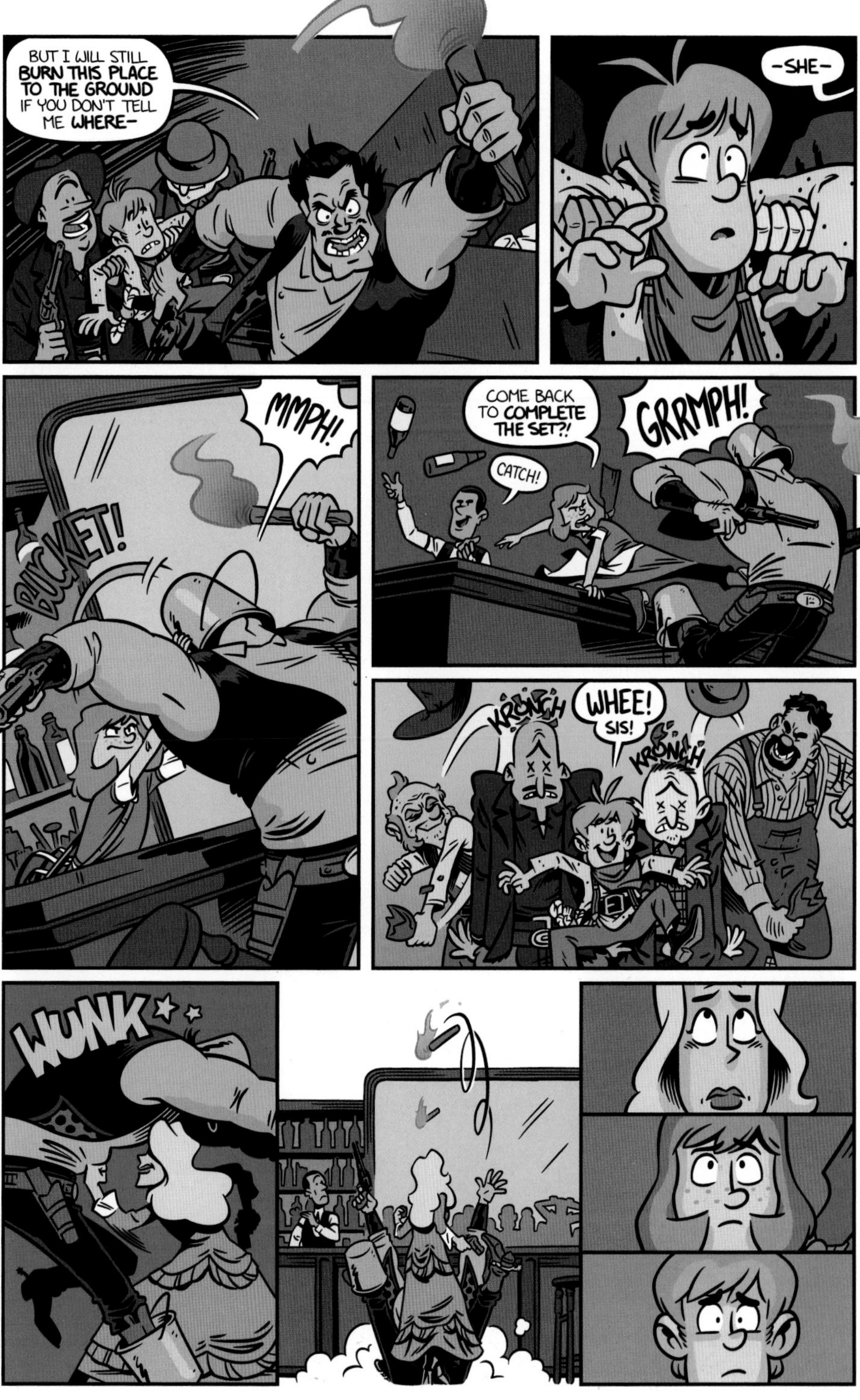
BUT I WILL STILL BURN THIS PLACE TO THE GROUND IF YOU DON'T TELL ME WHERE-
-SHE-
MMPH!
BUCKET!
COME BACK TO COMPLETE THE SET?!
CATCH!
GRRMPH!
KRONCH
WHEE! SIS!
KRONCH
WUNK

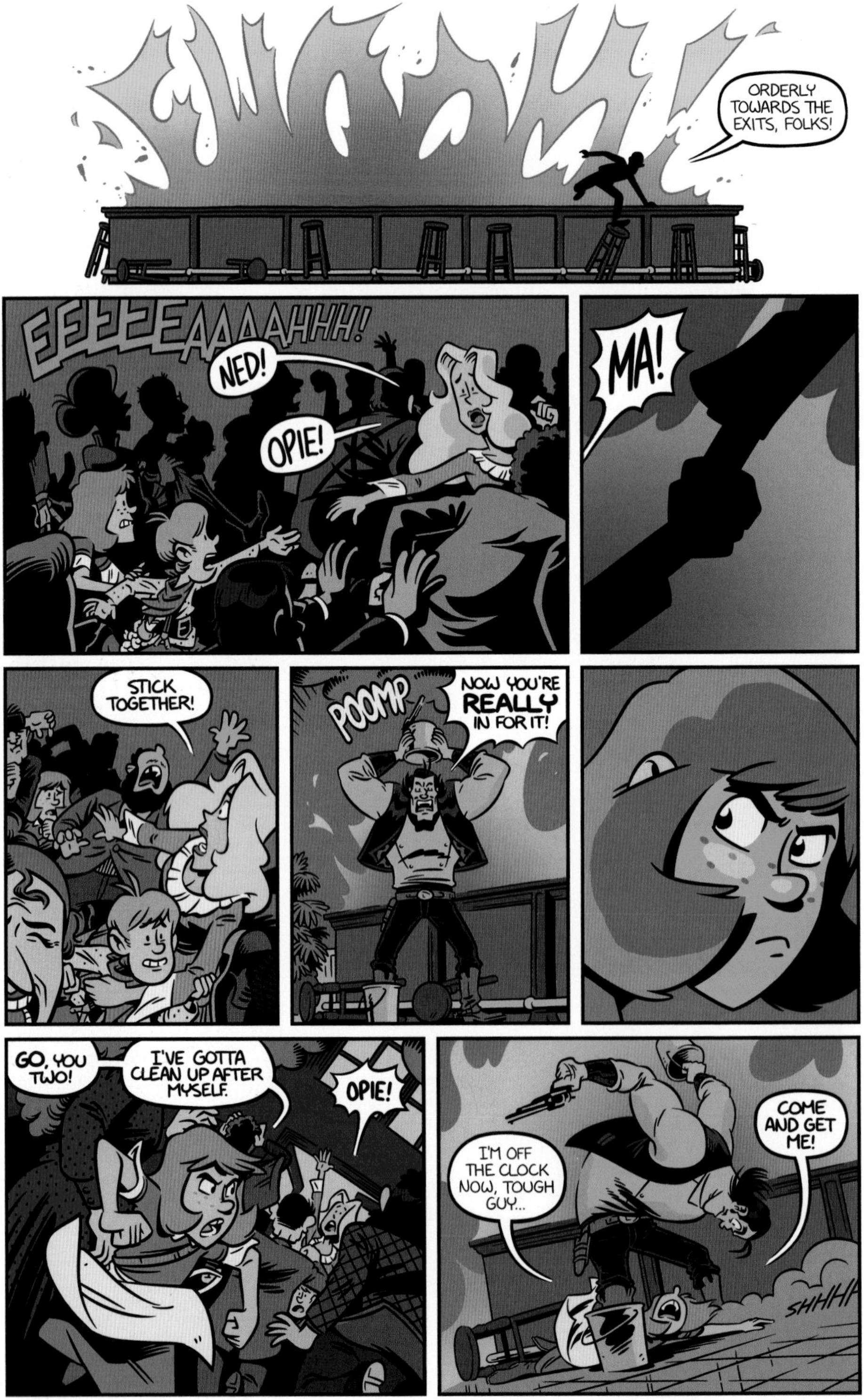
FWOOOM!
ORDERLY TOWARDS THE EXITS, FOLKS!
EEEEEAAAAHHH!
NED!
OPIE!
MA!
STICK TOGETHER!
POOMP
NOW YOU'RE REALLY IN FOR IT!
GO, YOU TWO!
I'VE GOTTA CLEAN UP AFTER MYSELF.
OPIE!
I'M OFF THE CLOCK NOW, TOUGH GUY...
COME AND GET ME!
SHHH

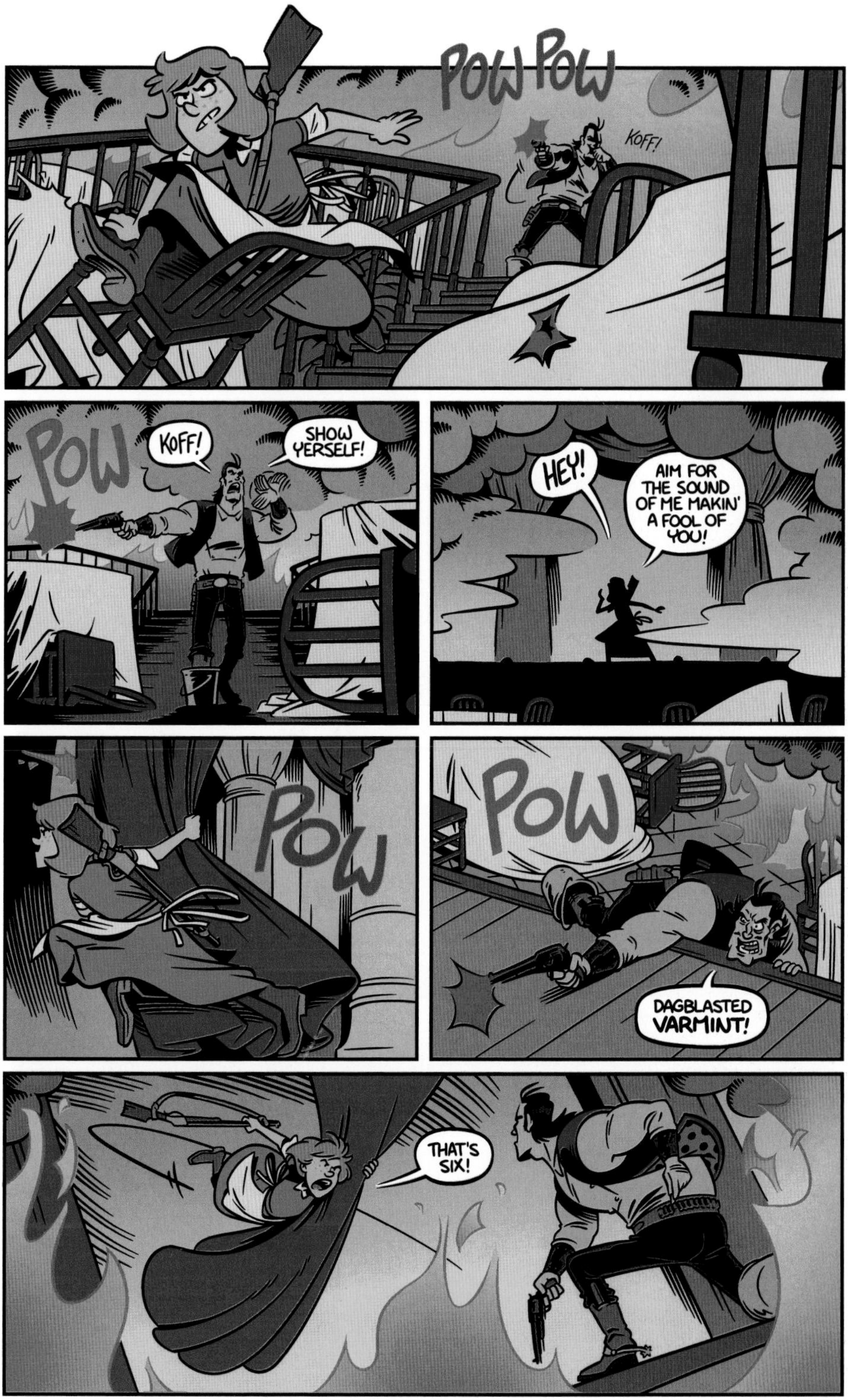
POW POW
KOFF!
POW
KOFF!
SHOW YERSELF!
HEY!
AIM FOR THE SOUND OF ME MAKIN' A FOOL OF YOU!
POW
POW
DAGBLASTED VARMINT!
THAT'S SIX!

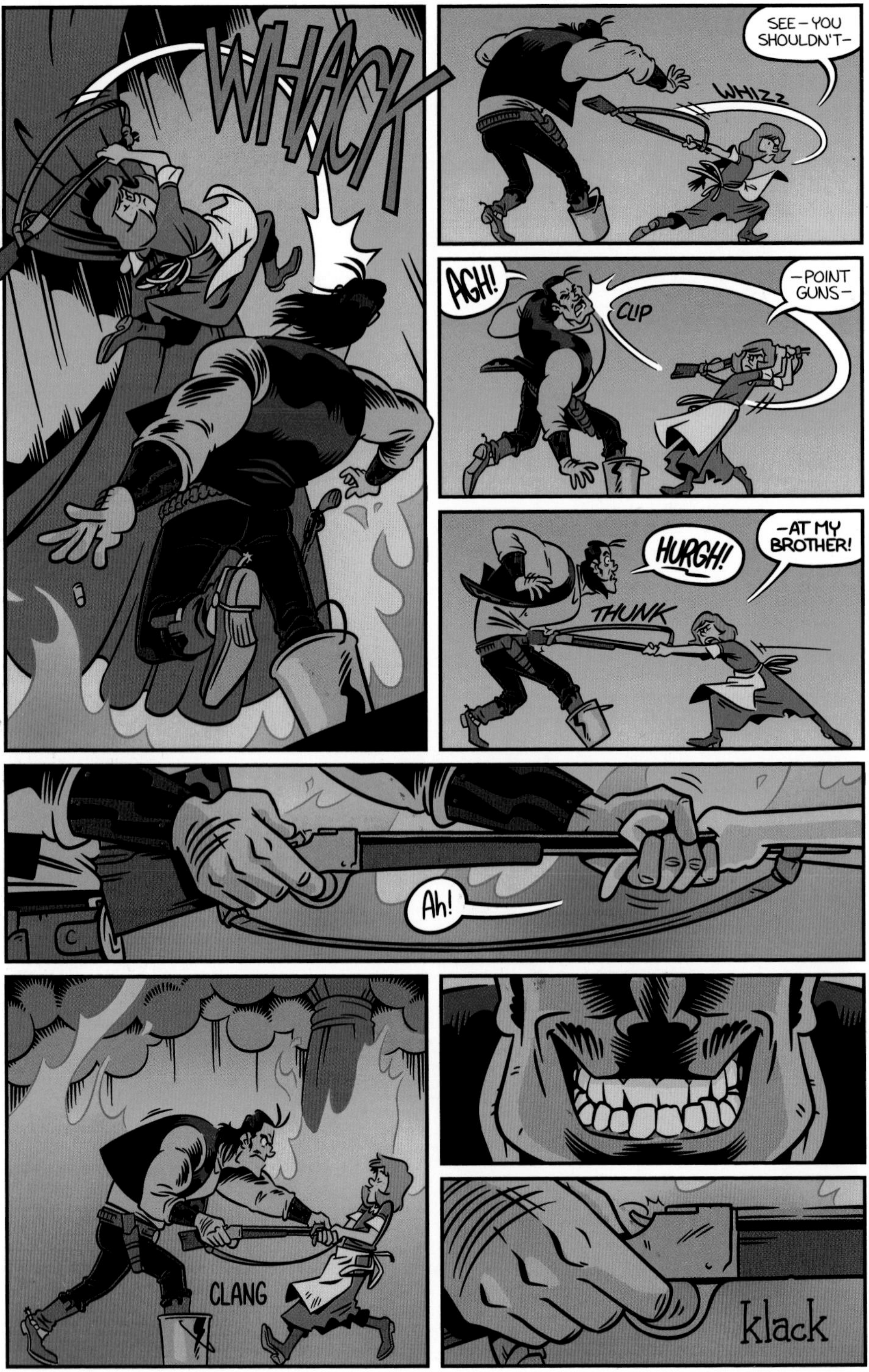
WHACK
SEE—YOU SHOULDN'T—
WHIZZ
AGH!
CLIP
—POINT GUNS—
HURGH!
—AT MY BROTHER!
THUNK
Ah!
CLANG
klack

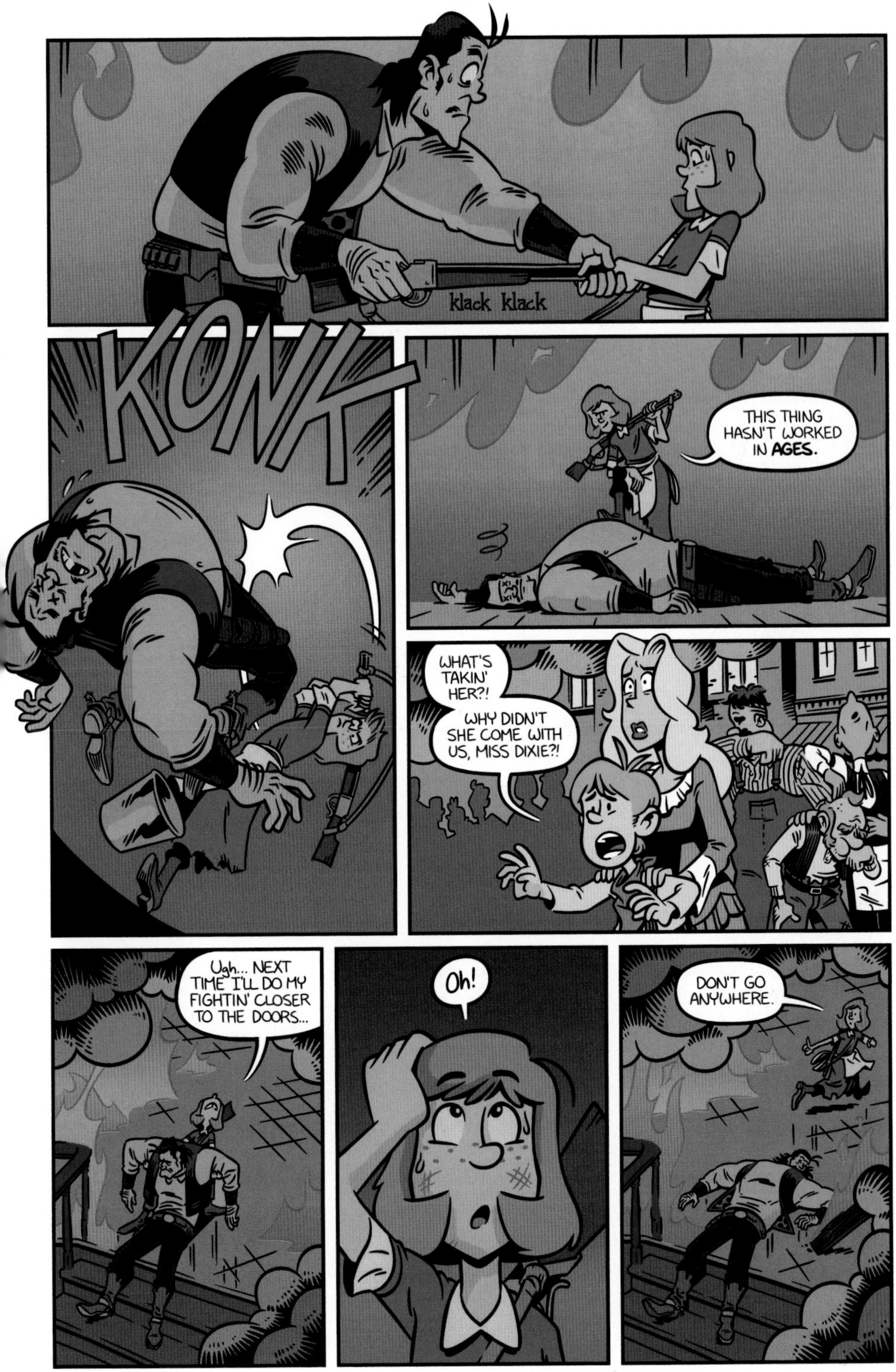
klack klack
KONK
THIS THING HASN'T WORKED IN AGES.
WHAT'S TAKIN' HER?!
WHY DIDN'T SHE COME WITH US, MISS DIXIE?!
Ugh... NEXT TIME I'LL DO MY FIGHTIN' CLOSER TO THE DOORS...
Oh!
DON'T GO ANYWHERE.

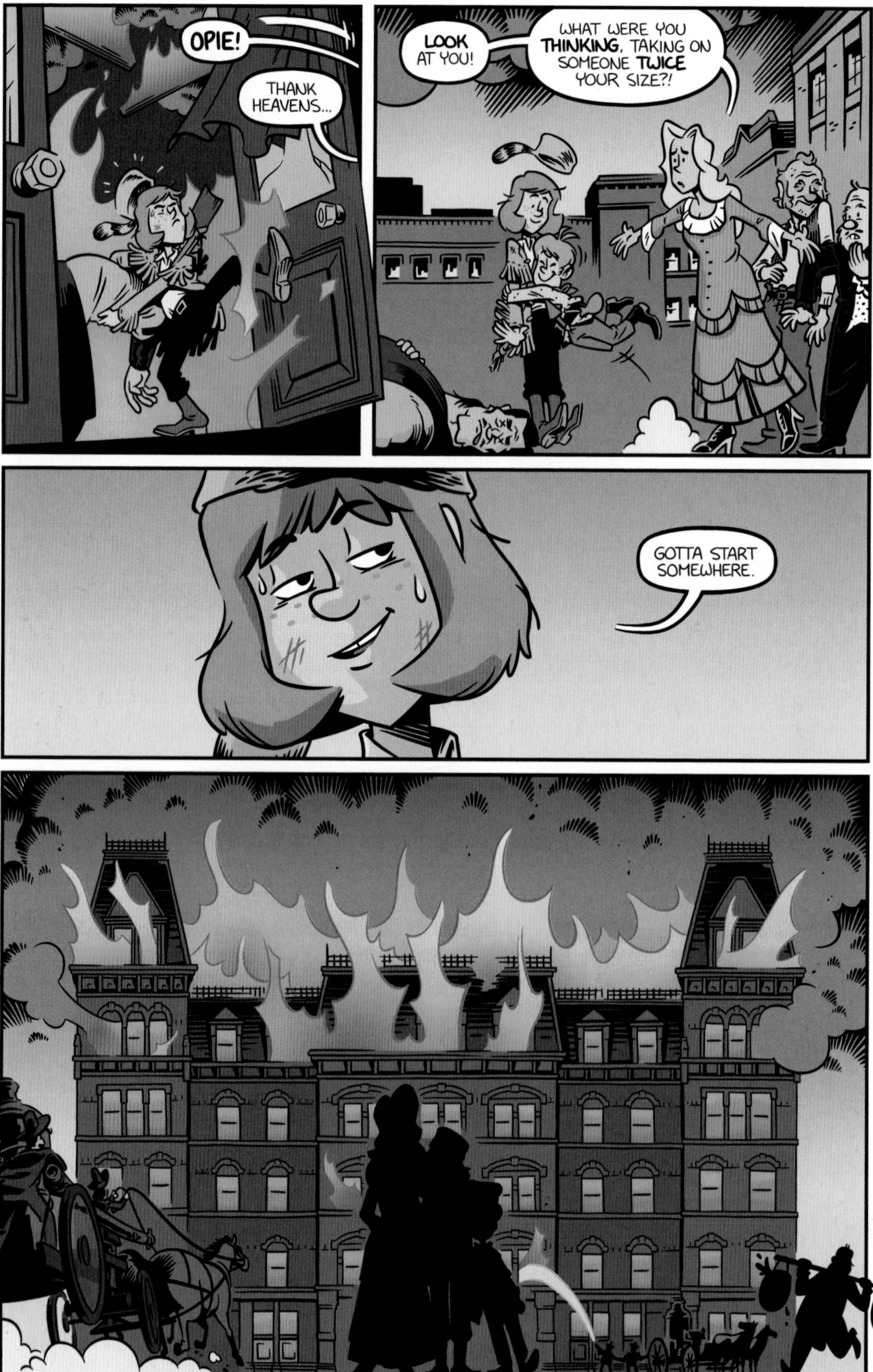
OPIE!
THANK HEAVENS...
LOOK AT YOU!
WHAT WERE YOU THINKING, TAKING ON SOMEONE TWICE YOUR SIZE?!
GOTTA START SOMEWHERE.

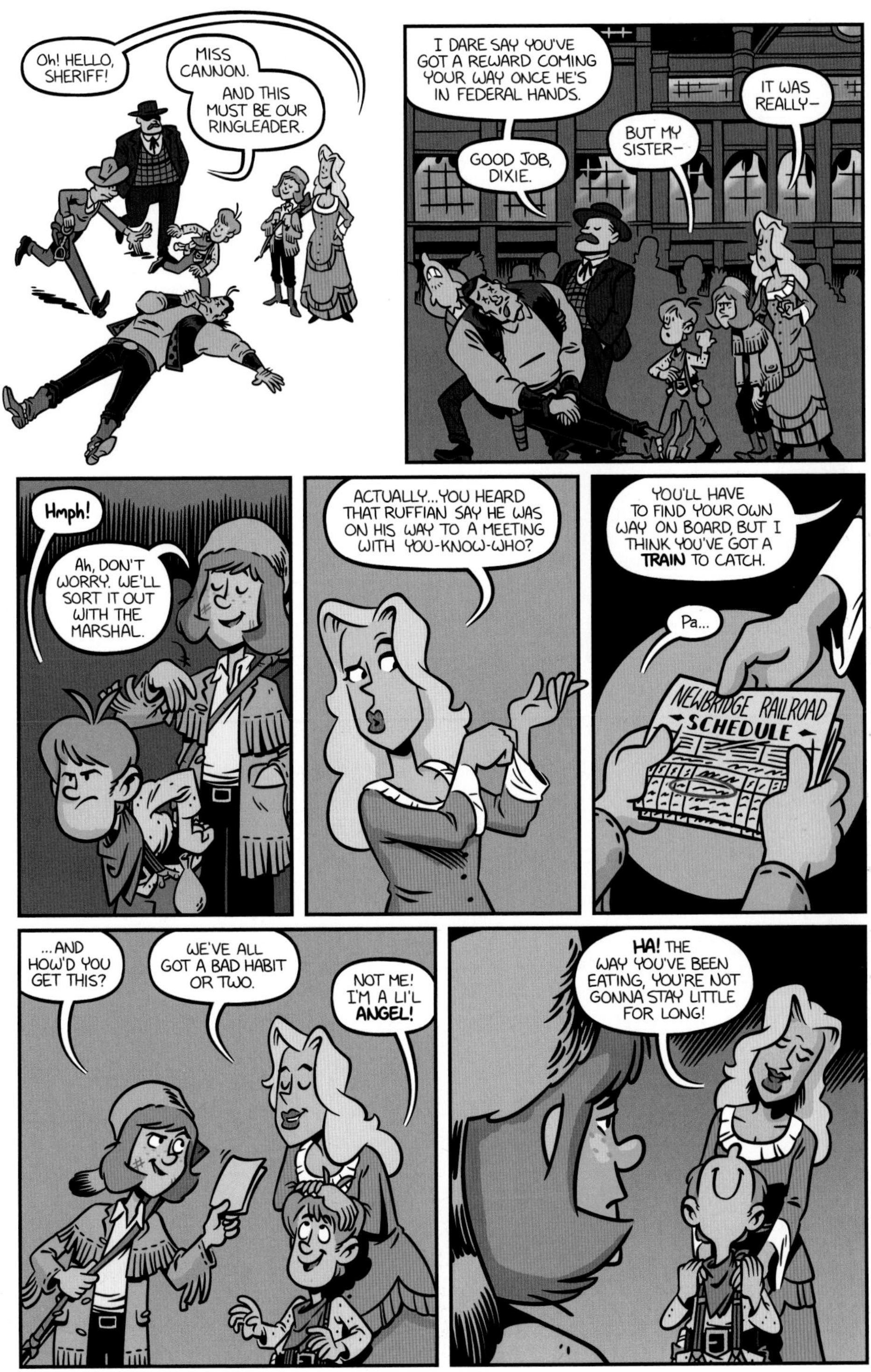
Oh! HELLO, SHERIFF!
MISS CANNON.
AND THIS MUST BE OUR RINGLEADER.
I DARE SAY YOU'VE GOT A REWARD COMING YOUR WAY ONCE HE'S IN FEDERAL HANDS.
GOOD JOB, DIXIE.
BUT MY SISTER—
IT WAS REALLY—
Hmph!
Ah, DON'T WORRY. WE'LL SORT IT OUT WITH THE MARSHAL.
ACTUALLY...YOU HEARD THAT RUFFIAN SAY HE WAS ON HIS WAY TO A MEETING WITH YOU-KNOW-WHO?
YOU'LL HAVE TO FIND YOUR OWN WAY ON BOARD, BUT I THINK YOU'VE GOT A TRAIN TO CATCH.
Pa...
NEWBRIDGE RAILROAD SCHEDULE
...AND HOW'D YOU GET THIS?
WE'VE ALL GOT A BAD HABIT OR TWO.
NOT ME! I'M A LI'L ANGEL!
HA! THE WAY YOU'VE BEEN EATING, YOU'RE NOT GONNA STAY LITTLE FOR LONG!

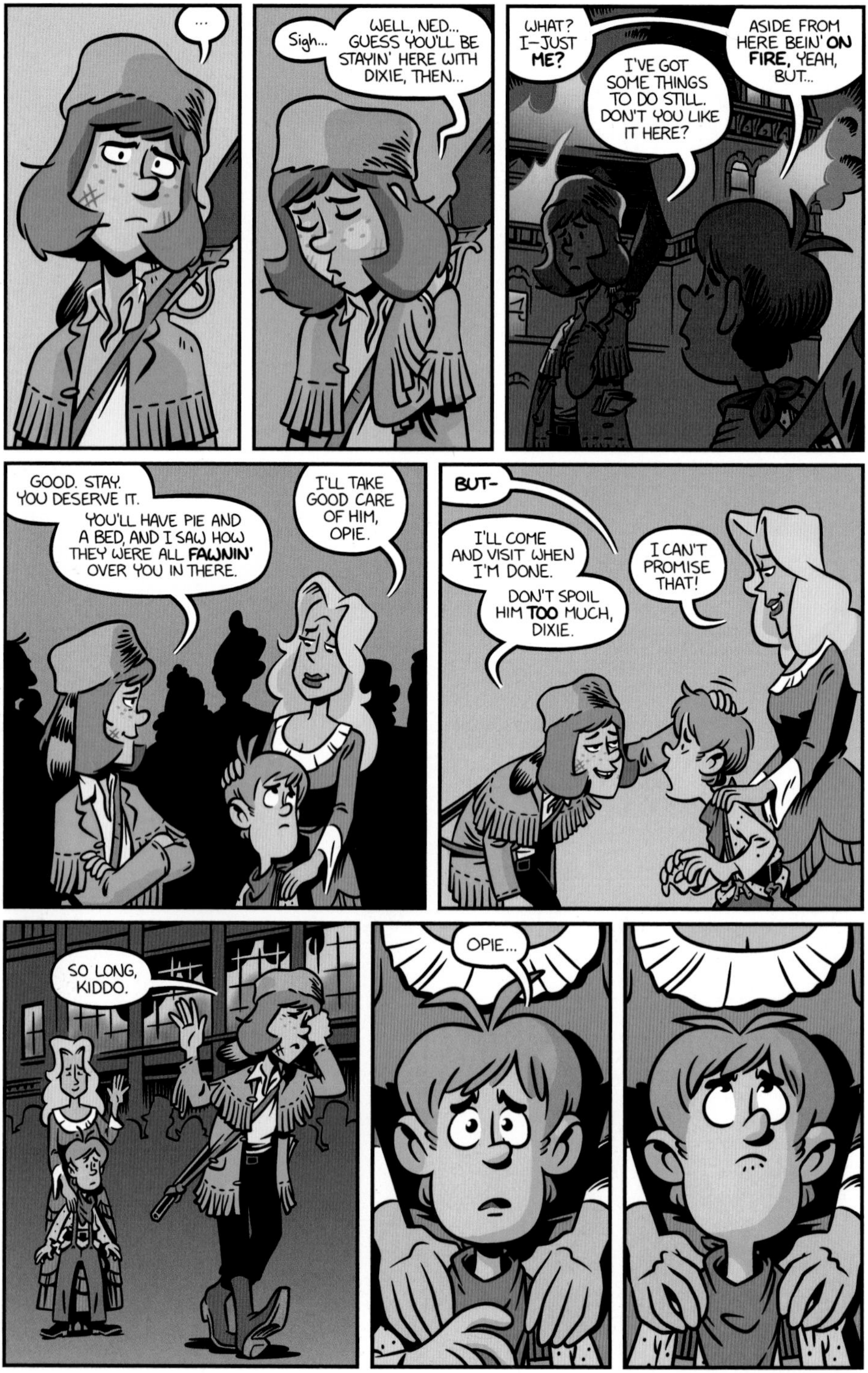
...
Sigh...
WELL, NED... GUESS YOU'LL BE STAYIN' HERE WITH DIXIE, THEN...
WHAT? I—JUST **ME?**
I'VE GOT SOME THINGS TO DO STILL. DON'T YOU LIKE IT HERE?
ASIDE FROM HERE BEIN' **ON FIRE,** YEAH, BUT...
GOOD. STAY. YOU DESERVE IT.
YOU'LL HAVE PIE AND A BED, AND I SAW HOW THEY WERE ALL **FAWNIN'** OVER YOU IN THERE.
I'LL TAKE GOOD CARE OF HIM, OPIE.
BUT-
I'LL COME AND VISIT WHEN I'M DONE.
DON'T SPOIL HIM **TOO** MUCH, DIXIE.
I CAN'T PROMISE THAT!
SO LONG, KIDDO.
OPIE...

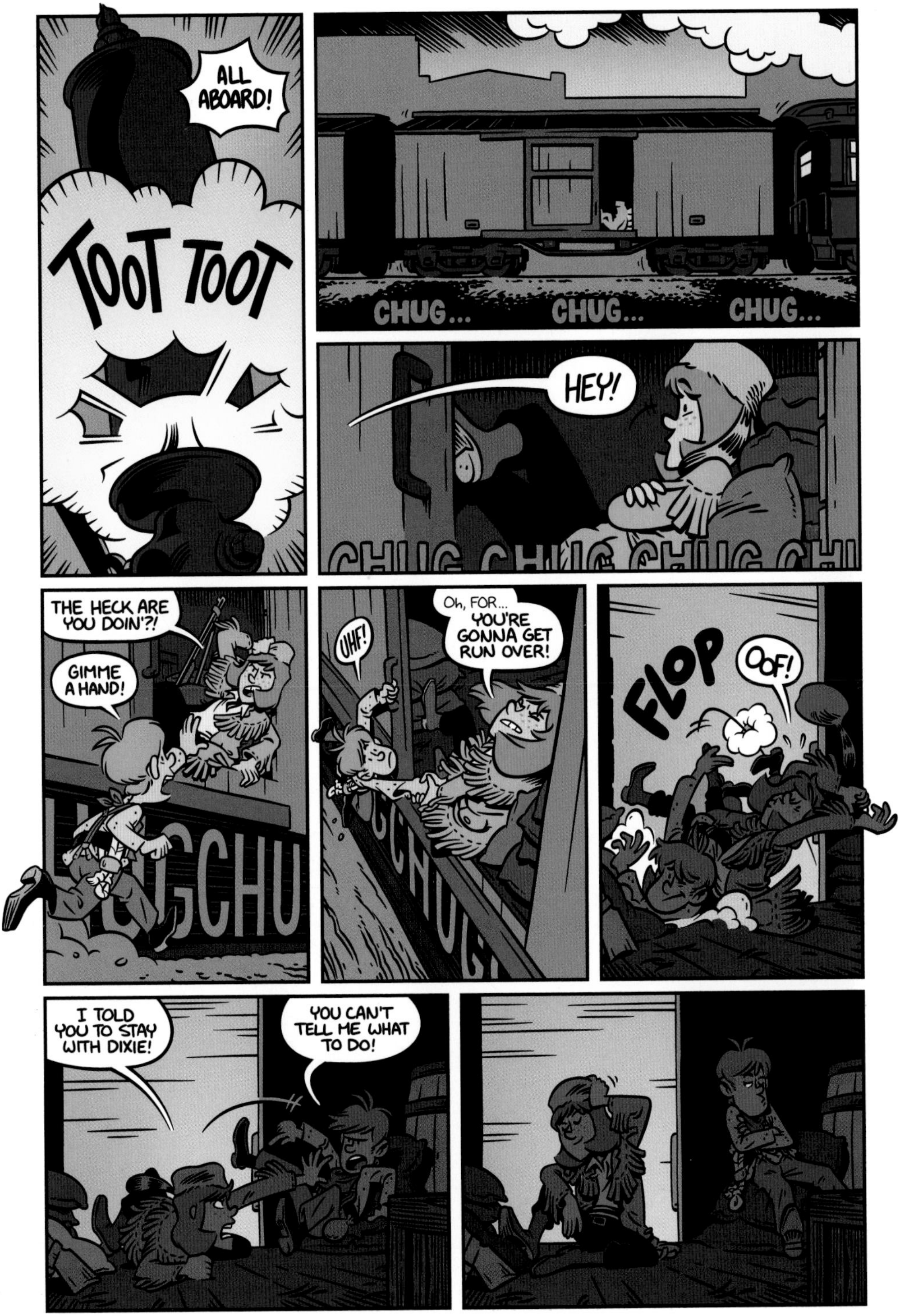
ALL ABOARD!
TOOT TOOT
CHUG... CHUG... CHUG...
HEY!
CHUG CHUG CHUG CHU
THE HECK ARE YOU DOIN'?!
GIMME A HAND!
CHUGCHU
UHF!
Oh, FOR... YOU'RE GONNA GET RUN OVER!
FLOP
OOF!
I TOLD YOU TO STAY WITH DIXIE!
YOU CAN'T TELL ME WHAT TO DO!

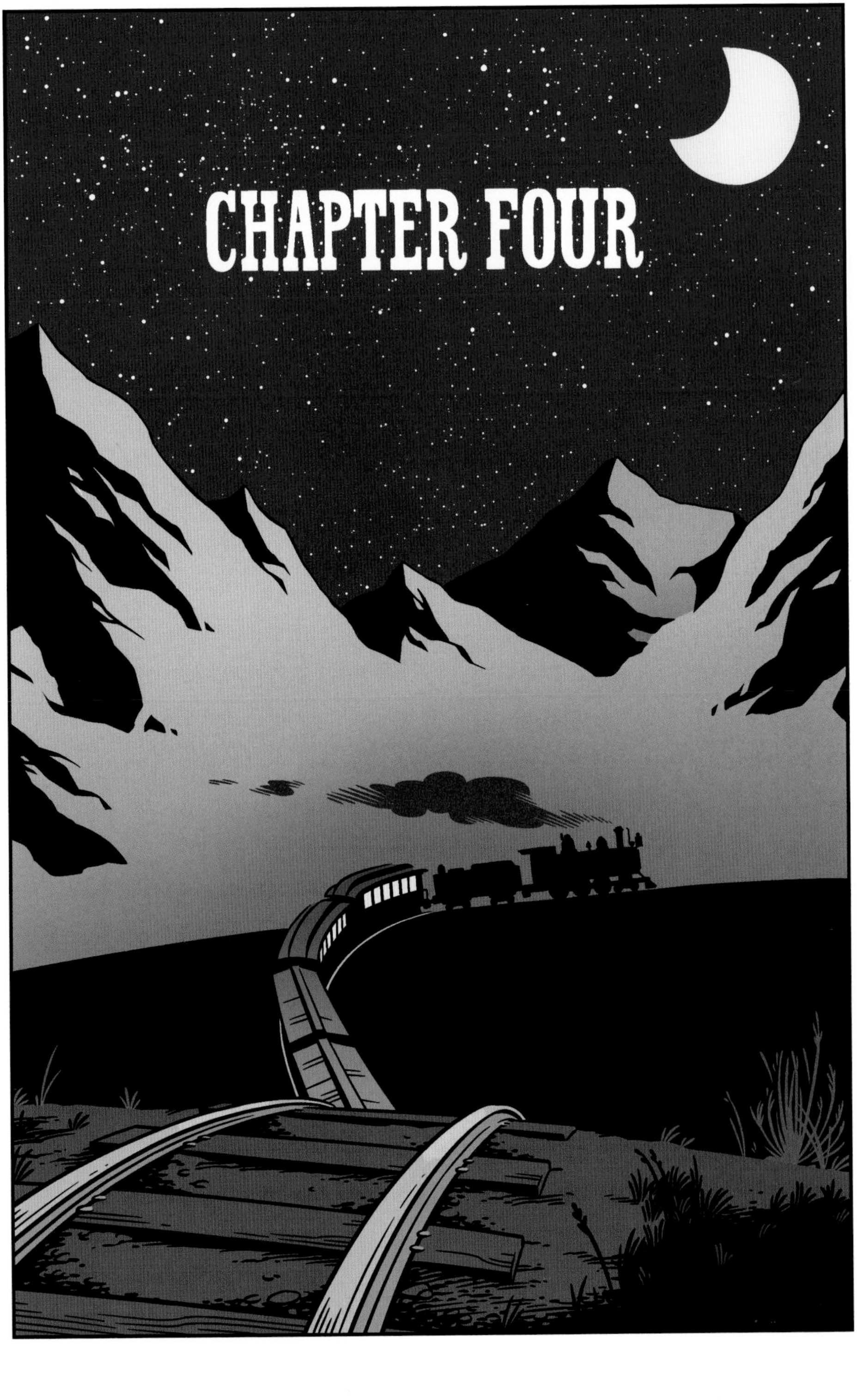
CHAPTER FOUR

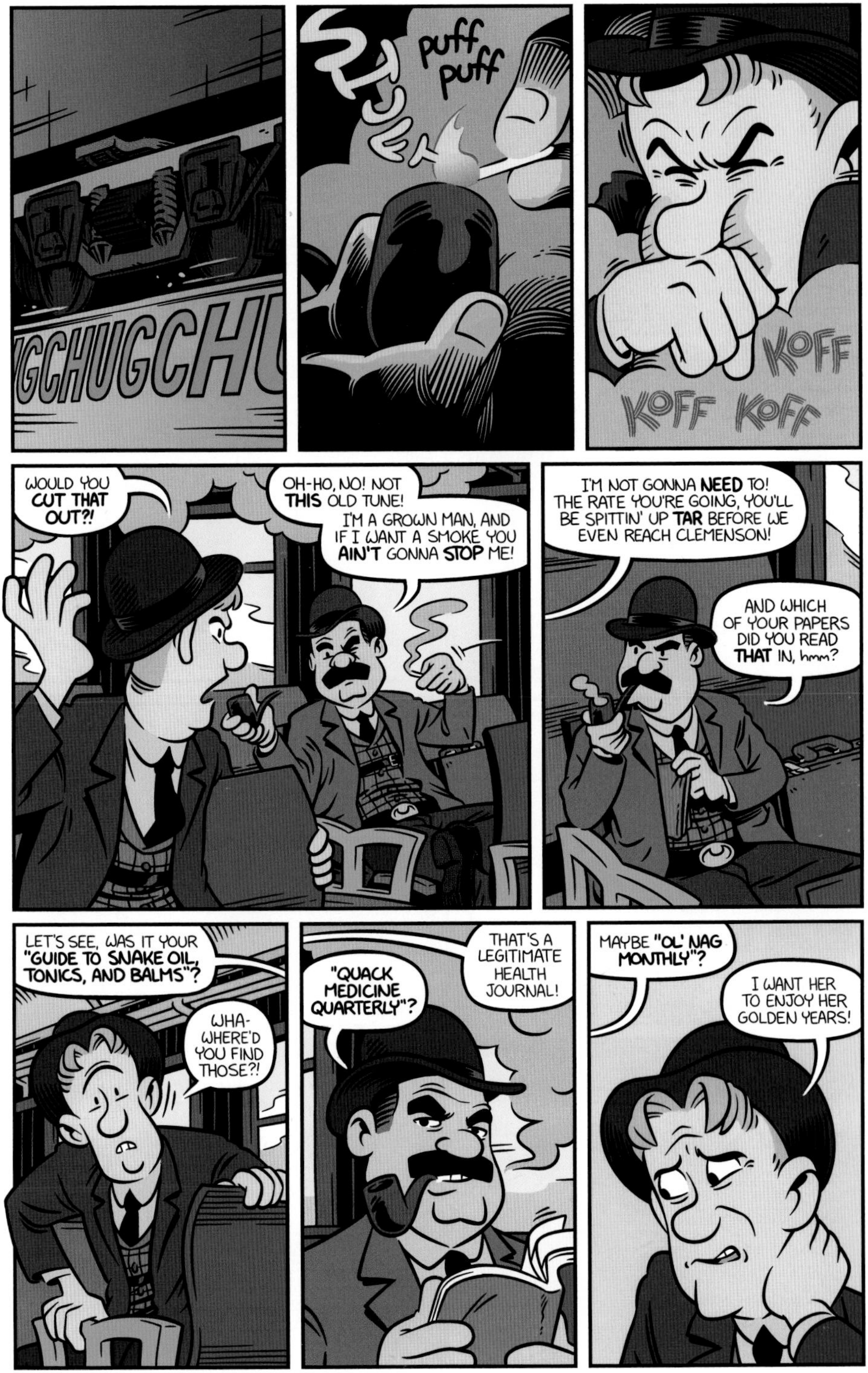
CHUGCHUGCHU
puff puff
SKRITCH
KOFF
KOFF KOFF
WOULD YOU CUT THAT OUT?!
OH-HO, NO! NOT THIS OLD TUNE!
I'M A GROWN MAN, AND IF I WANT A SMOKE YOU AIN'T GONNA STOP ME!
I'M NOT GONNA NEED TO! THE RATE YOU'RE GOING, YOU'LL BE SPITTIN' UP TAR BEFORE WE EVEN REACH CLEMENSON!
AND WHICH OF YOUR PAPERS DID YOU READ THAT IN, hmm?
LET'S SEE, WAS IT YOUR "GUIDE TO SNAKE OIL, TONICS, AND BALMS"?
WHA- WHERE'D YOU FIND THOSE?!
"QUACK MEDICINE QUARTERLY"?
THAT'S A LEGITIMATE HEALTH JOURNAL!
MAYBE "OL' NAG MONTHLY"?
I WANT HER TO ENJOY HER GOLDEN YEARS!

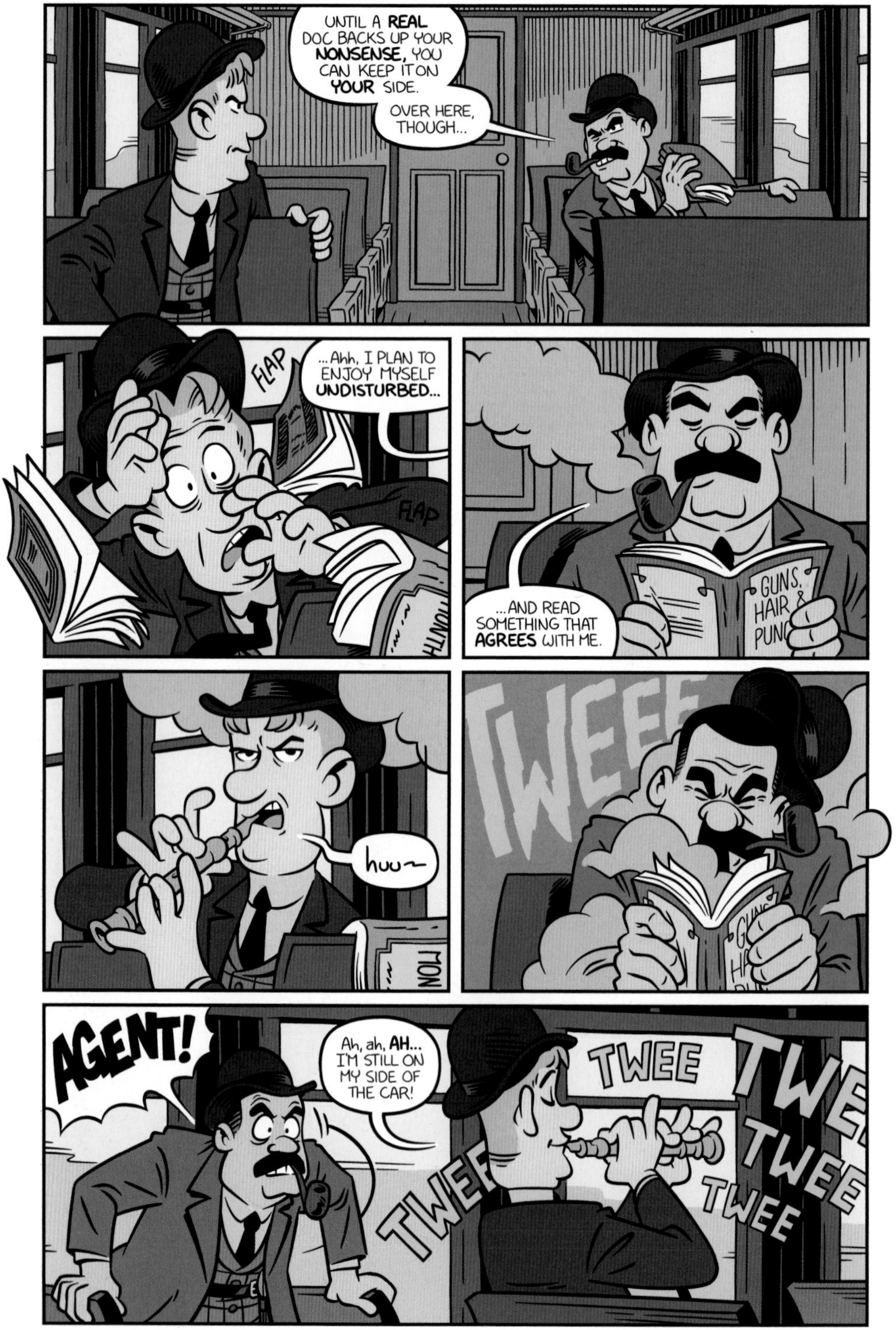
UNTIL A **REAL** DOC BACKS UP YOUR **NONSENSE,** YOU CAN KEEP IT ON **YOUR** SIDE.
OVER HERE, THOUGH...
FLAP
...Ahh, I PLAN TO ENJOY MYSELF **UNDISTURBED...**
FLAP
...AND READ SOMETHING THAT **AGREES** WITH ME.
GUNS, HAIR &
huu~
AGENT!
Ah, ah, **AH...** I'M STILL ON MY SIDE OF THE CAR!
TWEE
TWEE
TWEE
TWEE
TWEE

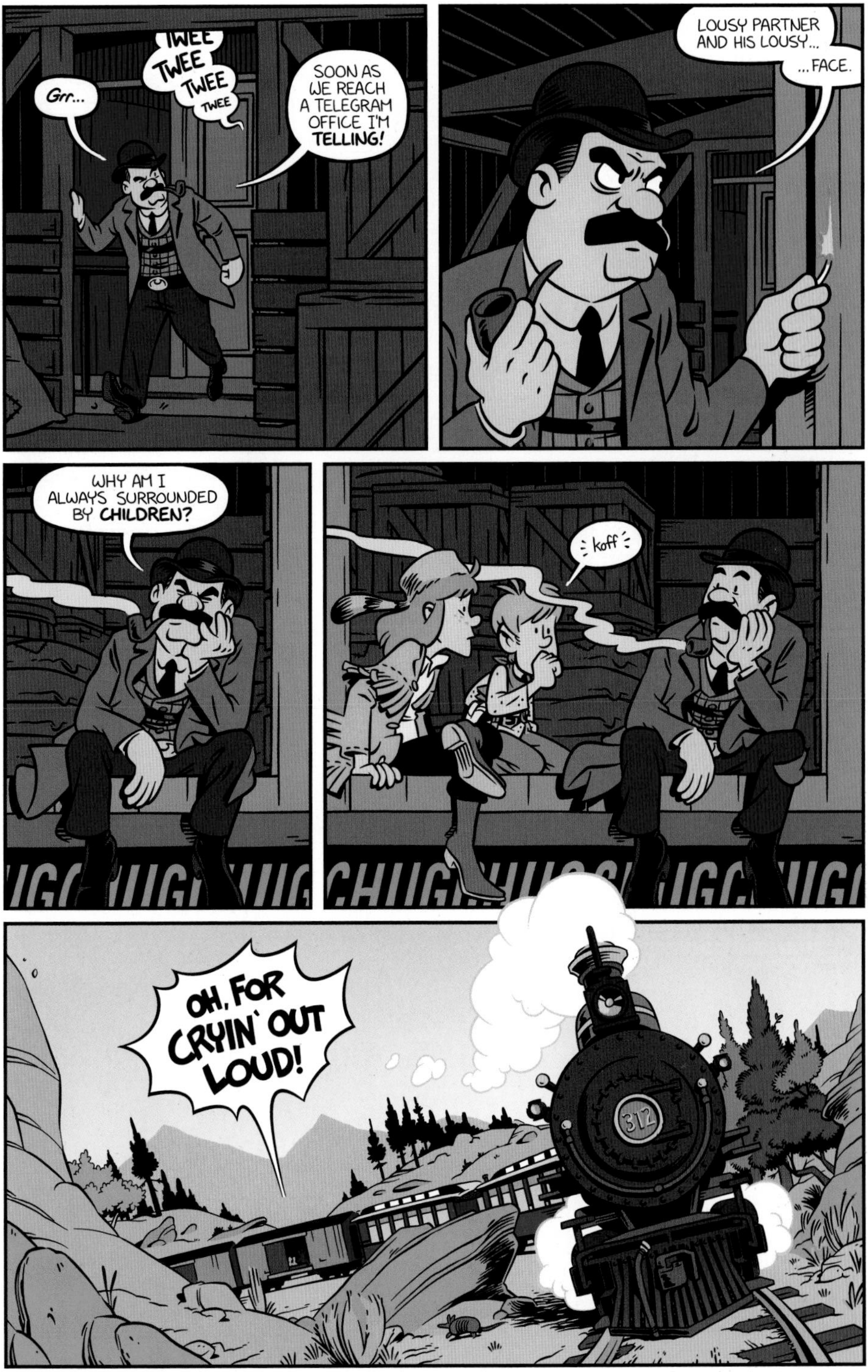
Grr...
TWEE TWEE TWEE TWEE
SOON AS WE REACH A TELEGRAM OFFICE I'M **TELLING!**
LOUSY PARTNER AND HIS LOUSY...
...FACE.
WHY AM I ALWAYS SURROUNDED BY **CHILDREN?**
koff
CHUGCHUGCHUG
OH, FOR CRYIN' OUT LOUD!
312

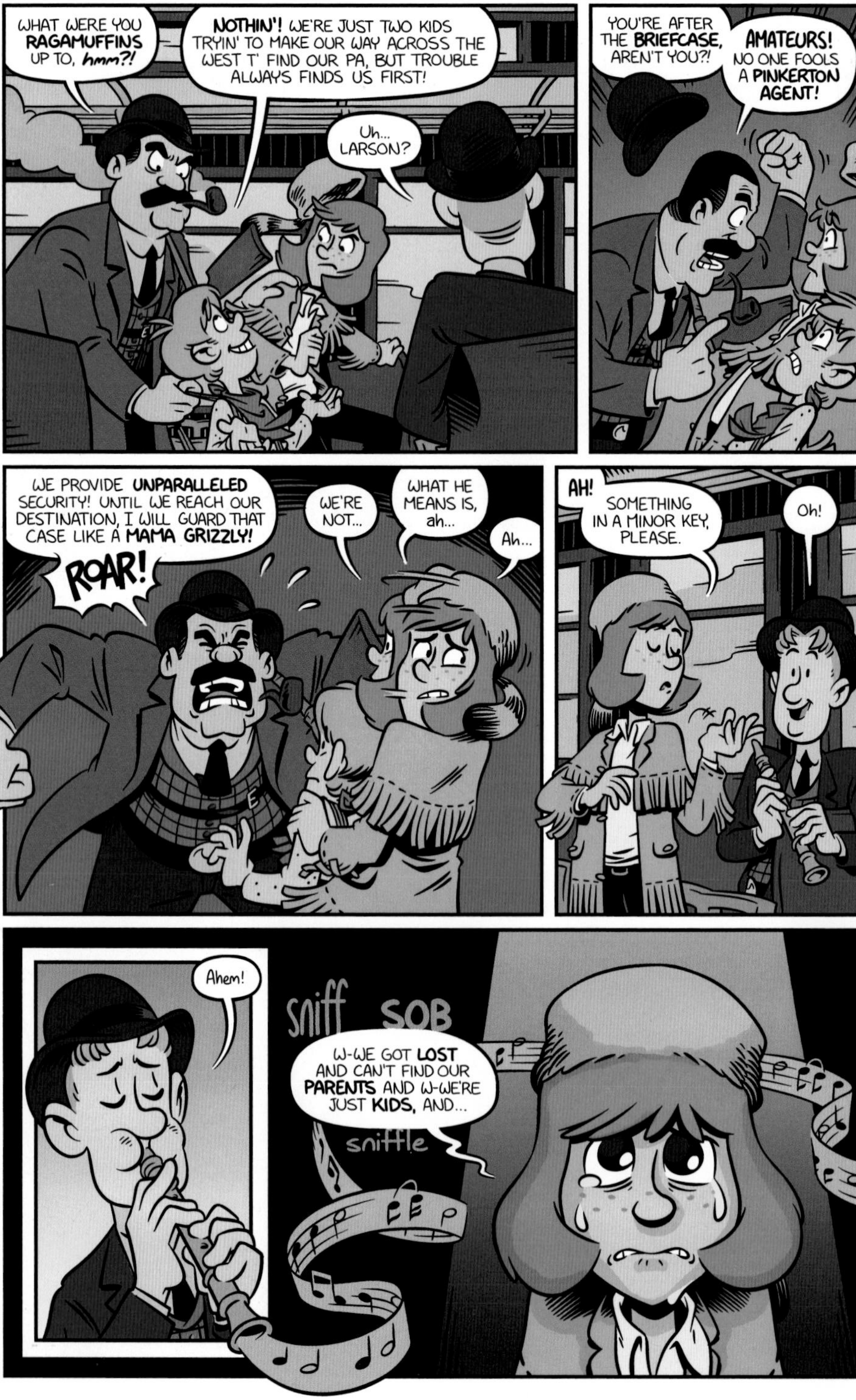
WHAT WERE YOU **RAGAMUFFINS** UP TO, *hmm?!*
NOTHIN'! WE'RE JUST TWO KIDS TRYIN' TO MAKE OUR WAY ACROSS THE WEST T' FIND OUR PA, BUT TROUBLE ALWAYS FINDS US FIRST!
Uh... LARSON?
YOU'RE AFTER THE **BRIEFCASE,** AREN'T YOU?!
AMATEURS! NO ONE FOOLS A **PINKERTON AGENT!**
WE PROVIDE **UNPARALLELED** SECURITY! UNTIL WE REACH OUR DESTINATION, I WILL GUARD THAT CASE LIKE A **MAMA GRIZZLY!**
ROAR!
WE'RE NOT...
WHAT HE MEANS IS, ah...
Ah...
AH!
SOMETHING IN A MINOR KEY, PLEASE.
Oh!
Ahem!
sniff
SOB
W-WE GOT **LOST** AND CAN'T FIND OUR **PARENTS** AND W-WE'RE JUST **KIDS,** AND...
sniffle

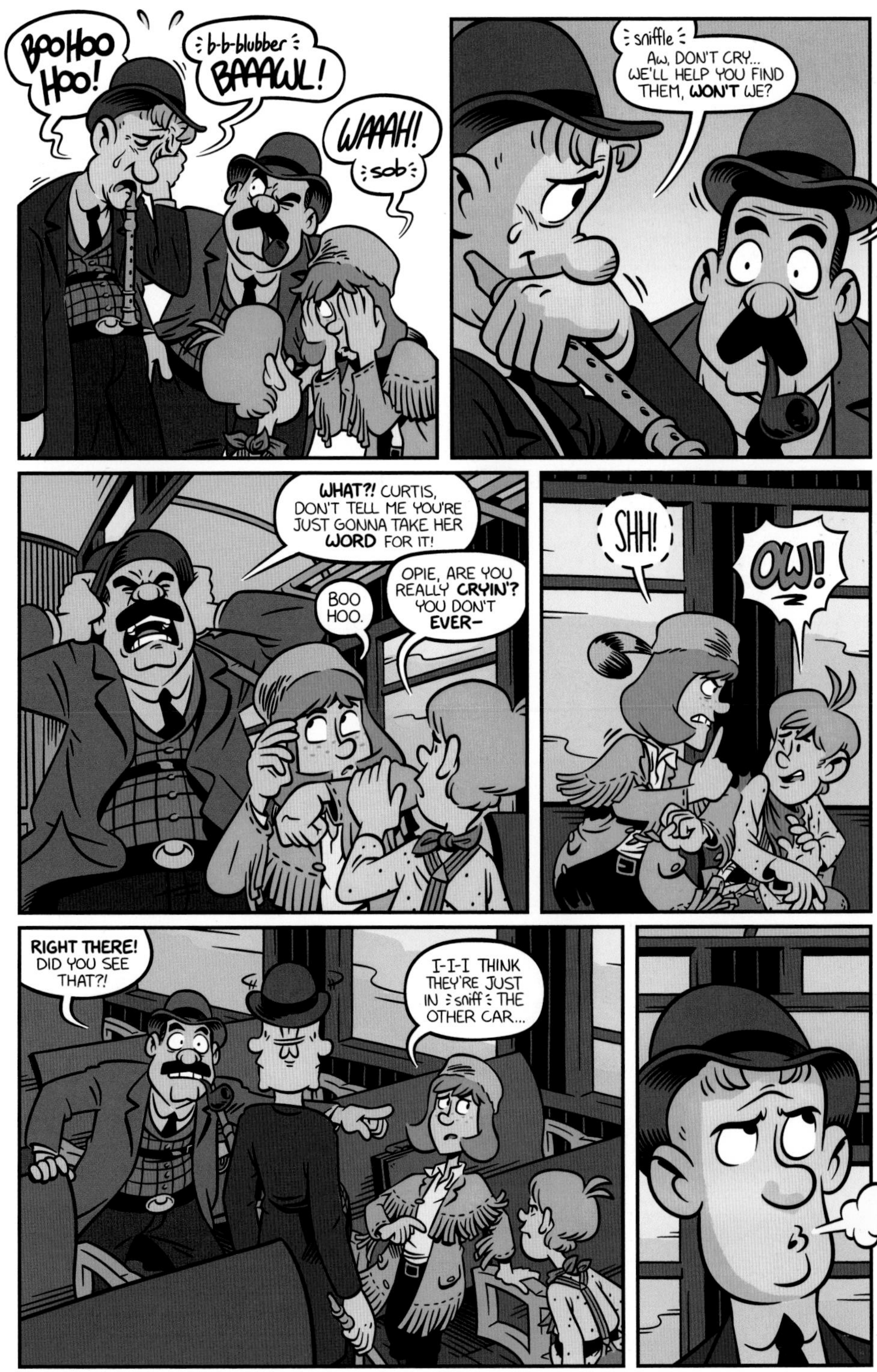
BOOHOO HOO!
b-b-blubber BAAAWL!
WAAAH! sob
sniffle Aw, DON'T CRY... WE'LL HELP YOU FIND THEM, WON'T WE?
WHAT?! CURTIS, DON'T TELL ME YOU'RE JUST GONNA TAKE HER WORD FOR IT!
BOO HOO.
OPIE, ARE YOU REALLY CRYIN'? YOU DON'T EVER–
SHH!
OW!
RIGHT THERE! DID YOU SEE THAT?!
I-I-I THINK THEY'RE JUST IN sniff THE OTHER CAR...

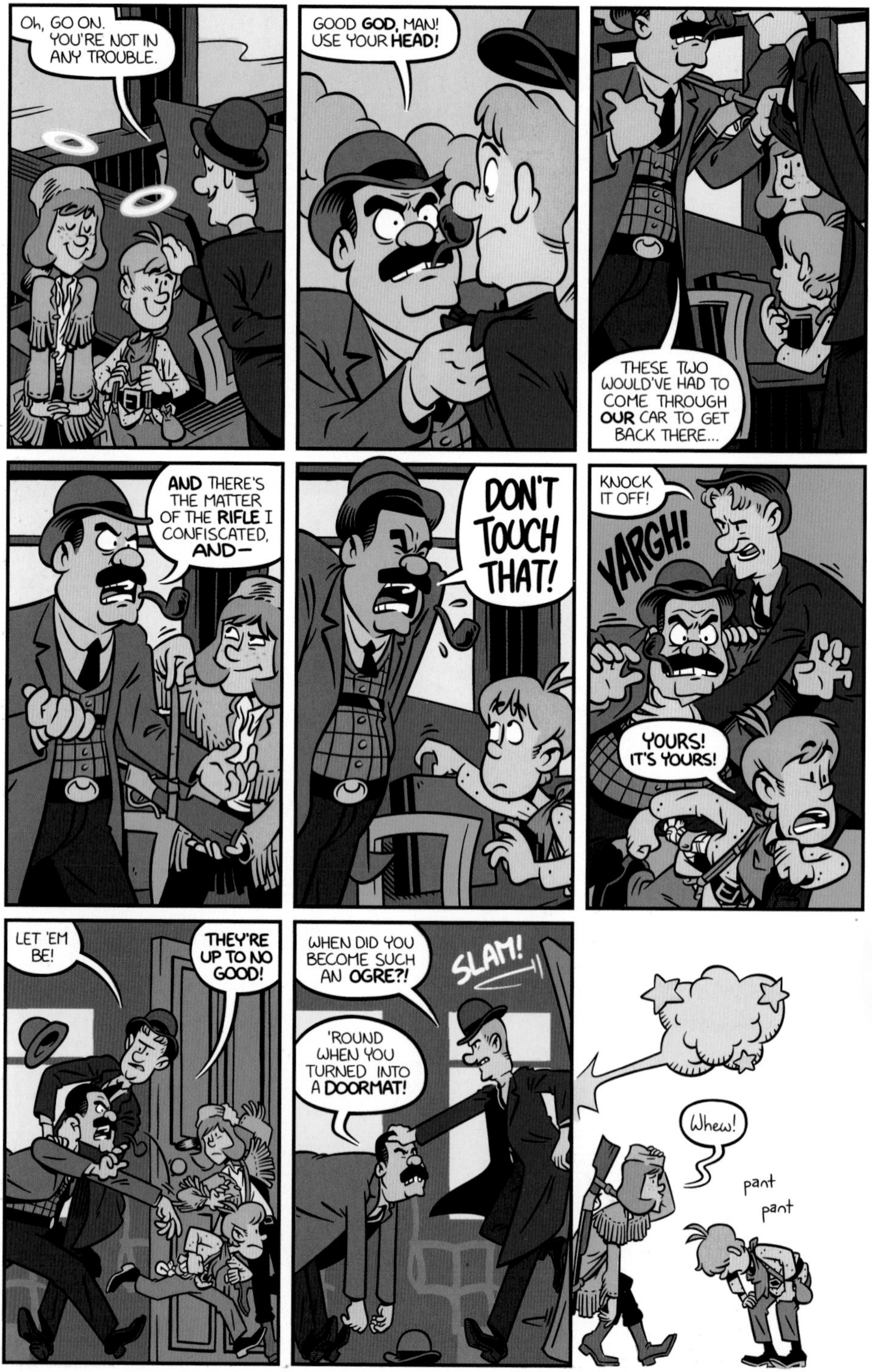
Oh, GO ON. YOU'RE NOT IN ANY TROUBLE.
GOOD GOD, MAN! USE YOUR HEAD!
THESE TWO WOULD'VE HAD TO COME THROUGH OUR CAR TO GET BACK THERE...
AND THERE'S THE MATTER OF THE RIFLE I CONFISCATED, AND—
DON'T TOUCH THAT!
KNOCK IT OFF!
YARGH!
YOURS! IT'S YOURS!
LET 'EM BE!
THEY'RE UP TO NO GOOD!
WHEN DID YOU BECOME SUCH AN OGRE?!
SLAM!
'ROUND WHEN YOU TURNED INTO A DOORMAT!
Whew!
pant
pant

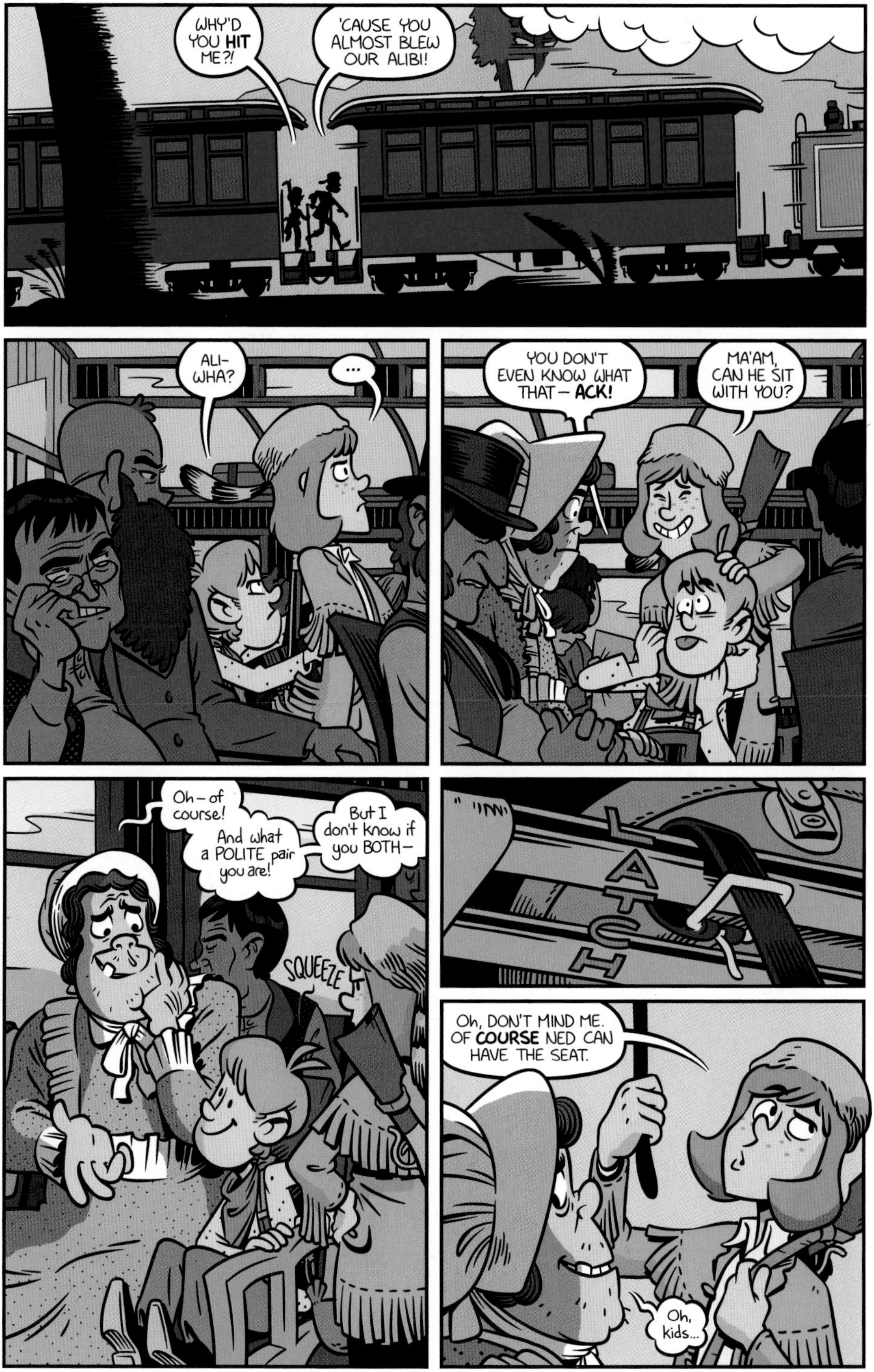
WHY'D YOU HIT ME?!
'CAUSE YOU ALMOST BLEW OUR ALIBI!
ALI-WHA?
...
YOU DON'T EVEN KNOW WHAT THAT— ACK!
MA'AM, CAN HE SIT WITH YOU?
Oh—of course!
And what a POLITE pair you are!
But I don't know if you BOTH—
SQUEEZE
LATCH
Oh, DON'T MIND ME. OF COURSE NED CAN HAVE THE SEAT.
Oh, kids...

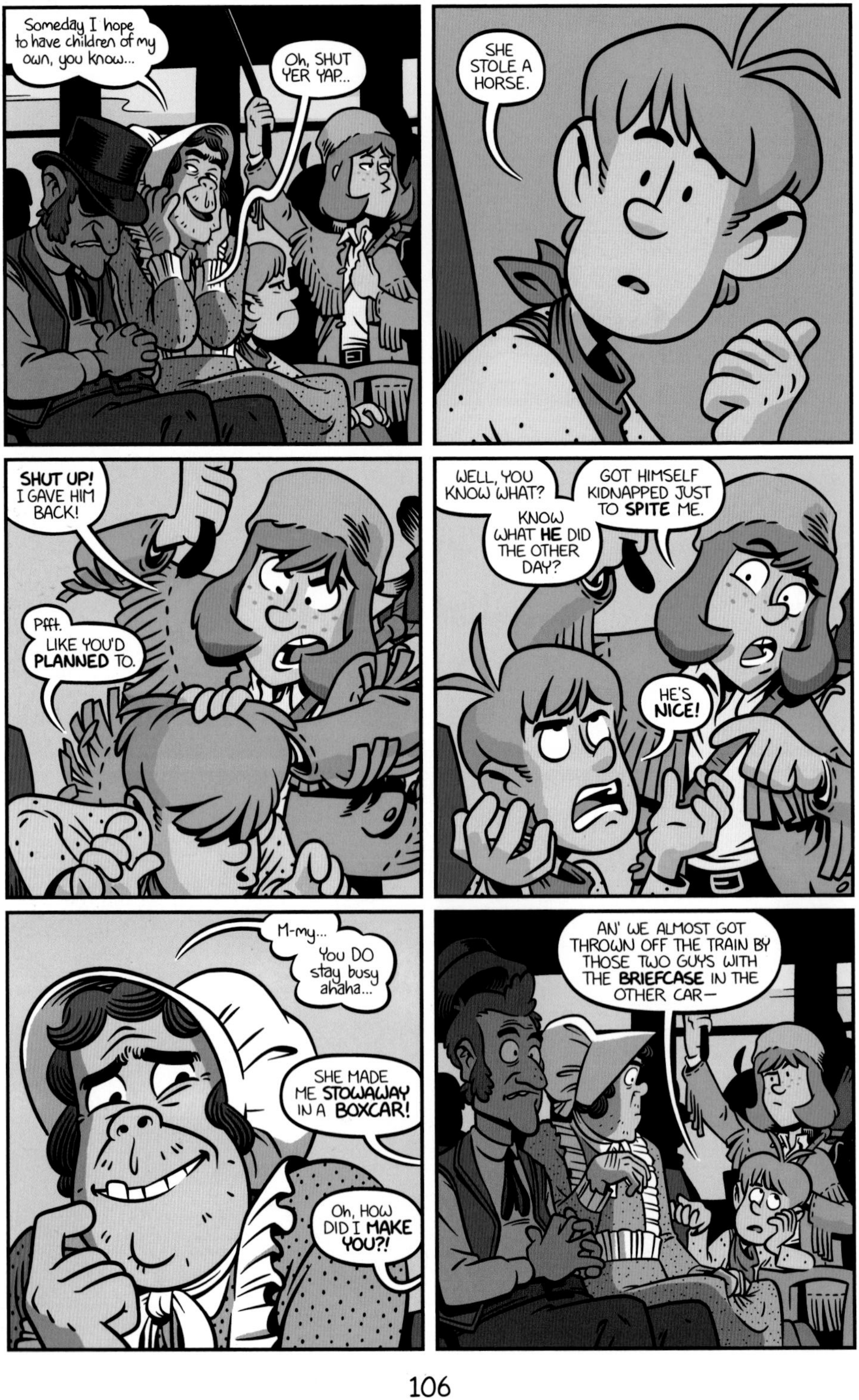

Someday I hope to have children of my own, you know...
Oh, SHUT YER YAP...
SHE STOLE A HORSE.
SHUT UP! I GAVE HIM BACK!
Pfft. LIKE YOU'D PLANNED TO.
WELL, YOU KNOW WHAT?
KNOW WHAT HE DID THE OTHER DAY?
GOT HIMSELF KIDNAPPED JUST TO SPITE ME.
HE'S NICE!
M-my...
You DO stay busy ahaha...
SHE MADE ME STOWAWAY IN A BOXCAR!
Oh, HOW DID I MAKE YOU?!
AN' WE ALMOST GOT THROWN OFF THE TRAIN BY THOSE TWO GUYS WITH THE BRIEFCASE IN THE OTHER CAR—

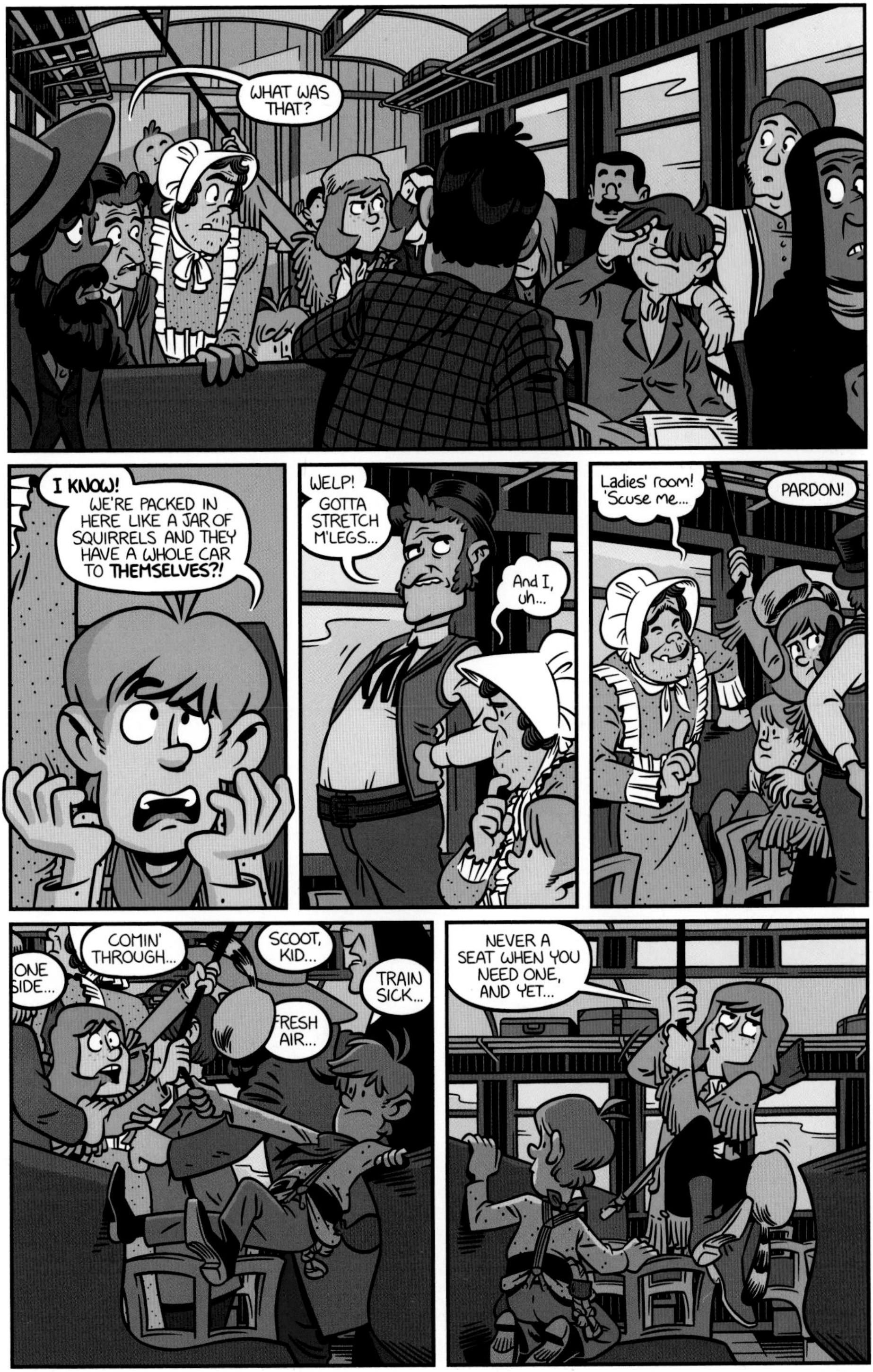
WHAT WAS THAT?
I KNOW! WE'RE PACKED IN HERE LIKE A JAR OF SQUIRRELS AND THEY HAVE A WHOLE CAR TO THEMSELVES?!
WELP! GOTTA STRETCH M'LEGS...
And I, uh...
Ladies' room! 'Scuse me...
PARDON!
COMIN' THROUGH...
SCOOT, KID...
TRAIN SICK...
FRESH AIR...
NEVER A SEAT WHEN YOU NEED ONE, AND YET...

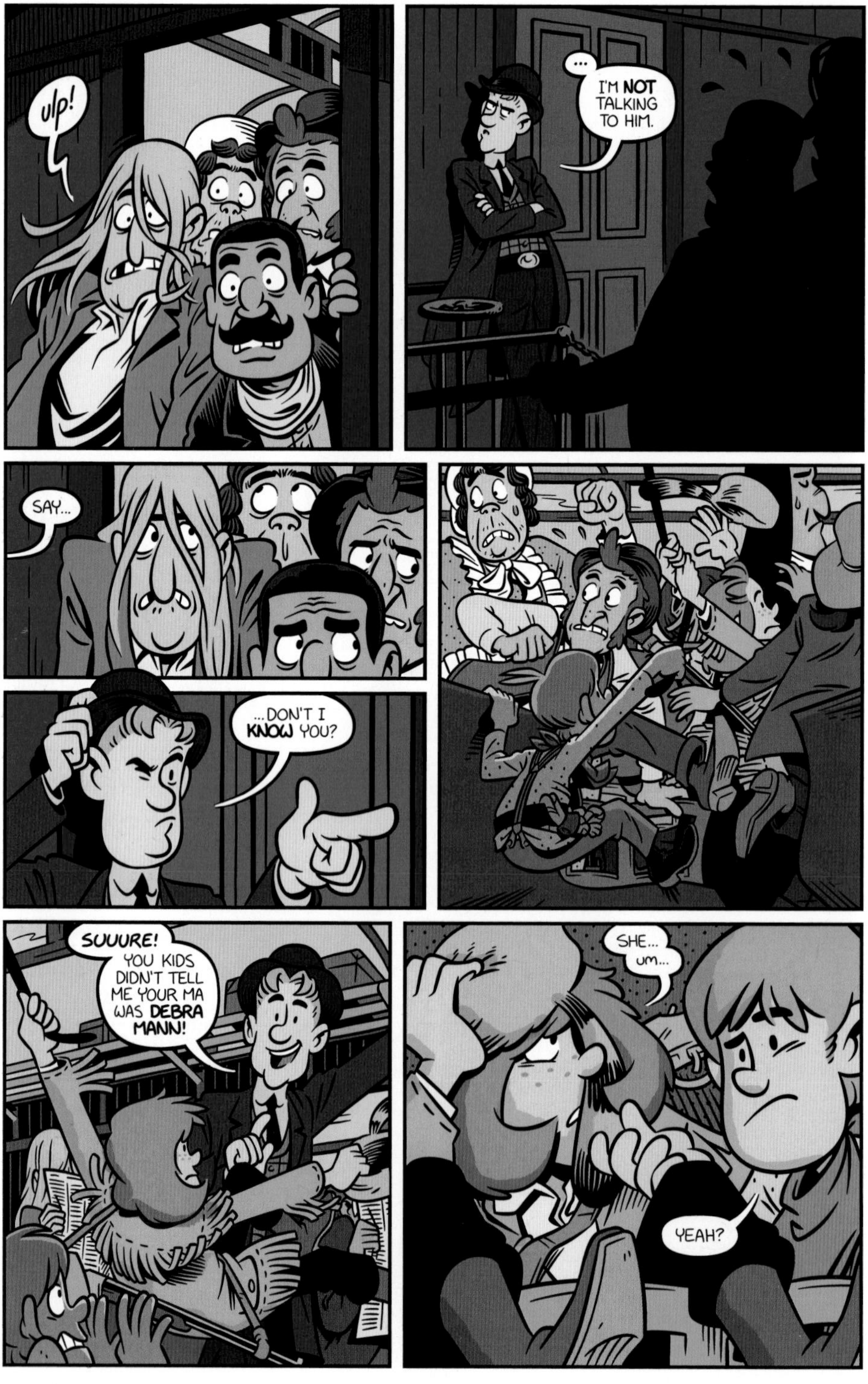
ulp!
...
I'M NOT TALKING TO HIM.
SAY...
...DON'T I KNOW YOU?
SUUURE! YOU KIDS DIDN'T TELL ME YOUR MA WAS DEBRA MANN!
SHE... um...
YEAH?

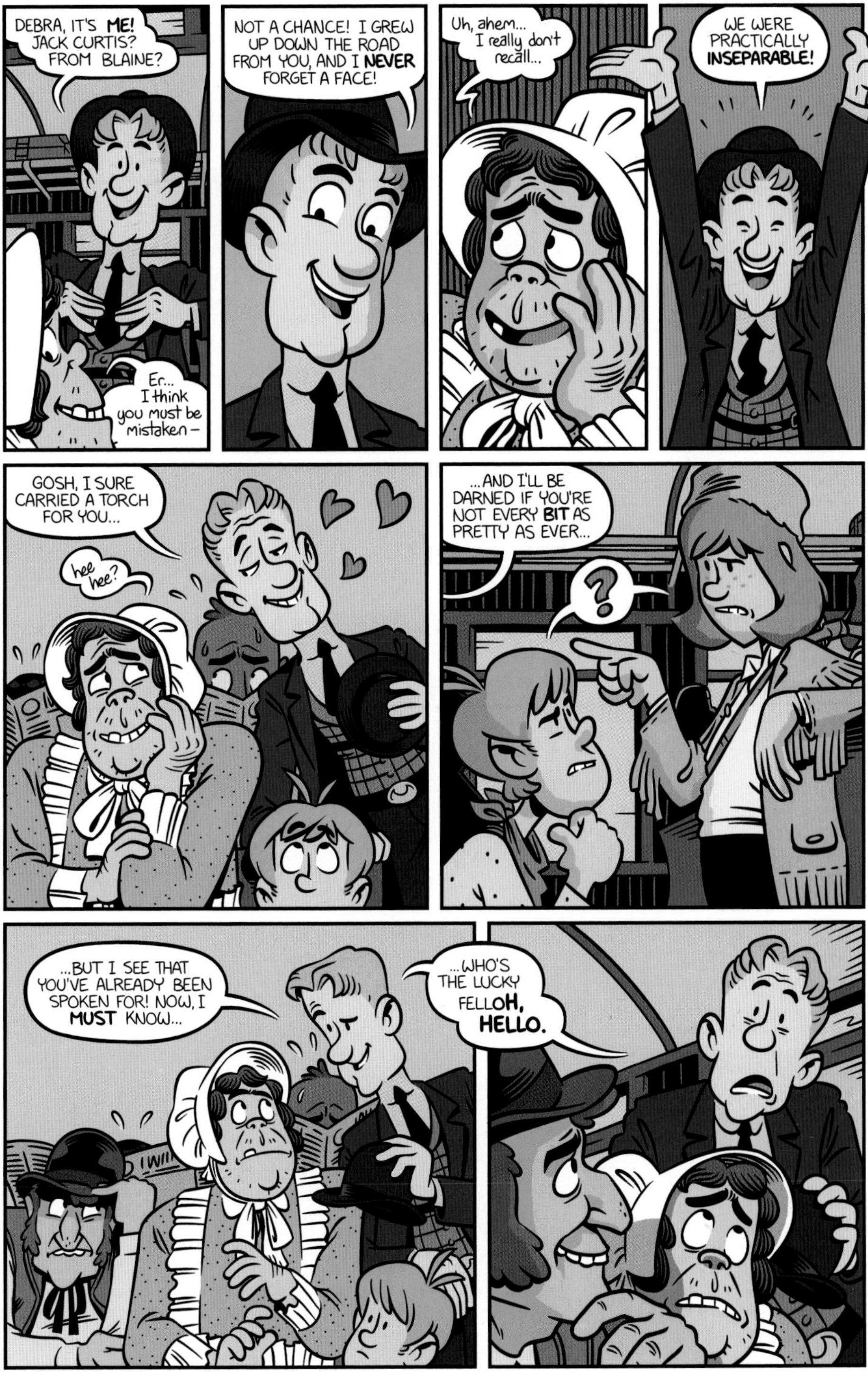
DEBRA, IT'S **ME!** JACK CURTIS? FROM BLAINE?
Er... I think you must be mistaken—
NOT A CHANCE! I GREW UP DOWN THE ROAD FROM YOU, AND I **NEVER** FORGET A FACE!
Uh, ahem... I really don't recall...
WE WERE PRACTICALLY **INSEPARABLE!**
GOSH, I SURE CARRIED A TORCH FOR YOU...
hee hee?
...AND I'LL BE DARNED IF YOU'RE NOT EVERY **BIT** AS PRETTY AS EVER...
?
...BUT I SEE THAT YOU'VE ALREADY BEEN SPOKEN FOR! NOW, I **MUST** KNOW...
...WHO'S THE LUCKY FELL**OH, HELLO.**

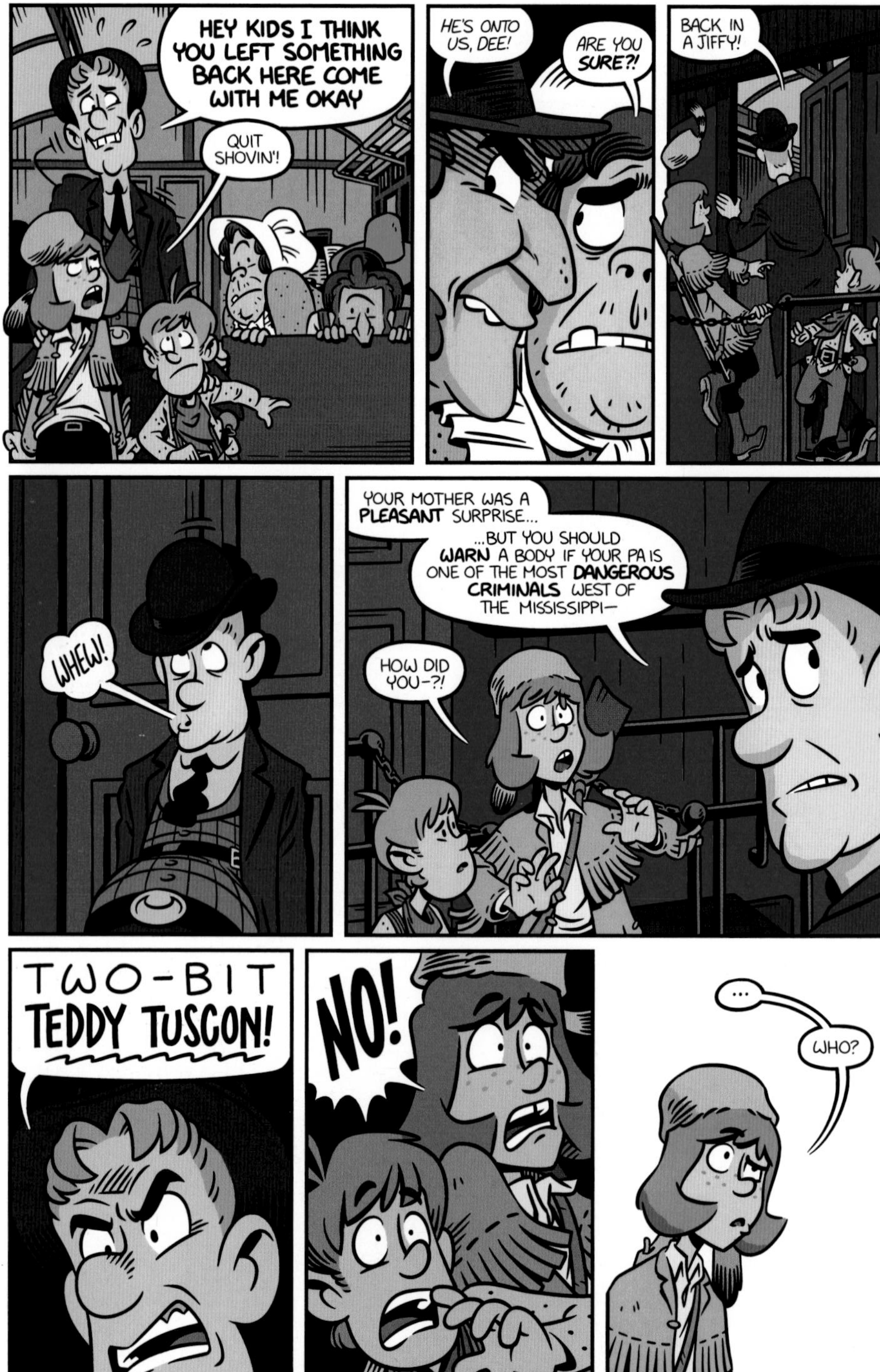
HEY KIDS I THINK YOU LEFT SOMETHING BACK HERE COME WITH ME OKAY
QUIT SHOVIN'!
HE'S ONTO US, DEE!
ARE YOU SURE?!
BACK IN A JIFFY!
WHEW!
YOUR MOTHER WAS A PLEASANT SURPRISE...
...BUT YOU SHOULD WARN A BODY IF YOUR PA IS ONE OF THE MOST DANGEROUS CRIMINALS WEST OF THE MISSISSIPPI—
HOW DID YOU-?!
TWO-BIT TEDDY TUSCON!
NO!
...
WHO?

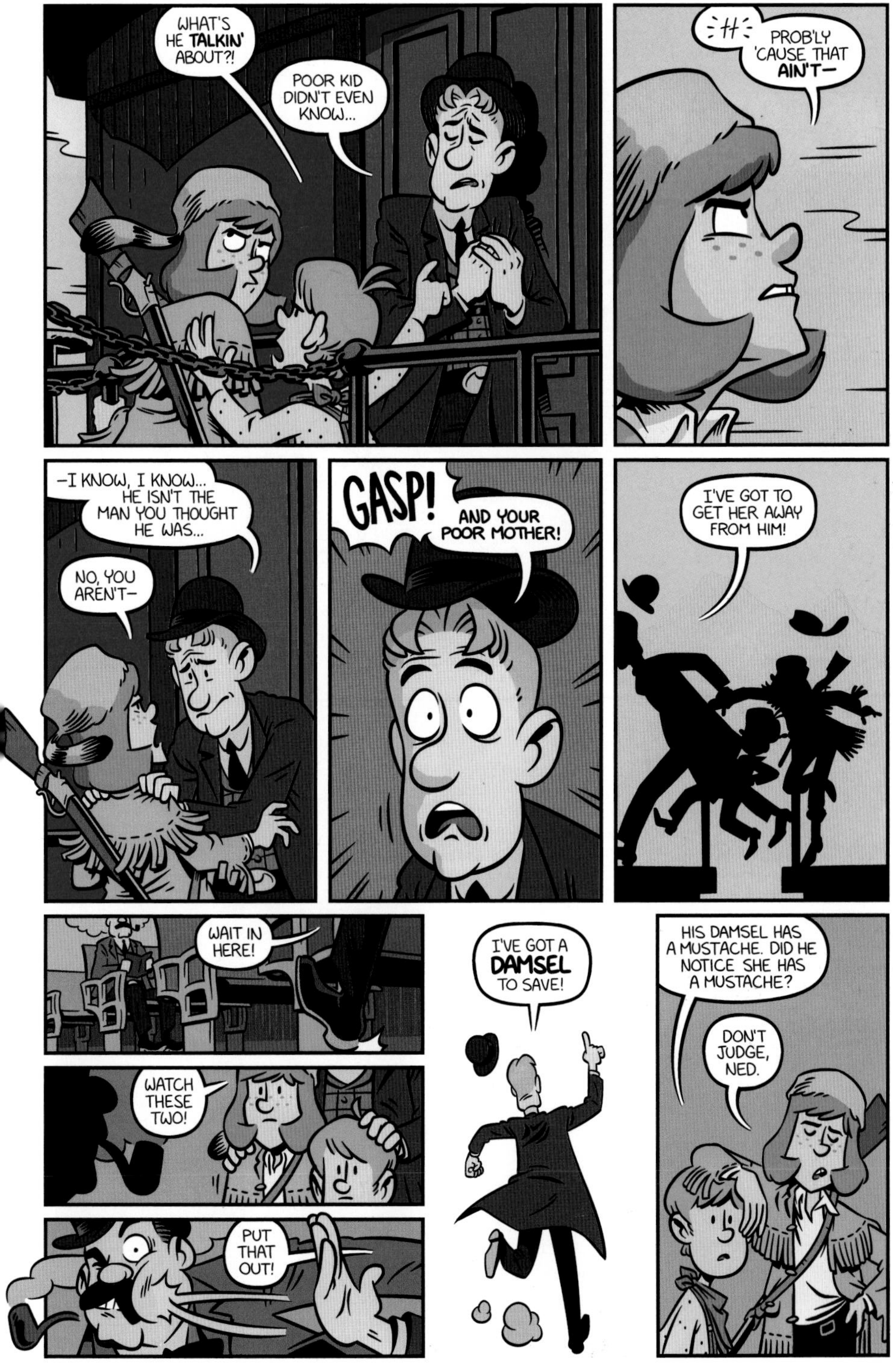
WHAT'S HE **TALKIN'** ABOUT?!
POOR KID DIDN'T EVEN KNOW...
PROB'LY 'CAUSE THAT **AIN'T—**
—I KNOW, I KNOW... HE ISN'T THE MAN YOU THOUGHT HE WAS...
NO, YOU AREN'T—
GASP!
AND YOUR POOR MOTHER!
I'VE GOT TO GET HER AWAY FROM HIM!
WAIT IN HERE!
WATCH THESE TWO!
PUT THAT OUT!
I'VE GOT A **DAMSEL** TO SAVE!
HIS DAMSEL HAS A MUSTACHE. DID HE NOTICE SHE HAS A MUSTACHE?
DON'T JUDGE, NED.

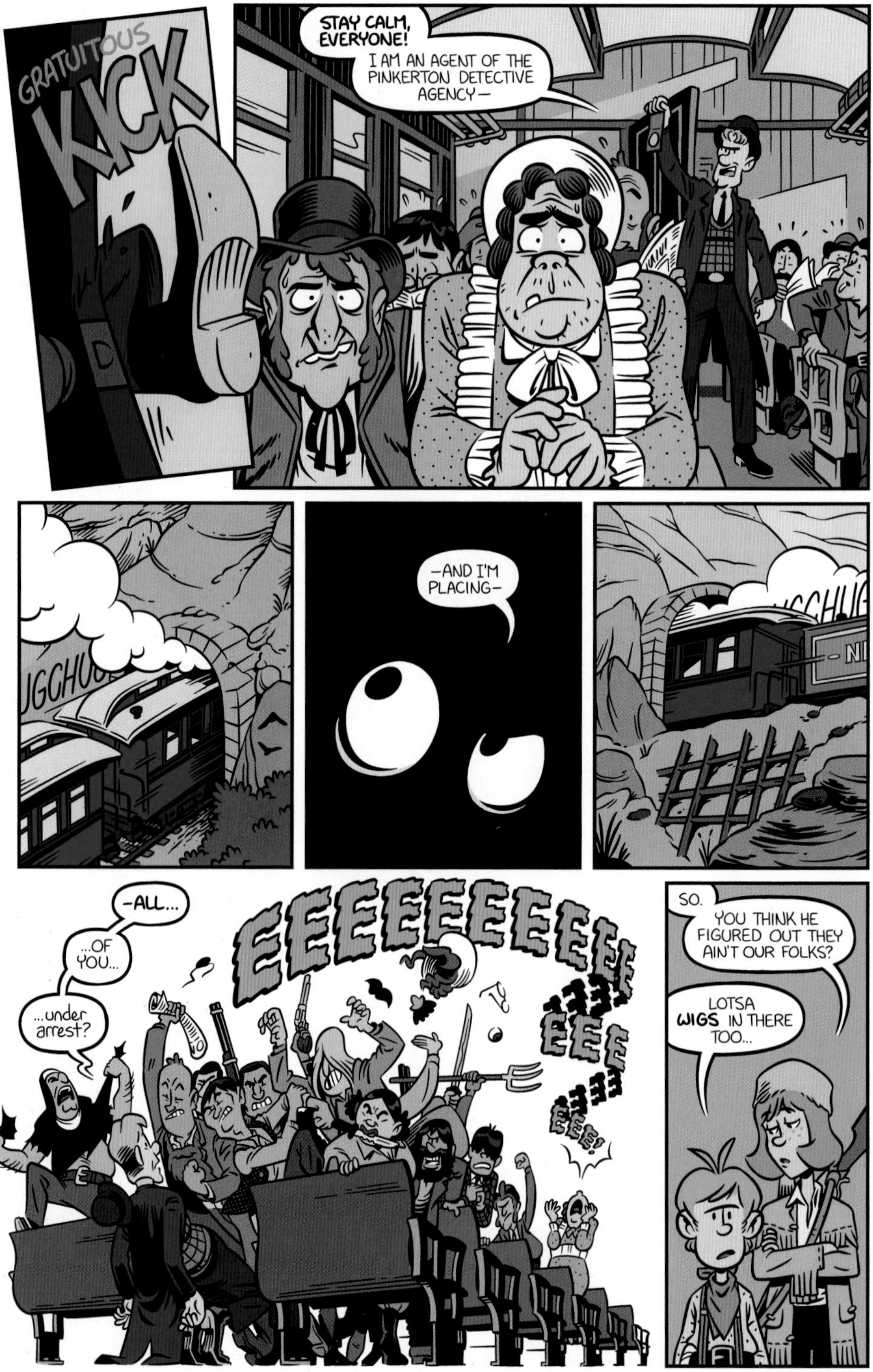
GRATUITOUS
KICK
STAY CALM, EVERYONE!
I AM AN AGENT OF THE PINKERTON DETECTIVE AGENCY—
—AND I'M PLACING—
-ALL...
...OF YOU...
...under arrest?
EEEEEEEEEEEEEEEEE
SO.
YOU THINK HE FIGURED OUT THEY AIN'T OUR FOLKS?
LOTSA WIGS IN THERE TOO...

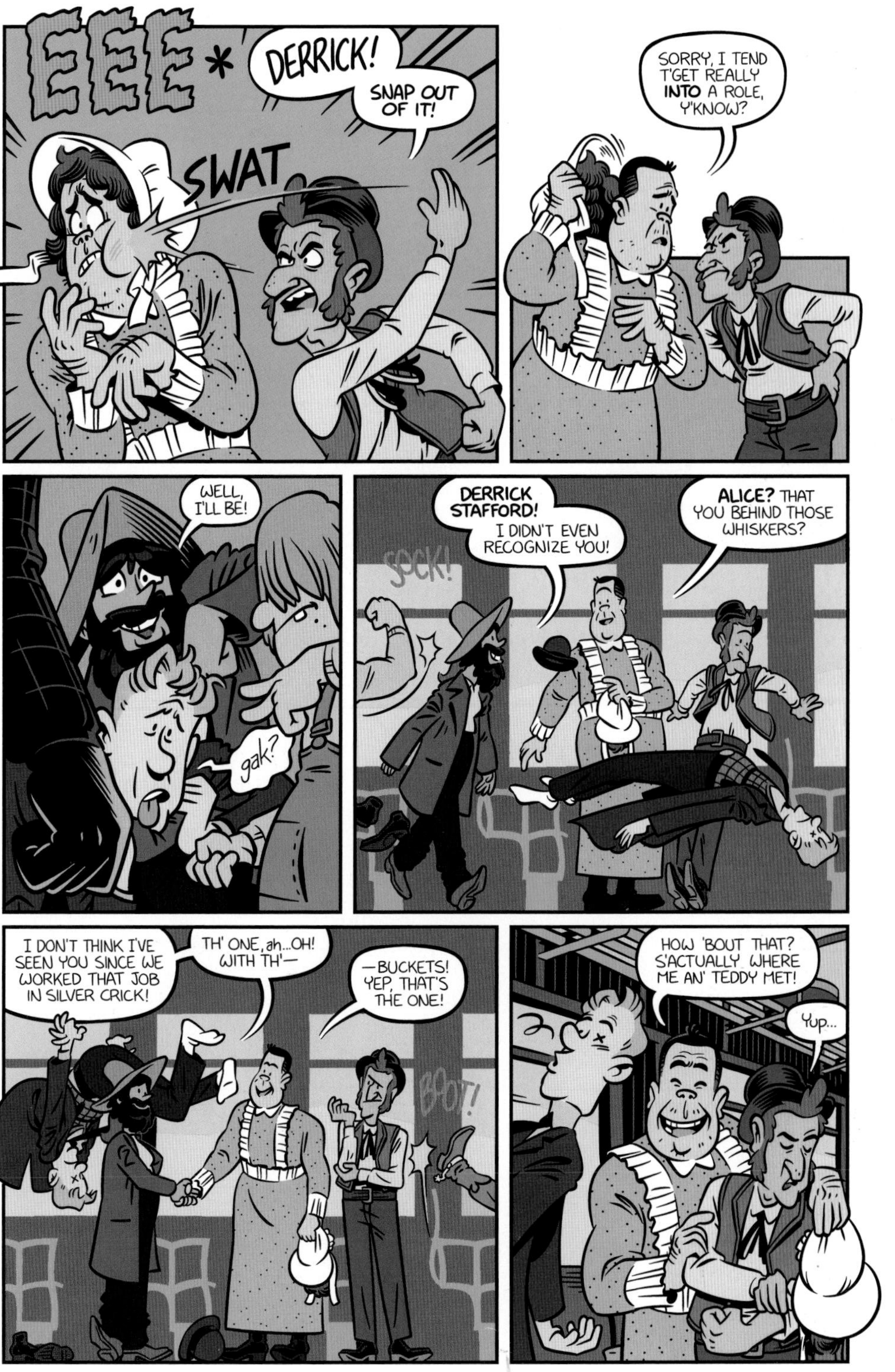
EEE*
DERRICK!
SNAP OUT OF IT!
SWAT
SORRY, I TEND T'GET REALLY **INTO** A ROLE, Y'KNOW?
WELL, I'LL BE!
gak?
DERRICK STAFFORD! I DIDN'T EVEN RECOGNIZE YOU!
ALICE? THAT YOU BEHIND THOSE WHISKERS?
SOCK!
I DON'T THINK I'VE SEEN YOU SINCE WE WORKED THAT JOB IN SILVER CRICK!
TH' ONE, ah...OH! WITH TH'—
—BUCKETS! YEP, THAT'S THE ONE!
BOOT!
HOW 'BOUT THAT? S'ACTUALLY WHERE ME AN' TEDDY MET!
Yup...

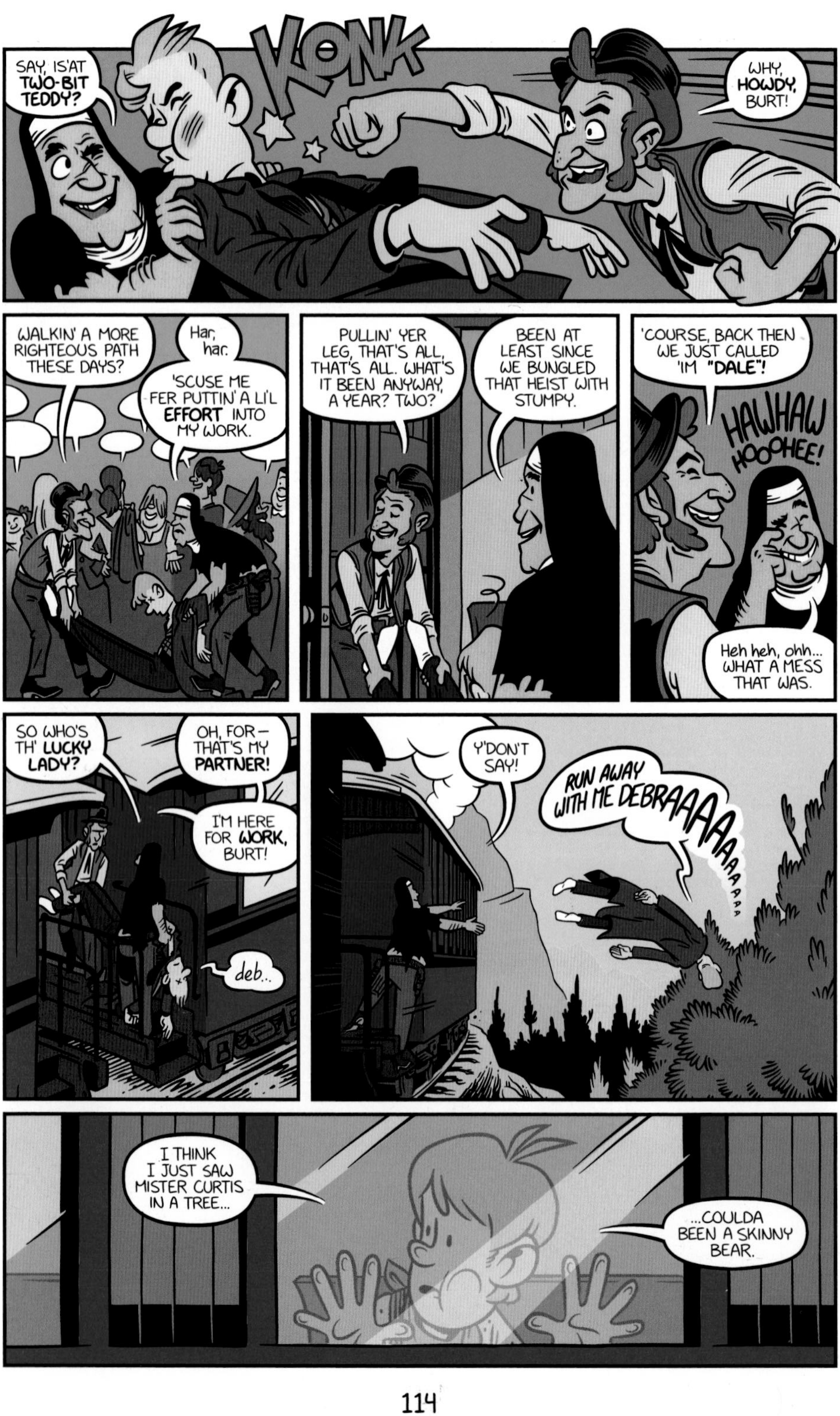
SAY, IS'AT TWO-BIT TEDDY?
KONK
WHY, HOWDY, BURT!
WALKIN' A MORE RIGHTEOUS PATH THESE DAYS?
Har, har.
'SCUSE ME FER PUTTIN' A LI'L EFFORT INTO MY WORK.
PULLIN' YER LEG, THAT'S ALL, THAT'S ALL. WHAT'S IT BEEN ANYWAY, A YEAR? TWO?
BEEN AT LEAST SINCE WE BUNGLED THAT HEIST WITH STUMPY.
'COURSE, BACK THEN WE JUST CALLED 'IM "DALE"!
HAWHAW HOOOHEE!
Heh heh, ohh... WHAT A MESS THAT WAS.
SO WHO'S TH' LUCKY LADY?
OH, FOR— THAT'S MY PARTNER!
I'M HERE FOR WORK, BURT!
deb...
Y'DON'T SAY!
RUN AWAY WITH ME DEBRAAAAAAAAAA
I THINK I JUST SAW MISTER CURTIS IN A TREE...
...COULDA BEEN A SKINNY BEAR.

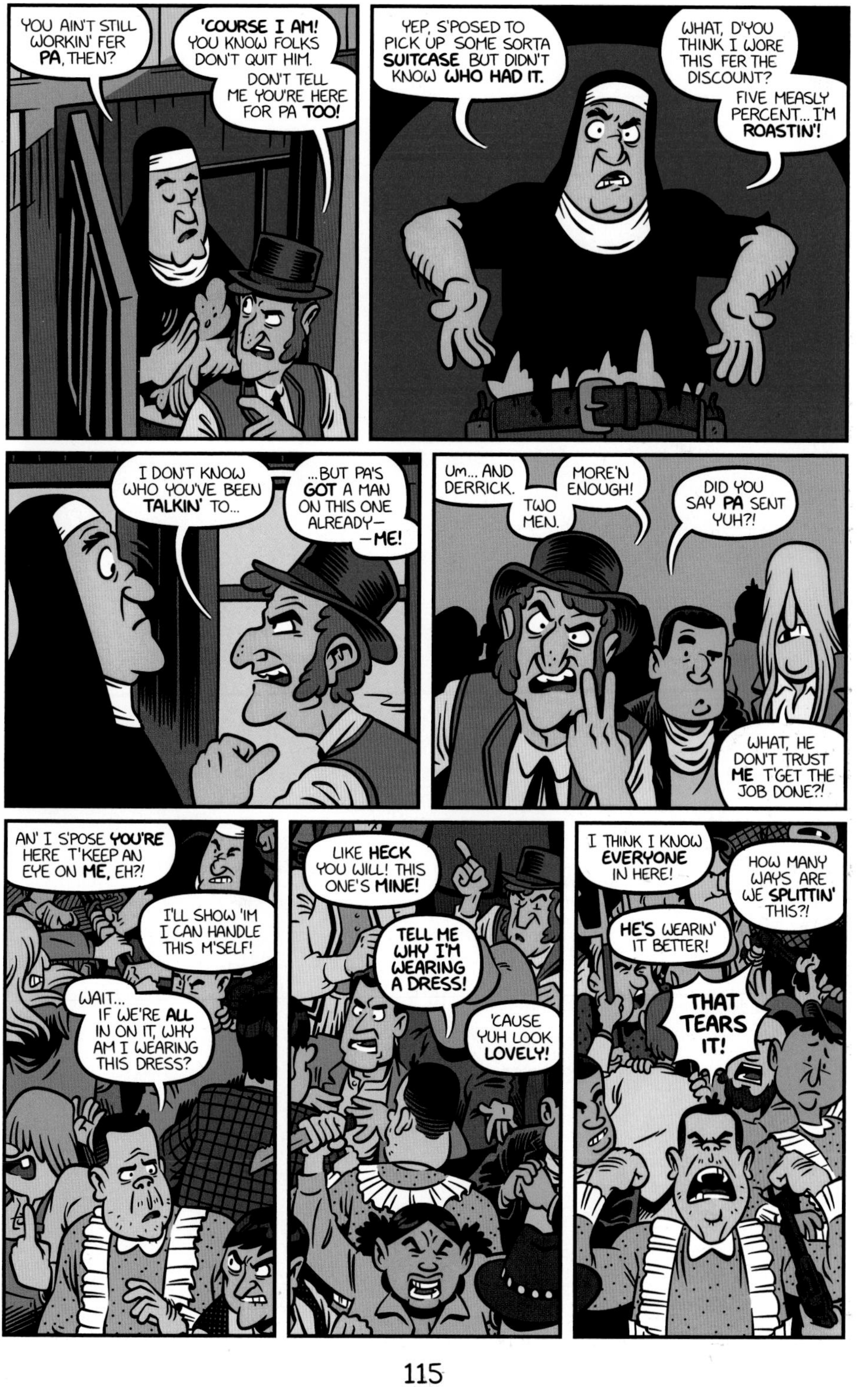

YOU AIN'T STILL WORKIN' FER PA, THEN?
'COURSE I AM! YOU KNOW FOLKS DON'T QUIT HIM.
DON'T TELL ME YOU'RE HERE FOR PA TOO!
YEP, S'POSED TO PICK UP SOME SORTA SUITCASE BUT DIDN'T KNOW WHO HAD IT.
WHAT, D'YOU THINK I WORE THIS FER THE DISCOUNT?
FIVE MEASLY PERCENT... I'M ROASTIN'!
I DON'T KNOW WHO YOU'VE BEEN TALKIN' TO...
...BUT PA'S GOT A MAN ON THIS ONE ALREADY—
—ME!
Um... AND DERRICK.
TWO MEN.
MORE'N ENOUGH!
DID YOU SAY PA SENT YUH?!
WHAT, HE DON'T TRUST ME T'GET THE JOB DONE?!
AN' I S'POSE YOU'RE HERE T'KEEP AN EYE ON ME, EH?!
I'LL SHOW 'IM I CAN HANDLE THIS M'SELF!
WAIT... IF WE'RE ALL IN ON IT, WHY AM I WEARING THIS DRESS?
LIKE HECK YOU WILL! THIS ONE'S MINE!
TELL ME WHY I'M WEARING A DRESS!
'CAUSE YUH LOOK LOVELY!
I THINK I KNOW EVERYONE IN HERE!
HOW MANY WAYS ARE WE SPLITTIN' THIS?!
HE'S WEARIN' IT BETTER!
THAT TEARS IT!

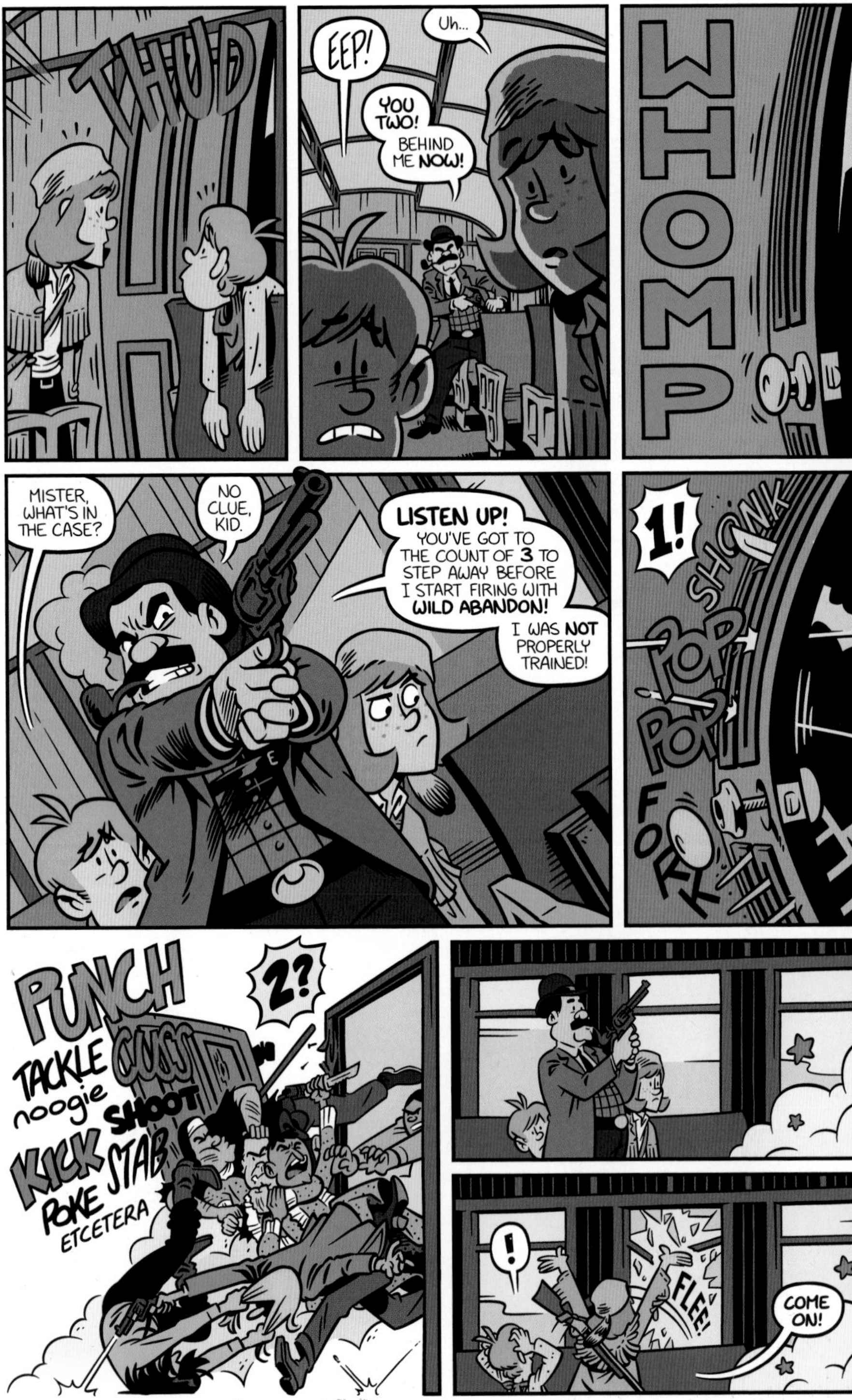
THUD
EEP!
Uh...
YOU TWO!
BEHIND ME NOW!
WHOMP
MISTER, WHAT'S IN THE CASE?
NO CLUE, KID.
LISTEN UP! YOU'VE GOT TO THE COUNT OF 3 TO STEP AWAY BEFORE I START FIRING WITH WILD ABANDON!
I WAS NOT PROPERLY TRAINED!
1!
SHONK
POP
POP
FORK
PUNCH
TACKLE
CUSS
noogie
SHOOT
KICK
STAB
POKE
ETCETERA
2?
!
FLEE!
COME ON!

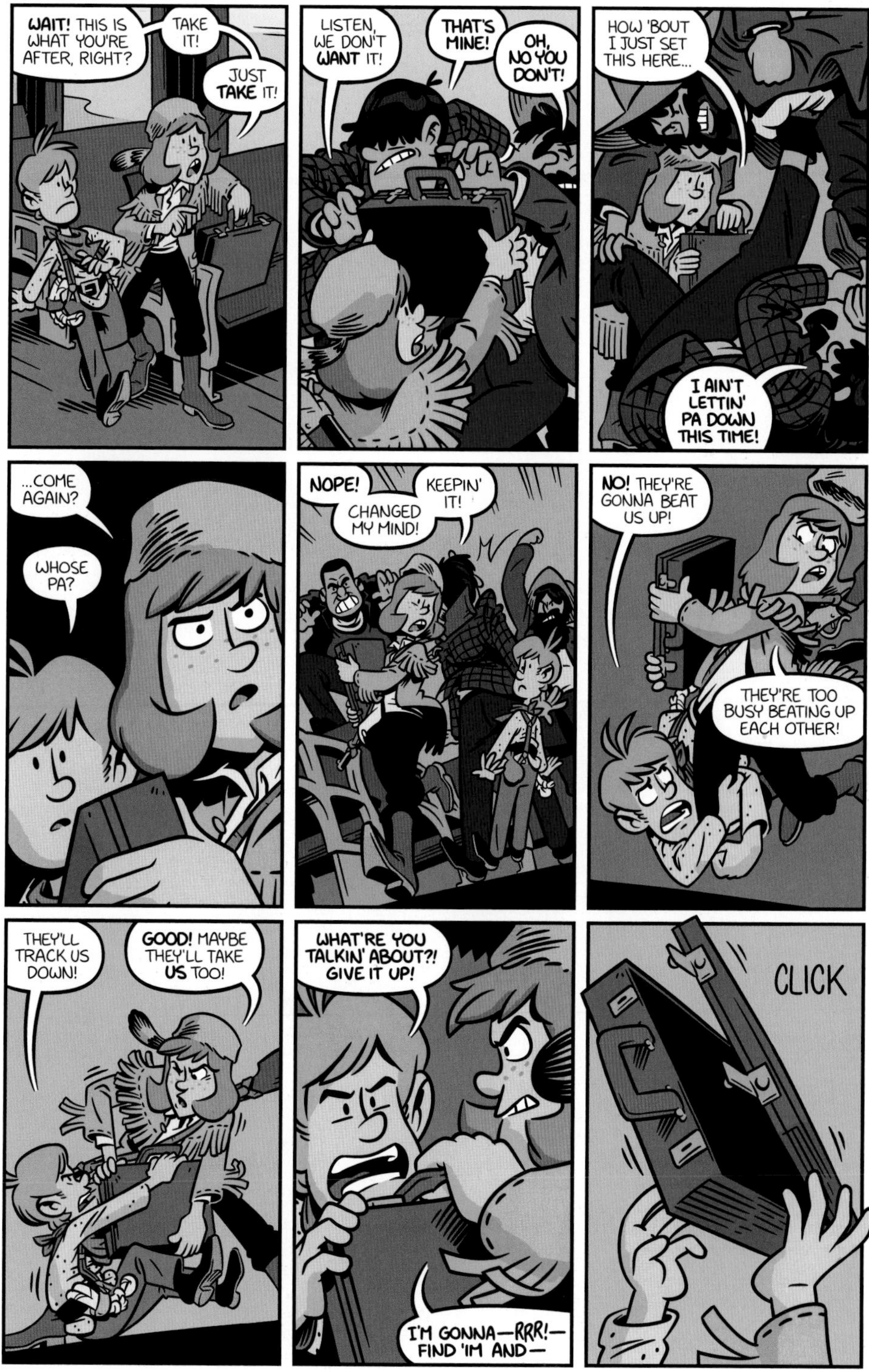
WAIT! THIS IS WHAT YOU'RE AFTER, RIGHT?
TAKE IT!
JUST **TAKE** IT!
LISTEN, WE DON'T **WANT** IT!
THAT'S MINE!
OH, NO YOU DON'T!
HOW 'BOUT I JUST SET THIS HERE...
I AIN'T LETTIN' PA DOWN THIS TIME!
...COME AGAIN?
WHOSE PA?
NOPE!
CHANGED MY MIND!
KEEPIN' IT!
NO! THEY'RE GONNA BEAT US UP!
THEY'RE TOO BUSY BEATING UP EACH OTHER!
THEY'LL TRACK US DOWN!
GOOD! MAYBE THEY'LL TAKE **US** TOO!
WHAT'RE YOU TALKIN' ABOUT?! GIVE IT UP!
I'M GONNA—RRR!— FIND 'IM AND—
CLICK

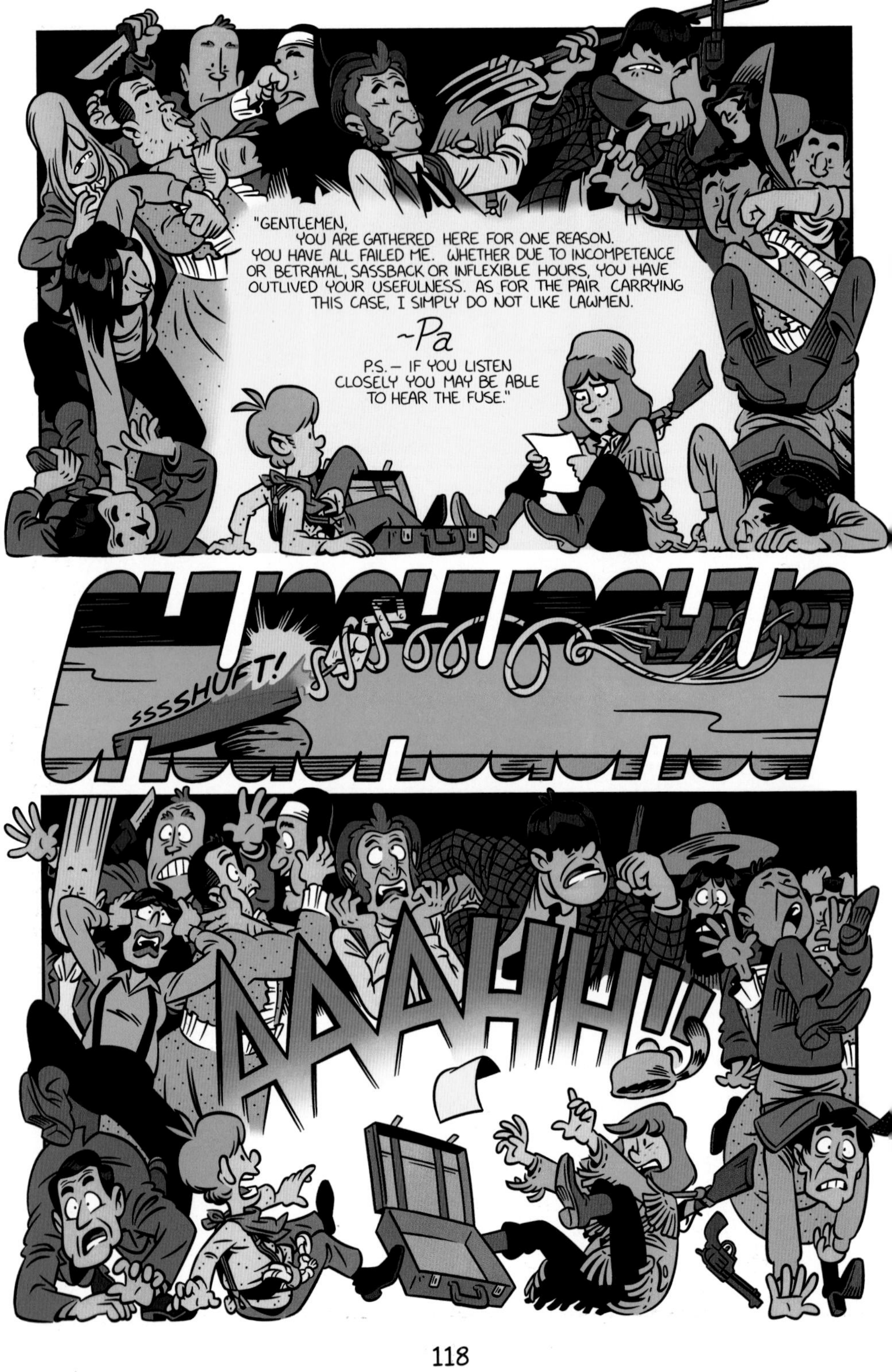
"GENTLEMEN,
YOU ARE GATHERED HERE FOR ONE REASON.
YOU HAVE ALL FAILED ME. WHETHER DUE TO INCOMPETENCE
OR BETRAYAL, SASSBACK OR INFLEXIBLE HOURS, YOU HAVE
OUTLIVED YOUR USEFULNESS. AS FOR THE PAIR CARRYING
THIS CASE, I SIMPLY DO NOT LIKE LAWMEN.
~Pa
P.S. – IF YOU LISTEN
CLOSELY YOU MAY BE ABLE
TO HEAR THE FUSE."
SSSSHUFT!
AAAHH!!

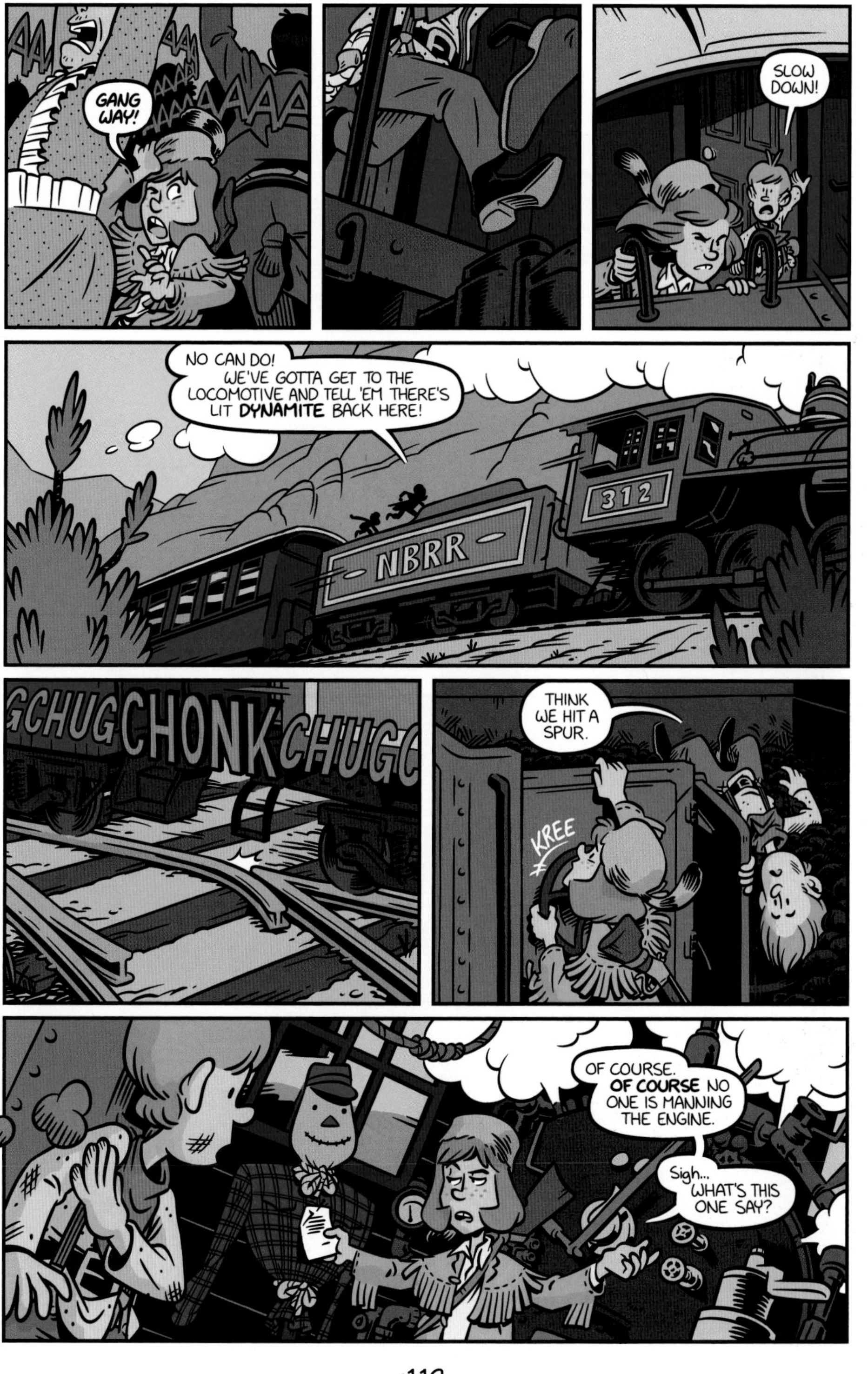
AAA
AAAA
AAAAA
GANG WAY!
SLOW DOWN!
NO CAN DO! WE'VE GOTTA GET TO THE LOCOMOTIVE AND TELL 'EM THERE'S LIT **DYNAMITE** BACK HERE!
312
NBRR
GCHUGCHONKCHUGC
THINK WE HIT A SPUR.
KREE
OF COURSE. **OF COURSE** NO ONE IS MANNING THE ENGINE.
Sigh... WHAT'S THIS ONE SAY?

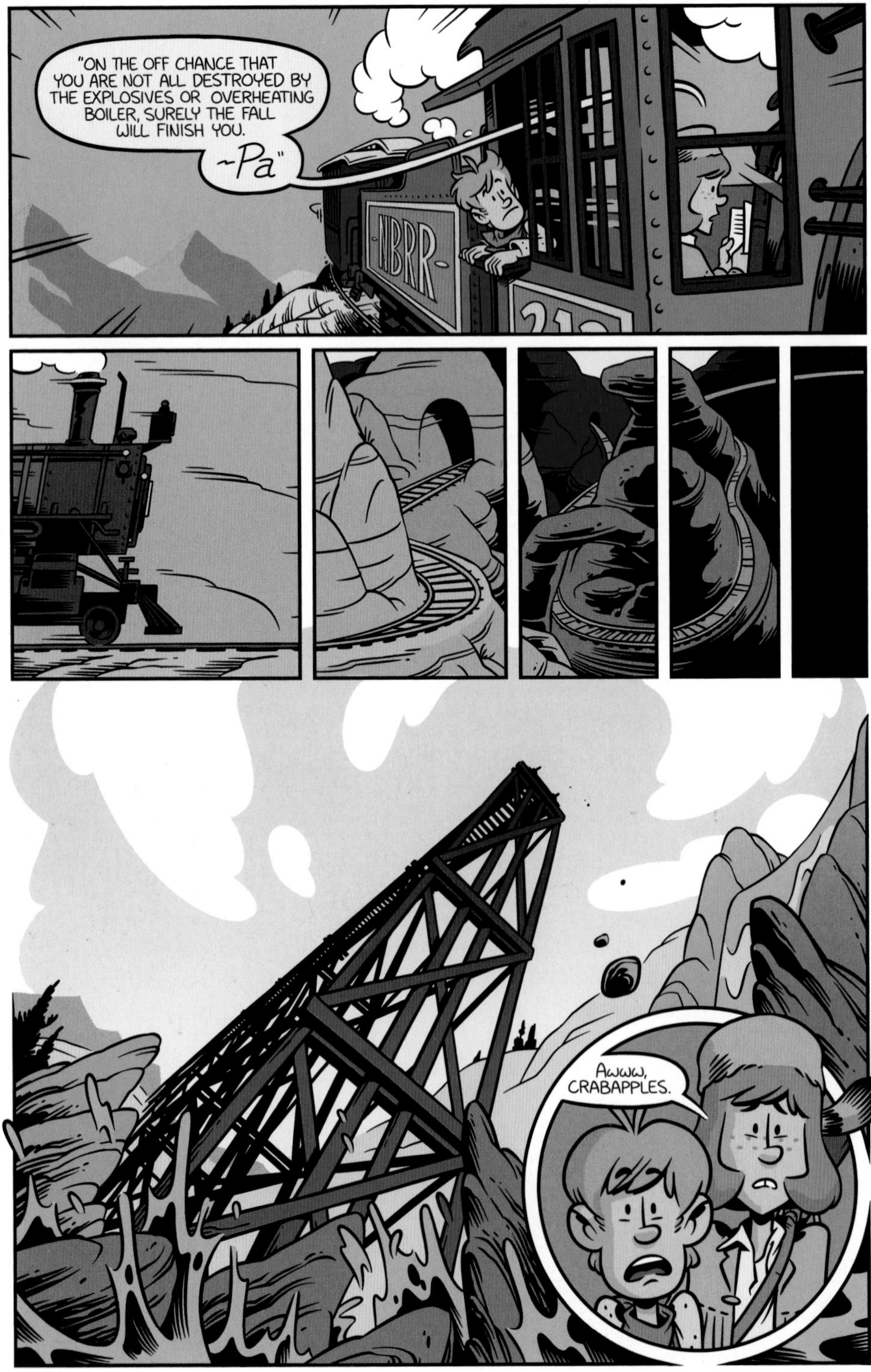
"ON THE OFF CHANCE THAT YOU ARE NOT ALL DESTROYED BY THE EXPLOSIVES OR OVERHEATING BOILER, SURELY THE FALL WILL FINISH YOU.
~Pa"
NBRR
AWWW, CRABAPPLES.

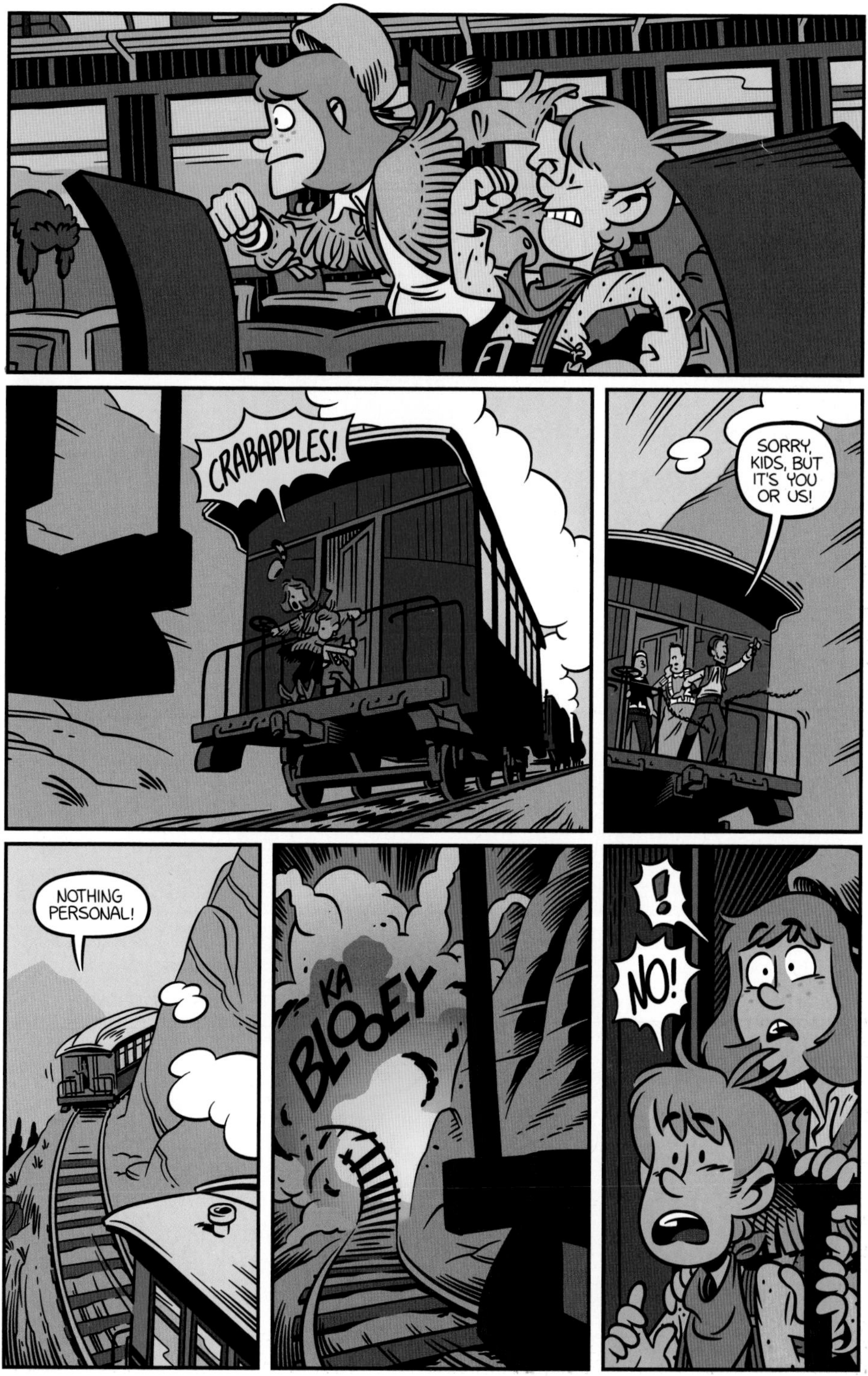

CRABAPPLES!
SORRY, KIDS, BUT IT'S YOU OR US!
NOTHING PERSONAL!
KA BLOOEY
!
NO!

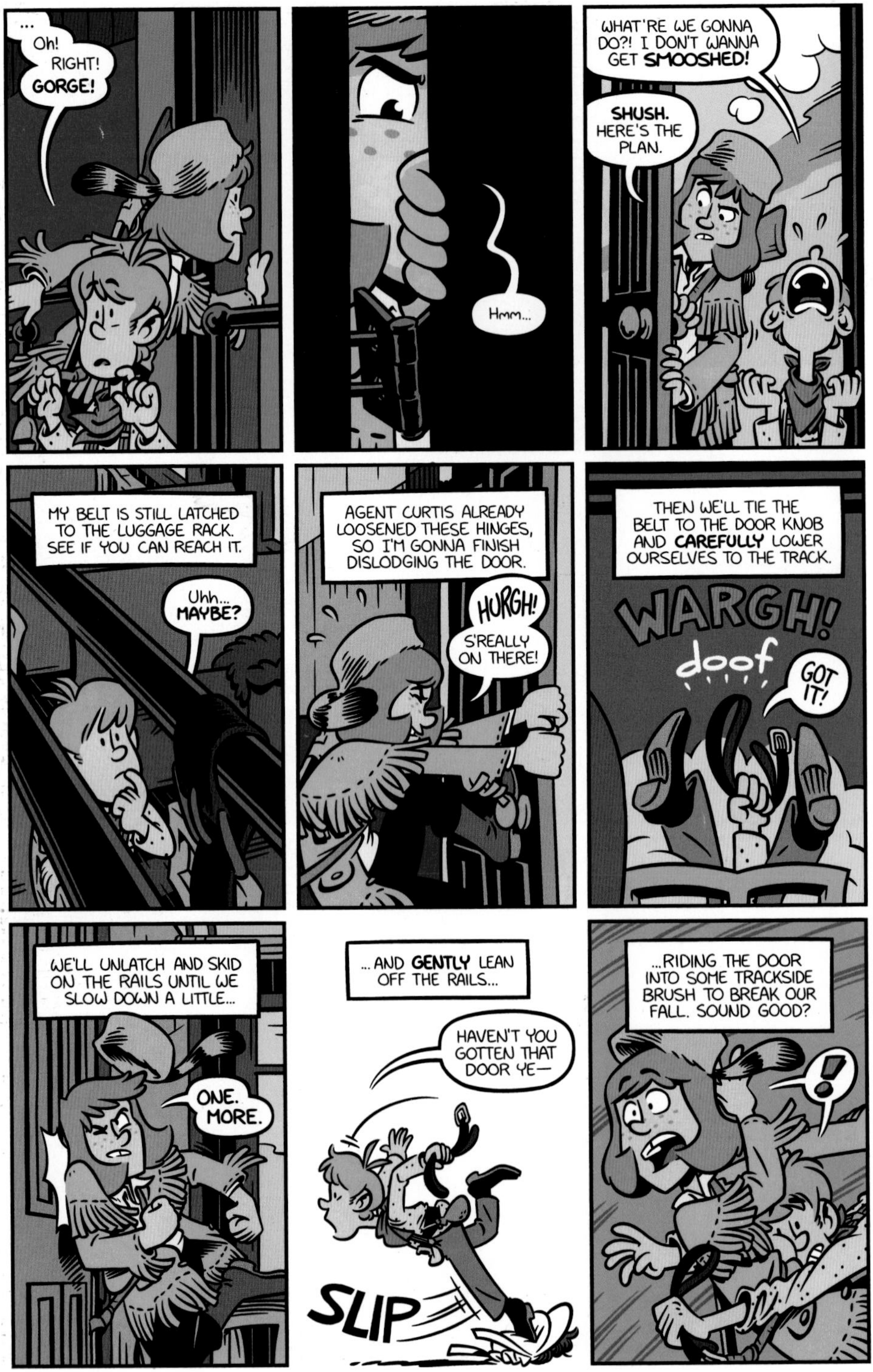
...
Oh! RIGHT! GORGE!
Hmm...
WHAT'RE WE GONNA DO?! I DON'T WANNA GET SMOOSHED!
SHUSH. HERE'S THE PLAN.
MY BELT IS STILL LATCHED TO THE LUGGAGE RACK. SEE IF YOU CAN REACH IT.
Uhh... MAYBE?
AGENT CURTIS ALREADY LOOSENED THESE HINGES, SO I'M GONNA FINISH DISLODGING THE DOOR.
HURGH!
S'REALLY ON THERE!
THEN WE'LL TIE THE BELT TO THE DOOR KNOB AND CAREFULLY LOWER OURSELVES TO THE TRACK.
WARGH!
doof
GOT IT!
WE'LL UNLATCH AND SKID ON THE RAILS UNTIL WE SLOW DOWN A LITTLE...
ONE. MORE.
...AND GENTLY LEAN OFF THE RAILS...
HAVEN'T YOU GOTTEN THAT DOOR YE—
SLIP
...RIDING THE DOOR INTO SOME TRACKSIDE BRUSH TO BREAK OUR FALL. SOUND GOOD?
!

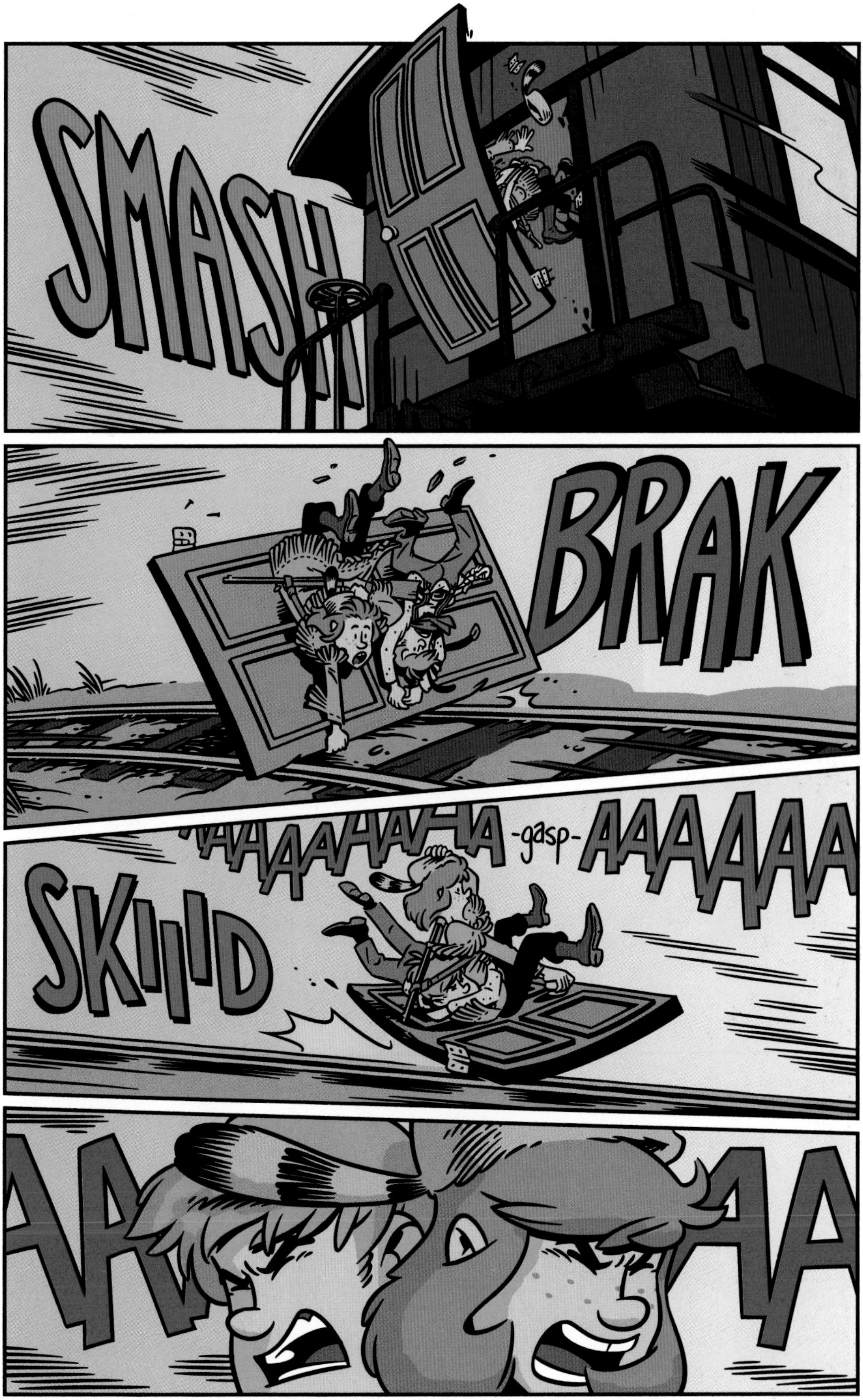
SMASH
BRAK
AAAAAAHAAHA -gasp- AAAAAA
SKIIID
AA
AA

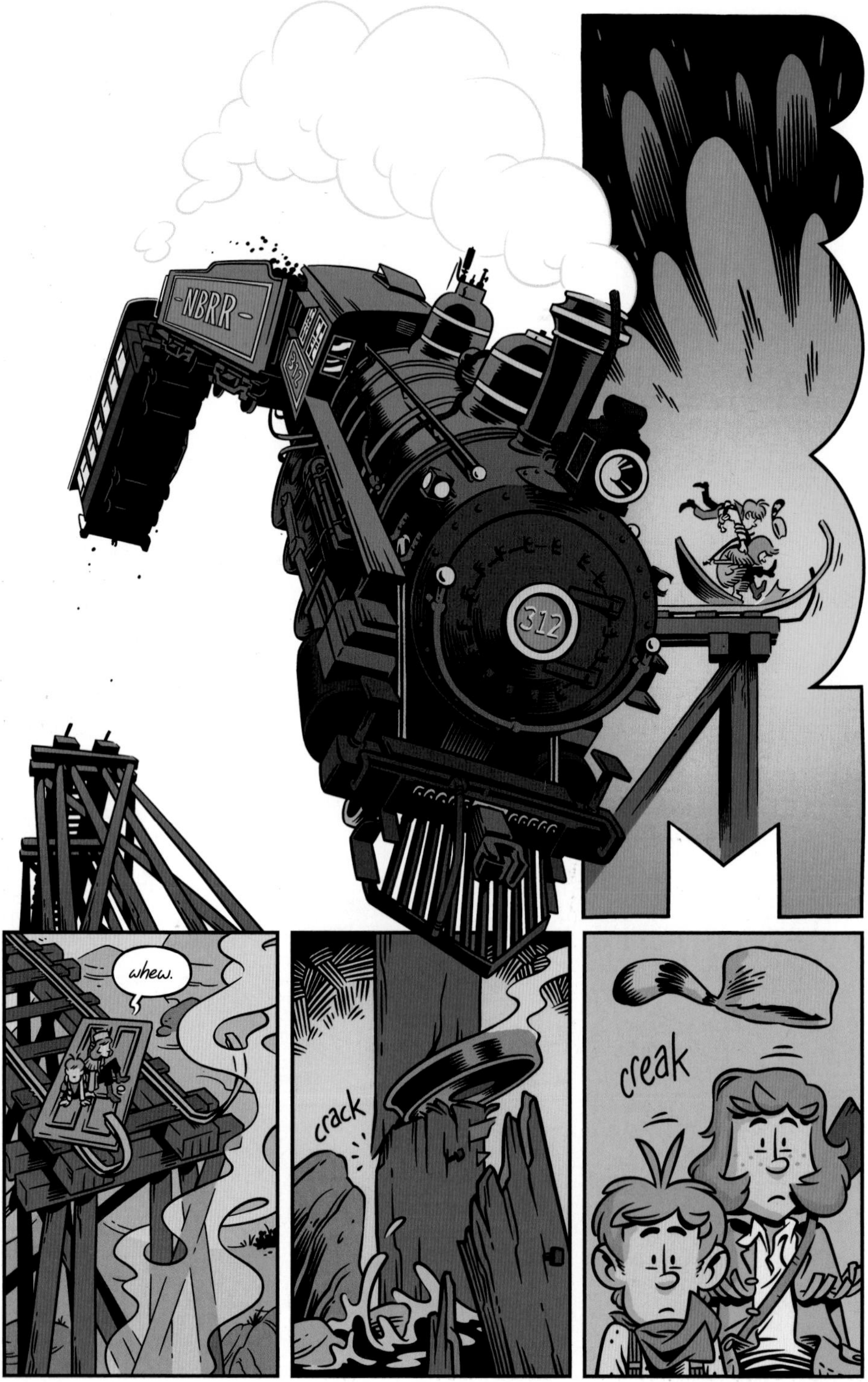
NBRR
312
312
whew.
crack
creak

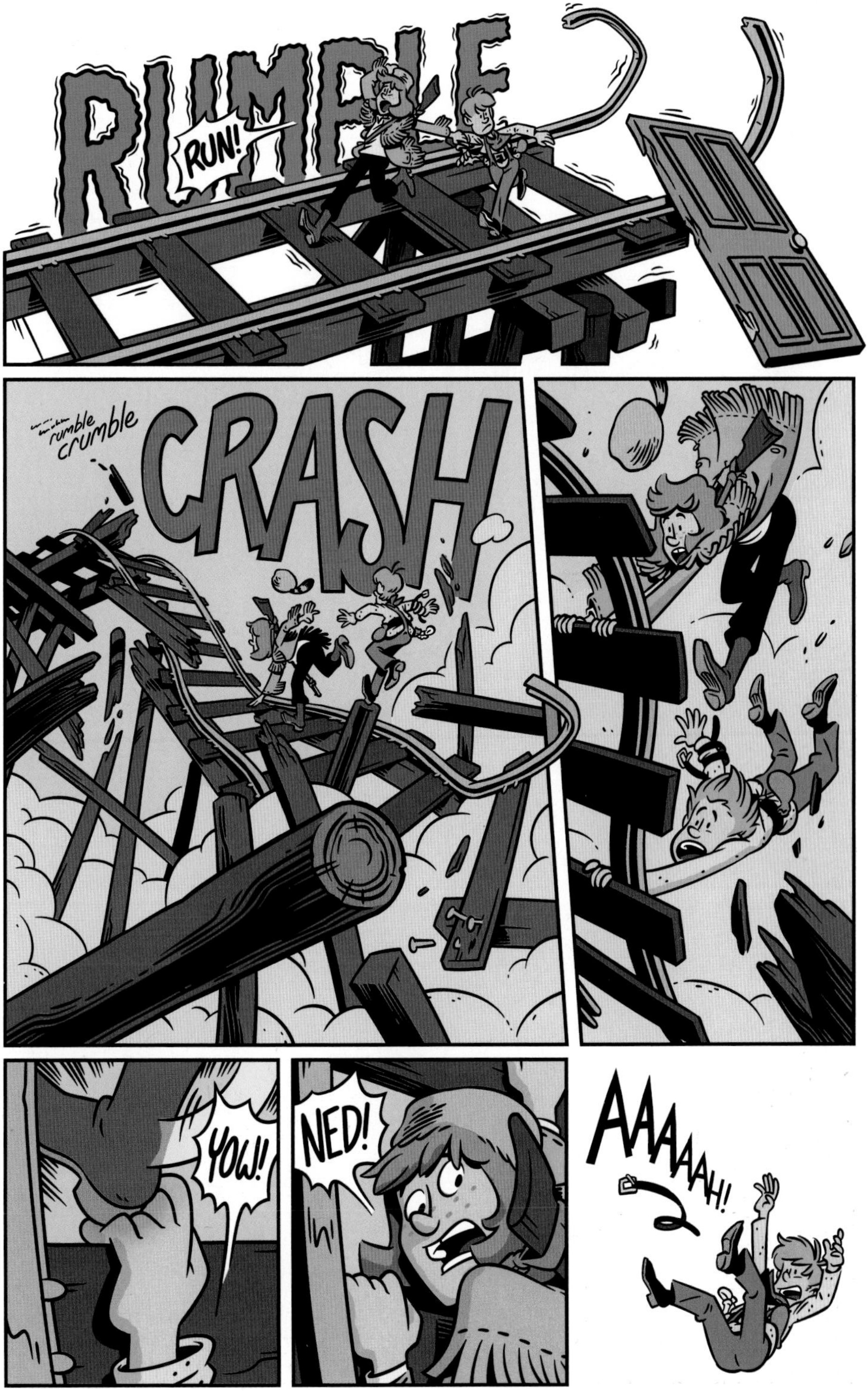
RUMBLE
RUN!
rumble
crumble
CRASH
YOW!
NED!
AAAAAAH!

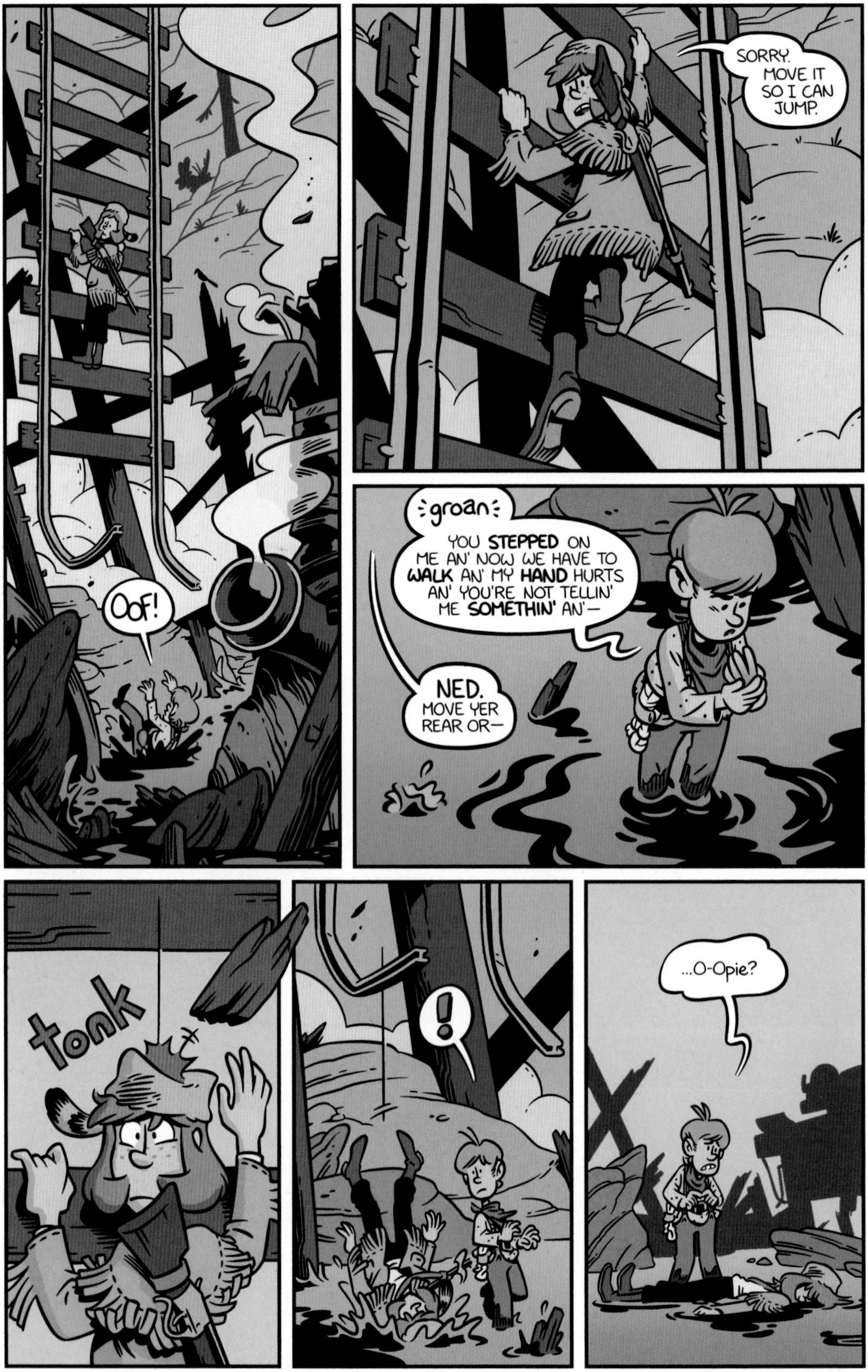
OOF!
SORRY. MOVE IT SO I CAN JUMP.
groan
YOU STEPPED ON ME AN' NOW WE HAVE TO WALK AN' MY HAND HURTS AN' YOU'RE NOT TELLIN' ME SOMETHIN' AN'—
NED. MOVE YER REAR OR—
tonk
!
...O-Opie?

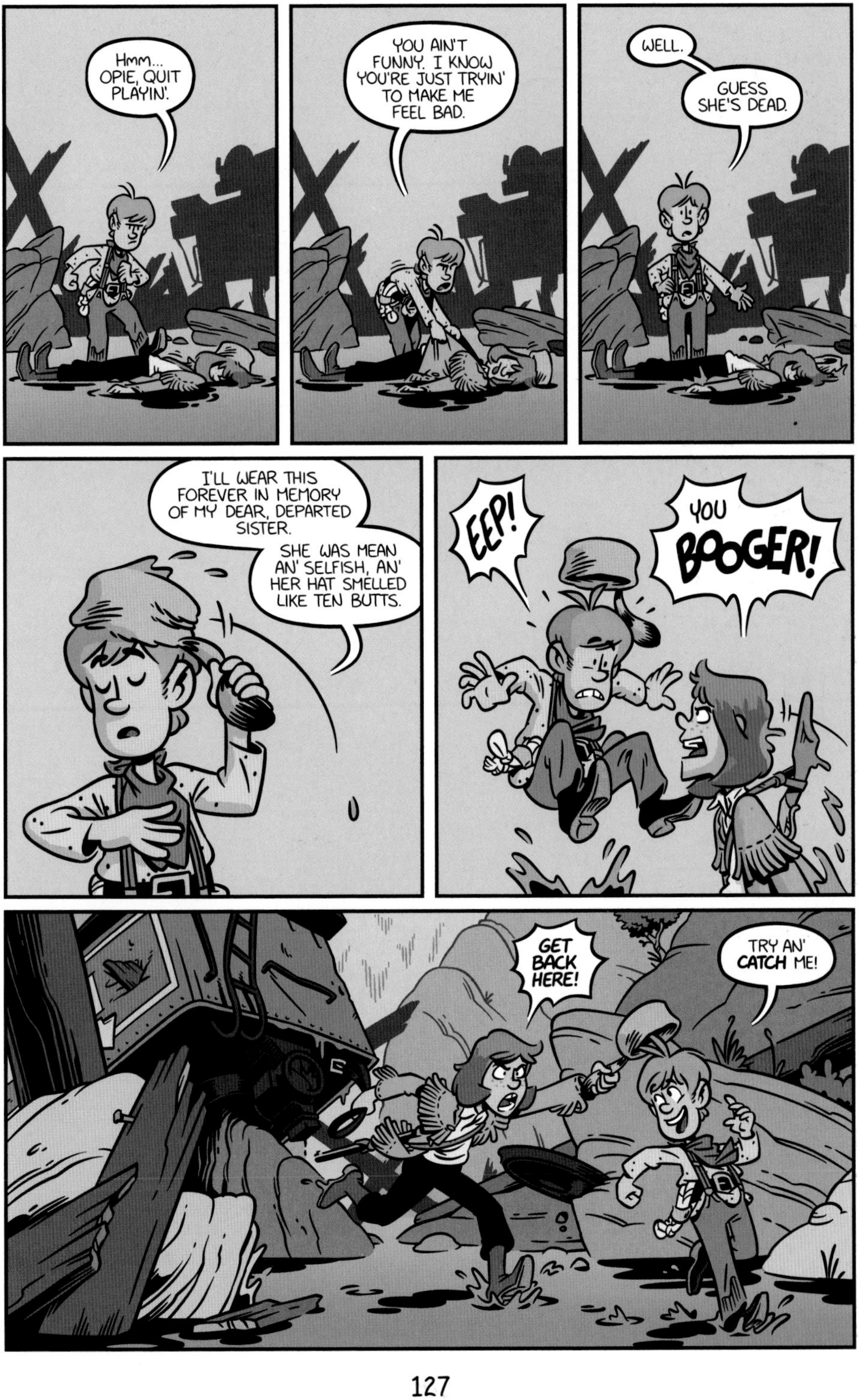
Hmm... OPIE, QUIT PLAYIN'.
YOU AIN'T FUNNY. I KNOW YOU'RE JUST TRYIN' TO MAKE ME FEEL BAD.
WELL.
GUESS SHE'S DEAD.
I'LL WEAR THIS FOREVER IN MEMORY OF MY DEAR, DEPARTED SISTER.
SHE WAS MEAN AN' SELFISH, AN' HER HAT SMELLED LIKE TEN BUTTS.
EEP!
YOU BOOGER!
GET BACK HERE!
TRY AN' CATCH ME!

CHAPTER FIVE

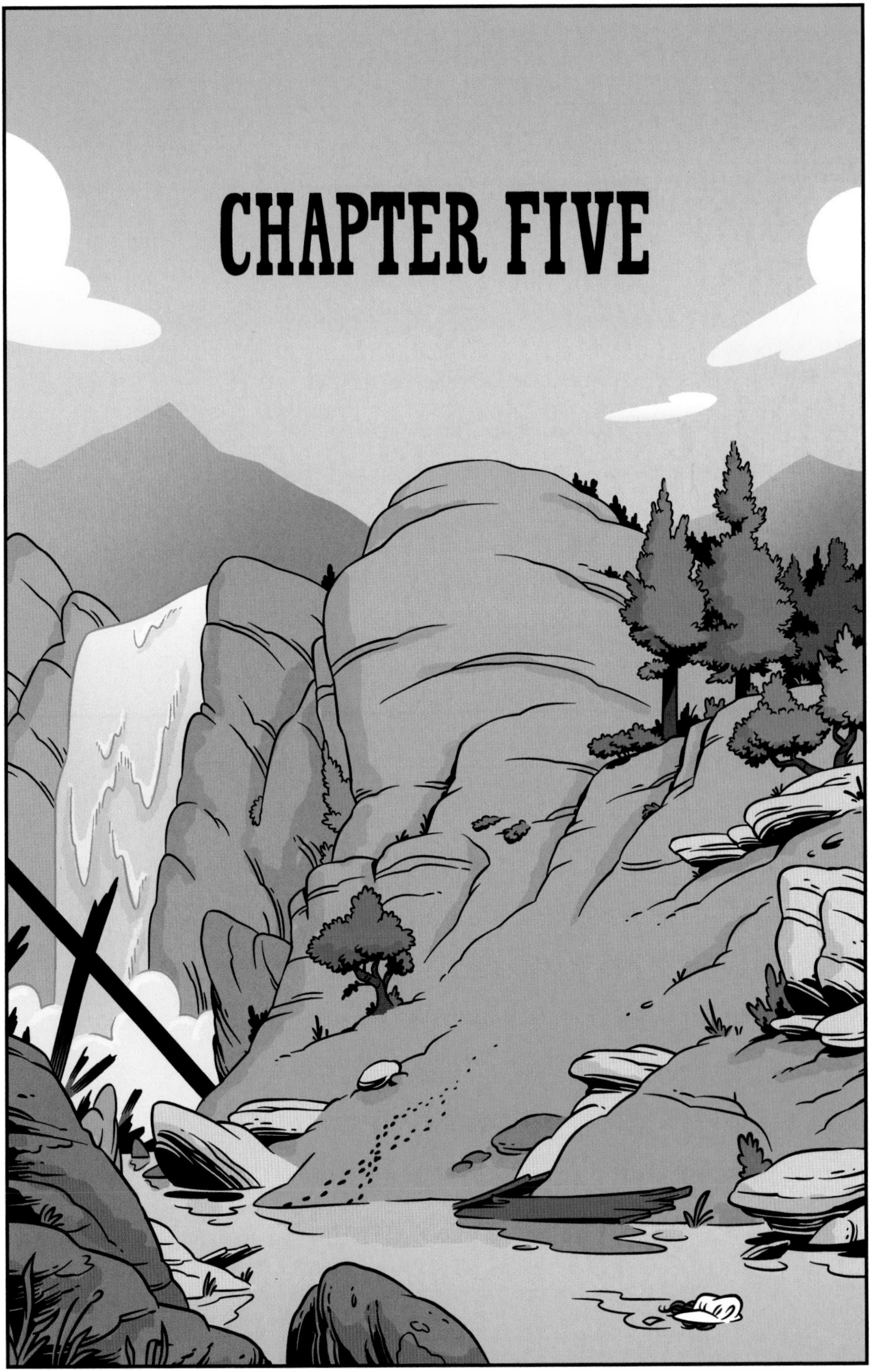

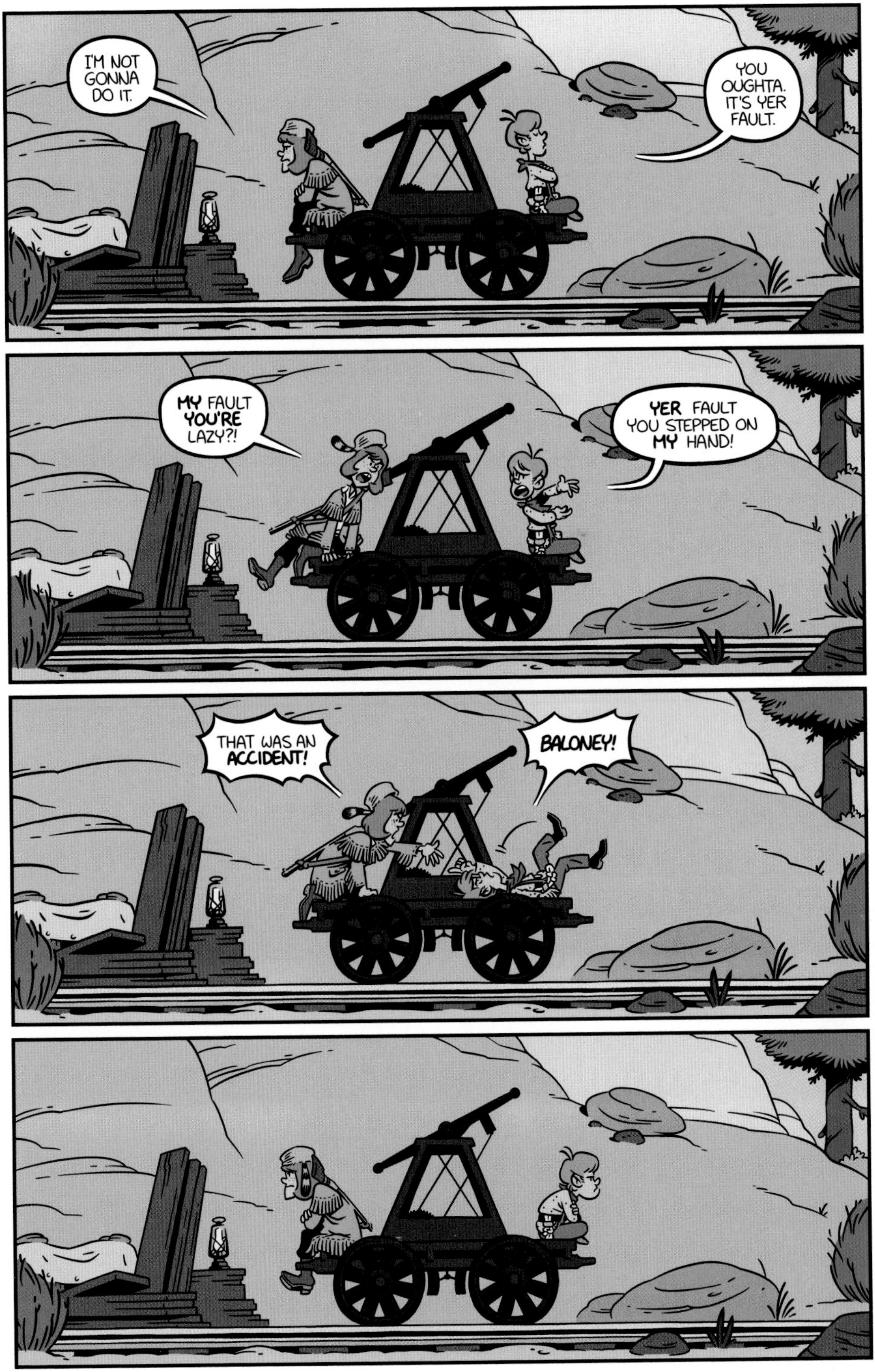
I'M NOT GONNA DO IT.
YOU OUGHTA. IT'S YER FAULT.
MY FAULT YOU'RE LAZY?!
YER FAULT YOU STEPPED ON MY HAND!
THAT WAS AN ACCIDENT!
BALONEY!

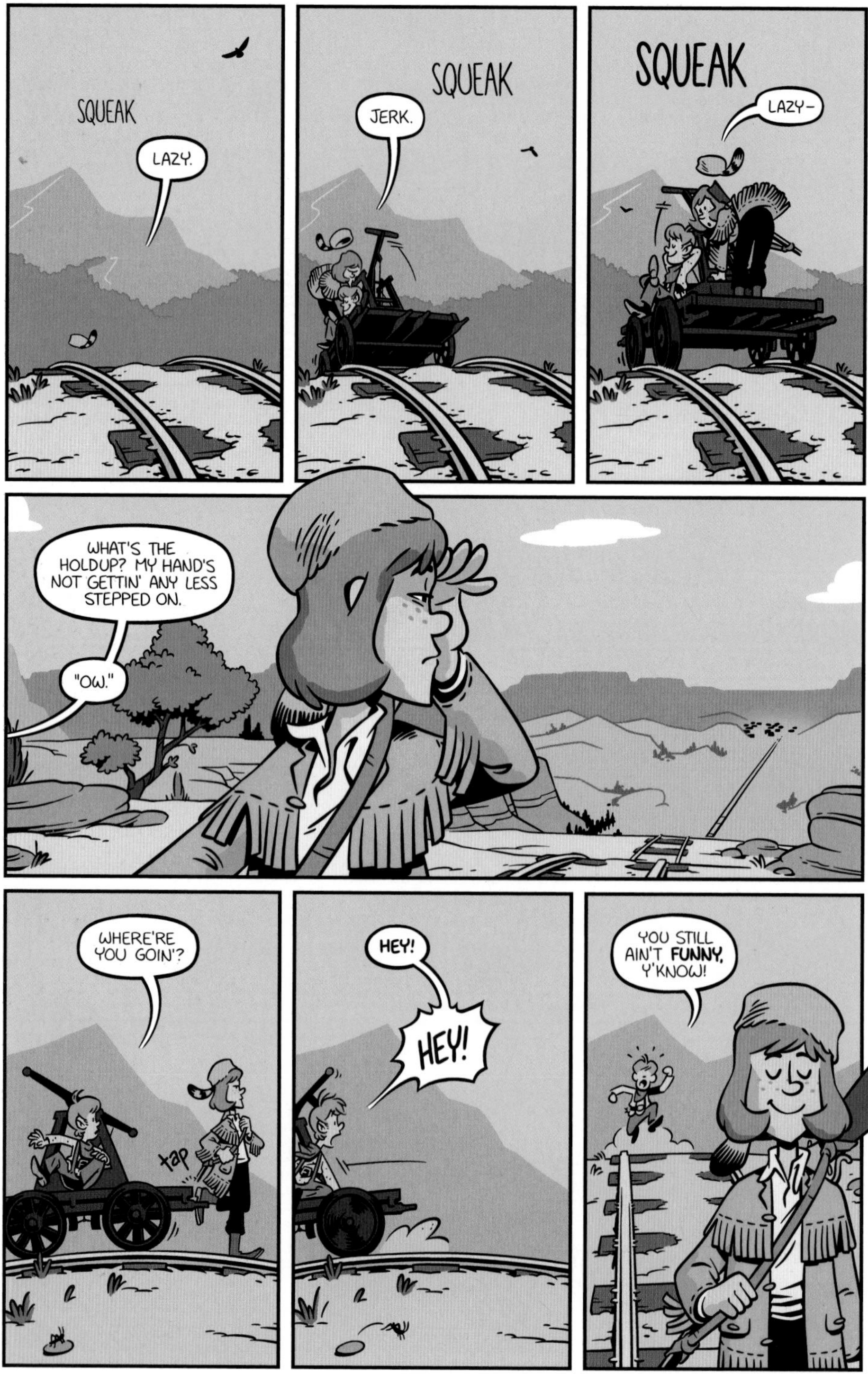
SQUEAK
LAZY.
SQUEAK
JERK.
SQUEAK
LAZY-
WHAT'S THE HOLDUP? MY HAND'S NOT GETTIN' ANY LESS STEPPED ON.
"OW."
WHERE'RE YOU GOIN'?
tap
HEY!
HEY!
YOU STILL AIN'T **FUNNY,** Y'KNOW!

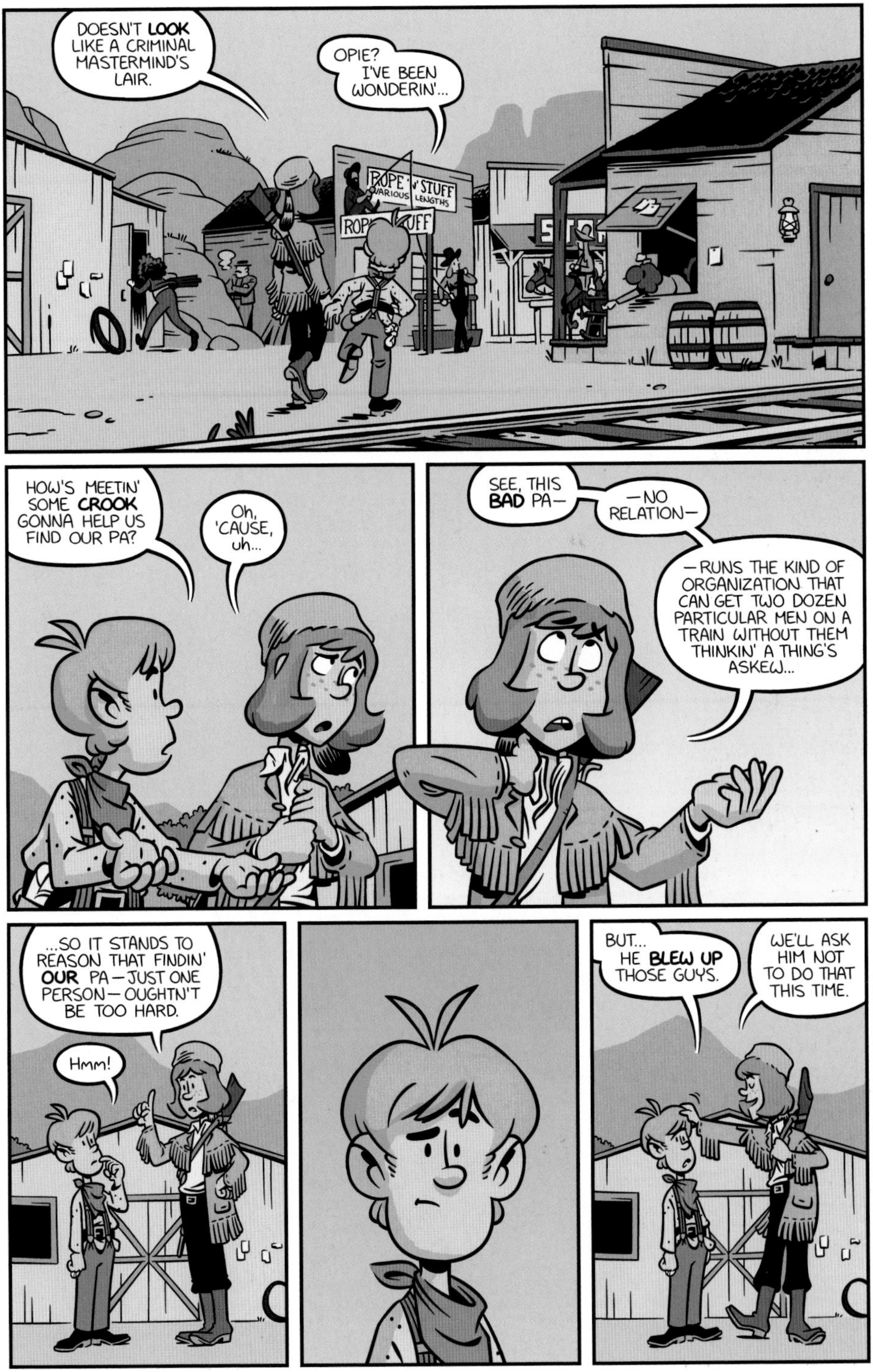
DOESN'T LOOK LIKE A CRIMINAL MASTERMIND'S LAIR.
OPIE? I'VE BEEN WONDERIN'...
ROPE 'N' STUFF VARIOUS LENGTHS
HOW'S MEETIN' SOME CROOK GONNA HELP US FIND OUR PA?
Oh, 'CAUSE, uh...
SEE, THIS BAD PA—
—NO RELATION—
—RUNS THE KIND OF ORGANIZATION THAT CAN GET TWO DOZEN PARTICULAR MEN ON A TRAIN WITHOUT THEM THINKIN' A THING'S ASKEW...
...SO IT STANDS TO REASON THAT FINDIN' OUR PA—JUST ONE PERSON—OUGHTN'T BE TOO HARD.
Hmm!
BUT... HE BLEW UP THOSE GUYS.
WE'LL ASK HIM NOT TO DO THAT THIS TIME.

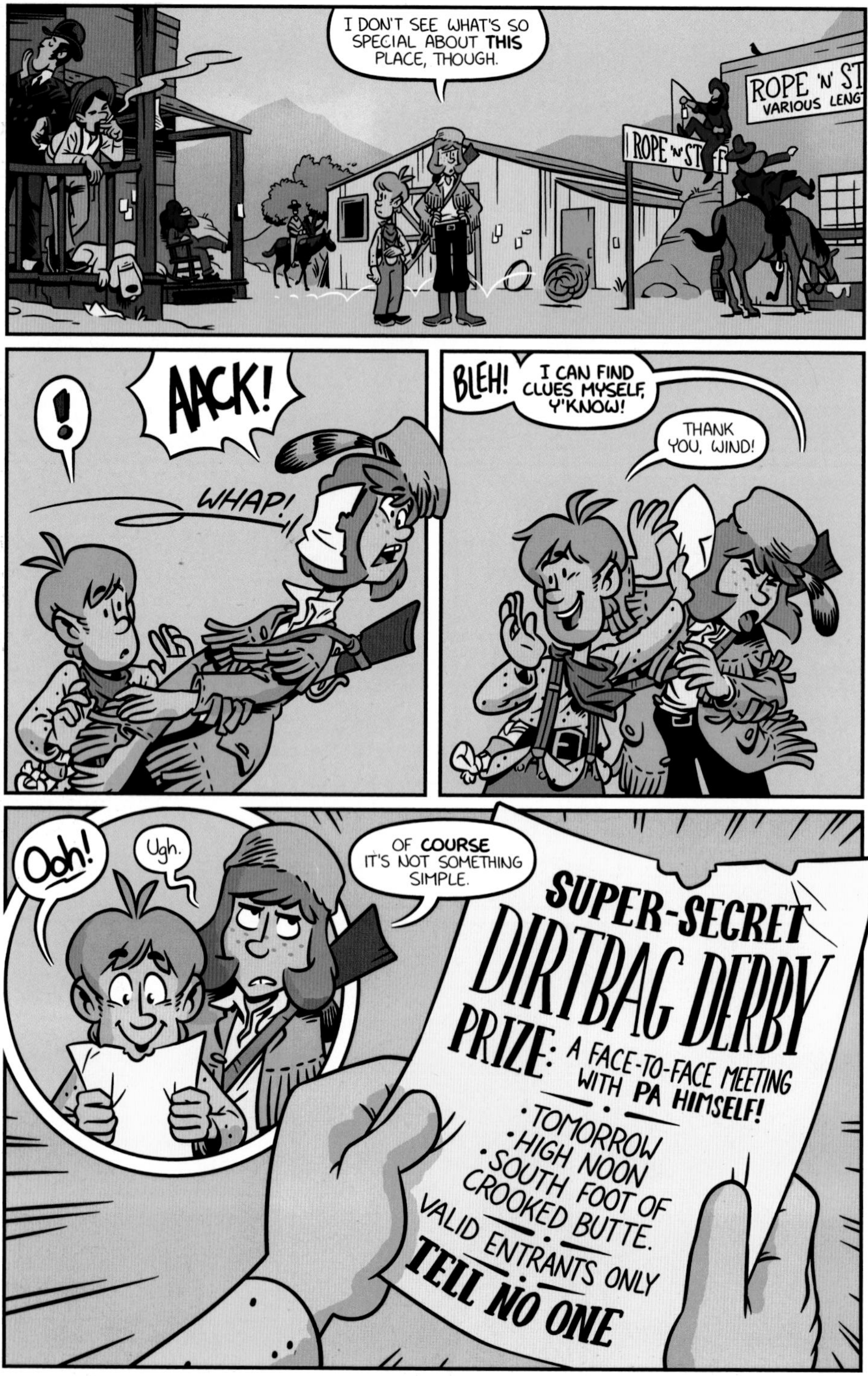

I DON'T SEE WHAT'S SO SPECIAL ABOUT THIS PLACE, THOUGH.
ROPE 'N' ST
VARIOUS LENG
ROPE 'N' ST
!
AACK!
WHAP!
BLEH!
I CAN FIND CLUES MYSELF, Y'KNOW!
THANK YOU, WIND!
Ooh!
Ugh.
OF COURSE IT'S NOT SOMETHING SIMPLE.
SUPER-SECRET
DIRTBAG DERBY
PRIZE: A FACE-TO-FACE MEETING WITH PA HIMSELF!
·TOMORROW
·HIGH NOON
·SOUTH FOOT OF CROOKED BUTTE.
VALID ENTRANTS ONLY
TELL NO ONE

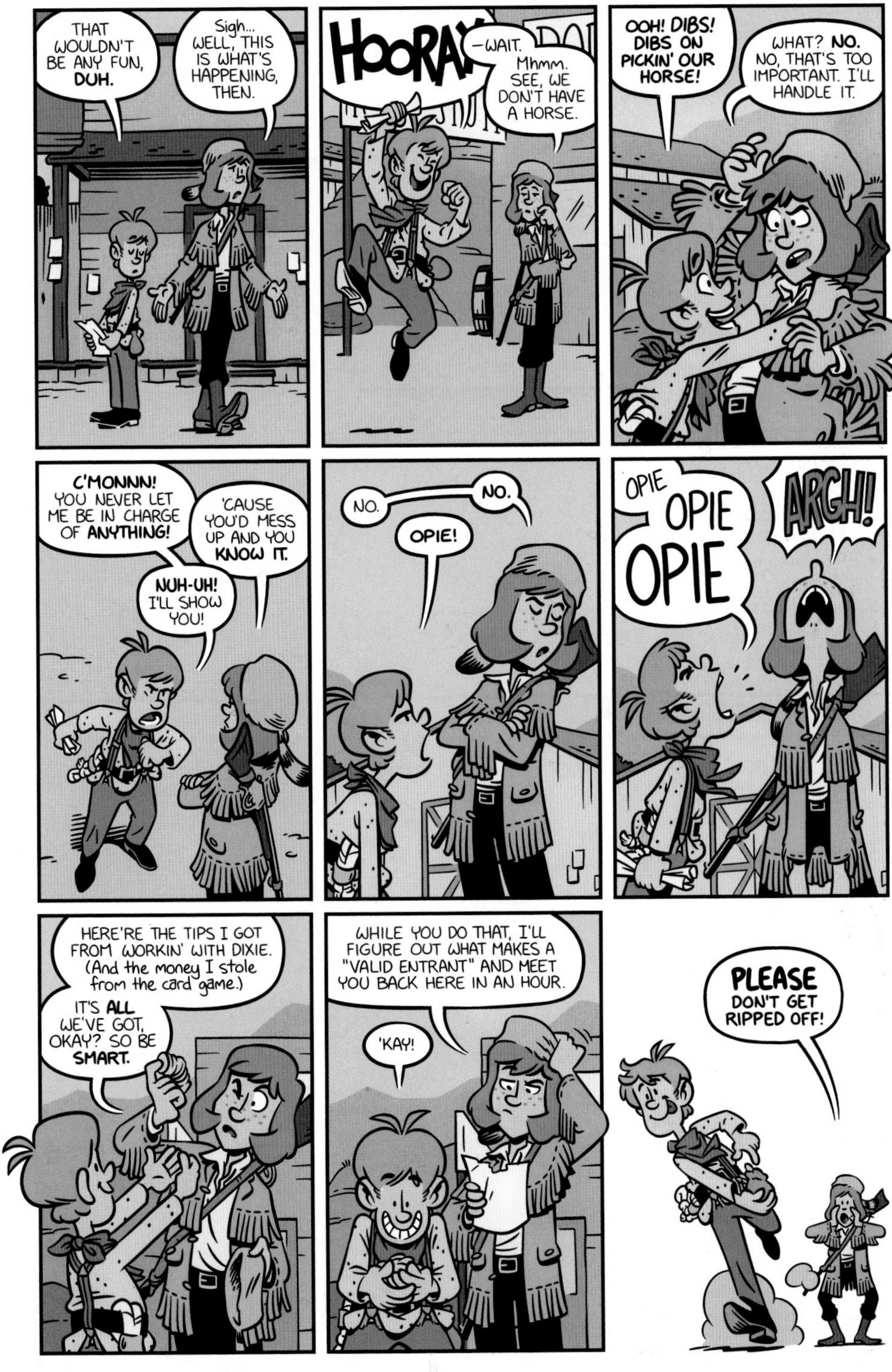
THAT WOULDN'T BE ANY FUN, **DUH.**
Sigh... WELL, THIS IS WHAT'S HAPPENING, THEN.
HOORAY
—WAIT.
Mhmm. SEE, WE DON'T HAVE A HORSE.
OOH! DIBS! DIBS ON PICKIN' OUR HORSE!
WHAT? **NO.** NO, THAT'S TOO IMPORTANT. I'LL HANDLE IT.
C'MONNN! YOU NEVER LET ME BE IN CHARGE OF **ANYTHING!**
'CAUSE YOU'D MESS UP AND YOU **KNOW IT.**
NUH-UH! I'LL SHOW YOU!
NO.
NO.
OPIE!
OPIE
OPIE
OPIE
ARGH!
HERE'RE THE TIPS I GOT FROM WORKIN' WITH DIXIE. (And the money I stole from the card game.)
IT'S **ALL** WE'VE GOT, OKAY? SO BE **SMART.**
WHILE YOU DO THAT, I'LL FIGURE OUT WHAT MAKES A "VALID ENTRANT" AND MEET YOU BACK HERE IN AN HOUR.
'KAY!
PLEASE DON'T GET RIPPED OFF!

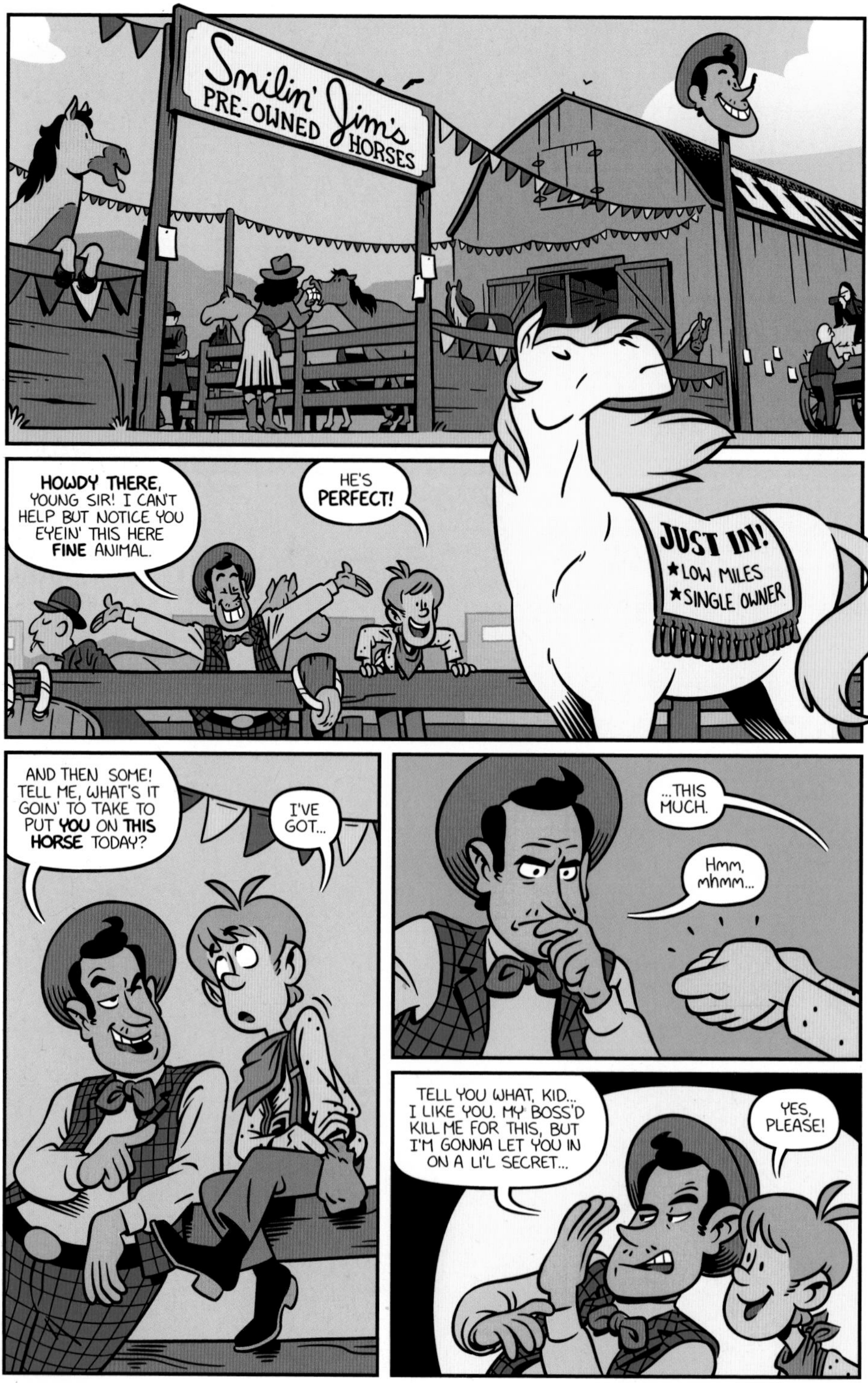

Smilin' Jim's PRE-OWNED HORSES
HOWDY THERE, YOUNG SIR! I CAN'T HELP BUT NOTICE YOU EYEIN' THIS HERE FINE ANIMAL.
HE'S PERFECT!
JUST IN! ★LOW MILES ★SINGLE OWNER
AND THEN SOME! TELL ME, WHAT'S IT GOIN' TO TAKE TO PUT YOU ON THIS HORSE TODAY?
I'VE GOT...
...THIS MUCH.
Hmm, mhmm...
TELL YOU WHAT, KID... I LIKE YOU. MY BOSS'D KILL ME FOR THIS, BUT I'M GONNA LET YOU IN ON A LI'L SECRET...
YES, PLEASE!

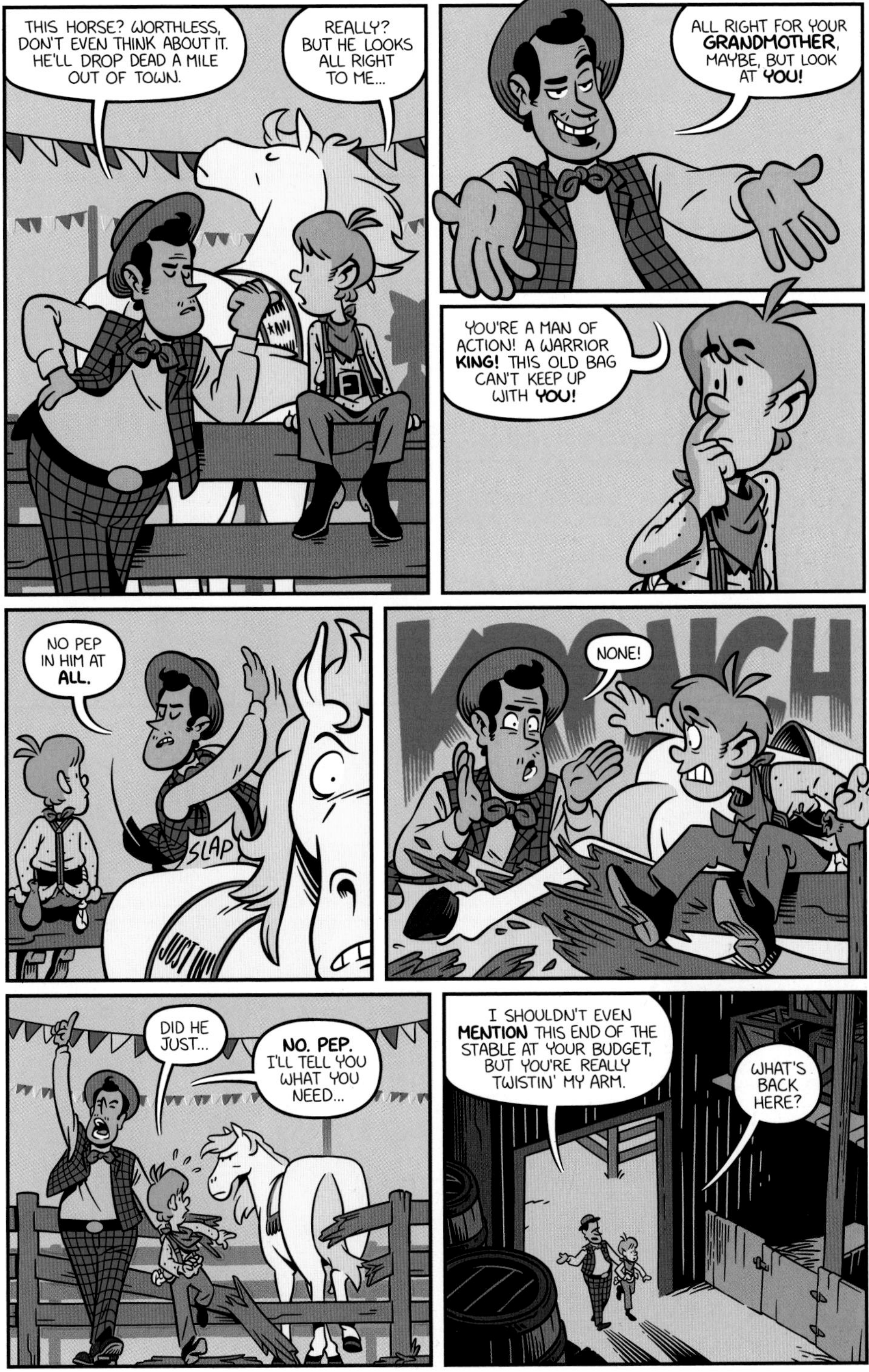
THIS HORSE? WORTHLESS, DON'T EVEN THINK ABOUT IT. HE'LL DROP DEAD A MILE OUT OF TOWN.
REALLY? BUT HE LOOKS ALL RIGHT TO ME...
ALL RIGHT FOR YOUR GRANDMOTHER, MAYBE, BUT LOOK AT YOU!
YOU'RE A MAN OF ACTION! A WARRIOR KING! THIS OLD BAG CAN'T KEEP UP WITH YOU!
NO PEP IN HIM AT ALL.
SLAP
NONE!
DID HE JUST...
NO. PEP. I'LL TELL YOU WHAT YOU NEED...
I SHOULDN'T EVEN MENTION THIS END OF THE STABLE AT YOUR BUDGET, BUT YOU'RE REALLY TWISTIN' MY ARM.
WHAT'S BACK HERE?

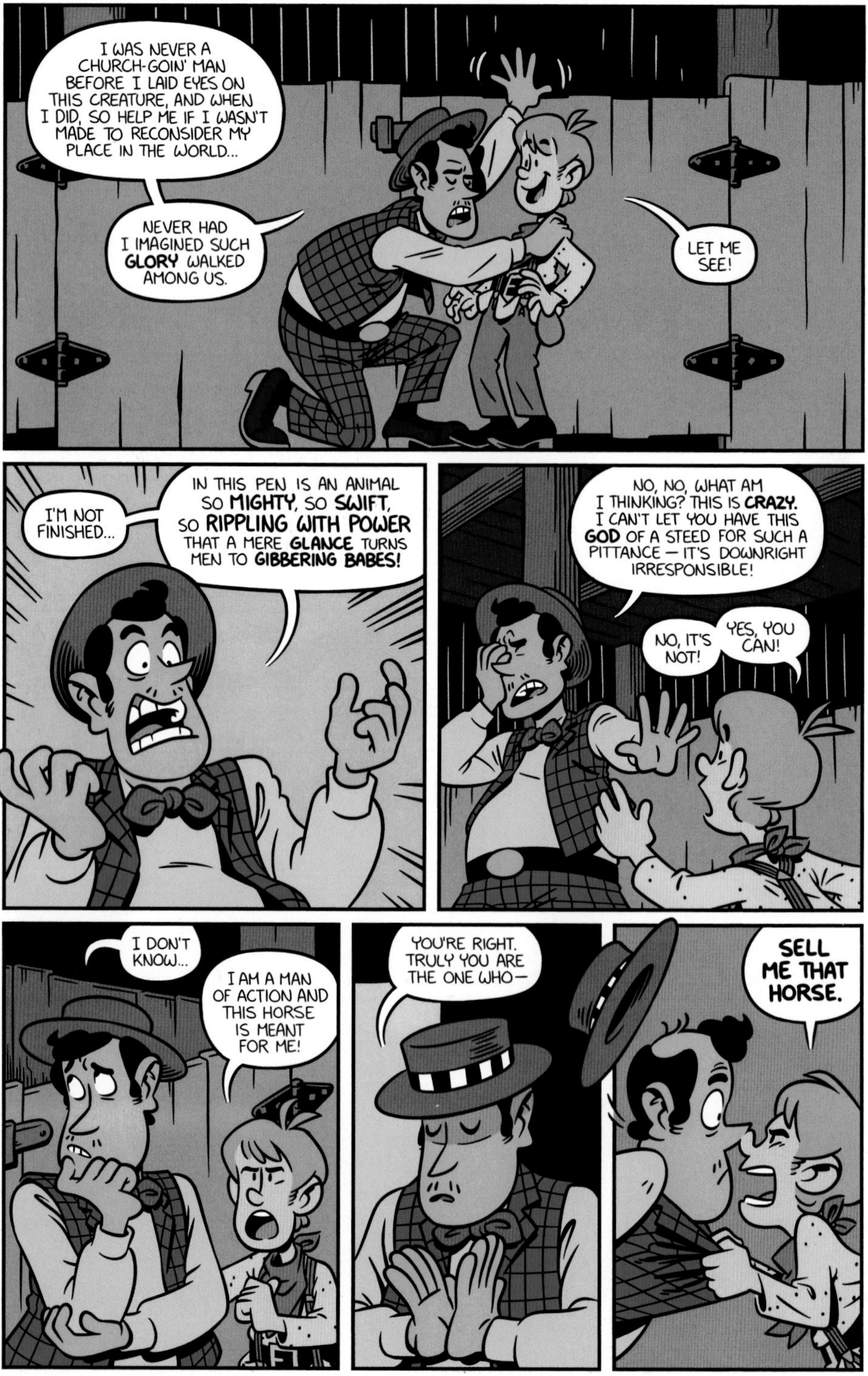
I WAS NEVER A CHURCH-GOIN' MAN BEFORE I LAID EYES ON THIS CREATURE, AND WHEN I DID, SO HELP ME IF I WASN'T MADE TO RECONSIDER MY PLACE IN THE WORLD...
NEVER HAD I IMAGINED SUCH GLORY WALKED AMONG US.
LET ME SEE!
I'M NOT FINISHED...
IN THIS PEN IS AN ANIMAL SO MIGHTY, SO SWIFT, SO RIPPLING WITH POWER THAT A MERE GLANCE TURNS MEN TO GIBBERING BABES!
NO, NO, WHAT AM I THINKING? THIS IS CRAZY. I CAN'T LET YOU HAVE THIS GOD OF A STEED FOR SUCH A PITTANCE — IT'S DOWNRIGHT IRRESPONSIBLE!
YES, YOU CAN!
NO, IT'S NOT!
I DON'T KNOW...
I AM A MAN OF ACTION AND THIS HORSE IS MEANT FOR ME!
YOU'RE RIGHT. TRULY YOU ARE THE ONE WHO—
SELL ME THAT HORSE.

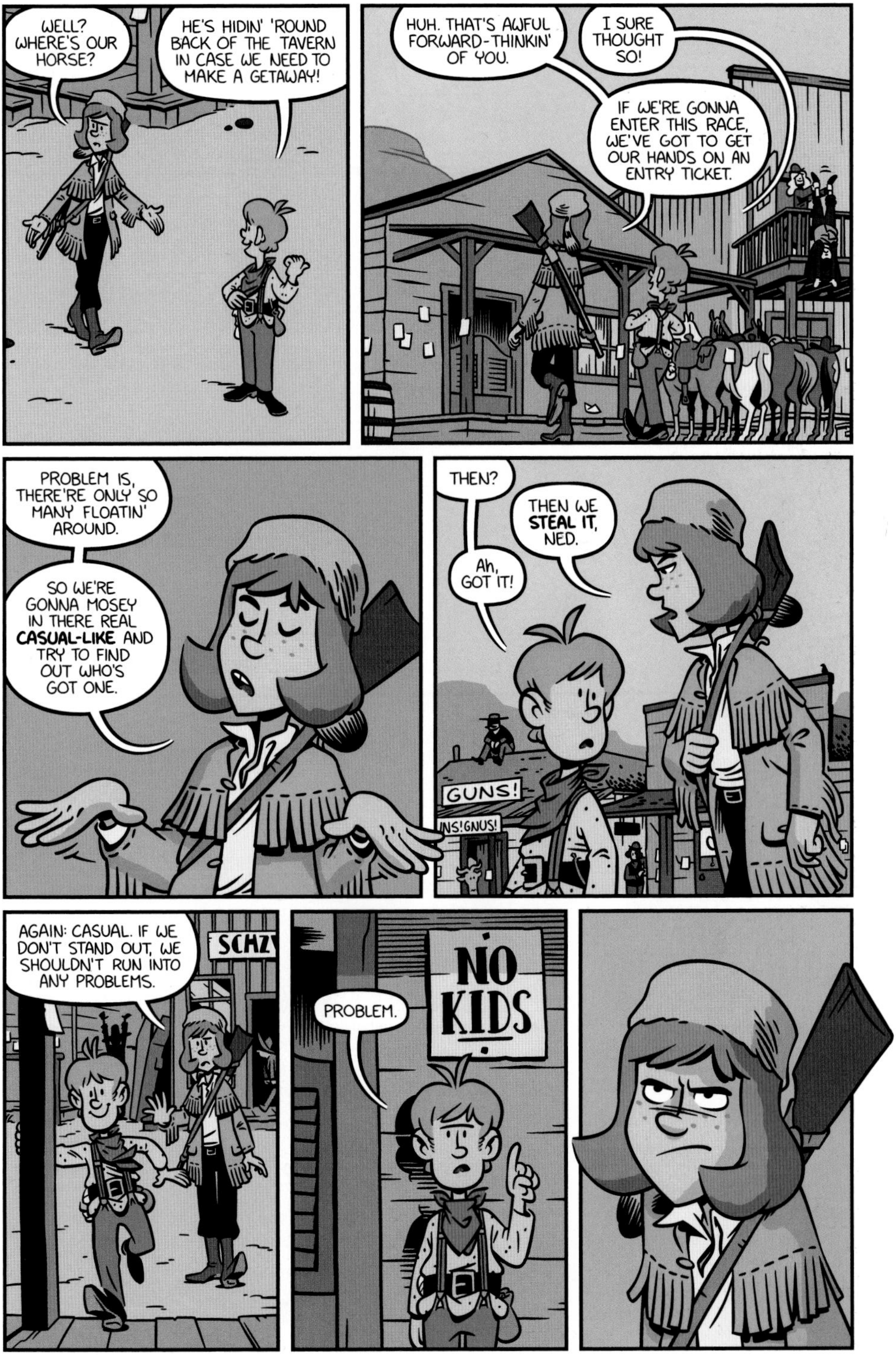
WELL? WHERE'S OUR HORSE?
HE'S HIDIN' 'ROUND BACK OF THE TAVERN IN CASE WE NEED TO MAKE A GETAWAY!
HUH. THAT'S AWFUL FORWARD-THINKIN' OF YOU.
I SURE THOUGHT SO!
IF WE'RE GONNA ENTER THIS RACE, WE'VE GOT TO GET OUR HANDS ON AN ENTRY TICKET.
PROBLEM IS, THERE'RE ONLY SO MANY FLOATIN' AROUND.
SO WE'RE GONNA MOSEY IN THERE REAL **CASUAL-LIKE** AND TRY TO FIND OUT WHO'S GOT ONE.
THEN?
THEN WE **STEAL IT**, NED.
Ah, GOT IT!
GUNS!
NS!GNUS!
AGAIN: CASUAL. IF WE DON'T STAND OUT, WE SHOULDN'T RUN INTO ANY PROBLEMS.
SCHZ
PROBLEM.
NO KIDS

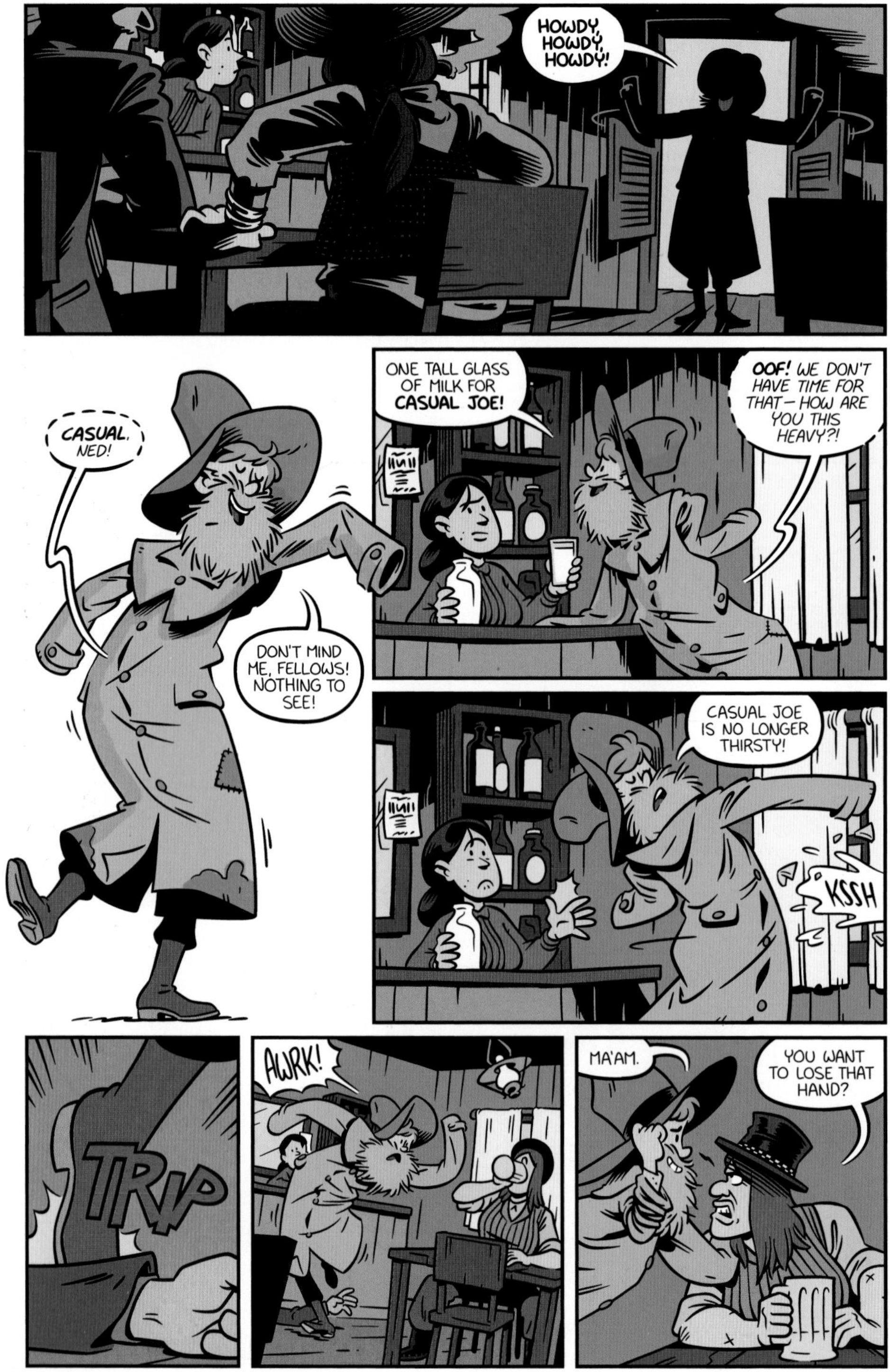
HOWDY, HOWDY, HOWDY!
CASUAL, NED!
DON'T MIND ME, FELLOWS! NOTHING TO SEE!
ONE TALL GLASS OF MILK FOR CASUAL JOE!
OOF! WE DON'T HAVE TIME FOR THAT—HOW ARE YOU THIS HEAVY?!
CASUAL JOE IS NO LONGER THIRSTY!
KSSH
TRIP
AWRK!
MA'AM.
YOU WANT TO LOSE THAT HAND?

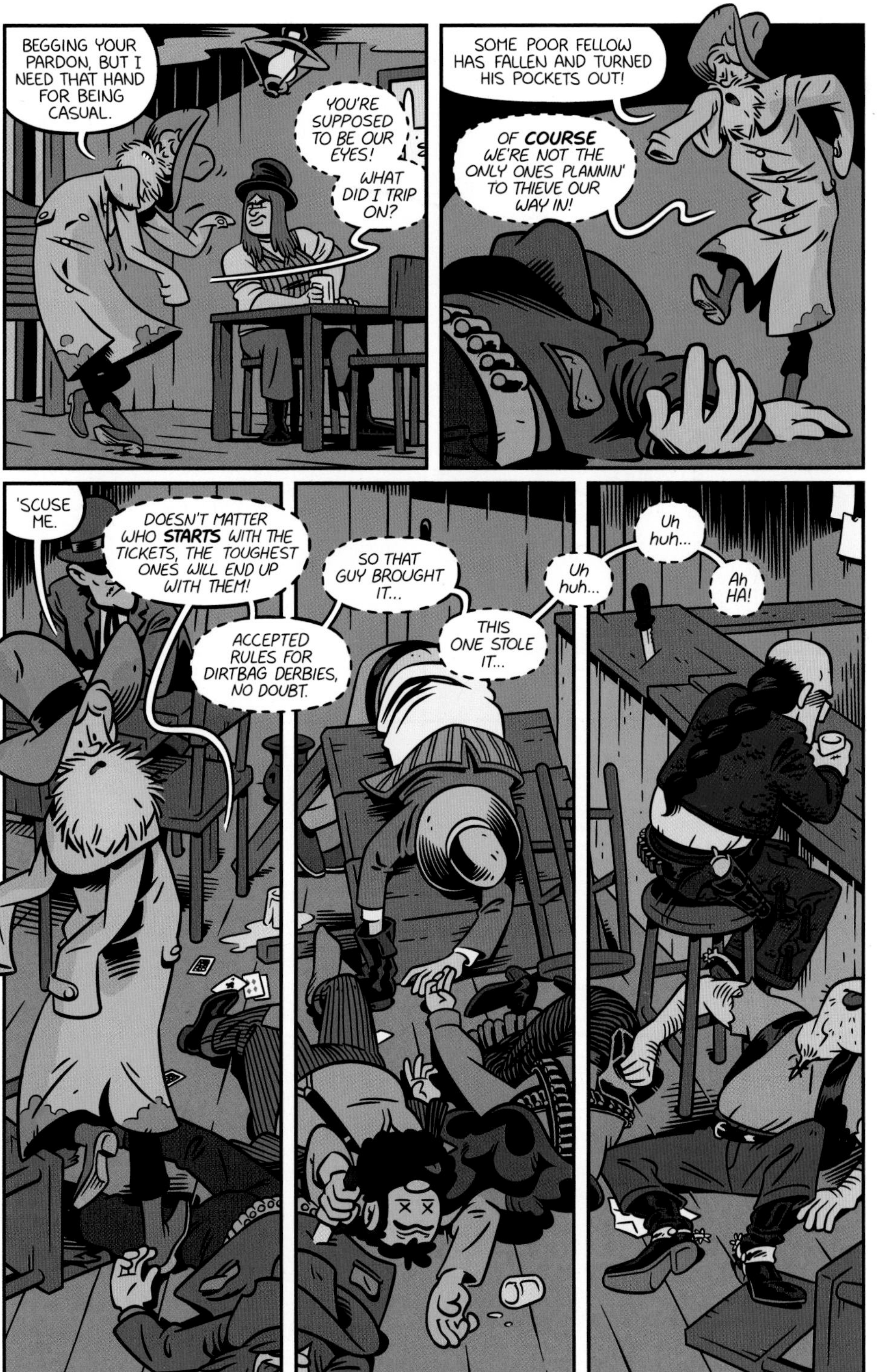
BEGGING YOUR PARDON, BUT I NEED THAT HAND FOR BEING CASUAL.
YOU'RE SUPPOSED TO BE OUR EYES!
WHAT DID I TRIP ON?
SOME POOR FELLOW HAS FALLEN AND TURNED HIS POCKETS OUT!
OF COURSE WE'RE NOT THE ONLY ONES PLANNIN' TO THIEVE OUR WAY IN!
'SCUSE ME.
DOESN'T MATTER WHO STARTS WITH THE TICKETS, THE TOUGHEST ONES WILL END UP WITH THEM!
ACCEPTED RULES FOR DIRTBAG DERBIES, NO DOUBT.
SO THAT GUY BROUGHT IT...
THIS ONE STOLE IT...
Uh huh...
Uh huh...
Ah HA!

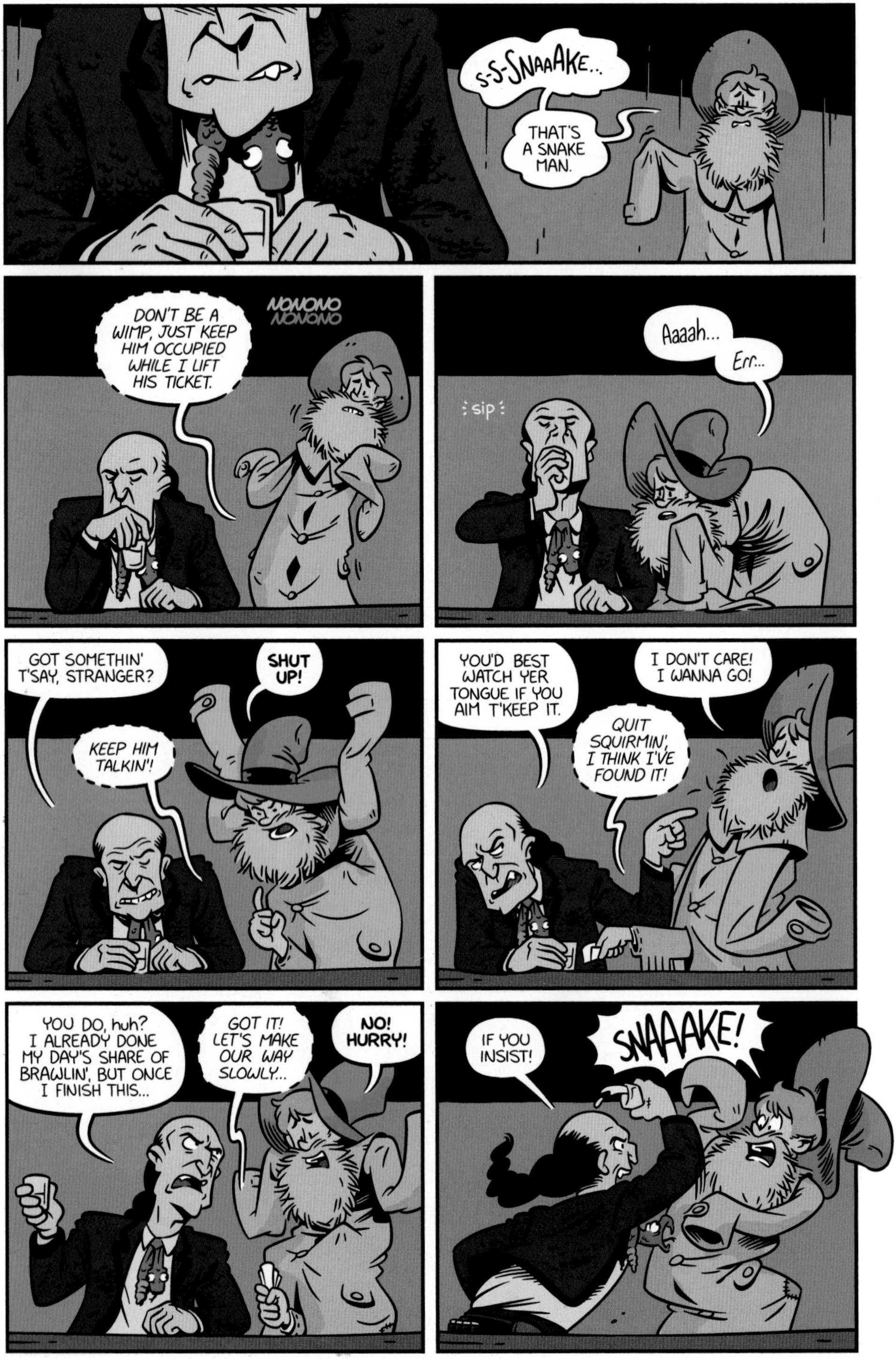
S-S-SNAAAKE...
THAT'S A SNAKE MAN.
DON'T BE A WIMP, JUST KEEP HIM OCCUPIED WHILE I LIFT HIS TICKET.
NONONO NONONO
Aaaah...
Err...
sip
GOT SOMETHIN' T'SAY, STRANGER?
SHUT UP!
KEEP HIM TALKIN'!
YOU'D BEST WATCH YER TONGUE IF YOU AIM T'KEEP IT.
I DON'T CARE! I WANNA GO!
QUIT SQUIRMIN', I THINK I'VE FOUND IT!
YOU DO, huh? I ALREADY DONE MY DAY'S SHARE OF BRAWLIN', BUT ONCE I FINISH THIS...
GOT IT! LET'S MAKE OUR WAY SLOWLY...
NO! HURRY!
IF YOU INSIST!
SNAAAKE!

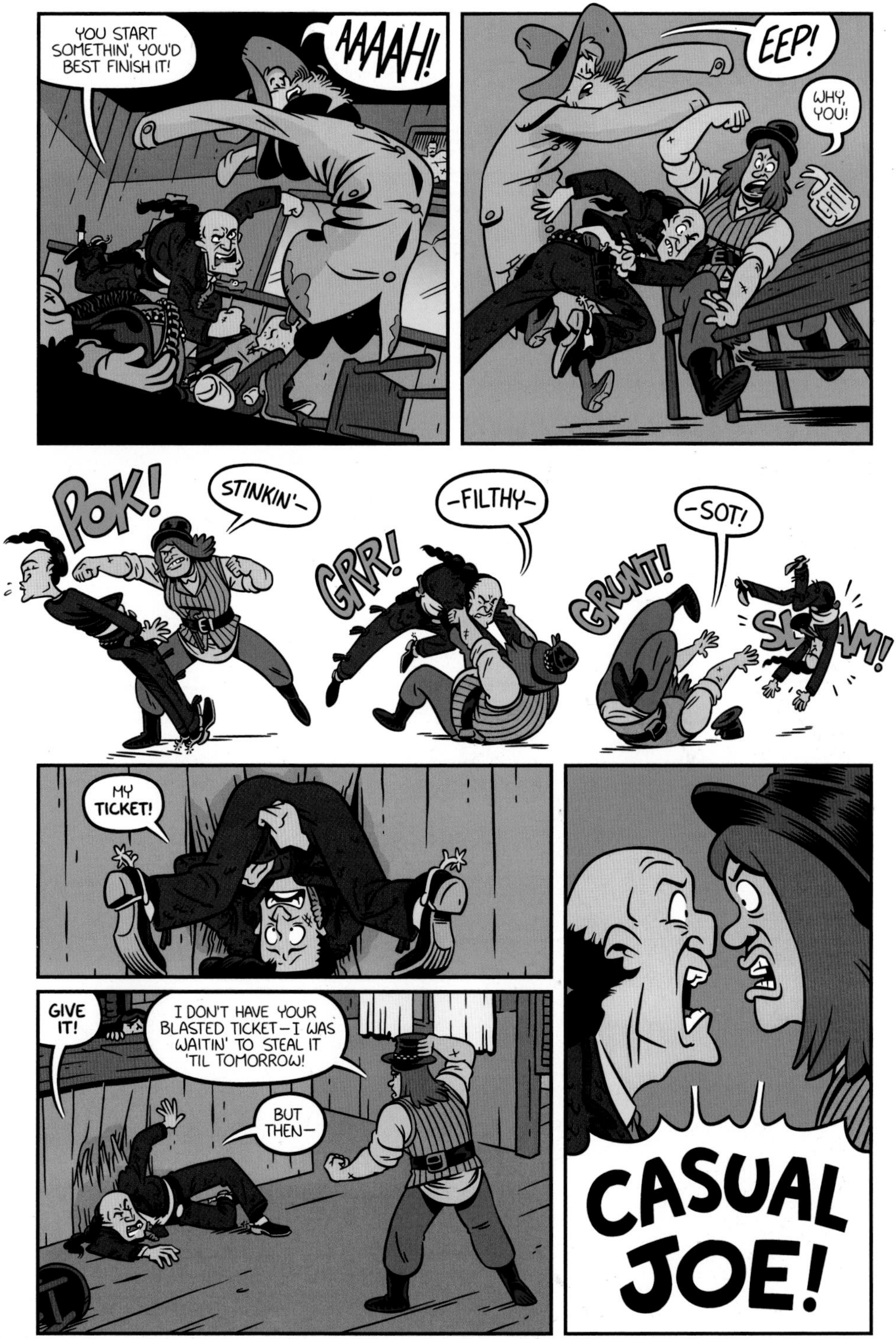

YOU START SOMETHIN', YOU'D BEST FINISH IT!
AAAAH!
EEP!
WHY, YOU!
POK!
STINKIN'-
-FILTHY-
GRR!
-SOT!
GRUNT!
MY TICKET!
GIVE IT!
I DON'T HAVE YOUR BLASTED TICKET—I WAS WAITIN' TO STEAL IT 'TIL TOMORROW!
BUT THEN—
CASUAL JOE!

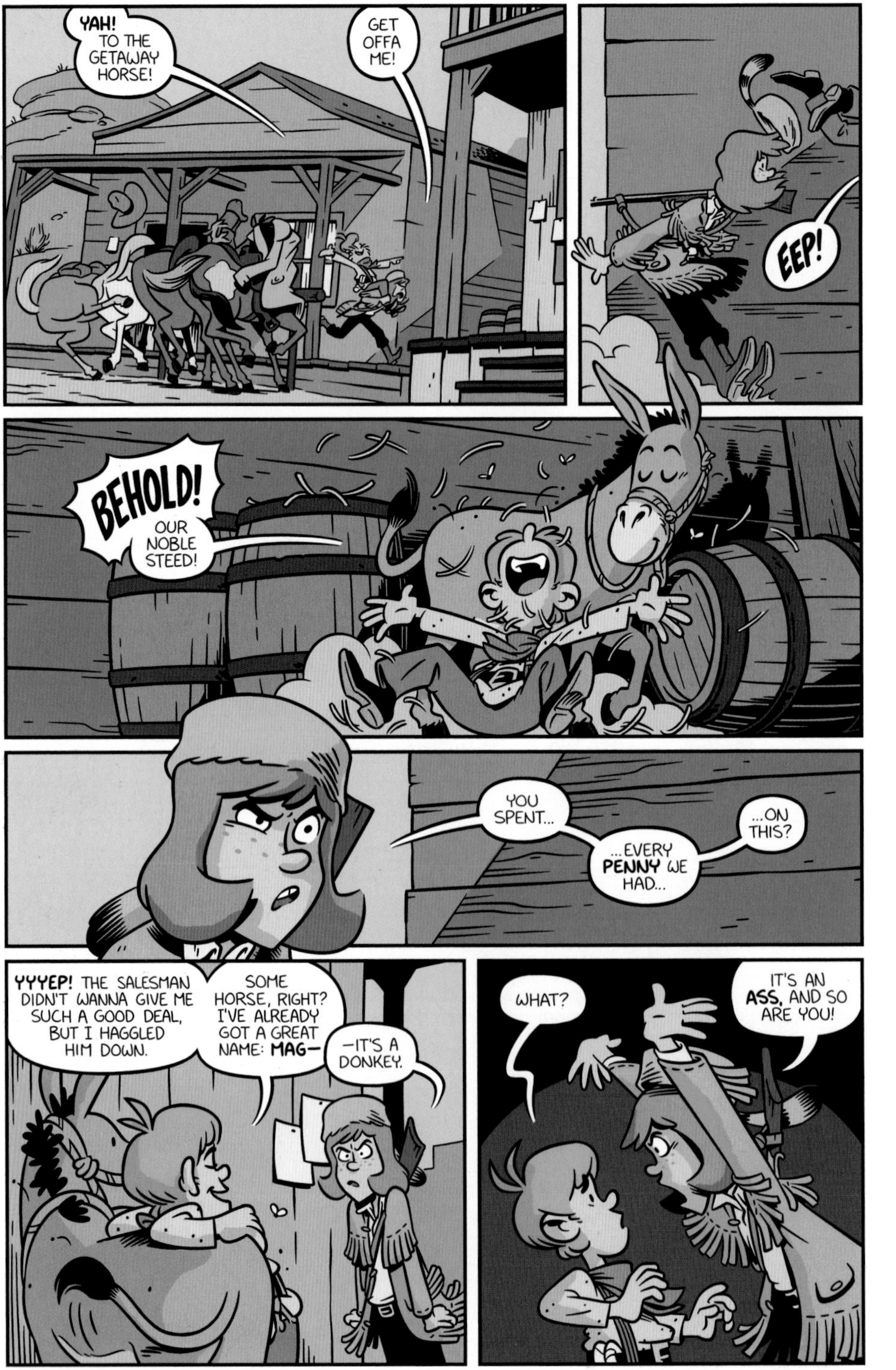
YAH! TO THE GETAWAY HORSE!
GET OFFA ME!
EEP!
BEHOLD!
OUR NOBLE STEED!
YOU SPENT...
...EVERY PENNY WE HAD...
...ON THIS?
YYYEP! THE SALESMAN DIDN'T WANNA GIVE ME SUCH A GOOD DEAL, BUT I HAGGLED HIM DOWN.
SOME HORSE, RIGHT? I'VE ALREADY GOT A GREAT NAME: MAG—
—IT'S A DONKEY.
WHAT?
IT'S AN ASS, AND SO ARE YOU!

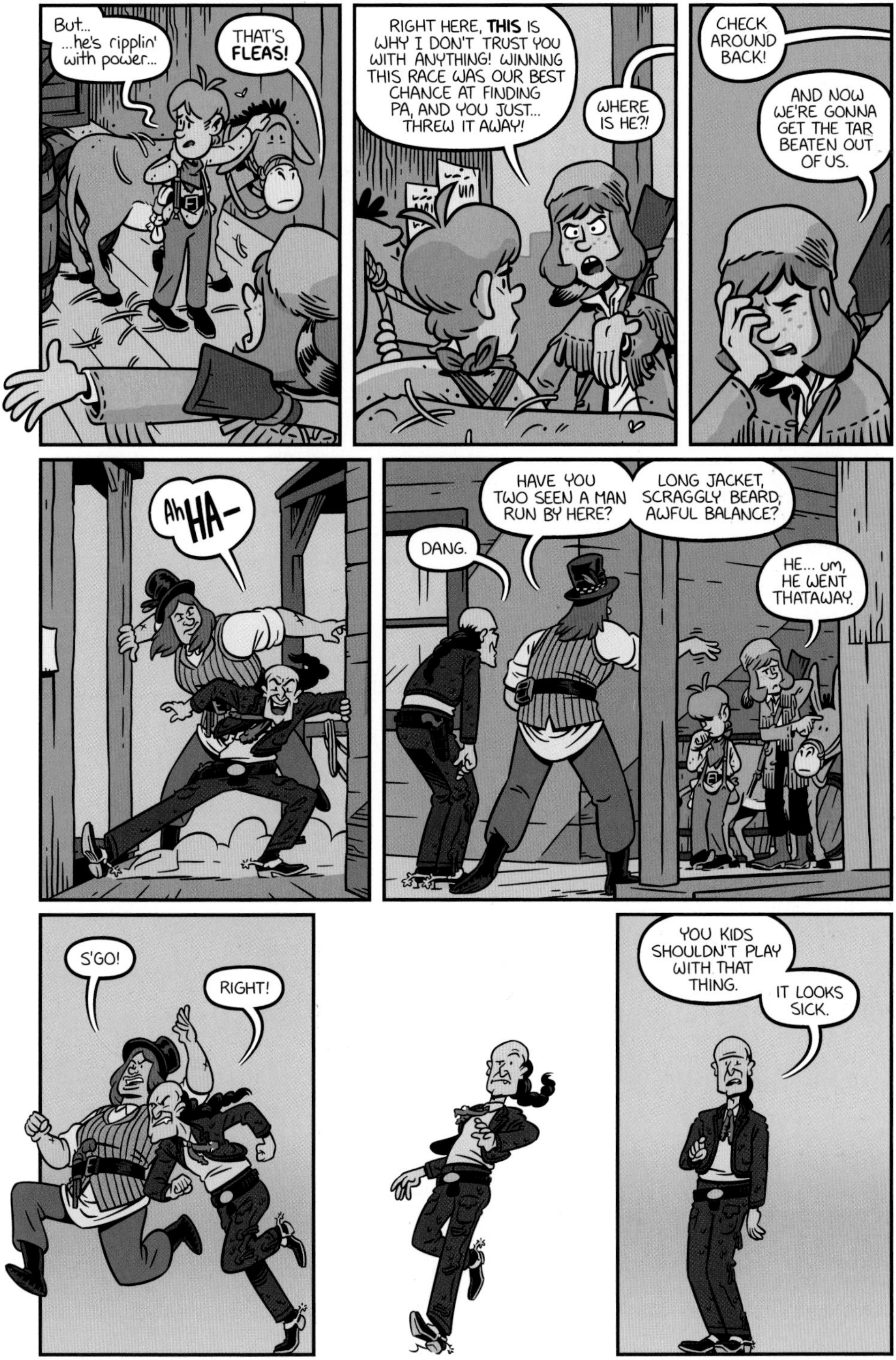
But... ...he's ripplin' with power...
THAT'S FLEAS!
RIGHT HERE, THIS IS WHY I DON'T TRUST YOU WITH ANYTHING! WINNING THIS RACE WAS OUR BEST CHANCE AT FINDING PA, AND YOU JUST... THREW IT AWAY!
WHERE IS HE?!
CHECK AROUND BACK!
AND NOW WE'RE GONNA GET THE TAR BEATEN OUT OF US.
Ah HA-
HAVE YOU TWO SEEN A MAN RUN BY HERE?
LONG JACKET, SCRAGGLY BEARD, AWFUL BALANCE?
DANG.
HE... um, HE WENT THATAWAY.
S'GO!
RIGHT!
YOU KIDS SHOULDN'T PLAY WITH THAT THING.
IT LOOKS SICK.

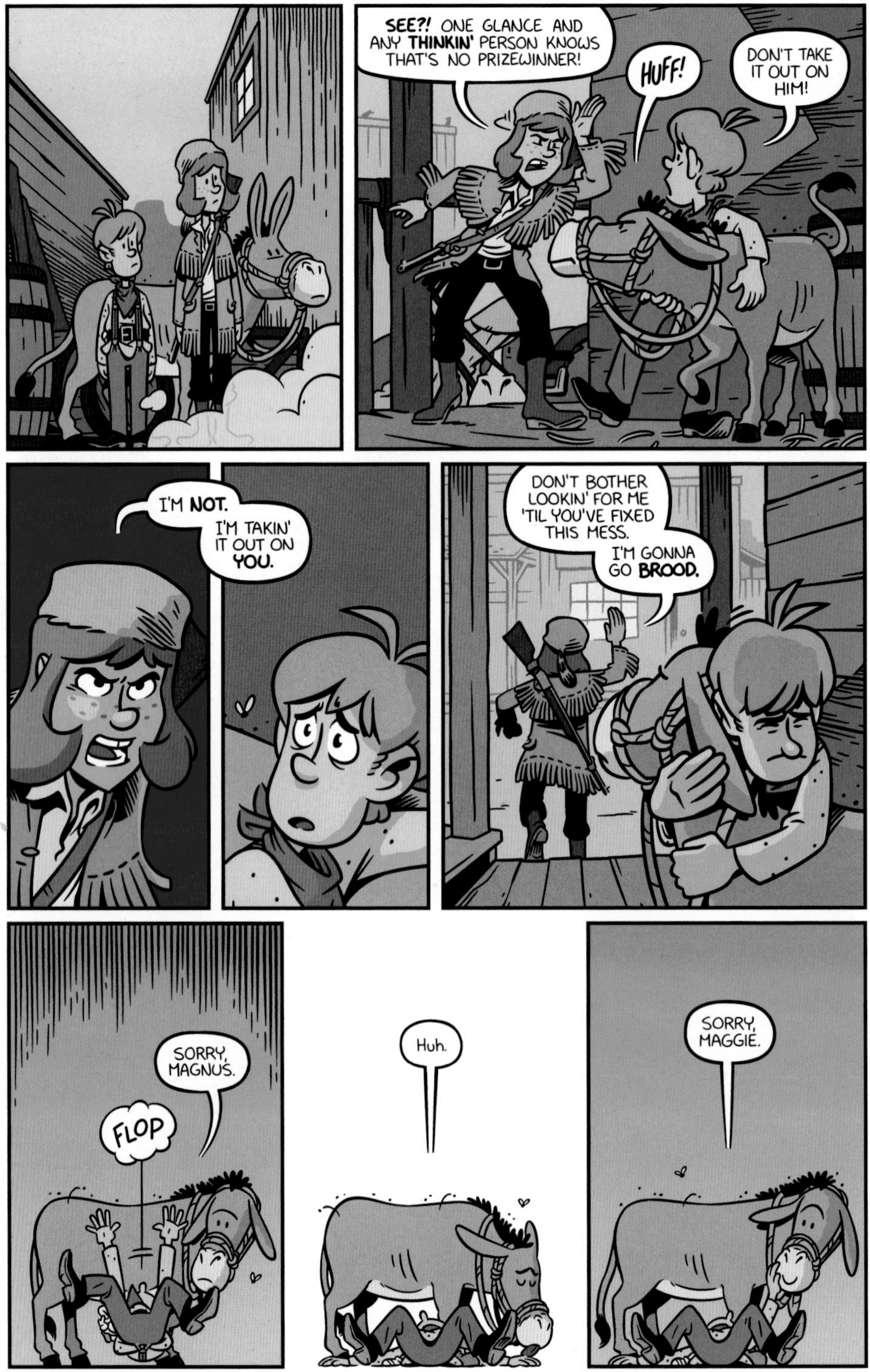
SEE?! ONE GLANCE AND ANY THINKIN' PERSON KNOWS THAT'S NO PRIZEWINNER!
HUFF!
DON'T TAKE IT OUT ON HIM!
I'M NOT.
I'M TAKIN' IT OUT ON YOU.
DON'T BOTHER LOOKIN' FOR ME 'TIL YOU'VE FIXED THIS MESS.
I'M GONNA GO BROOD.
SORRY, MAGNUS.
FLOP
Huh.
SORRY, MAGGIE.

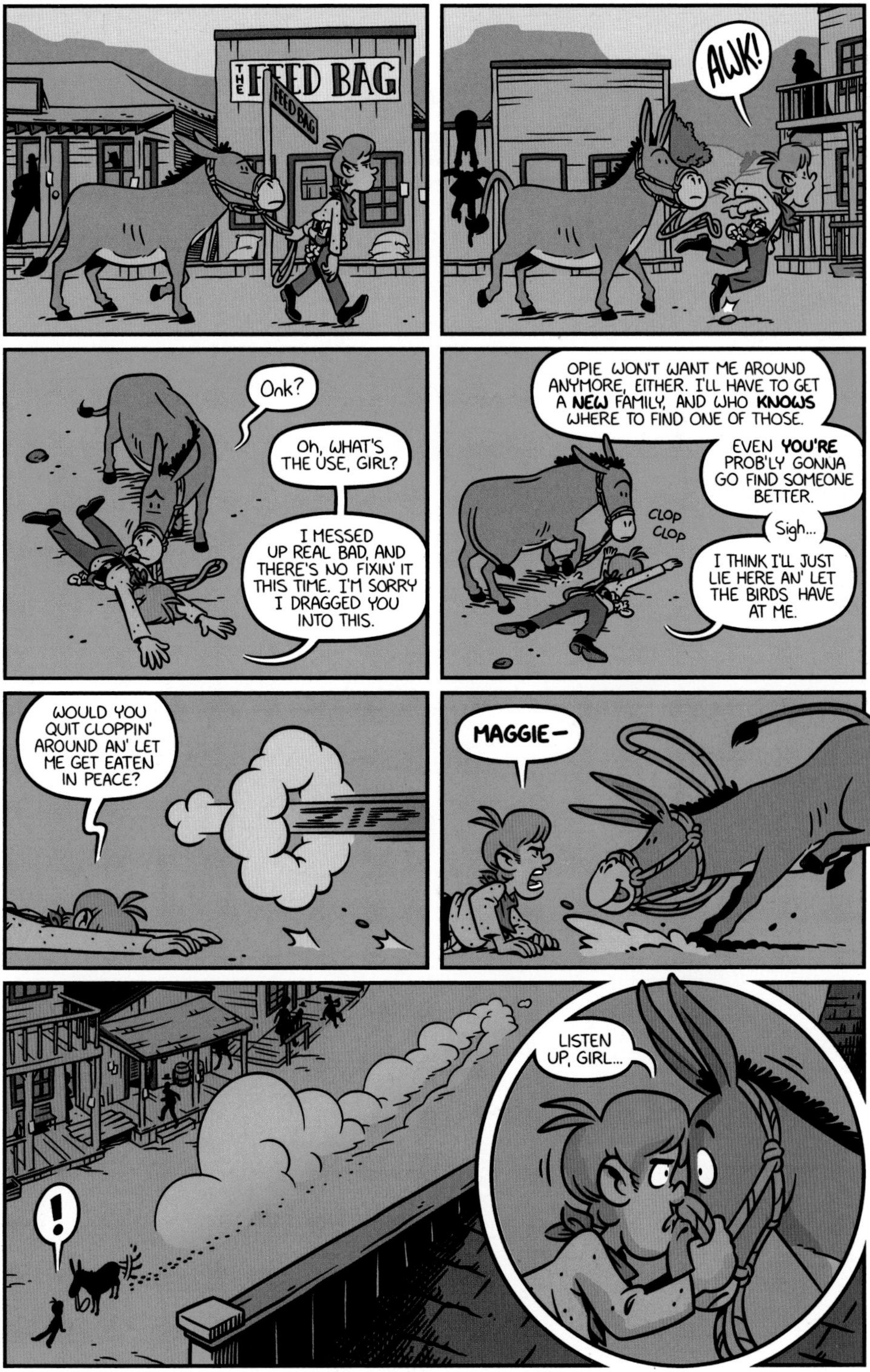
THE FEED BAG
FEED BAG
AWK!
Onk?
Oh, WHAT'S THE USE, GIRL?
I MESSED UP REAL BAD, AND THERE'S NO FIXIN' IT THIS TIME. I'M SORRY I DRAGGED YOU INTO THIS.
OPIE WON'T WANT ME AROUND ANYMORE, EITHER. I'LL HAVE TO GET A NEW FAMILY, AND WHO KNOWS WHERE TO FIND ONE OF THOSE.
EVEN YOU'RE PROB'LY GONNA GO FIND SOMEONE BETTER.
CLOP CLOP
Sigh...
I THINK I'LL JUST LIE HERE AN' LET THE BIRDS HAVE AT ME.
WOULD YOU QUIT CLOPPIN' AROUND AN' LET ME GET EATEN IN PEACE?
ZIP
MAGGIE-
!
LISTEN UP, GIRL...

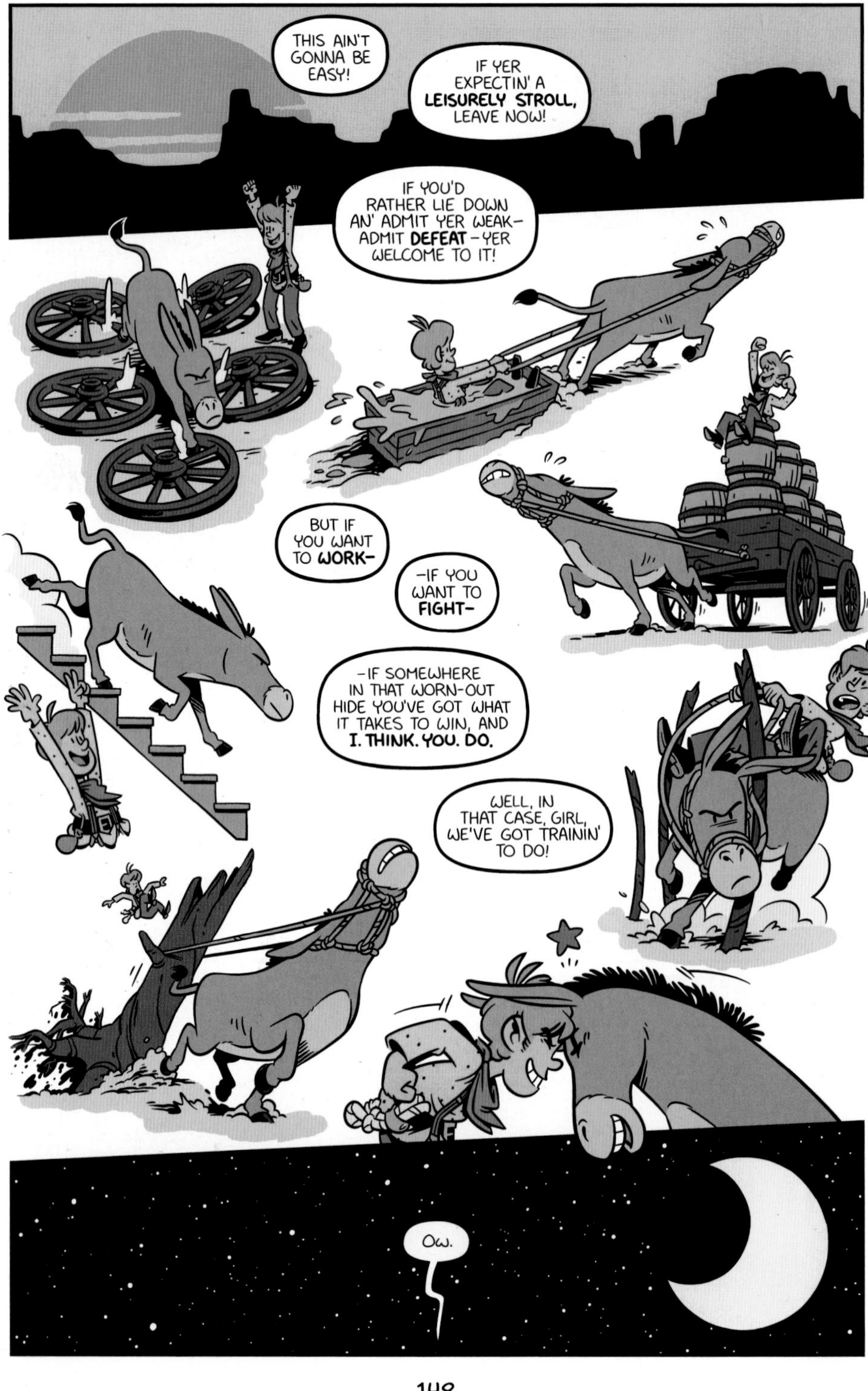
THIS AIN'T GONNA BE EASY!
IF YER EXPECTIN' A **LEISURELY STROLL,** LEAVE NOW!
IF YOU'D RATHER LIE DOWN AN' ADMIT YER WEAK— ADMIT **DEFEAT** —YER WELCOME TO IT!
BUT IF YOU WANT TO **WORK—**
—IF YOU WANT TO **FIGHT—**
—IF SOMEWHERE IN THAT WORN-OUT HIDE YOU'VE GOT WHAT IT TAKES TO WIN, AND **I. THINK. YOU. DO.**
WELL, IN THAT CASE, GIRL, WE'VE GOT TRAININ' TO DO!
Ow.

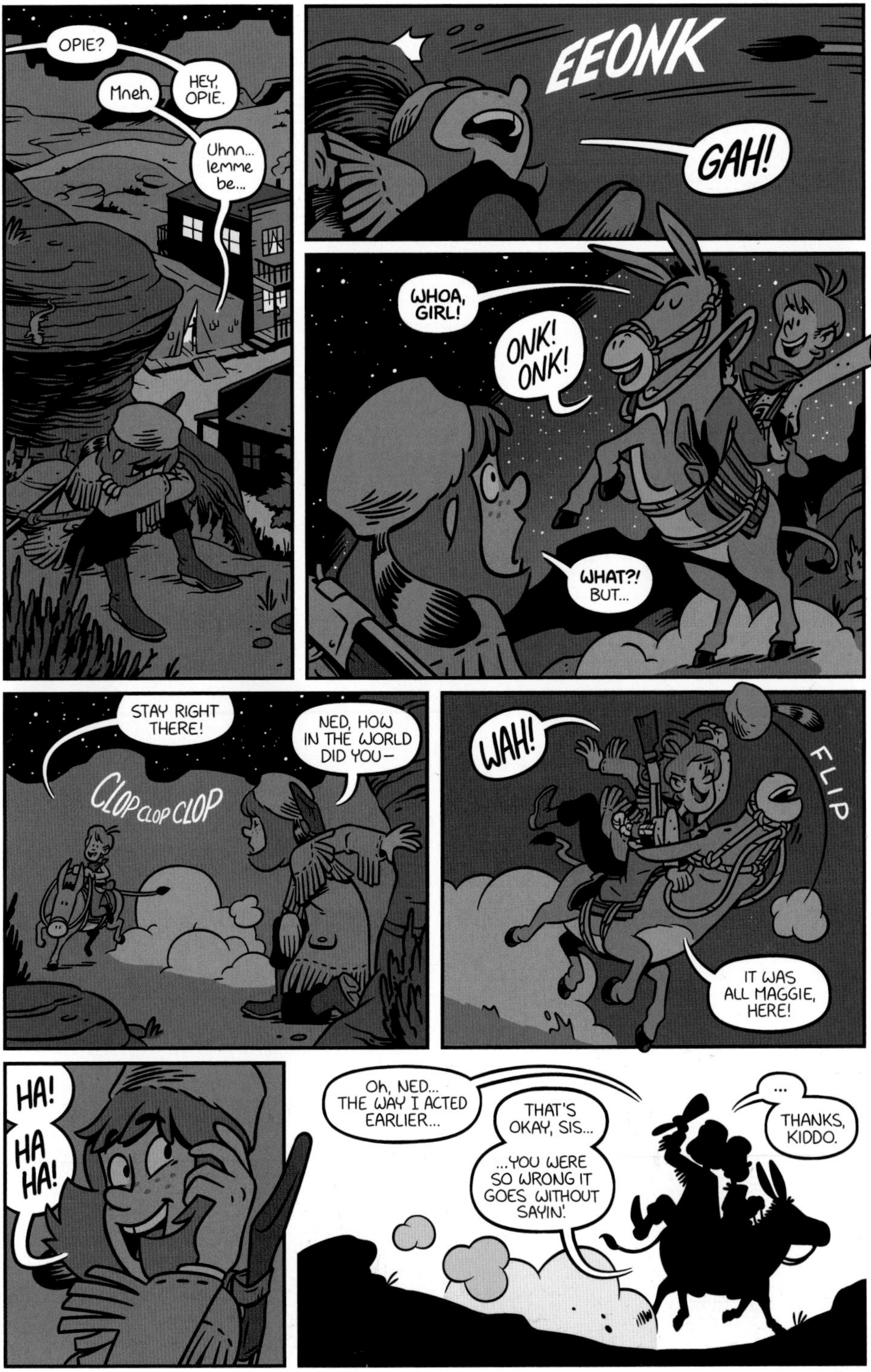
OPIE?
HEY, OPIE.
Mneh.
Uhnn... lemme be...
EEONK
GAH!
WHOA, GIRL!
ONK! ONK!
WHAT?! BUT...
STAY RIGHT THERE!
NED, HOW IN THE WORLD DID YOU—
CLOP CLOP CLOP
WAH!
FLIP
IT WAS ALL MAGGIE, HERE!
HA!
HA HA!
Oh, NED... THE WAY I ACTED EARLIER...
THAT'S OKAY, SIS...
...YOU WERE SO WRONG IT GOES WITHOUT SAYIN'.
...
THANKS, KIDDO.

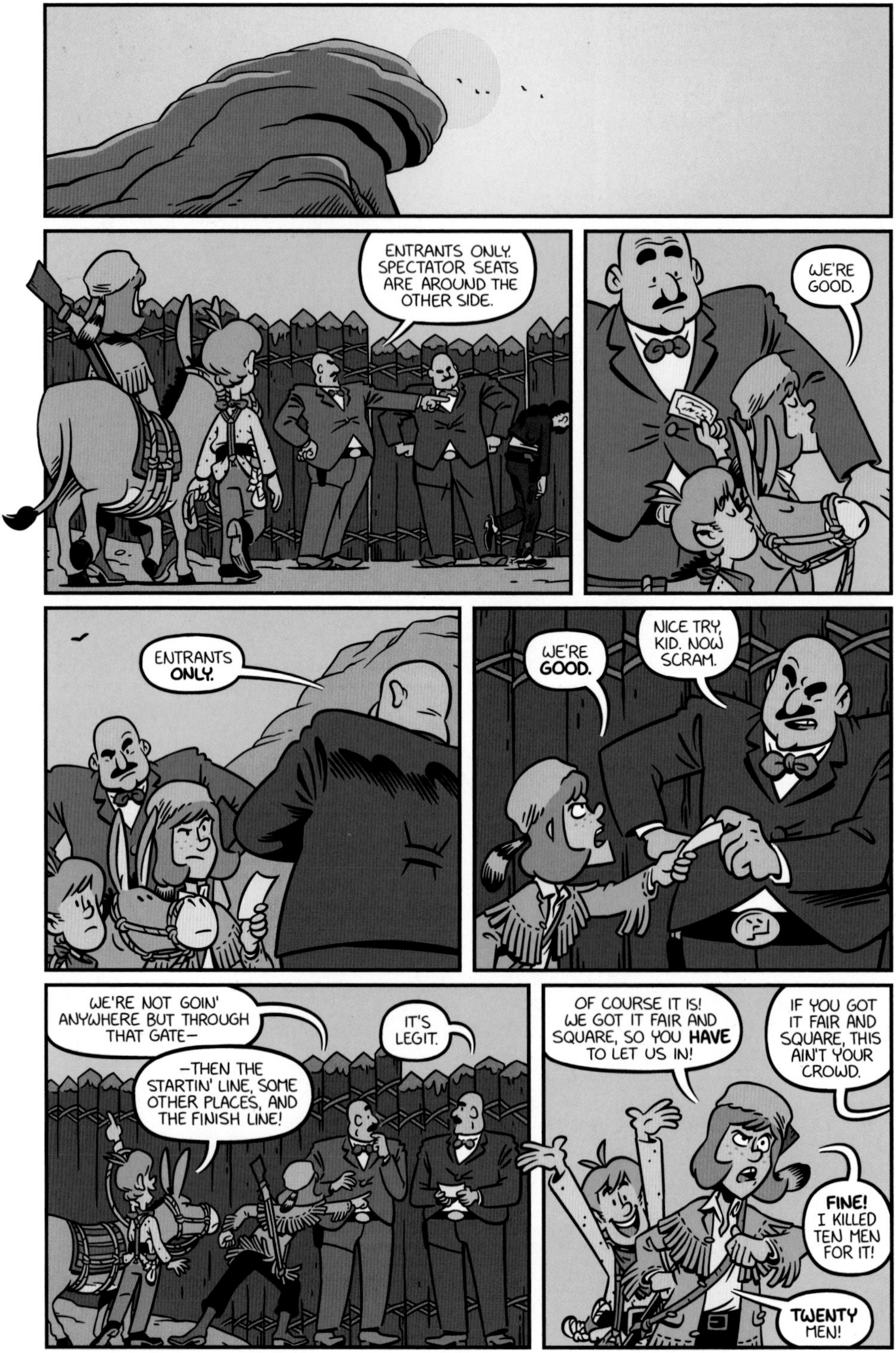
ENTRANTS ONLY. SPECTATOR SEATS ARE AROUND THE OTHER SIDE.
WE'RE GOOD.
ENTRANTS **ONLY.**
WE'RE **GOOD.**
NICE TRY, KID. NOW SCRAM.
WE'RE NOT GOIN' ANYWHERE BUT THROUGH THAT GATE—
—THEN THE STARTIN' LINE, SOME OTHER PLACES, AND THE FINISH LINE!
IT'S LEGIT.
OF COURSE IT IS! WE GOT IT FAIR AND SQUARE, SO YOU **HAVE** TO LET US IN!
IF YOU GOT IT FAIR AND SQUARE, THIS AIN'T YOUR CROWD.
FINE! I KILLED TEN MEN FOR IT!
TWENTY MEN!

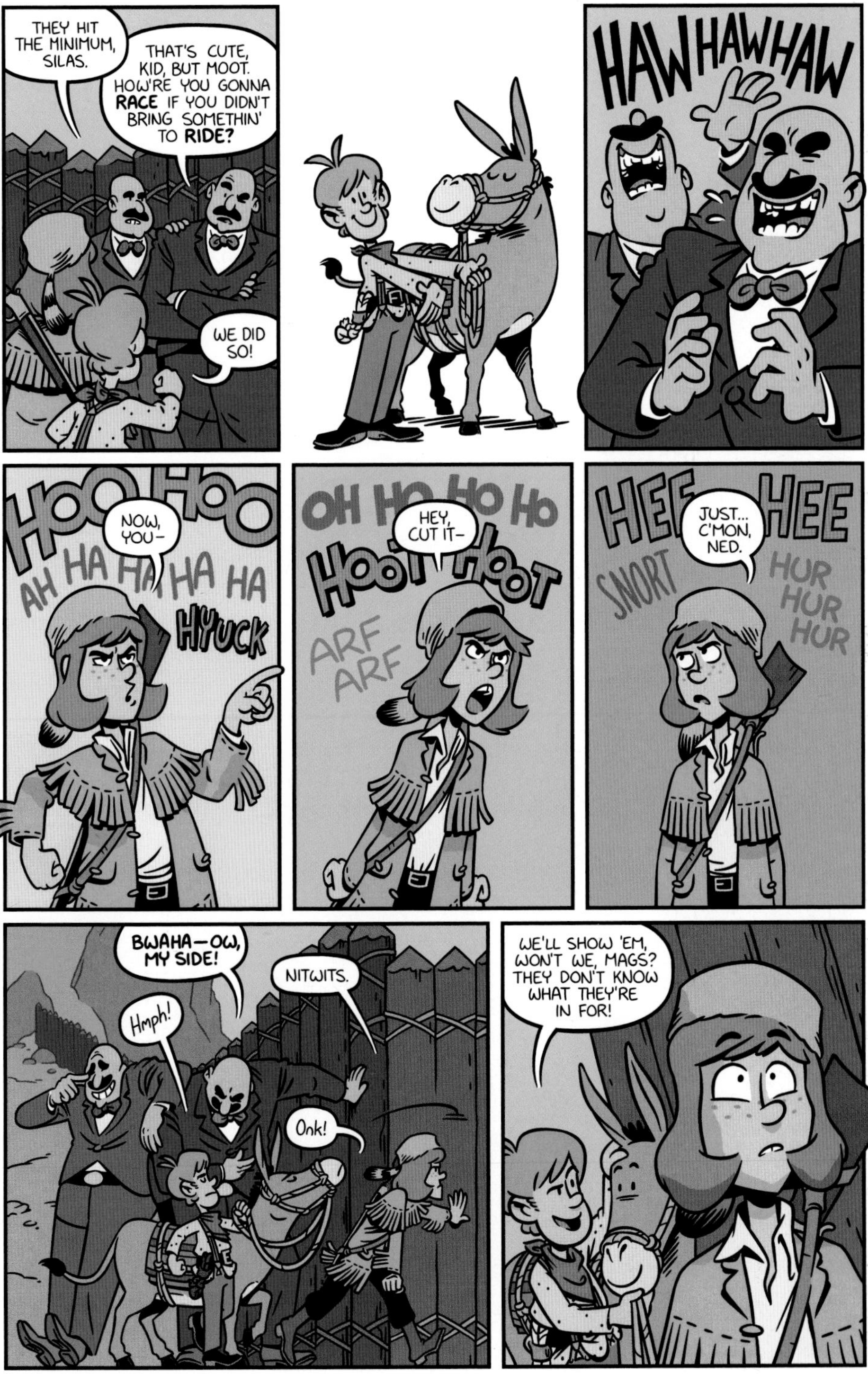
THEY HIT THE MINIMUM, SILAS.
THAT'S CUTE, KID, BUT MOOT. HOW'RE YOU GONNA **RACE** IF YOU DIDN'T BRING SOMETHIN' TO **RIDE?**
WE DID SO!
HAW HAW HAW HAW
HOO HOO
NOW, YOU—
AH HA HA HA HA
HYUCK
OH HO HO HO HO
HEY, CUT IT—
HOOT HOOT
ARF ARF
HEE HEE
JUST... C'MON, NED.
SNORT
HUR HUR HUR
BWAHA—OW, MY SIDE!
NITWITS.
Hmph!
Onk!
WE'LL SHOW 'EM, WON'T WE, MAGS? THEY DON'T KNOW WHAT THEY'RE IN FOR!

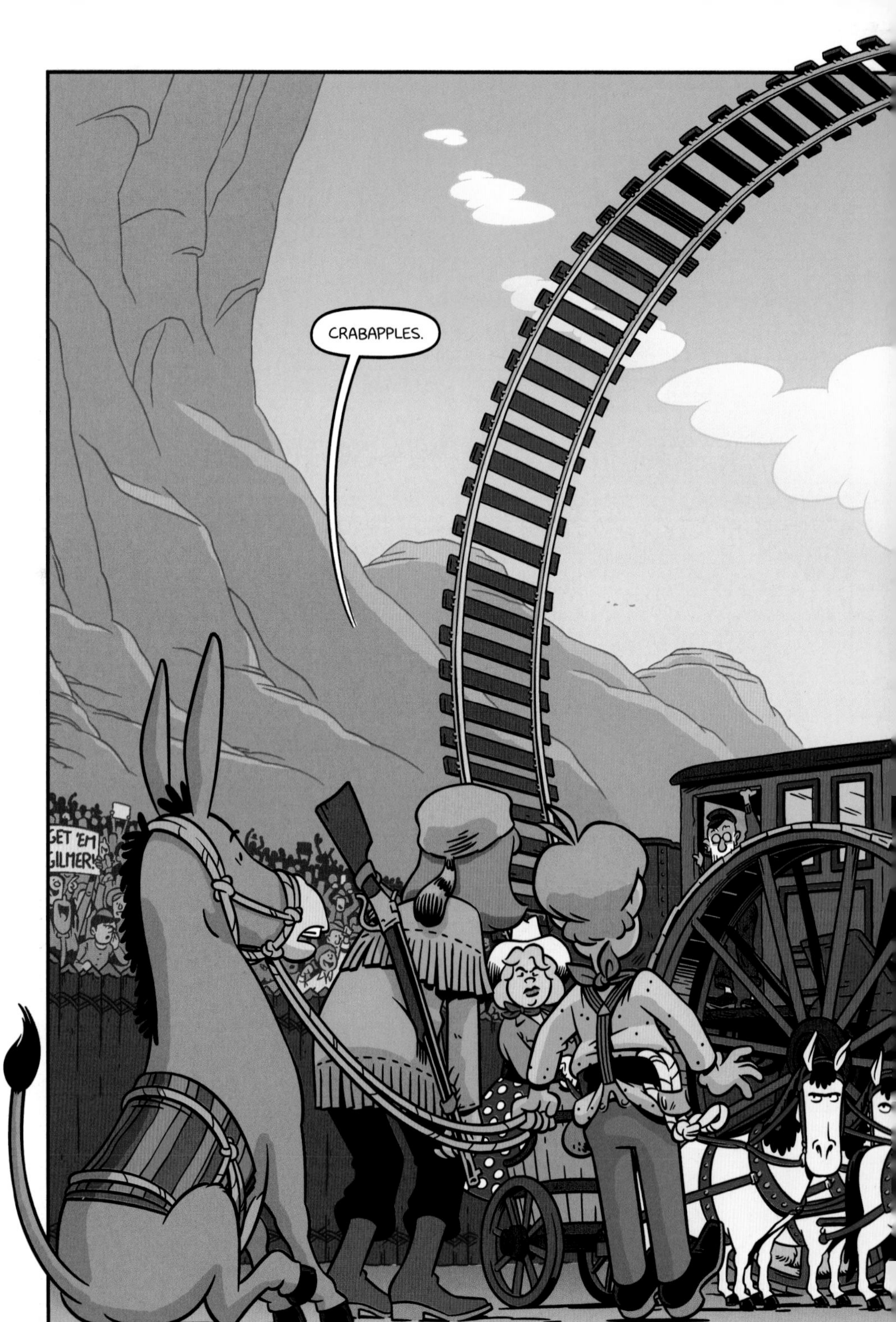
CRABAPPLES.
GET 'EM GILMER!

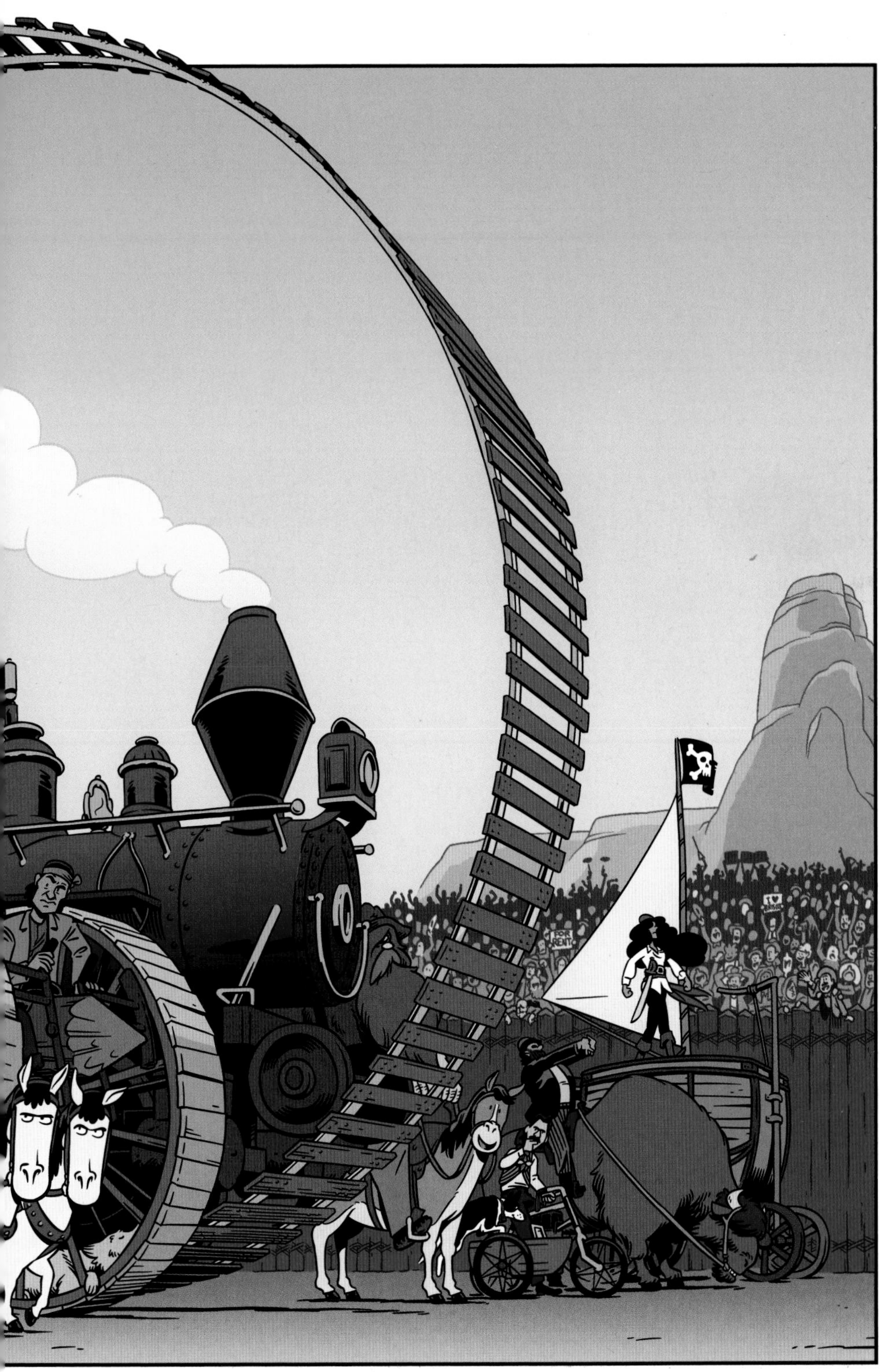
FOR RENT

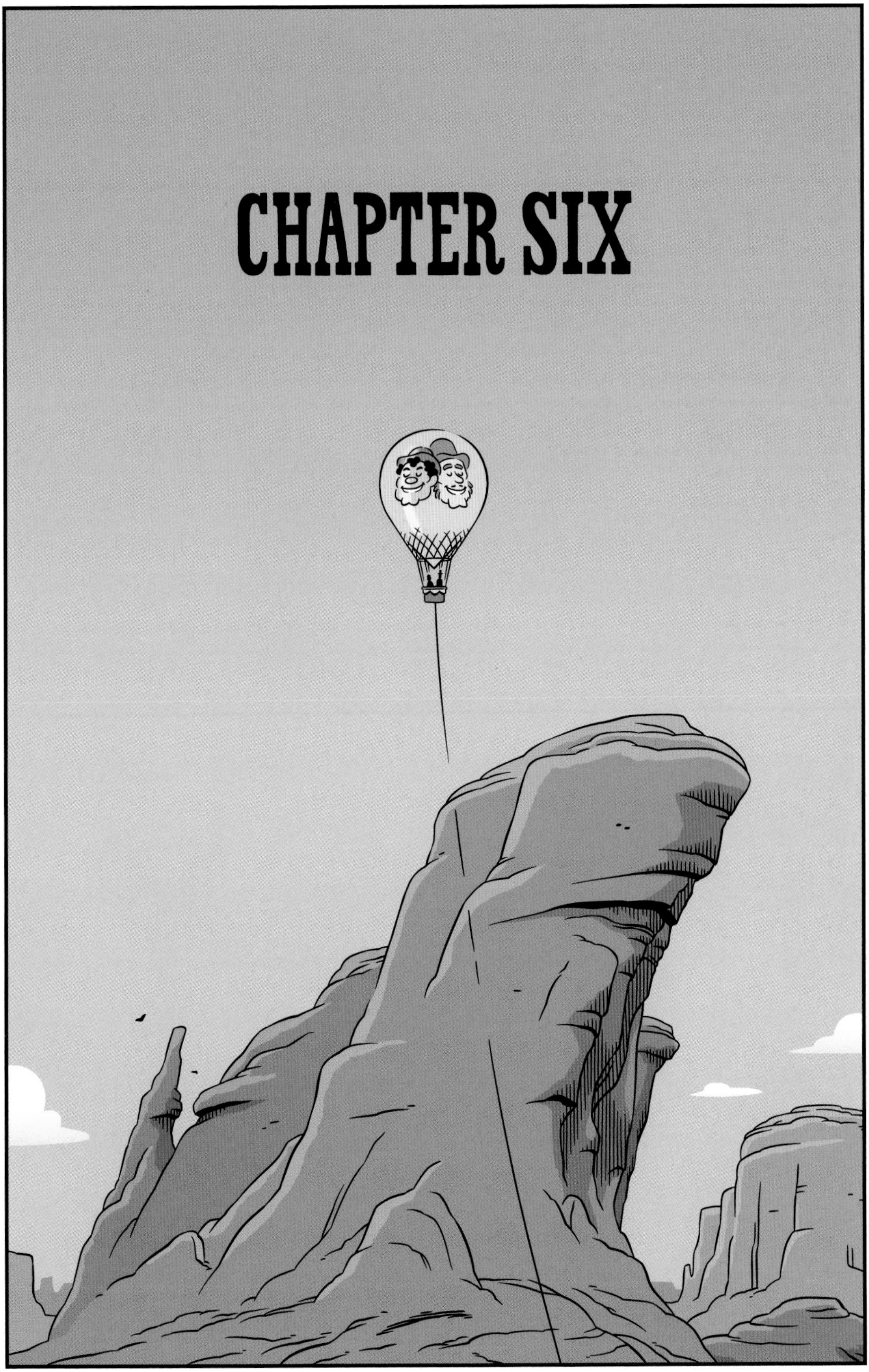
CHAPTER SIX

HELLOOOO RACE FANS!

I'M **CHIP DIPSON**—

—AND I'M **DIP DOPSON**, HERE COVERING THE FIRST **CROOKED BUTTE DIRTBAG DERBY!**

TELL US A LITTLE ABOUT THIS CONTEST, DIP!

WELL, CHIP, OUR ENTRANTS HAVE TRAVELED FROM FAR AND WIDE FOR THEIR CHANCE TO WIN A ONE-ON-ONE MEETING WITH THE NOTORIOUS **PA!**

CHIP + DIP

THE CRIMINAL KING OF THE WEST?!

THE VERY SAME! THOSE FAMILIAR WITH PA'S ORGANIZATION EXPECT HIM TO USE HIS CONSIDERABLE INFLUENCE TO GRANT A **BOON** TO WHOEVER WINS THE CHANCE TO ASK!

YOW! I KNOW WHAT I'M ASKING FOR—SOMEONE GIVE DIP A **BATH!**

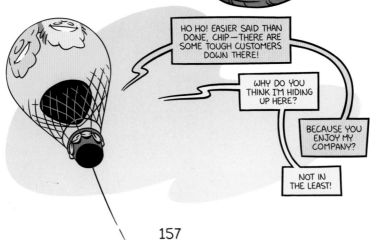

HO HO! EASIER SAID THAN DONE, CHIP—THERE ARE SOME TOUGH CUSTOMERS DOWN THERE!

WHY DO YOU THINK I'M HIDING UP HERE?

BECAUSE YOU ENJOY MY COMPANY?

NOT IN THE LEAST!

157

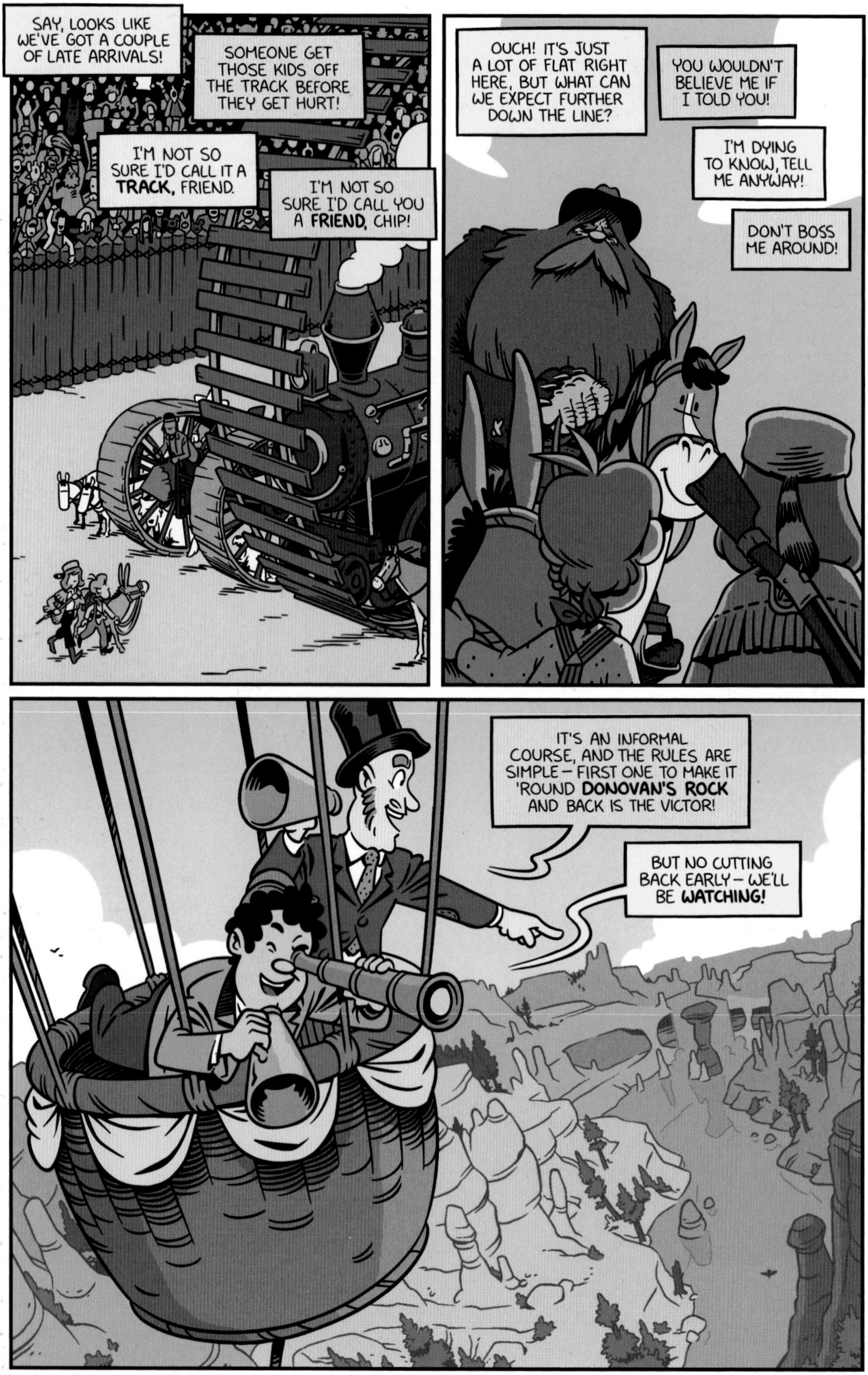
SAY, LOOKS LIKE WE'VE GOT A COUPLE OF LATE ARRIVALS!
SOMEONE GET THOSE KIDS OFF THE TRACK BEFORE THEY GET HURT!
I'M NOT SO SURE I'D CALL IT A **TRACK,** FRIEND.
I'M NOT SO SURE I'D CALL YOU A **FRIEND,** CHIP!
OUCH! IT'S JUST A LOT OF FLAT RIGHT HERE, BUT WHAT CAN WE EXPECT FURTHER DOWN THE LINE?
YOU WOULDN'T BELIEVE ME IF I TOLD YOU!
I'M DYING TO KNOW, TELL ME ANYWAY!
DON'T BOSS ME AROUND!
IT'S AN INFORMAL COURSE, AND THE RULES ARE SIMPLE – FIRST ONE TO MAKE IT 'ROUND **DONOVAN'S ROCK** AND BACK IS THE VICTOR!
BUT NO CUTTING BACK EARLY – WE'LL BE **WATCHING!**

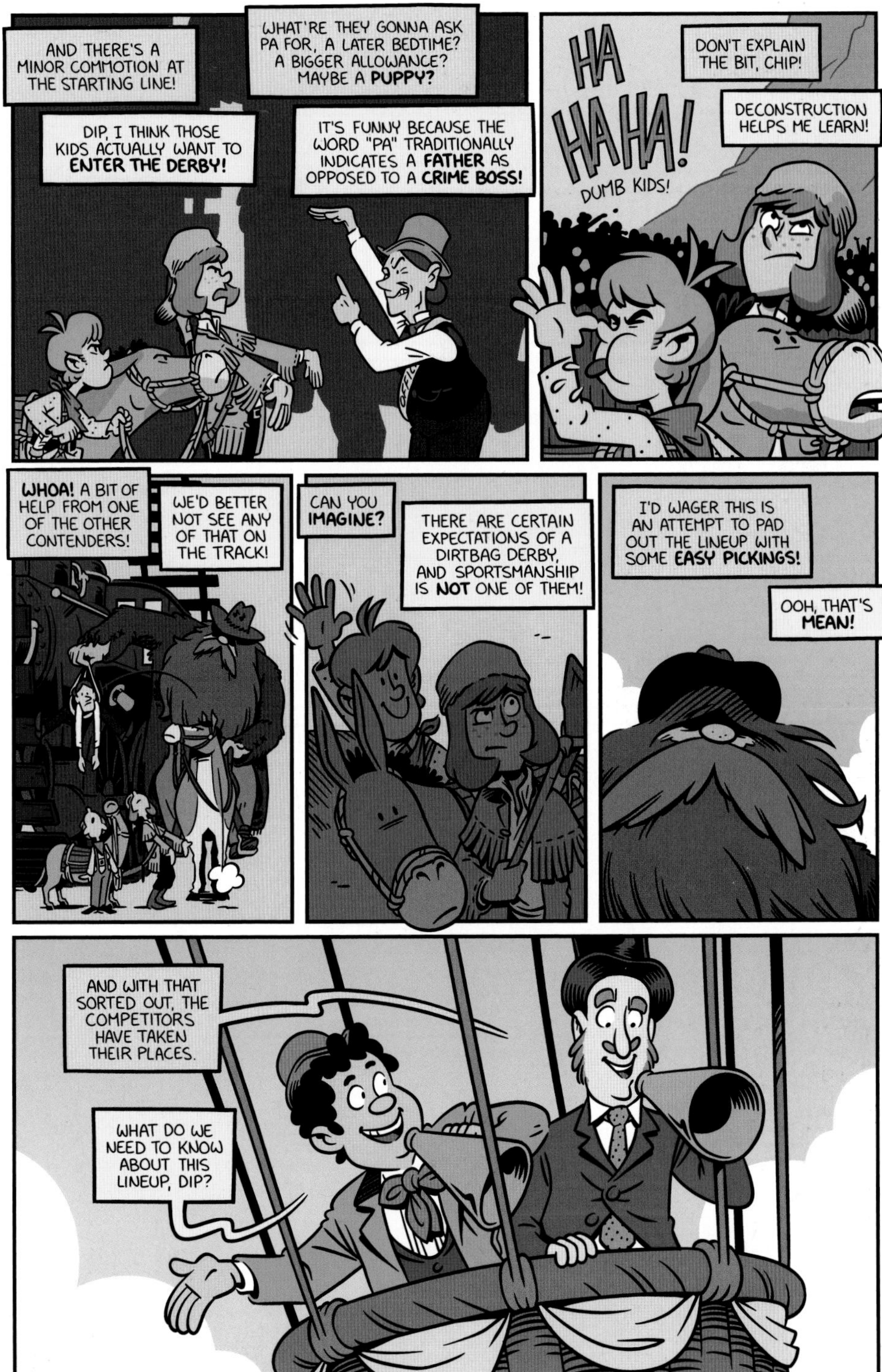
AND THERE'S A MINOR COMMOTION AT THE STARTING LINE!
WHAT'RE THEY GONNA ASK PA FOR, A LATER BEDTIME? A BIGGER ALLOWANCE? MAYBE A **PUPPY?**
DIP, I THINK THOSE KIDS ACTUALLY WANT TO **ENTER THE DERBY!**
IT'S FUNNY BECAUSE THE WORD "PA" TRADITIONALLY INDICATES A **FATHER** AS OPPOSED TO A **CRIME BOSS!**
HA HAHA!
DUMB KIDS!
DON'T EXPLAIN THE BIT, CHIP!
DECONSTRUCTION HELPS ME LEARN!
WHOA! A BIT OF HELP FROM ONE OF THE OTHER CONTENDERS!
WE'D BETTER NOT SEE ANY OF THAT ON THE TRACK!
CAN YOU **IMAGINE?**
THERE ARE CERTAIN EXPECTATIONS OF A DIRTBAG DERBY, AND SPORTSMANSHIP IS **NOT** ONE OF THEM!
I'D WAGER THIS IS AN ATTEMPT TO PAD OUT THE LINEUP WITH SOME **EASY PICKINGS!**
OOH, THAT'S **MEAN!**
AND WITH THAT SORTED OUT, THE COMPETITORS HAVE TAKEN THEIR PLACES.
WHAT DO WE NEED TO KNOW ABOUT THIS LINEUP, DIP?

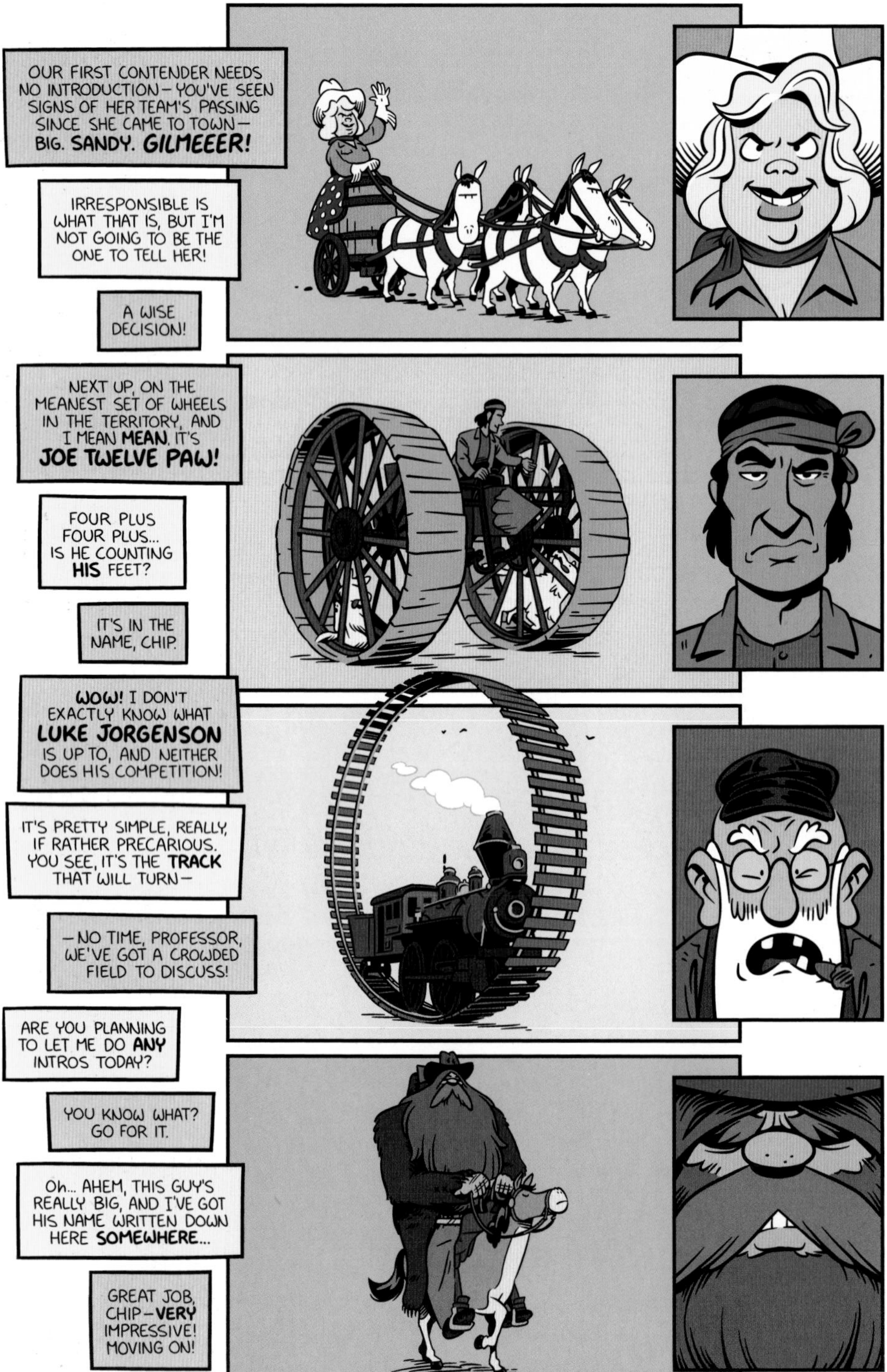
OUR FIRST CONTENDER NEEDS NO INTRODUCTION—YOU'VE SEEN SIGNS OF HER TEAM'S PASSING SINCE SHE CAME TO TOWN—BIG. SANDY. GILMEEER!
IRRESPONSIBLE IS WHAT THAT IS, BUT I'M NOT GOING TO BE THE ONE TO TELL HER!
A WISE DECISION!
NEXT UP, ON THE MEANEST SET OF WHEELS IN THE TERRITORY, AND I MEAN MEAN, IT'S JOE TWELVE PAW!
FOUR PLUS FOUR PLUS... IS HE COUNTING HIS FEET?
IT'S IN THE NAME, CHIP.
WOW! I DON'T EXACTLY KNOW WHAT LUKE JORGENSON IS UP TO, AND NEITHER DOES HIS COMPETITION!
IT'S PRETTY SIMPLE, REALLY, IF RATHER PRECARIOUS. YOU SEE, IT'S THE TRACK THAT WILL TURN—
—NO TIME, PROFESSOR, WE'VE GOT A CROWDED FIELD TO DISCUSS!
ARE YOU PLANNING TO LET ME DO ANY INTROS TODAY?
YOU KNOW WHAT? GO FOR IT.
Oh... AHEM, THIS GUY'S REALLY BIG, AND I'VE GOT HIS NAME WRITTEN DOWN HERE SOMEWHERE...
GREAT JOB, CHIP—VERY IMPRESSIVE! MOVING ON!

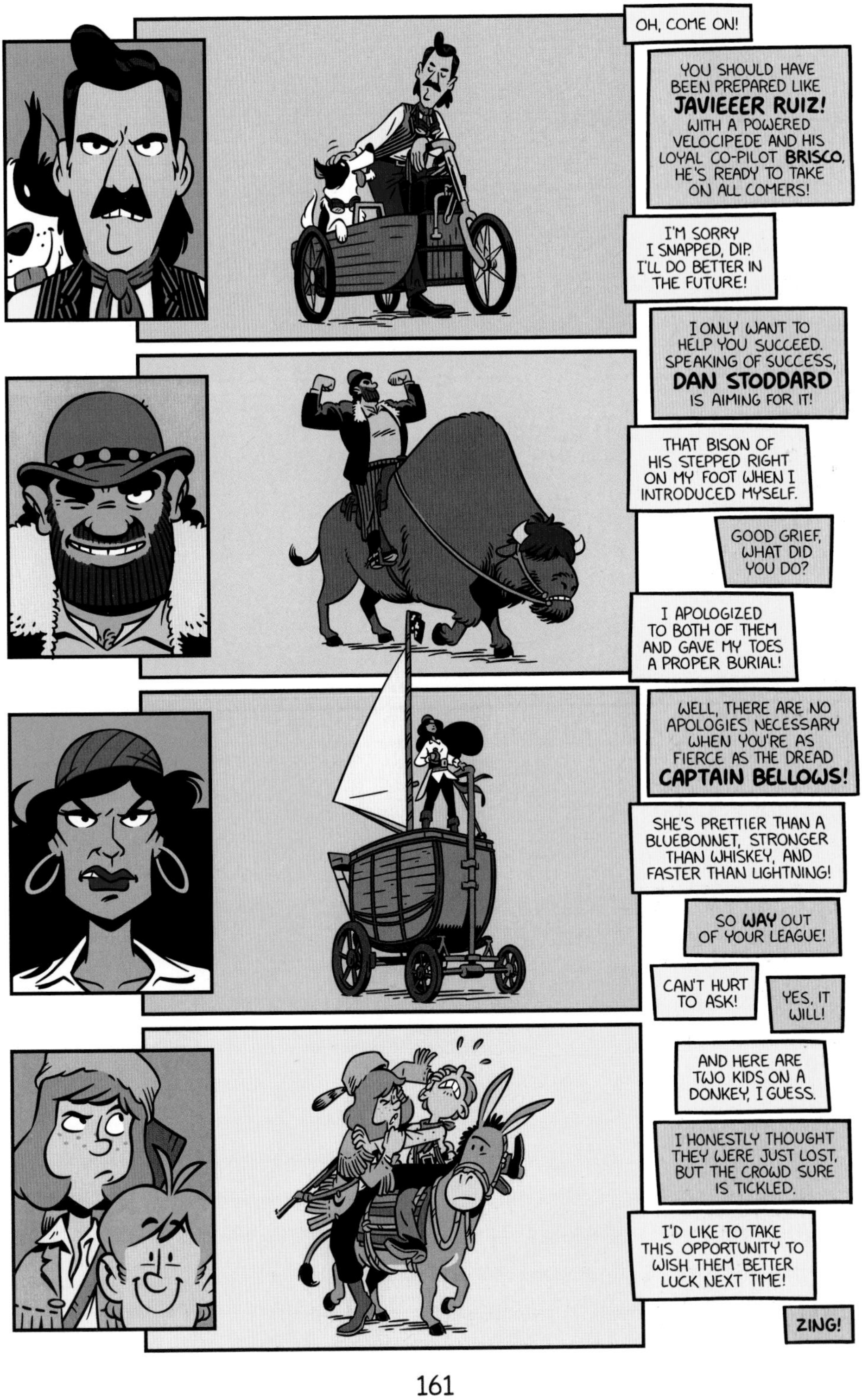

OH, COME ON!
YOU SHOULD HAVE BEEN PREPARED LIKE JAVIEEER RUIZ! WITH A POWERED VELOCIPEDE AND HIS LOYAL CO-PILOT BRISCO, HE'S READY TO TAKE ON ALL COMERS!
I'M SORRY I SNAPPED, DIP. I'LL DO BETTER IN THE FUTURE!
I ONLY WANT TO HELP YOU SUCCEED. SPEAKING OF SUCCESS, DAN STODDARD IS AIMING FOR IT!
THAT BISON OF HIS STEPPED RIGHT ON MY FOOT WHEN I INTRODUCED MYSELF.
GOOD GRIEF, WHAT DID YOU DO?
I APOLOGIZED TO BOTH OF THEM AND GAVE MY TOES A PROPER BURIAL!
WELL, THERE ARE NO APOLOGIES NECESSARY WHEN YOU'RE AS FIERCE AS THE DREAD CAPTAIN BELLOWS!
SHE'S PRETTIER THAN A BLUEBONNET, STRONGER THAN WHISKEY, AND FASTER THAN LIGHTNING!
SO WAY OUT OF YOUR LEAGUE!
CAN'T HURT TO ASK!
YES, IT WILL!
AND HERE ARE TWO KIDS ON A DONKEY, I GUESS.
I HONESTLY THOUGHT THEY WERE JUST LOST, BUT THE CROWD SURE IS TICKLED.
I'D LIKE TO TAKE THIS OPPORTUNITY TO WISH THEM BETTER LUCK NEXT TIME!
ZING!

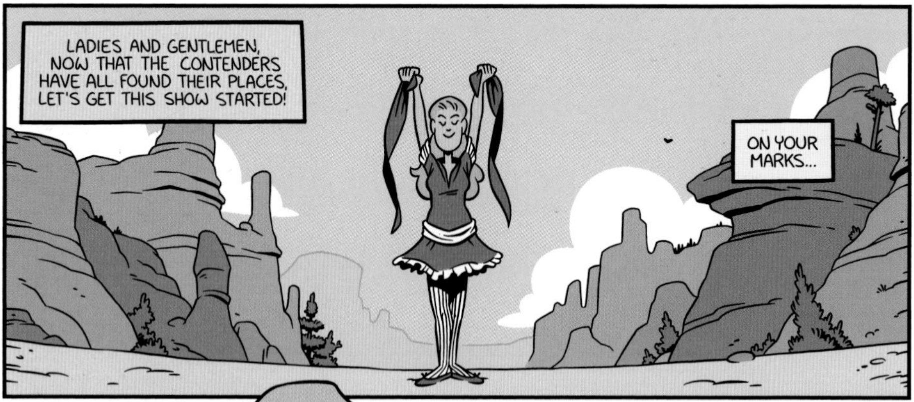
LADIES AND GENTLEMEN, NOW THAT THE CONTENDERS HAVE ALL FOUND THEIR PLACES, LET'S GET THIS SHOW STARTED!
ON YOUR MARKS...

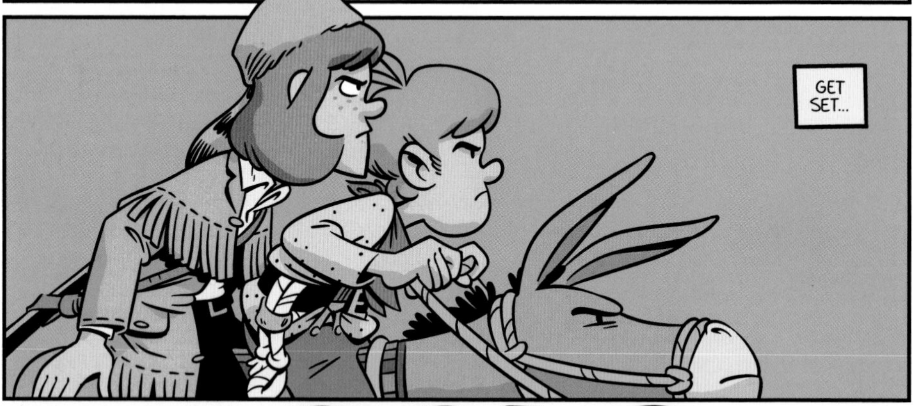
GET SET...

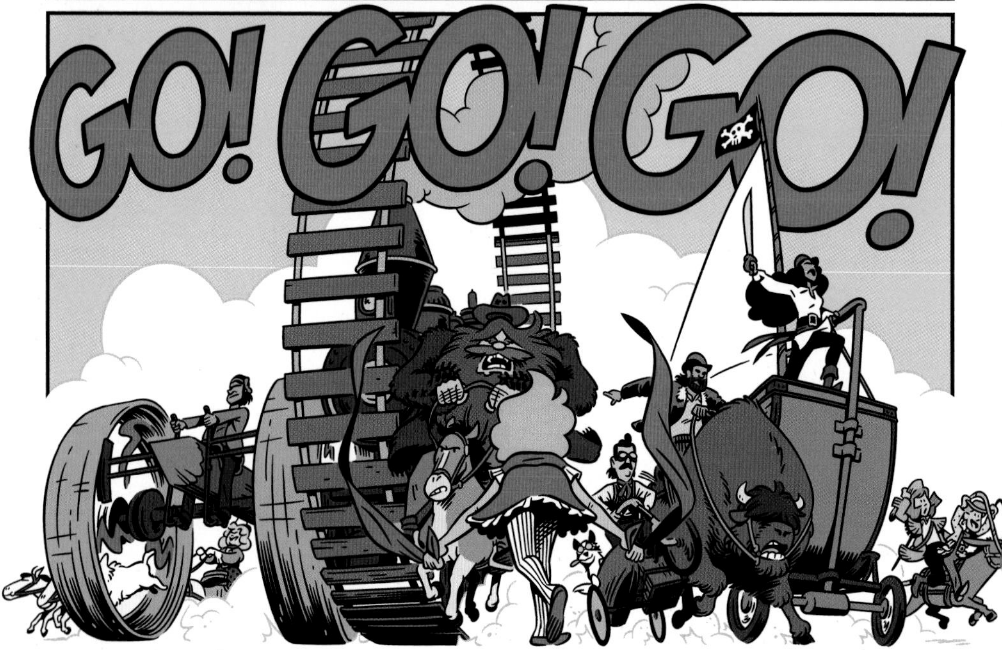
GO! GO! GO!

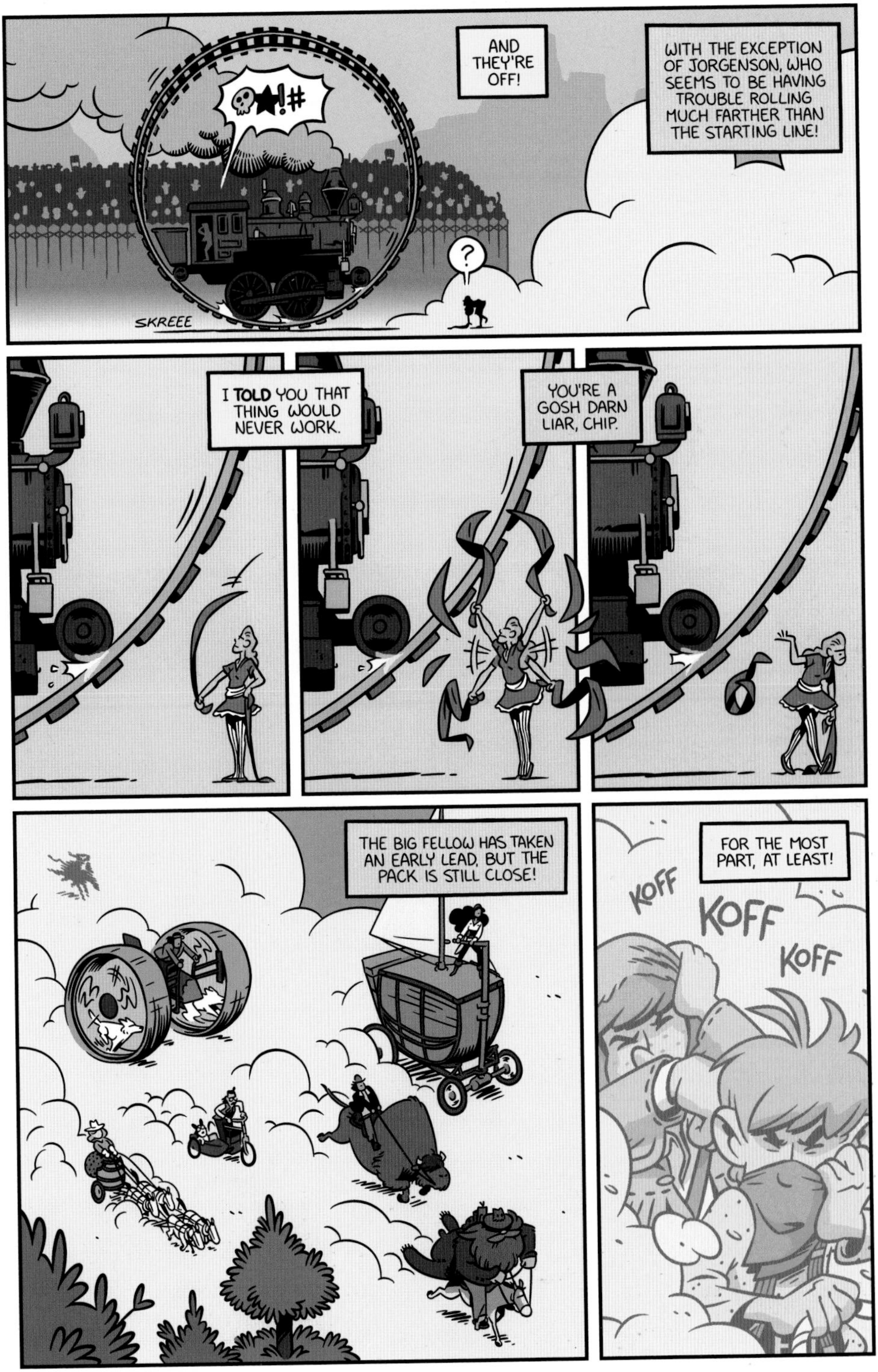

AND THEY'RE OFF!
WITH THE EXCEPTION OF JORGENSON, WHO SEEMS TO BE HAVING TROUBLE ROLLING MUCH FARTHER THAN THE STARTING LINE!
?
SKREEE
I **TOLD** YOU THAT THING WOULD NEVER WORK.
YOU'RE A GOSH DARN LIAR, CHIP.
THE BIG FELLOW HAS TAKEN AN EARLY LEAD, BUT THE PACK IS STILL CLOSE!
FOR THE MOST PART, AT LEAST!
KOFF
KOFF
KOFF

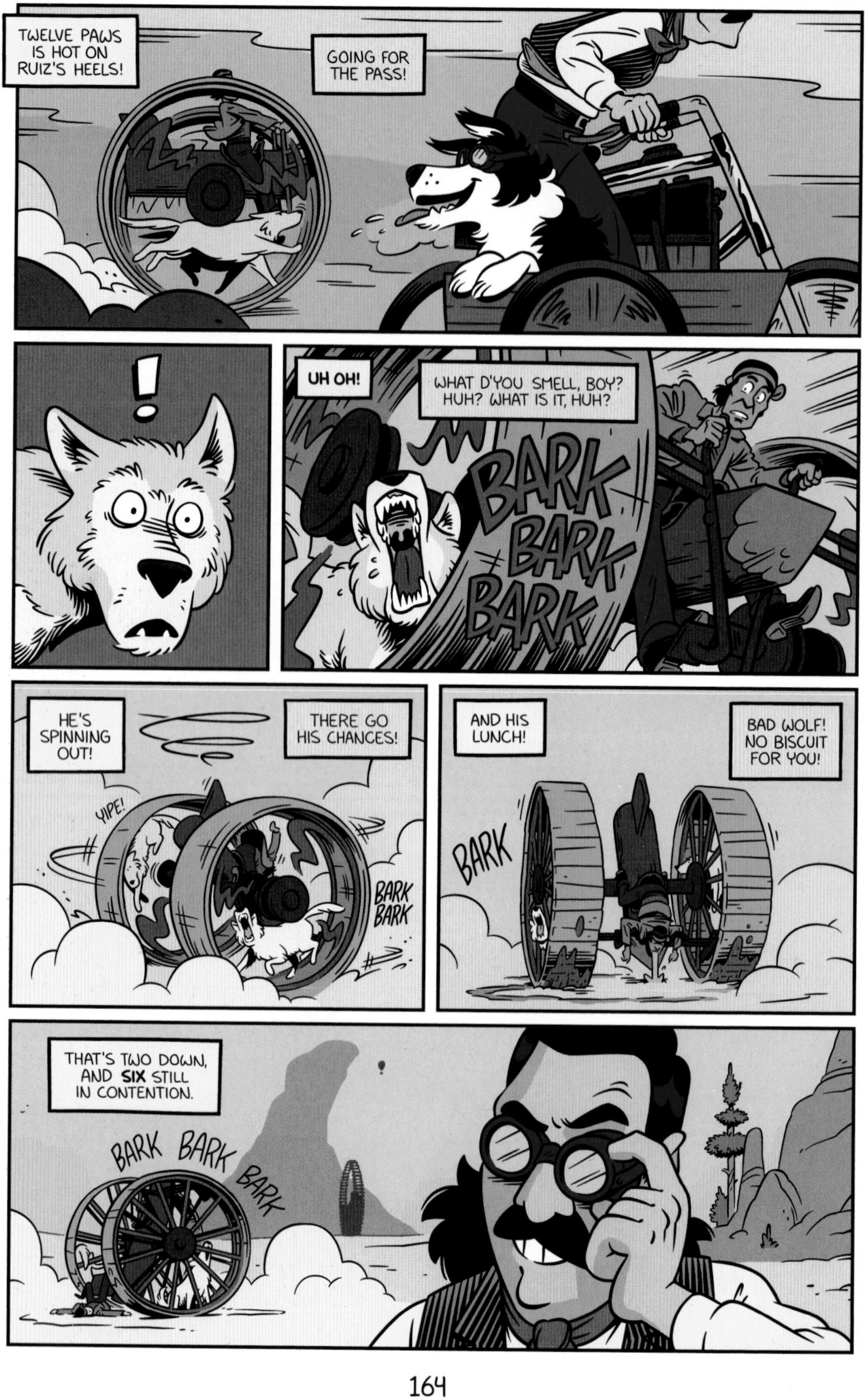
TWELVE PAWS IS HOT ON RUIZ'S HEELS!
GOING FOR THE PASS!
!
UH OH!
WHAT D'YOU SMELL, BOY? HUH? WHAT IS IT, HUH?
BARK BARK BARK
HE'S SPINNING OUT!
THERE GO HIS CHANCES!
YIPE!
BARK BARK
AND HIS LUNCH!
BAD WOLF! NO BISCUIT FOR YOU!
BARK
THAT'S TWO DOWN, AND **SIX** STILL IN CONTENTION.
BARK BARK BARK

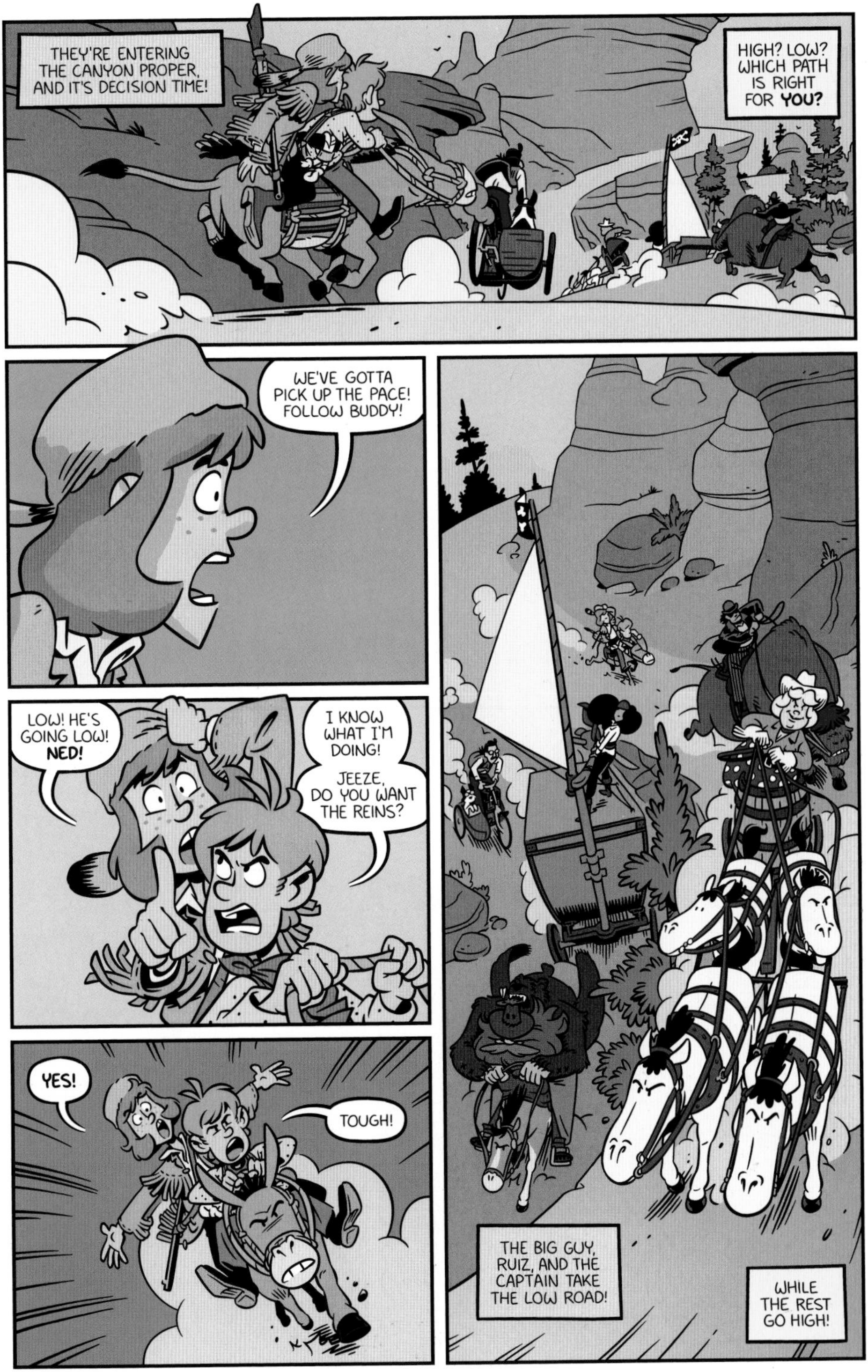
THEY'RE ENTERING THE CANYON PROPER, AND IT'S DECISION TIME!
HIGH? LOW? WHICH PATH IS RIGHT FOR **YOU?**
WE'VE GOTTA PICK UP THE PACE! FOLLOW BUDDY!
LOW! HE'S GOING LOW! **NED!**
I KNOW WHAT I'M DOING!
JEEZE, DO YOU WANT THE REINS?
YES!
TOUGH!
THE BIG GUY, RUIZ, AND THE CAPTAIN TAKE THE LOW ROAD!
WHILE THE REST GO HIGH!

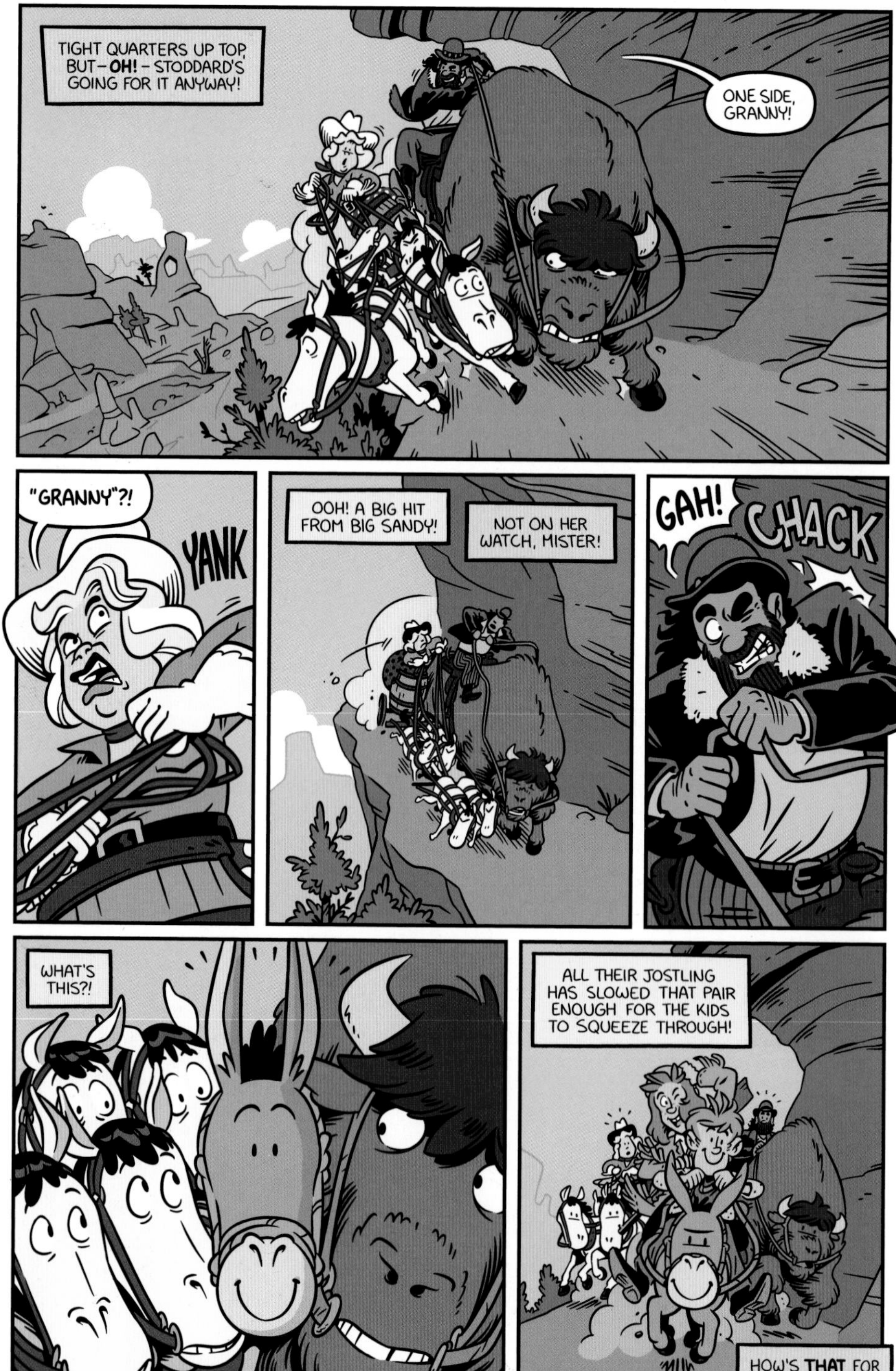
TIGHT QUARTERS UP TOP, BUT—**OH!**—STODDARD'S GOING FOR IT ANYWAY!
ONE SIDE, GRANNY!
"GRANNY"?!
YANK
OOH! A BIG HIT FROM BIG SANDY!
NOT ON HER WATCH, MISTER!
GAH!
CHACK
WHAT'S THIS?!
ALL THEIR JOSTLING HAS SLOWED THAT PAIR ENOUGH FOR THE KIDS TO SQUEEZE THROUGH!
HOW'S **THAT** FOR EMBARRASSING?

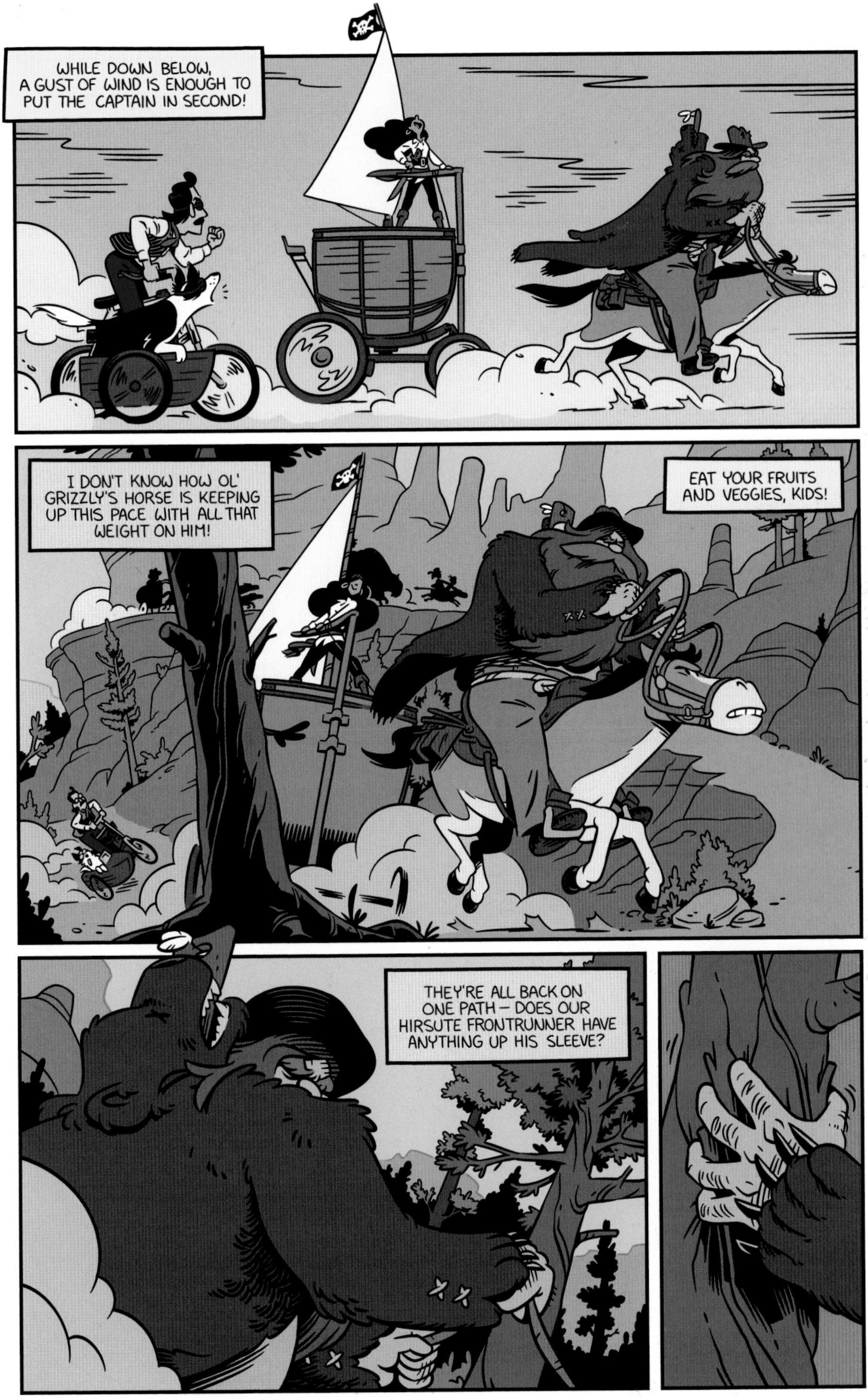
WHILE DOWN BELOW, A GUST OF WIND IS ENOUGH TO PUT THE CAPTAIN IN SECOND!
I DON'T KNOW HOW OL' GRIZZLY'S HORSE IS KEEPING UP THIS PACE WITH ALL THAT WEIGHT ON HIM!
EAT YOUR FRUITS AND VEGGIES, KIDS!
THEY'RE ALL BACK ON ONE PATH — DOES OUR HIRSUTE FRONTRUNNER HAVE ANYTHING UP HIS SLEEVE?

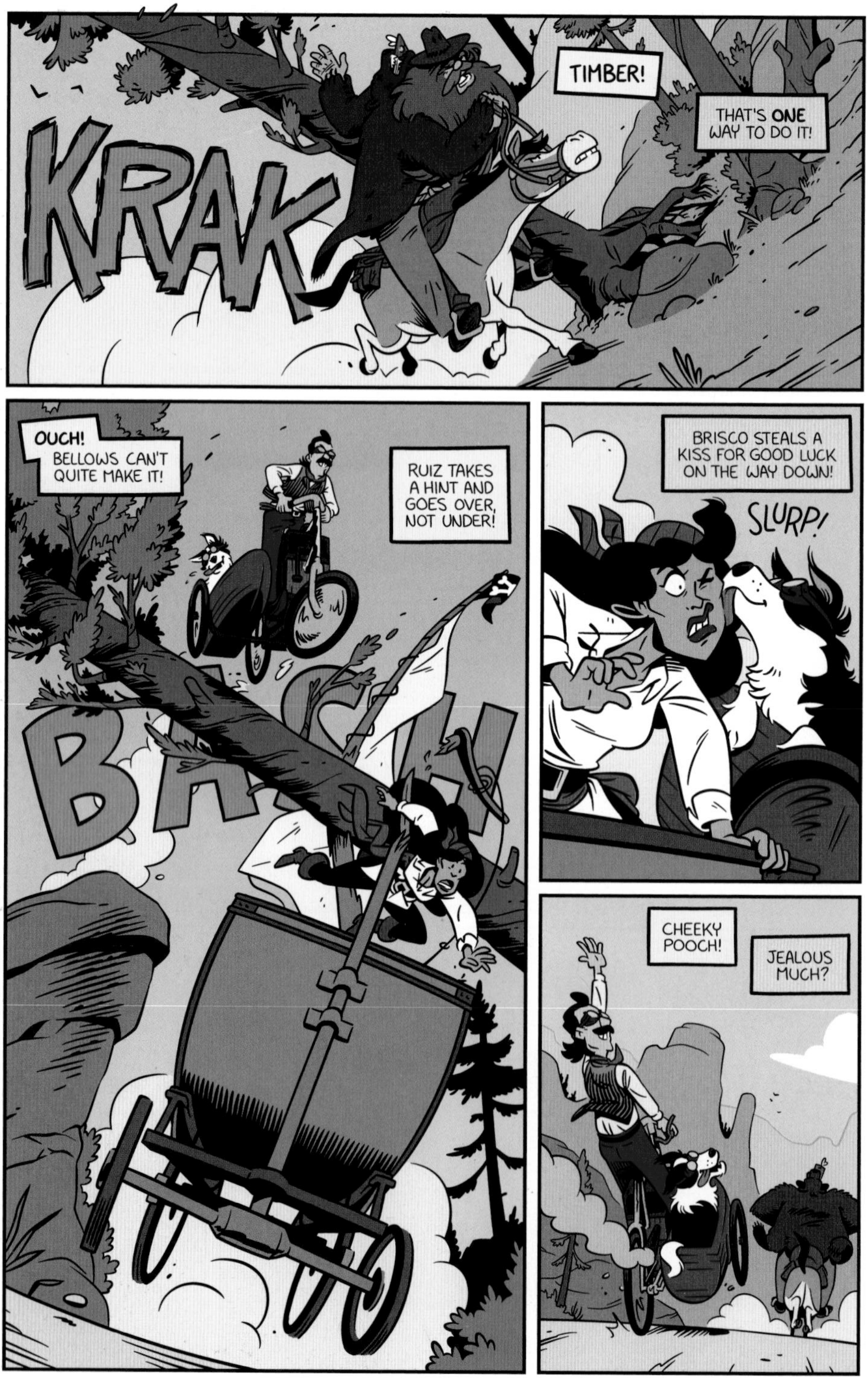
KRAK
TIMBER!
THAT'S **ONE** WAY TO DO IT!
OUCH!
BELLOWS CAN'T QUITE MAKE IT!
RUIZ TAKES A HINT AND GOES OVER, NOT UNDER!
BRISCO STEALS A KISS FOR GOOD LUCK ON THE WAY DOWN!
SLURP!
CHEEKY POOCH!
JEALOUS MUCH?

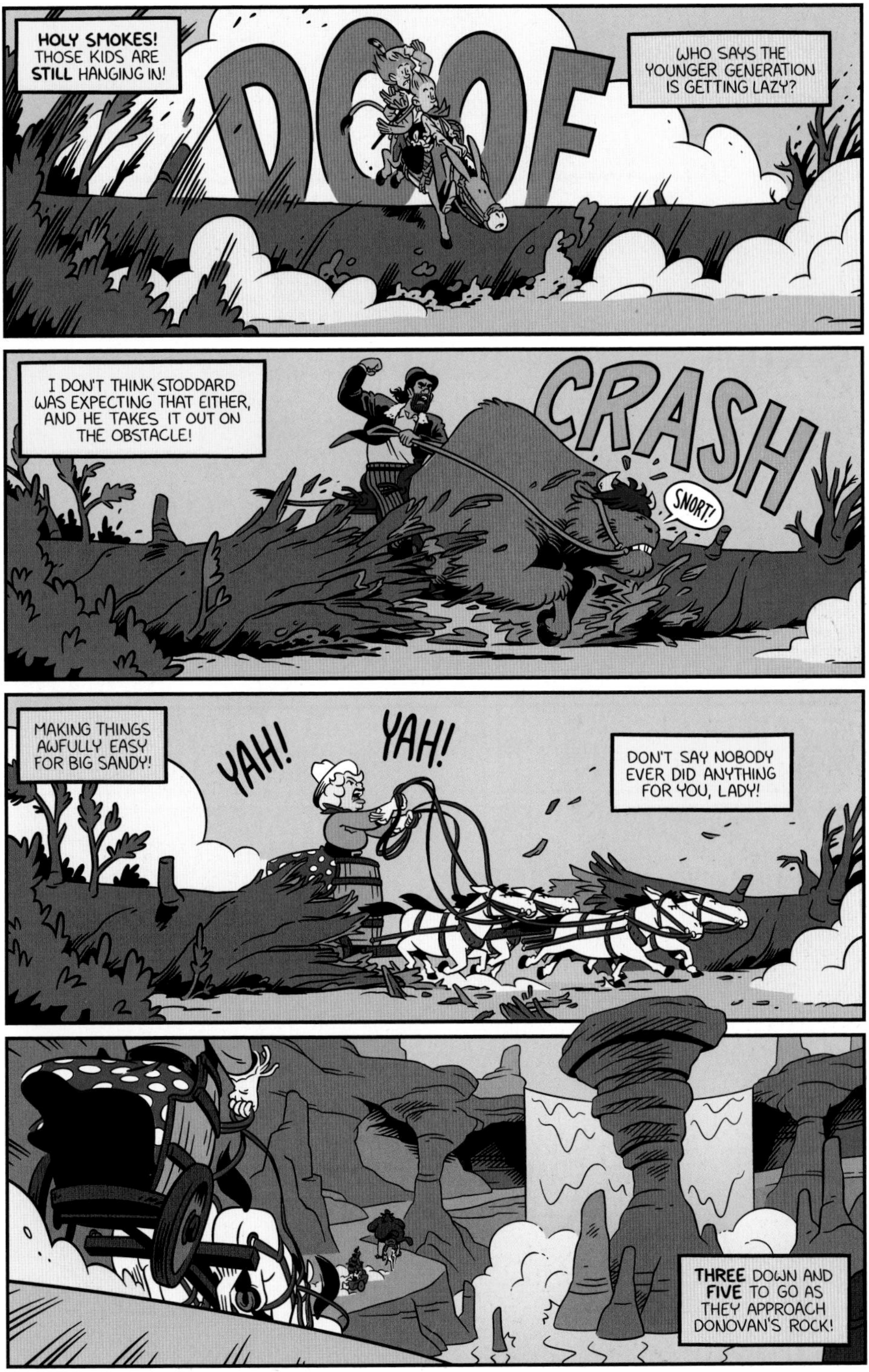
HOLY SMOKES! THOSE KIDS ARE STILL HANGING IN!
DOOF
WHO SAYS THE YOUNGER GENERATION IS GETTING LAZY?
I DON'T THINK STODDARD WAS EXPECTING THAT EITHER, AND HE TAKES IT OUT ON THE OBSTACLE!
CRASH
SNORT!
MAKING THINGS AWFULLY EASY FOR BIG SANDY!
YAH!
YAH!
DON'T SAY NOBODY EVER DID ANYTHING FOR YOU, LADY!
THREE DOWN AND FIVE TO GO AS THEY APPROACH DONOVAN'S ROCK!

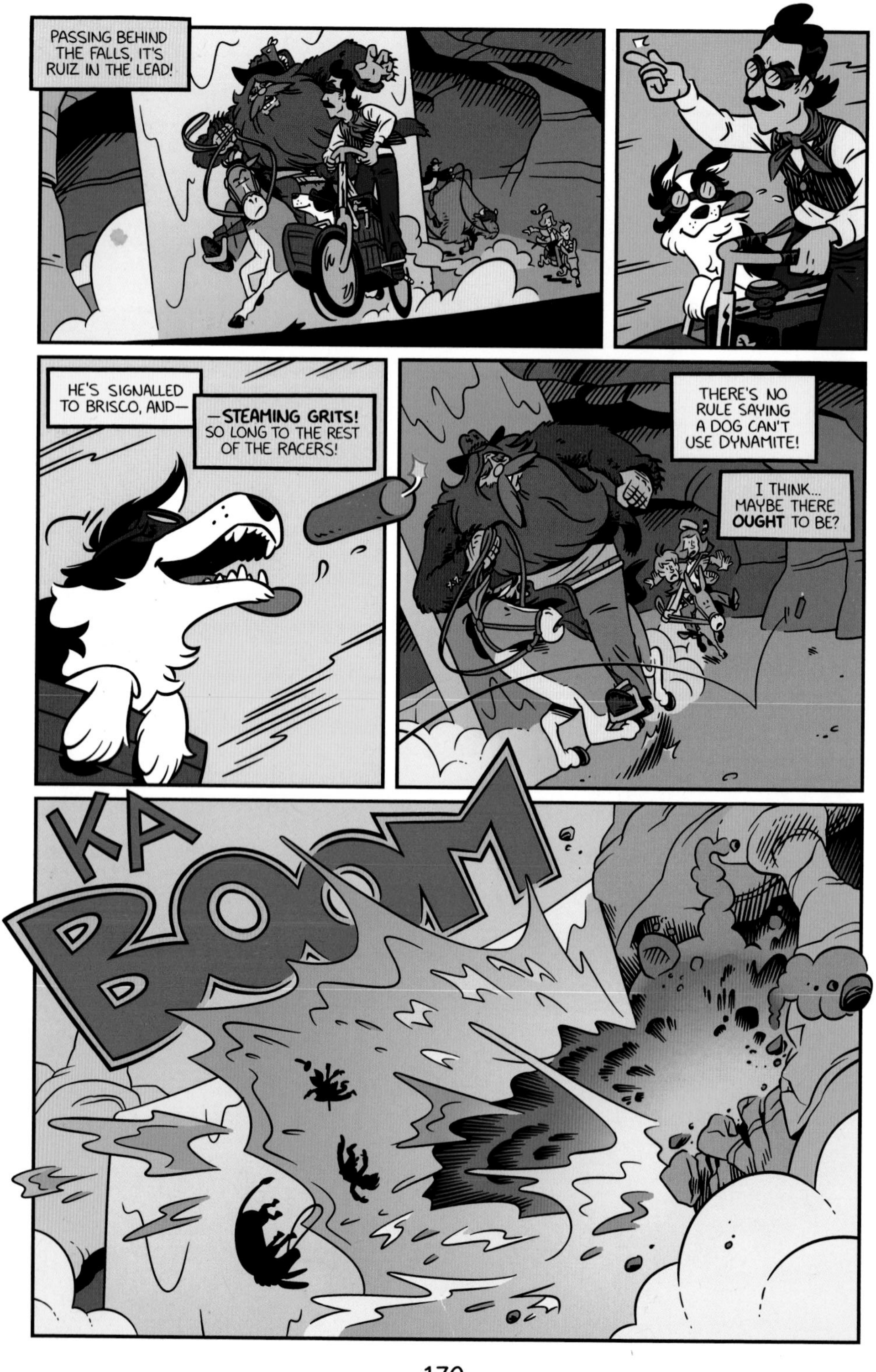
PASSING BEHIND THE FALLS, IT'S RUIZ IN THE LEAD!
HE'S SIGNALLED TO BRISCO, AND—
—STEAMING GRITS! SO LONG TO THE REST OF THE RACERS!
THERE'S NO RULE SAYING A DOG CAN'T USE DYNAMITE!
I THINK... MAYBE THERE OUGHT TO BE?
KA BOOM

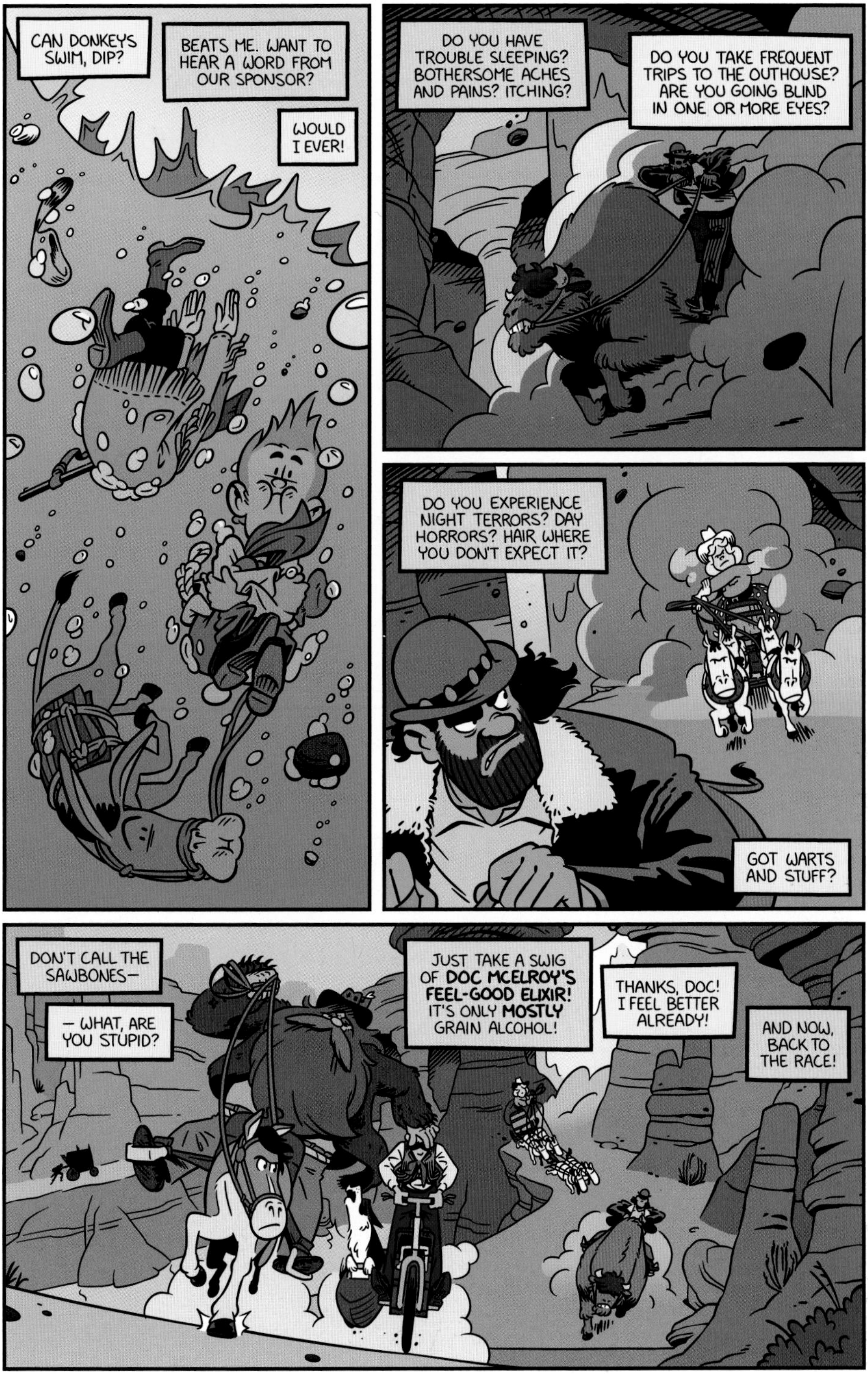
CAN DONKEYS SWIM, DIP?
BEATS ME. WANT TO HEAR A WORD FROM OUR SPONSOR?
WOULD I EVER!
DO YOU HAVE TROUBLE SLEEPING? BOTHERSOME ACHES AND PAINS? ITCHING?
DO YOU TAKE FREQUENT TRIPS TO THE OUTHOUSE? ARE YOU GOING BLIND IN ONE OR MORE EYES?
DO YOU EXPERIENCE NIGHT TERRORS? DAY HORRORS? HAIR WHERE YOU DON'T EXPECT IT?
GOT WARTS AND STUFF?
DON'T CALL THE SAWBONES—
— WHAT, ARE YOU STUPID?
JUST TAKE A SWIG OF **DOC MCELROY'S FEEL-GOOD ELIXIR!** IT'S ONLY **MOSTLY** GRAIN ALCOHOL!
THANKS, DOC! I FEEL BETTER ALREADY!
AND NOW, BACK TO THE RACE!

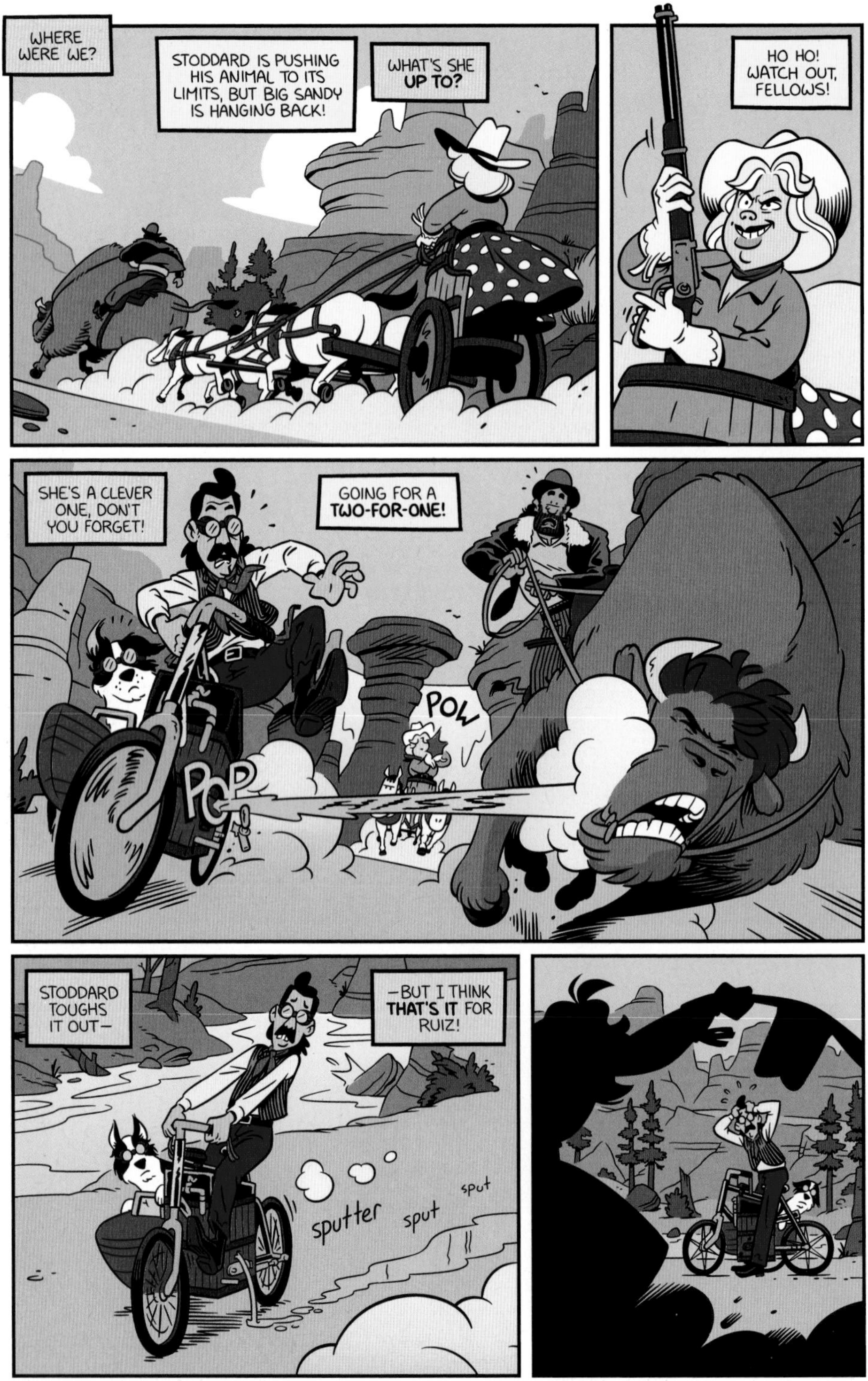
WHERE WERE WE?
STODDARD IS PUSHING HIS ANIMAL TO ITS LIMITS, BUT BIG SANDY IS HANGING BACK!
WHAT'S SHE **UP TO?**
HO HO! WATCH OUT, FELLOWS!
SHE'S A CLEVER ONE, DON'T YOU FORGET!
GOING FOR A **TWO-FOR-ONE!**
POW
POP
STODDARD TOUGHS IT OUT—
—BUT I THINK **THAT'S IT** FOR RUIZ!
sputter
sput
sput

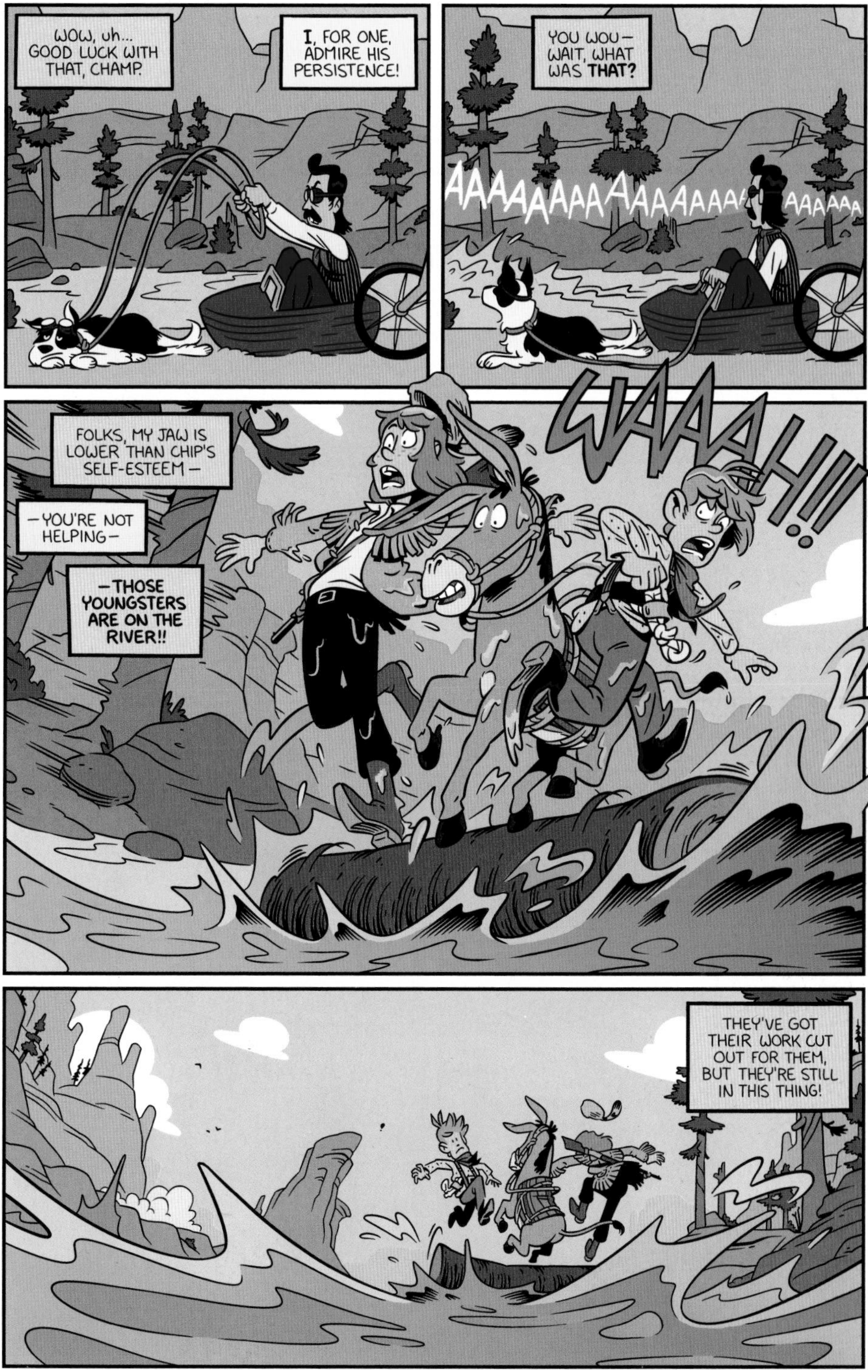
WOW, uh... GOOD LUCK WITH THAT, CHAMP.
I, FOR ONE, ADMIRE HIS PERSISTENCE!
YOU WOU— WAIT, WHAT WAS THAT?
AAAAAAAAAAAAAAAAAAAAA
WAAAAH!!!
FOLKS, MY JAW IS LOWER THAN CHIP'S SELF-ESTEEM—
—YOU'RE NOT HELPING—
—THOSE YOUNGSTERS ARE ON THE RIVER!!
THEY'VE GOT THEIR WORK CUT OUT FOR THEM, BUT THEY'RE STILL IN THIS THING!

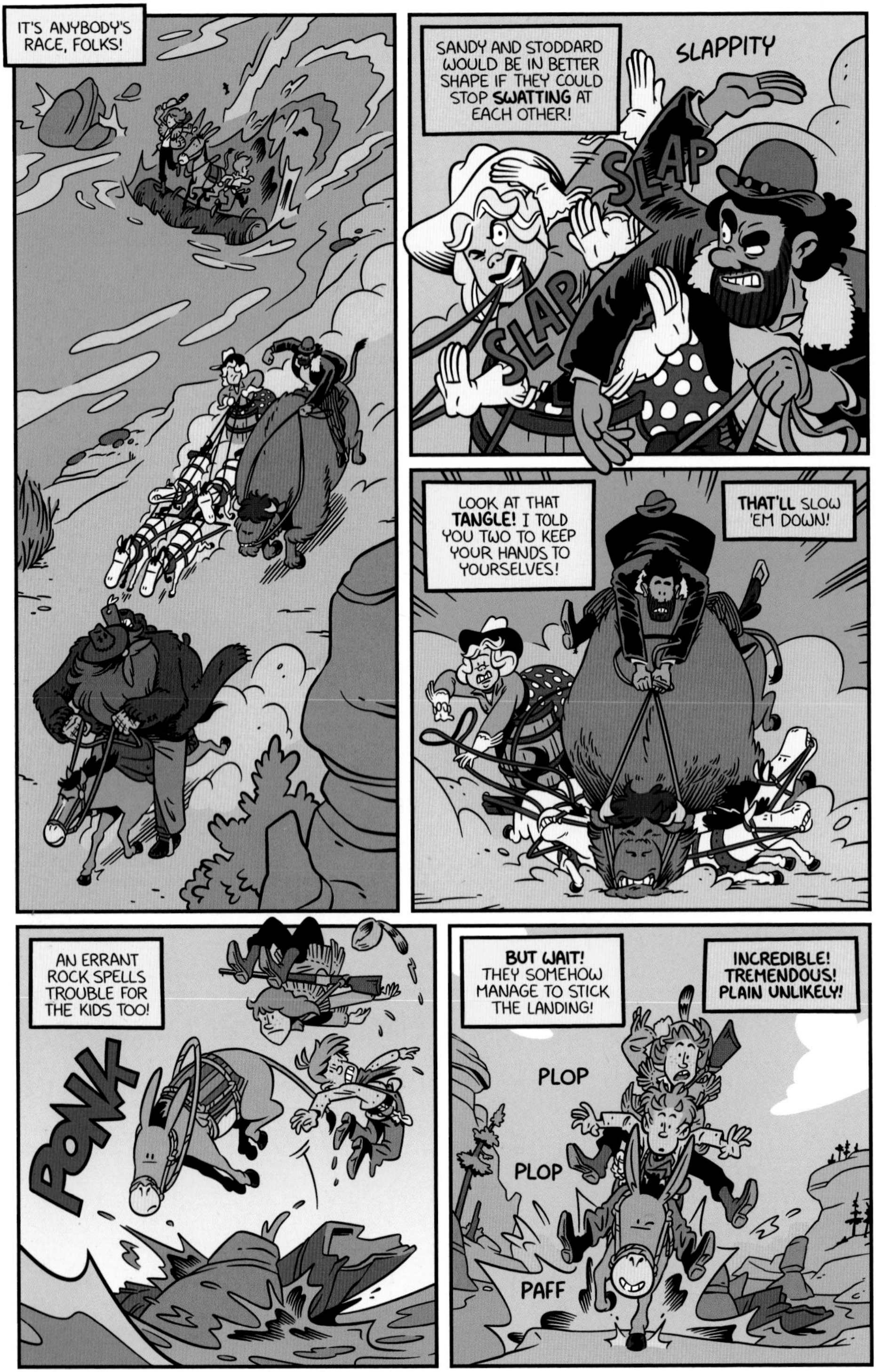
IT'S ANYBODY'S RACE, FOLKS!
SANDY AND STODDARD WOULD BE IN BETTER SHAPE IF THEY COULD STOP SWATTING AT EACH OTHER!
SLAPPITY
SLAP
SLAP
SLAP
LOOK AT THAT TANGLE! I TOLD YOU TWO TO KEEP YOUR HANDS TO YOURSELVES!
THAT'LL SLOW 'EM DOWN!
AN ERRANT ROCK SPELLS TROUBLE FOR THE KIDS TOO!
PONK
BUT WAIT! THEY SOMEHOW MANAGE TO STICK THE LANDING!
INCREDIBLE! TREMENDOUS! PLAIN UNLIKELY!
PLOP
PLOP
PAFF

WITH THE FINISH IN VIEW, THEY'RE NIPPING AT THE BIG GUY'S HEELS!

AW, POOR JORGENSON NEVER DID GET THAT THING WORKING.

IT WOULD'VE BEEN SO NEAT, TOO.

TUNK

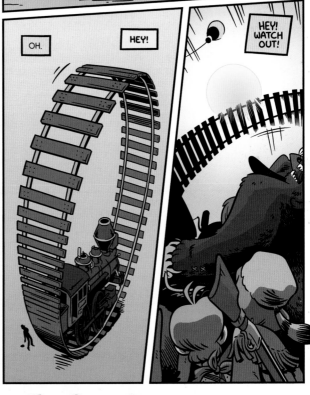

OH.

HEY!

HEY! WATCH OUT!

CHOOM

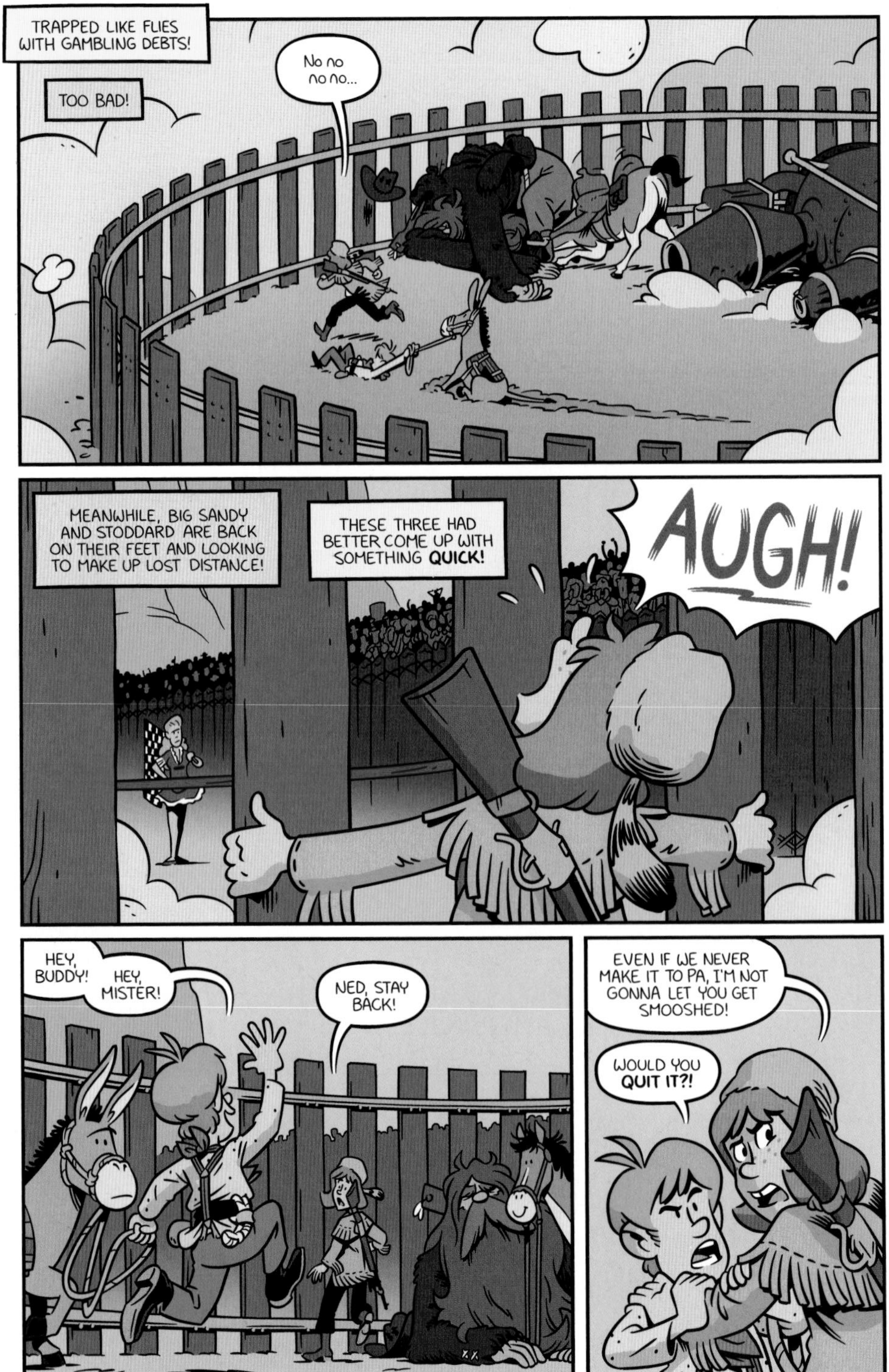
TRAPPED LIKE FLIES WITH GAMBLING DEBTS!
TOO BAD!
No no no no...
MEANWHILE, BIG SANDY AND STODDARD ARE BACK ON THEIR FEET AND LOOKING TO MAKE UP LOST DISTANCE!
THESE THREE HAD BETTER COME UP WITH SOMETHING **QUICK!**
AUGH!
HEY, BUDDY!
HEY, MISTER!
NED, STAY BACK!
EVEN IF WE NEVER MAKE IT TO PA, I'M NOT GONNA LET YOU GET SMOOSHED!
WOULD YOU **QUIT IT?!**

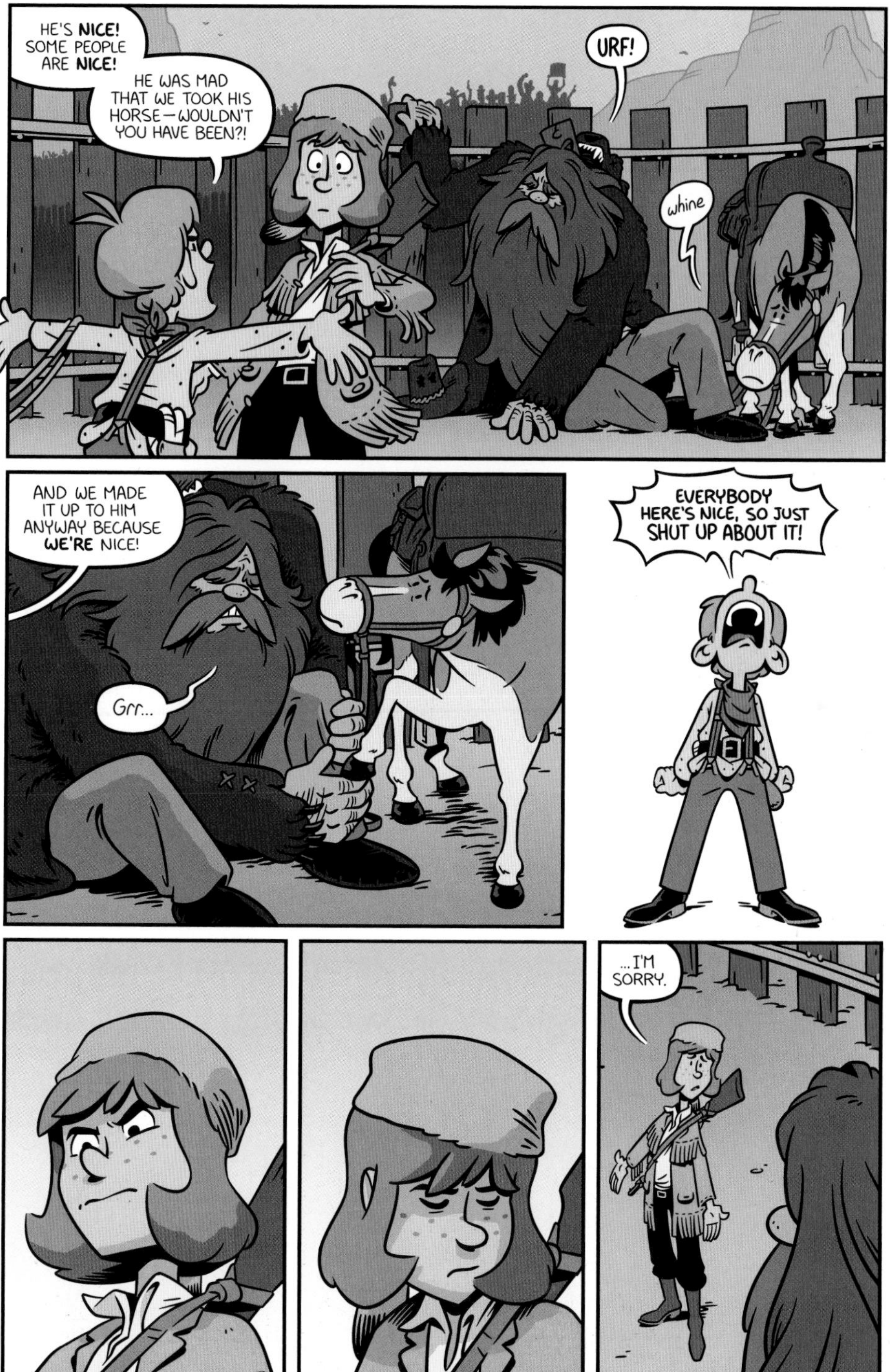
HE'S **NICE!** SOME PEOPLE ARE **NICE!**
HE WAS MAD THAT WE TOOK HIS HORSE—WOULDN'T YOU HAVE BEEN?!
URF!
whine
AND WE MADE IT UP TO HIM ANYWAY BECAUSE **WE'RE** NICE!
Grr...
EVERYBODY HERE'S NICE, SO JUST **SHUT UP ABOUT IT!**
...I'M SORRY.

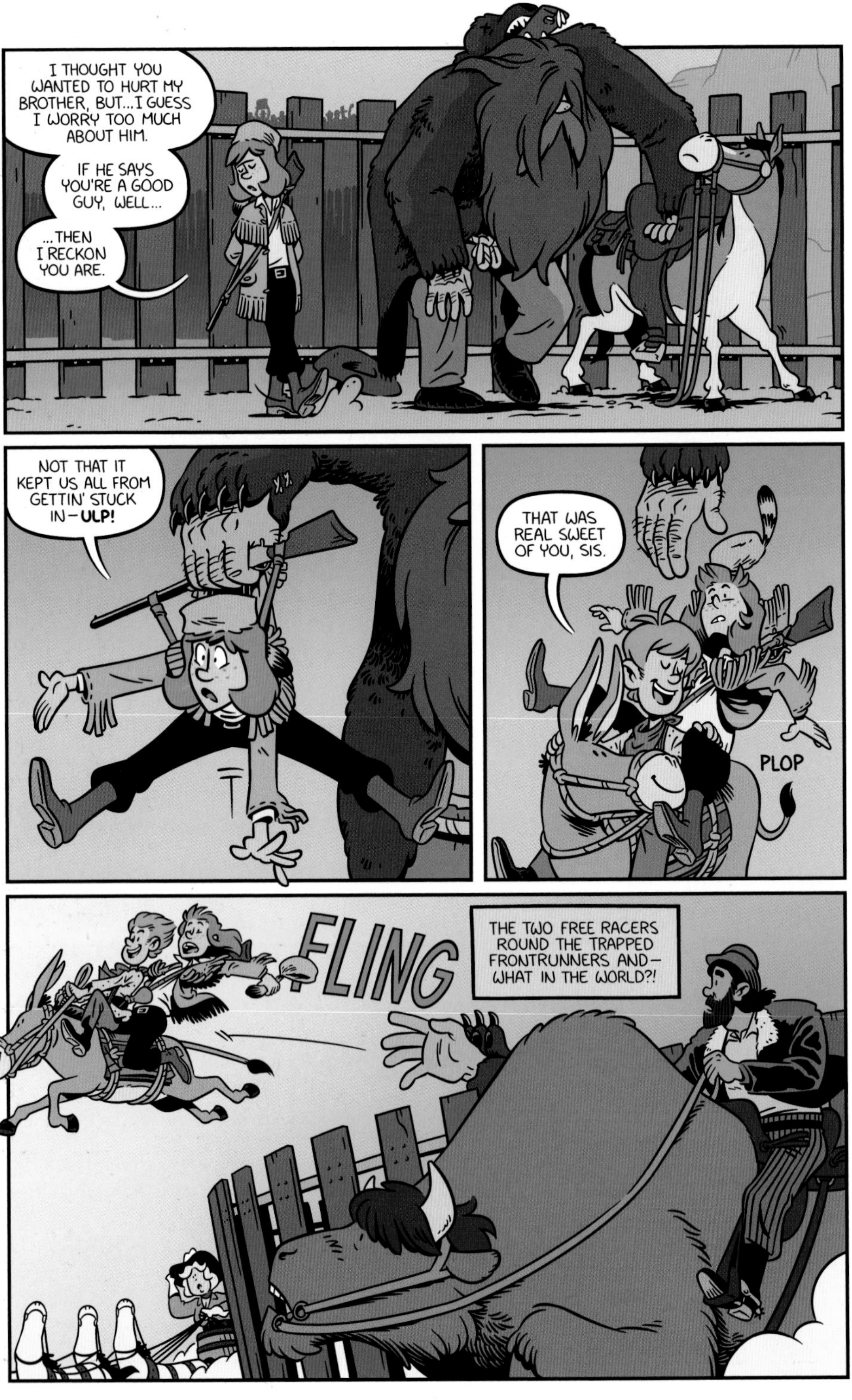
I THOUGHT YOU WANTED TO HURT MY BROTHER, BUT...I GUESS I WORRY TOO MUCH ABOUT HIM.
IF HE SAYS YOU'RE A GOOD GUY, WELL...
...THEN I RECKON YOU ARE.
NOT THAT IT KEPT US ALL FROM GETTIN' STUCK IN—**ULP!**
THAT WAS REAL SWEET OF YOU, SIS.
PLOP
FLING
THE TWO FREE RACERS ROUND THE TRAPPED FRONTRUNNERS AND— WHAT IN THE WORLD?!

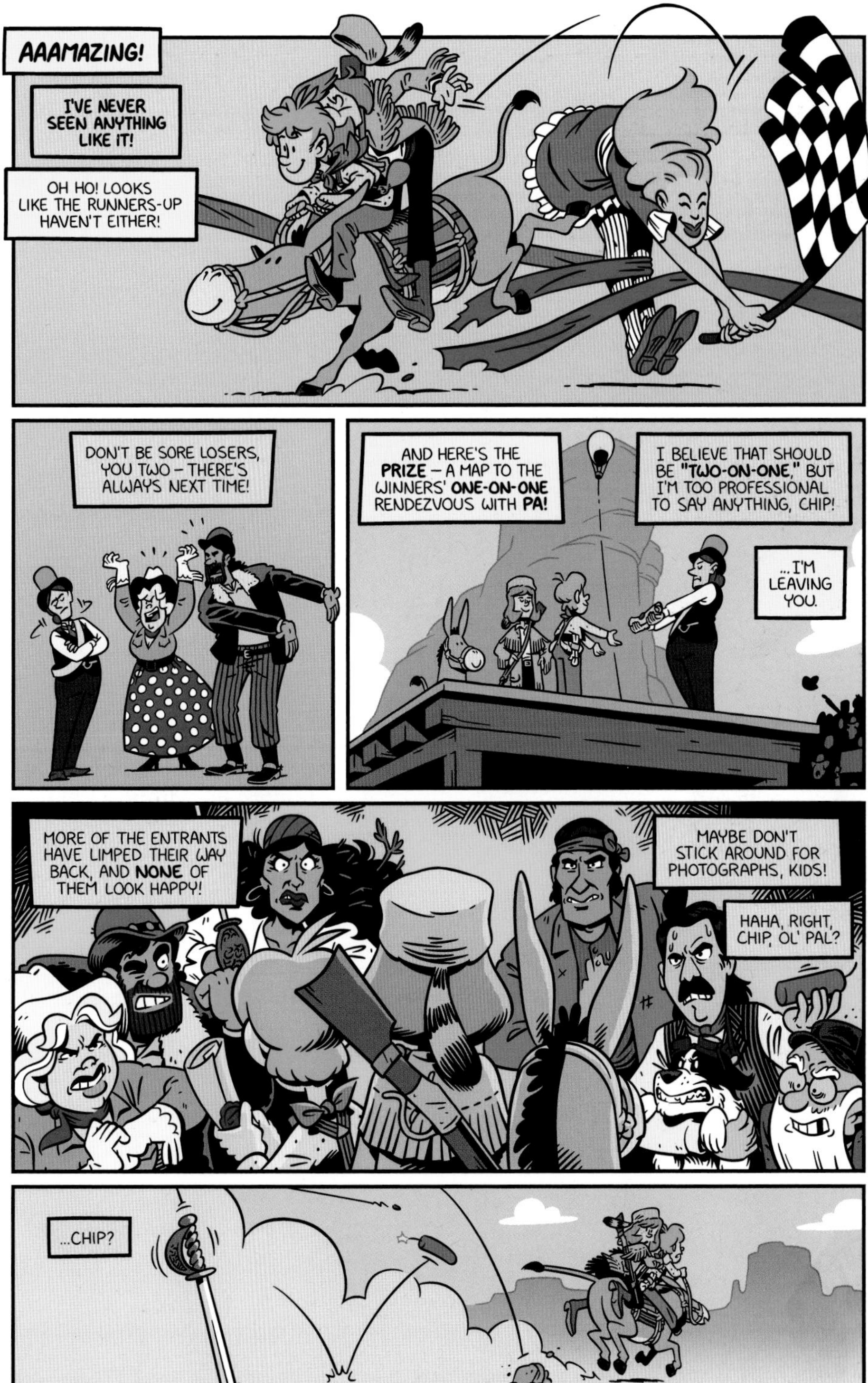
AAAMAZING!
I'VE NEVER SEEN ANYTHING LIKE IT!
OH HO! LOOKS LIKE THE RUNNERS-UP HAVEN'T EITHER!
DON'T BE SORE LOSERS, YOU TWO – THERE'S ALWAYS NEXT TIME!
AND HERE'S THE PRIZE – A MAP TO THE WINNERS' ONE-ON-ONE RENDEZVOUS WITH PA!
I BELIEVE THAT SHOULD BE "TWO-ON-ONE," BUT I'M TOO PROFESSIONAL TO SAY ANYTHING, CHIP!
...I'M LEAVING YOU.
MORE OF THE ENTRANTS HAVE LIMPED THEIR WAY BACK, AND NONE OF THEM LOOK HAPPY!
MAYBE DON'T STICK AROUND FOR PHOTOGRAPHS, KIDS!
HAHA, RIGHT, CHIP, OL' PAL?
...CHIP?

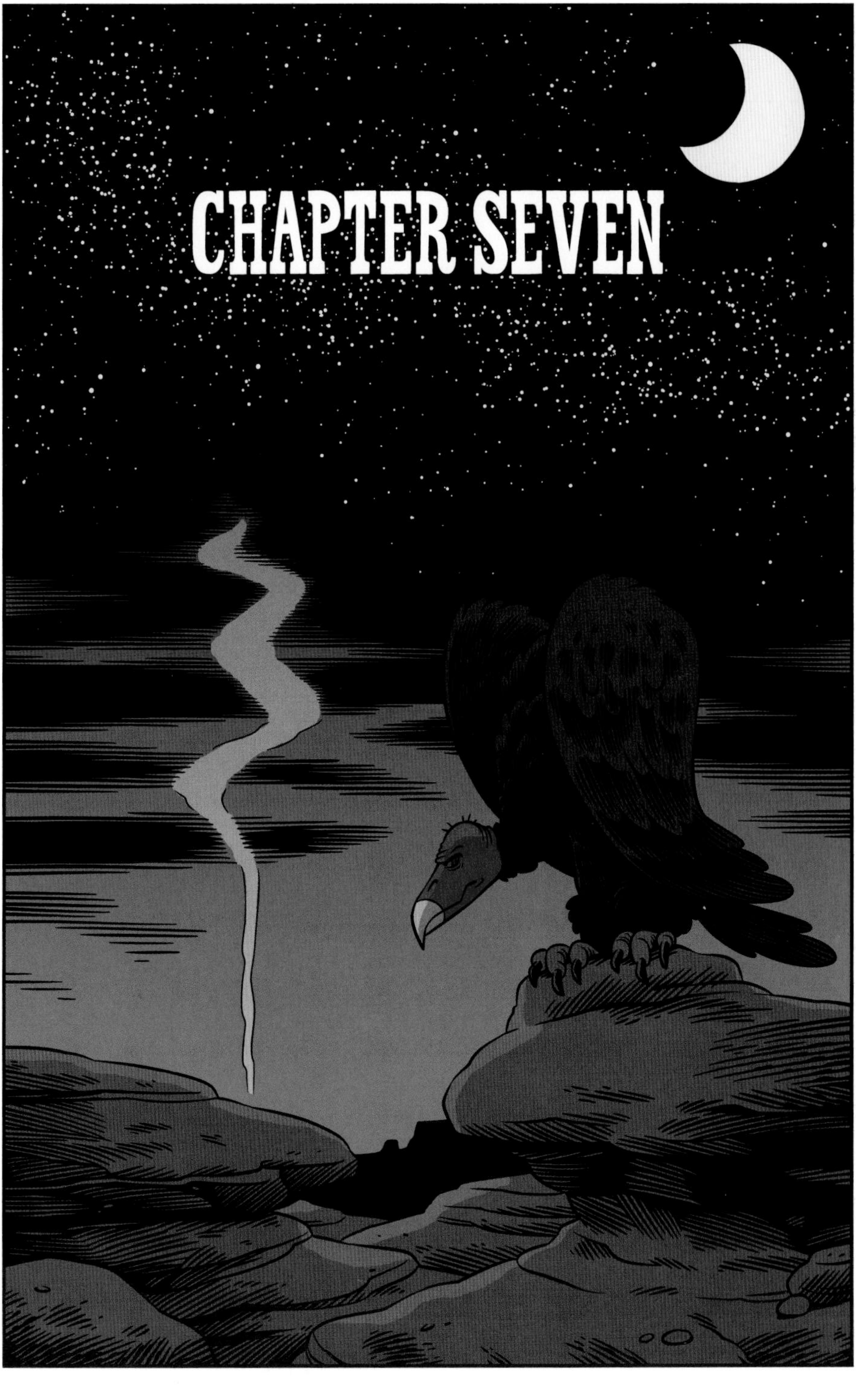
CHAPTER SEVEN

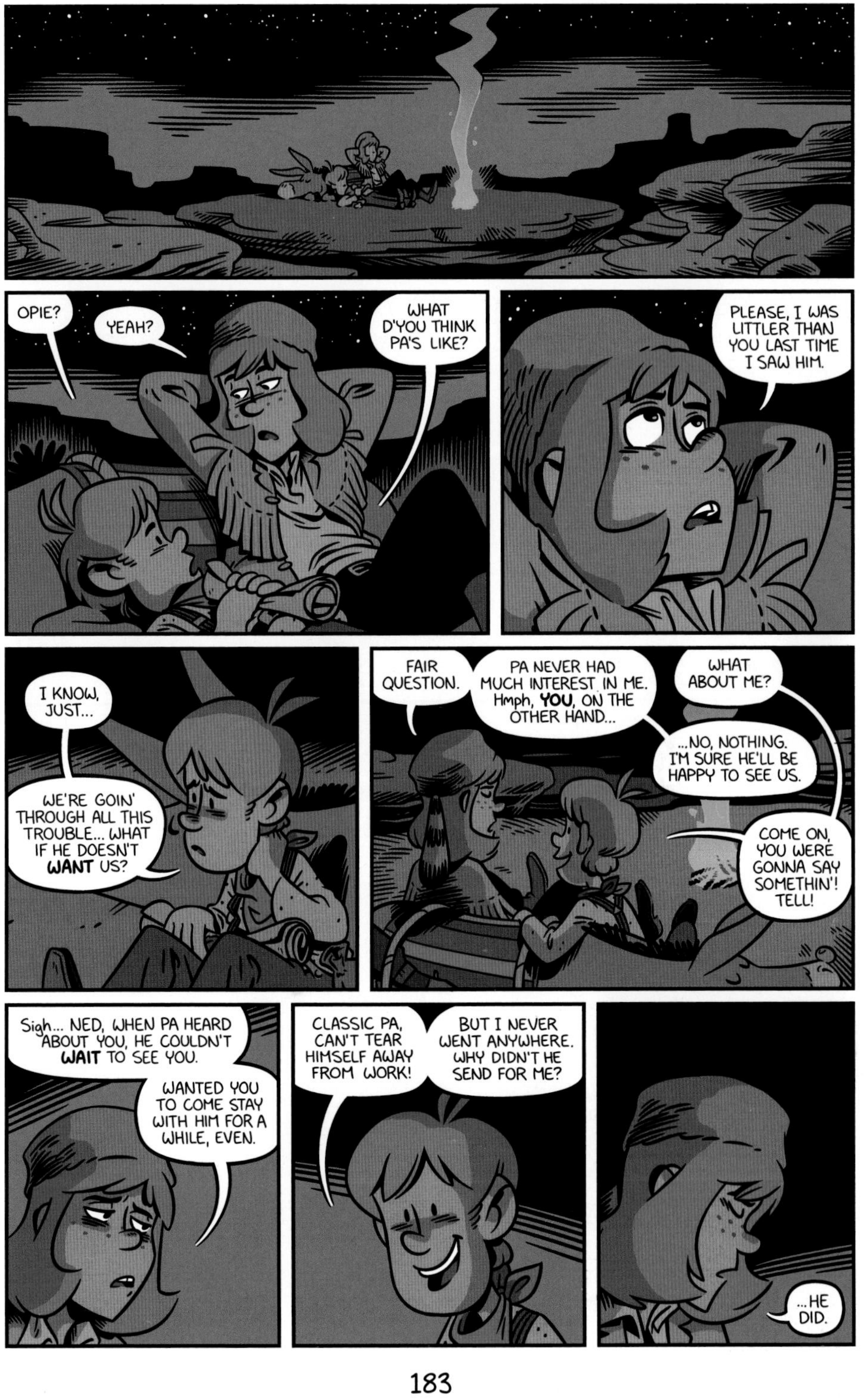
OPIE?
YEAH?
WHAT D'YOU THINK PA'S LIKE?
PLEASE, I WAS LITTLER THAN YOU LAST TIME I SAW HIM.
I KNOW, JUST...
WE'RE GOIN' THROUGH ALL THIS TROUBLE... WHAT IF HE DOESN'T **WANT** US?
FAIR QUESTION.
PA NEVER HAD MUCH INTEREST IN ME. Hmph, **YOU**, ON THE OTHER HAND...
WHAT ABOUT ME?
...NO, NOTHING. I'M SURE HE'LL BE HAPPY TO SEE US.
COME ON, YOU WERE GONNA SAY SOMETHIN'! TELL!
Sigh... NED, WHEN PA HEARD ABOUT YOU, HE COULDN'T **WAIT** TO SEE YOU.
WANTED YOU TO COME STAY WITH HIM FOR A WHILE, EVEN.
CLASSIC PA, CAN'T TEAR HIMSELF AWAY FROM WORK!
BUT I NEVER WENT ANYWHERE. WHY DIDN'T HE SEND FOR ME?
...HE DID.

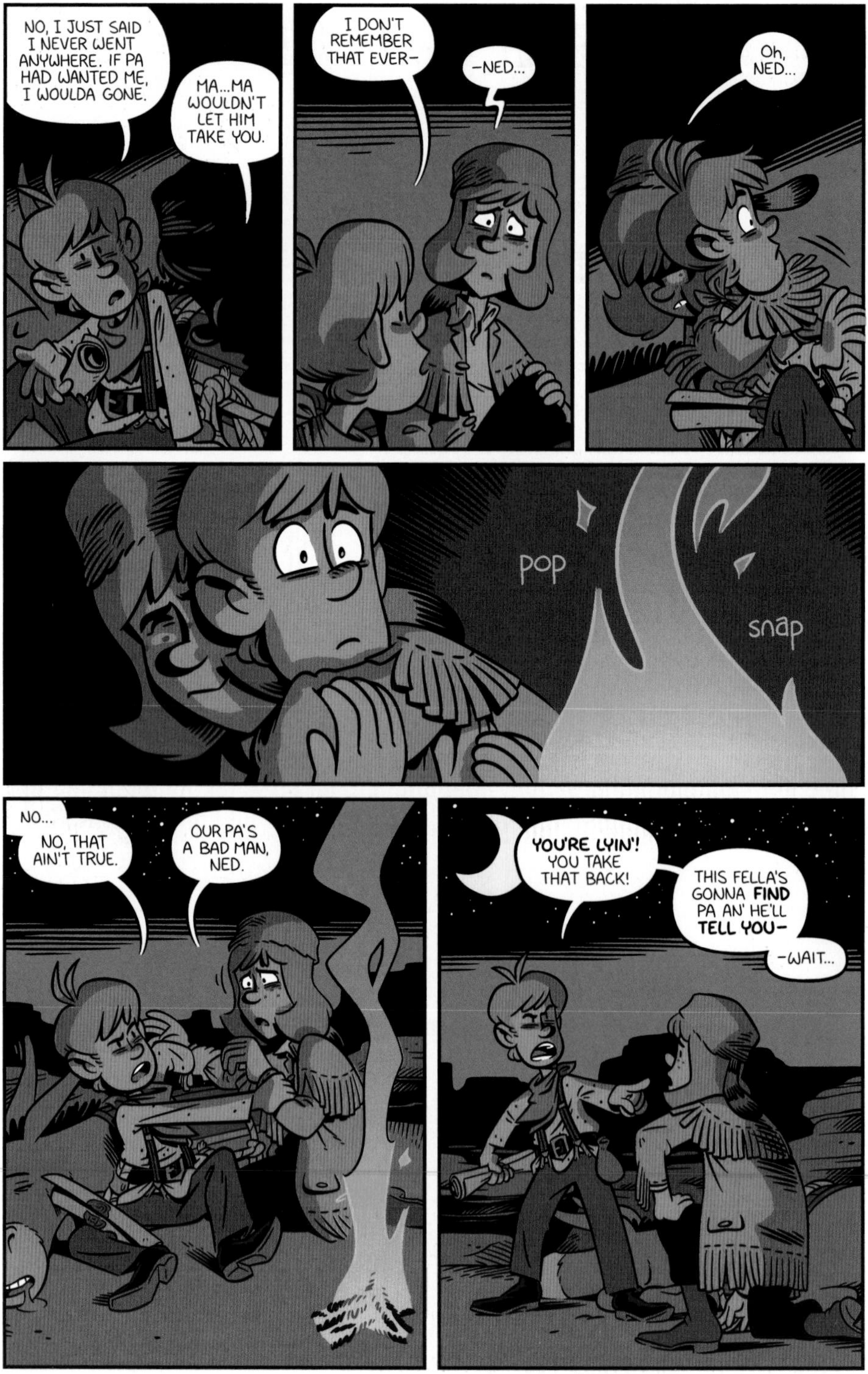
NO, I JUST SAID I NEVER WENT ANYWHERE. IF PA HAD WANTED ME, I WOULDA GONE.
MA...MA WOULDN'T LET HIM TAKE YOU.
I DON'T REMEMBER THAT EVER-
-NED...
Oh, NED...
pop
snap
NO...
NO, THAT AIN'T TRUE.
OUR PA'S A BAD MAN, NED.
YOU'RE LYIN'! YOU TAKE THAT BACK!
THIS FELLA'S GONNA **FIND** PA AN' HE'LL **TELL YOU-**
-WAIT...

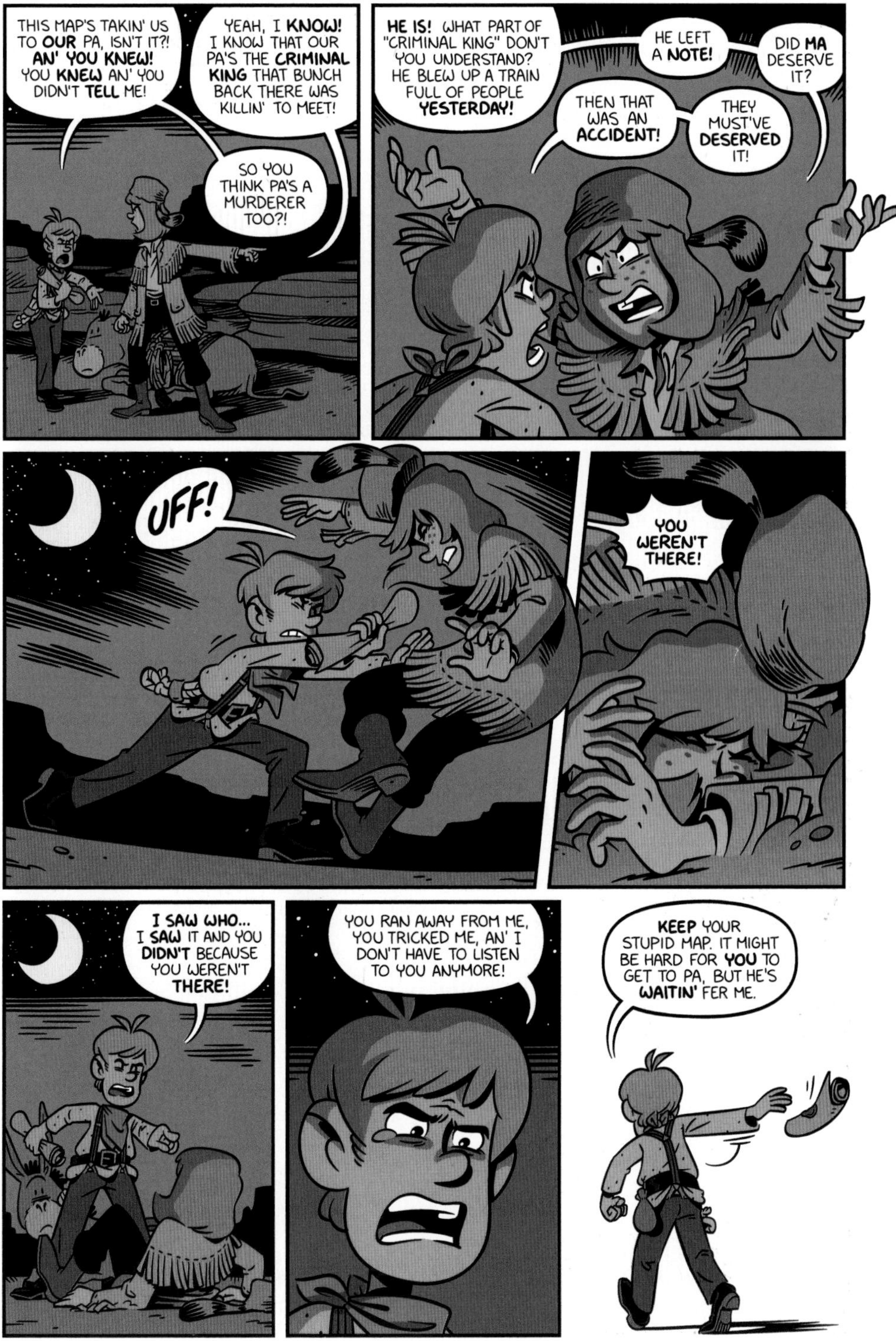
THIS MAP'S TAKIN' US TO OUR PA, ISN'T IT?! AN' YOU KNEW! YOU KNEW AN' YOU DIDN'T TELL ME!
YEAH, I KNOW! I KNOW THAT OUR PA'S THE CRIMINAL KING THAT BUNCH BACK THERE WAS KILLIN' TO MEET!
SO YOU THINK PA'S A MURDERER TOO?!
HE IS! WHAT PART OF "CRIMINAL KING" DON'T YOU UNDERSTAND? HE BLEW UP A TRAIN FULL OF PEOPLE YESTERDAY!
THEN THAT WAS AN ACCIDENT!
HE LEFT A NOTE!
THEY MUST'VE DESERVED IT!
DID MA DESERVE IT?
UFF!
YOU WEREN'T THERE!
I SAW WHO... I SAW IT AND YOU DIDN'T BECAUSE YOU WEREN'T THERE!
YOU RAN AWAY FROM ME, YOU TRICKED ME, AN' I DON'T HAVE TO LISTEN TO YOU ANYMORE!
KEEP YOUR STUPID MAP. IT MIGHT BE HARD FOR YOU TO GET TO PA, BUT HE'S WAITIN' FER ME.

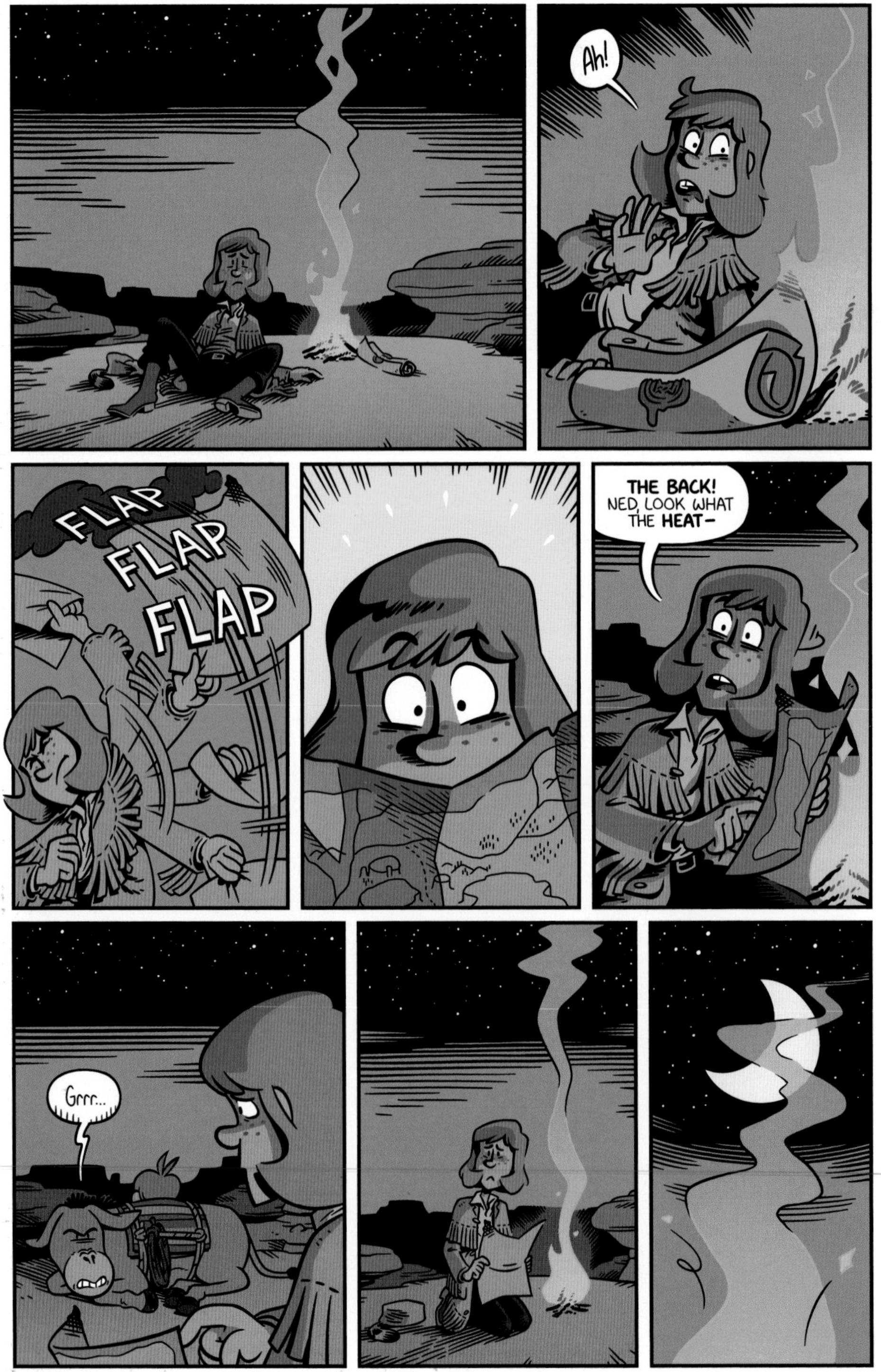
Ah!
FLAP
FLAP
FLAP
THE BACK! NED, LOOK WHAT THE HEAT–
Grrr...

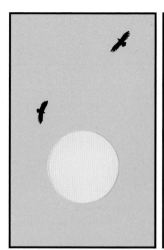

ONK!

ONK ONK!

Ugh... MAGGIEEE...

YAWN! YOU FEELIN' FRIENDLIER, NED? LOOK WHAT I FOUND LAST—

NED?

ONK!

COME ON, DON'T BE A WIMP!

ONK!

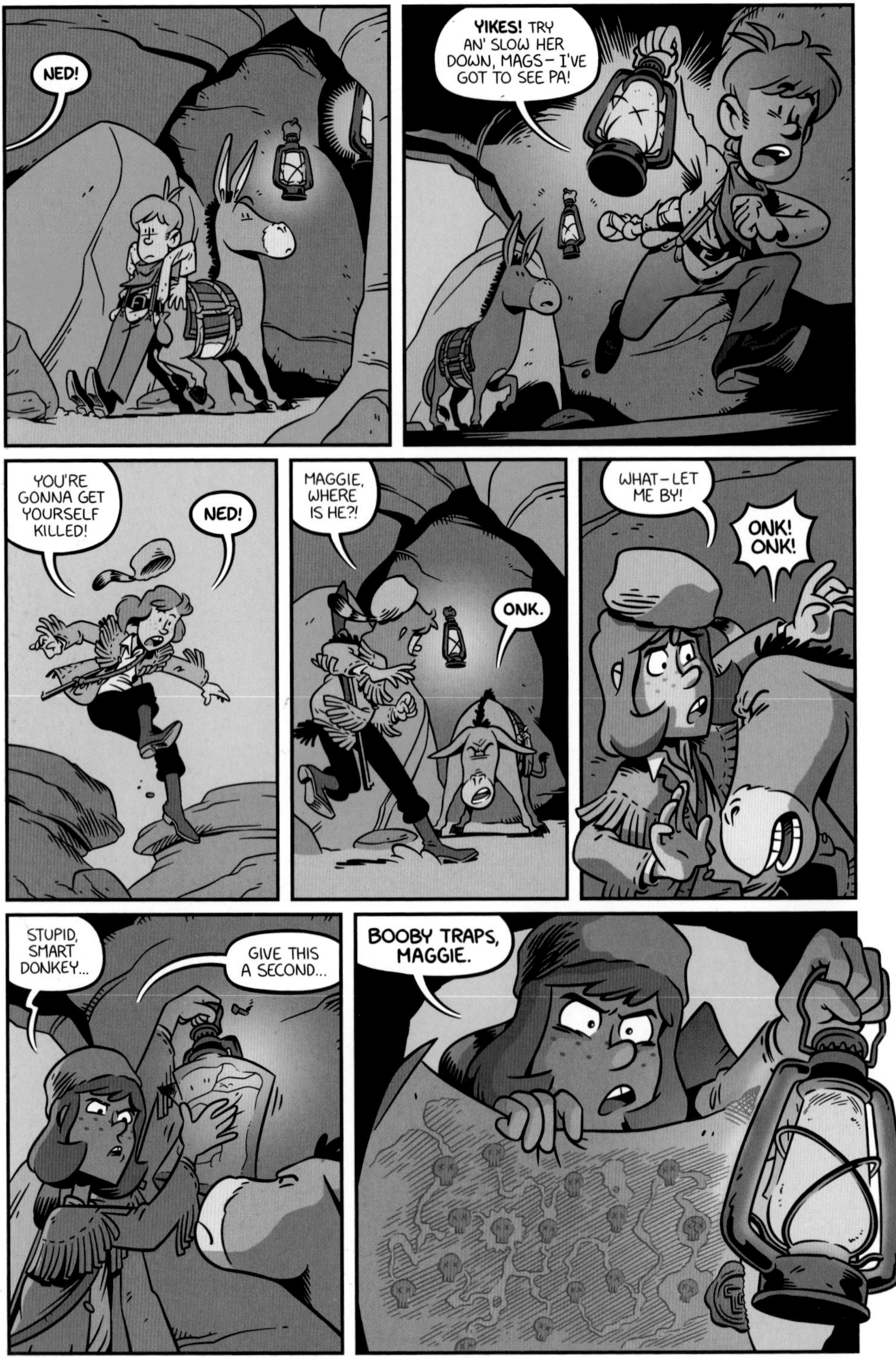
NED!
YIKES! TRY AN' SLOW HER DOWN, MAGS– I'VE GOT TO SEE PA!
YOU'RE GONNA GET YOURSELF KILLED!
NED!
MAGGIE, WHERE IS HE?!
ONK.
WHAT– LET ME BY!
ONK! ONK!
STUPID, SMART DONKEY...
GIVE THIS A SECOND...
BOOBY TRAPS, MAGGIE.

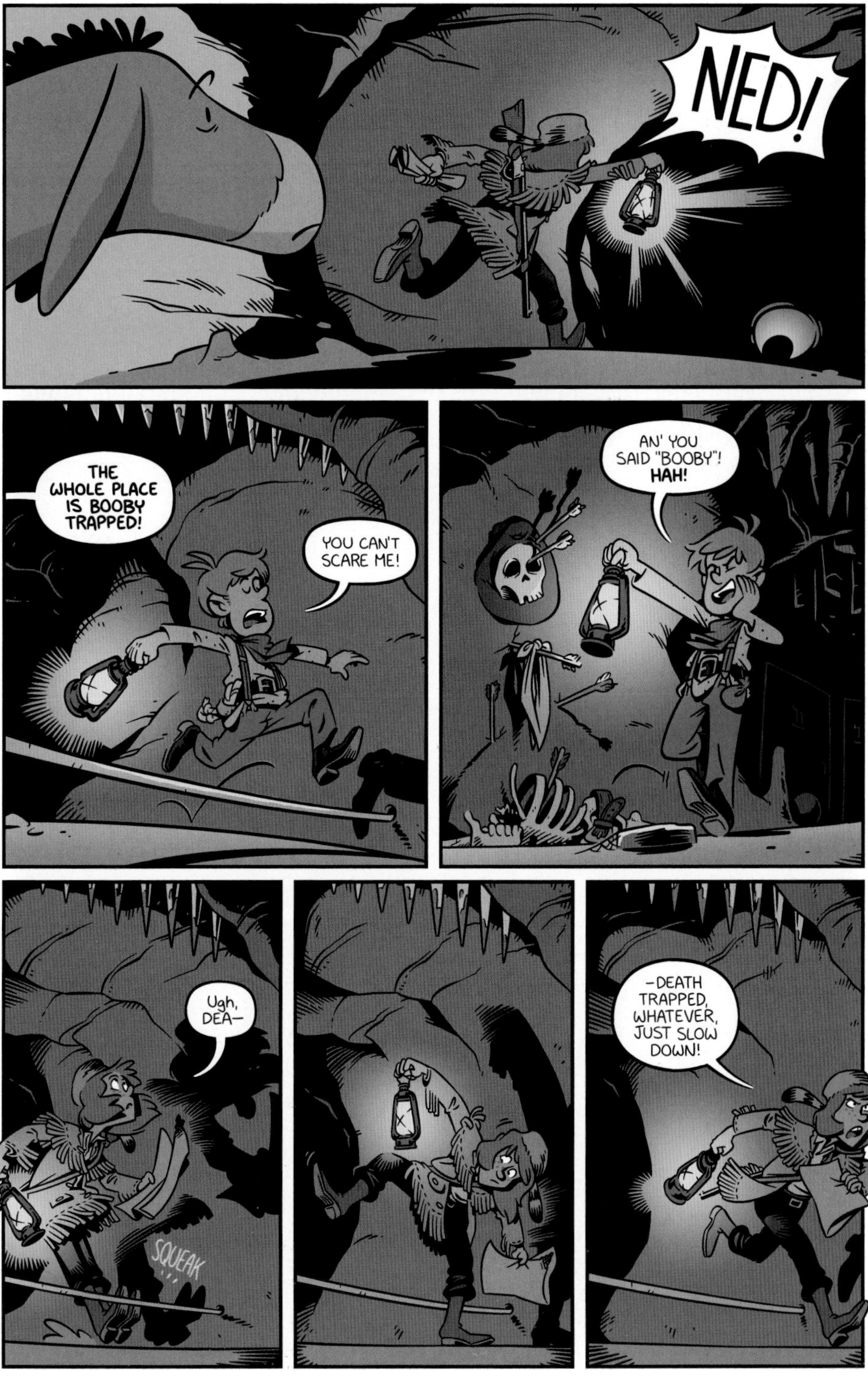

NED!
THE WHOLE PLACE IS BOOBY TRAPPED!
YOU CAN'T SCARE ME!
AN' YOU SAID "BOOBY"! HAH!
Ugh, DEA—
SQUEAK
—DEATH TRAPPED, WHATEVER, JUST SLOW DOWN!

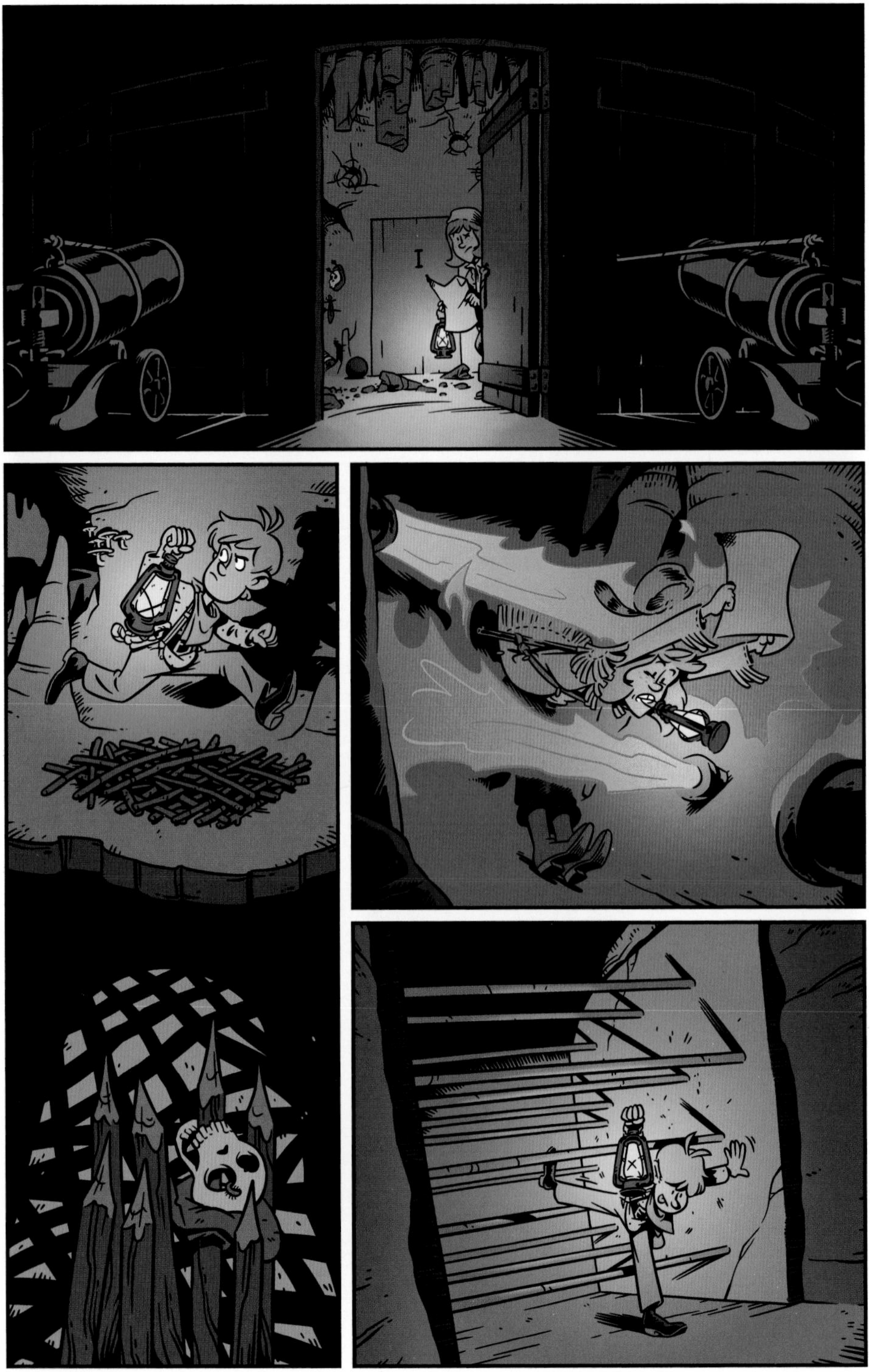
I

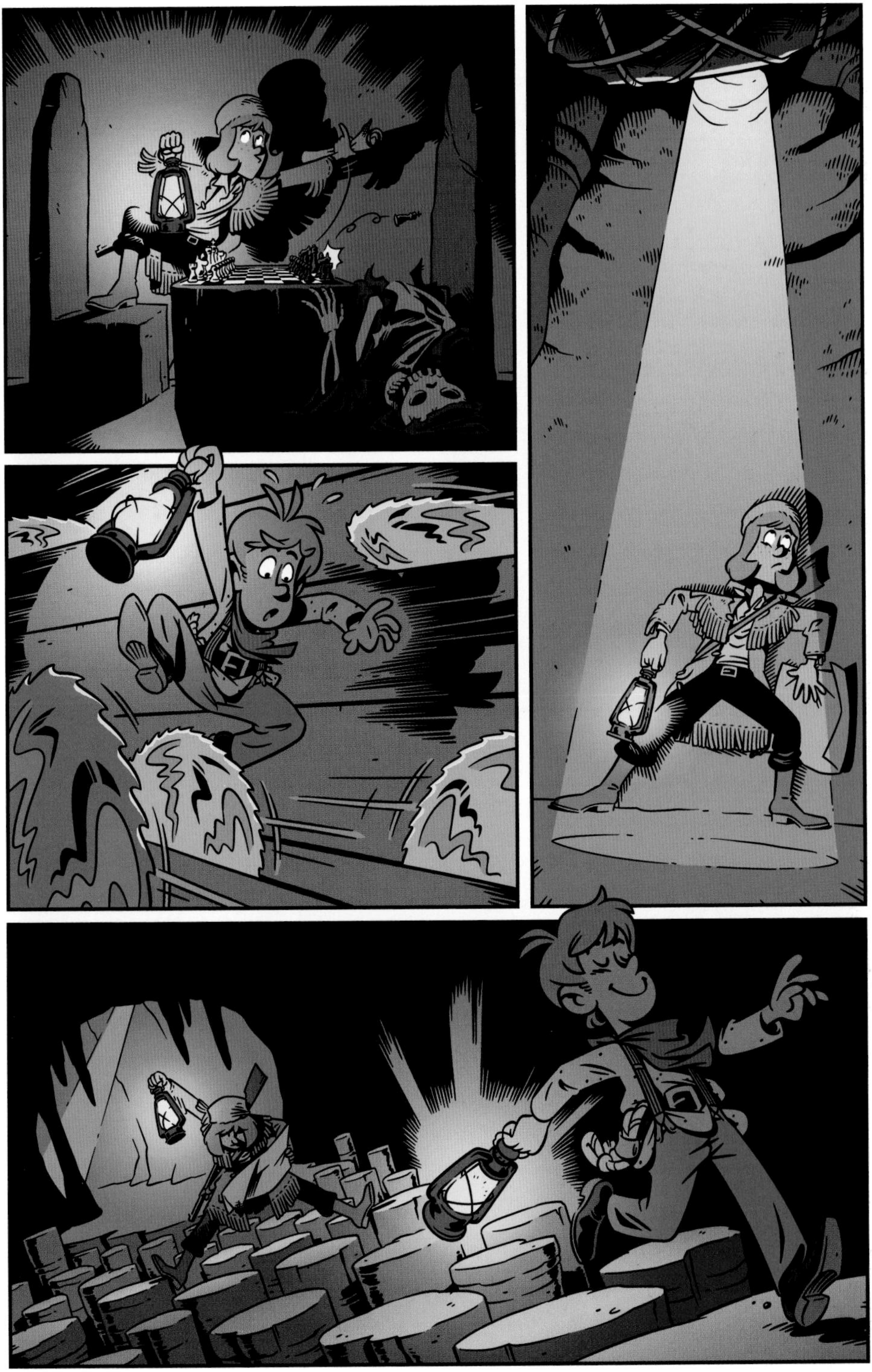

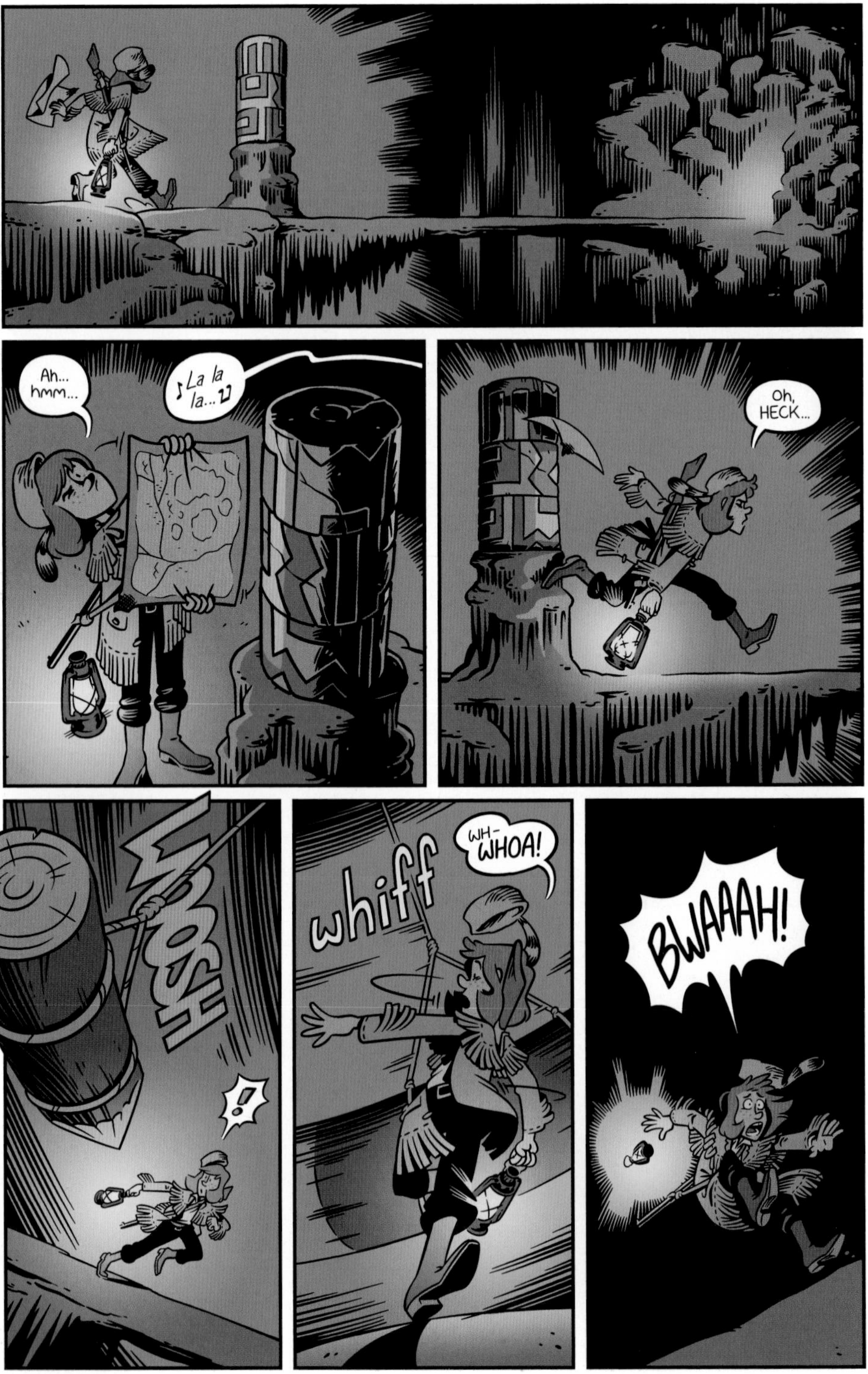
Ah... hmm...
♪La la la...♫
Oh, HECK...
WHOOSH
!
whiff
WH- WHOA!
BWAAAH!

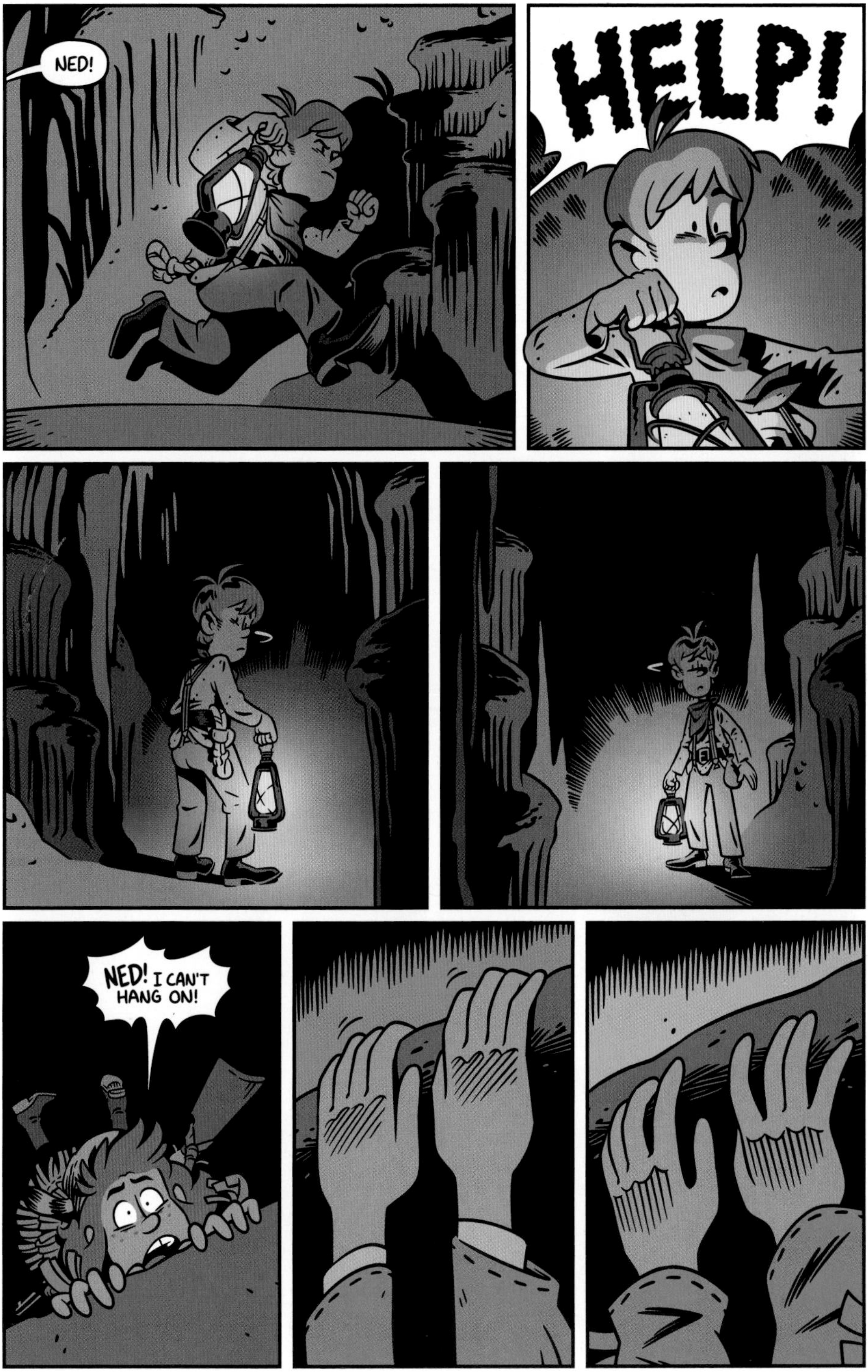
NED!
HELP!
NED! I CAN'T HANG ON!

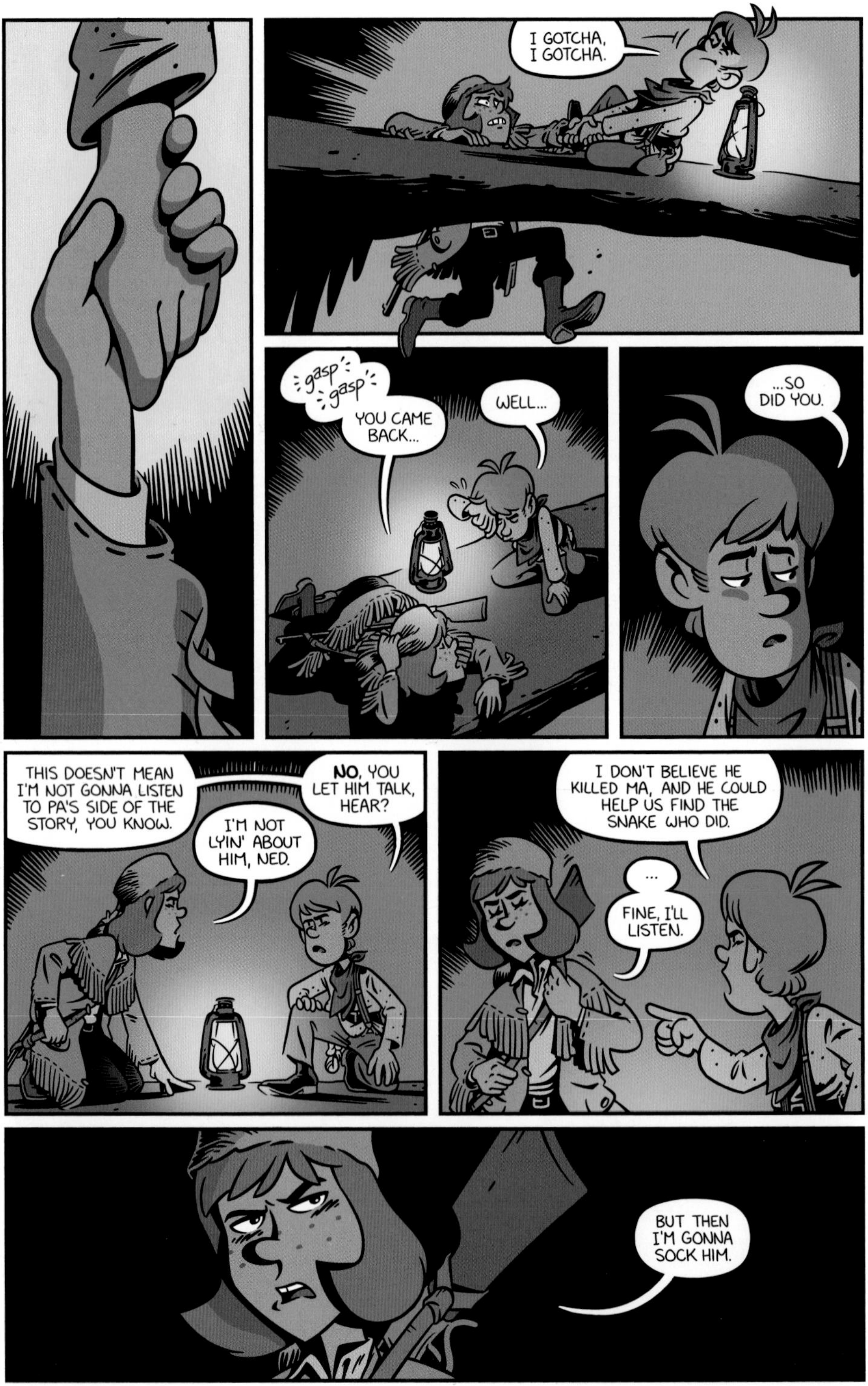
I GOTCHA, I GOTCHA.
gasp gasp
YOU CAME BACK...
WELL...
...SO DID YOU.
THIS DOESN'T MEAN I'M NOT GONNA LISTEN TO PA'S SIDE OF THE STORY, YOU KNOW.
NO, YOU LET HIM TALK, HEAR?
I'M NOT LYIN' ABOUT HIM, NED.
I DON'T BELIEVE HE KILLED MA, AND HE COULD HELP US FIND THE SNAKE WHO DID.
...
FINE, I'LL LISTEN.
BUT THEN I'M GONNA SOCK HIM.

AH, THE VICTOR HAS FINALLY ARRIVED...

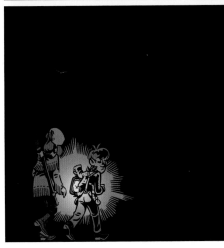

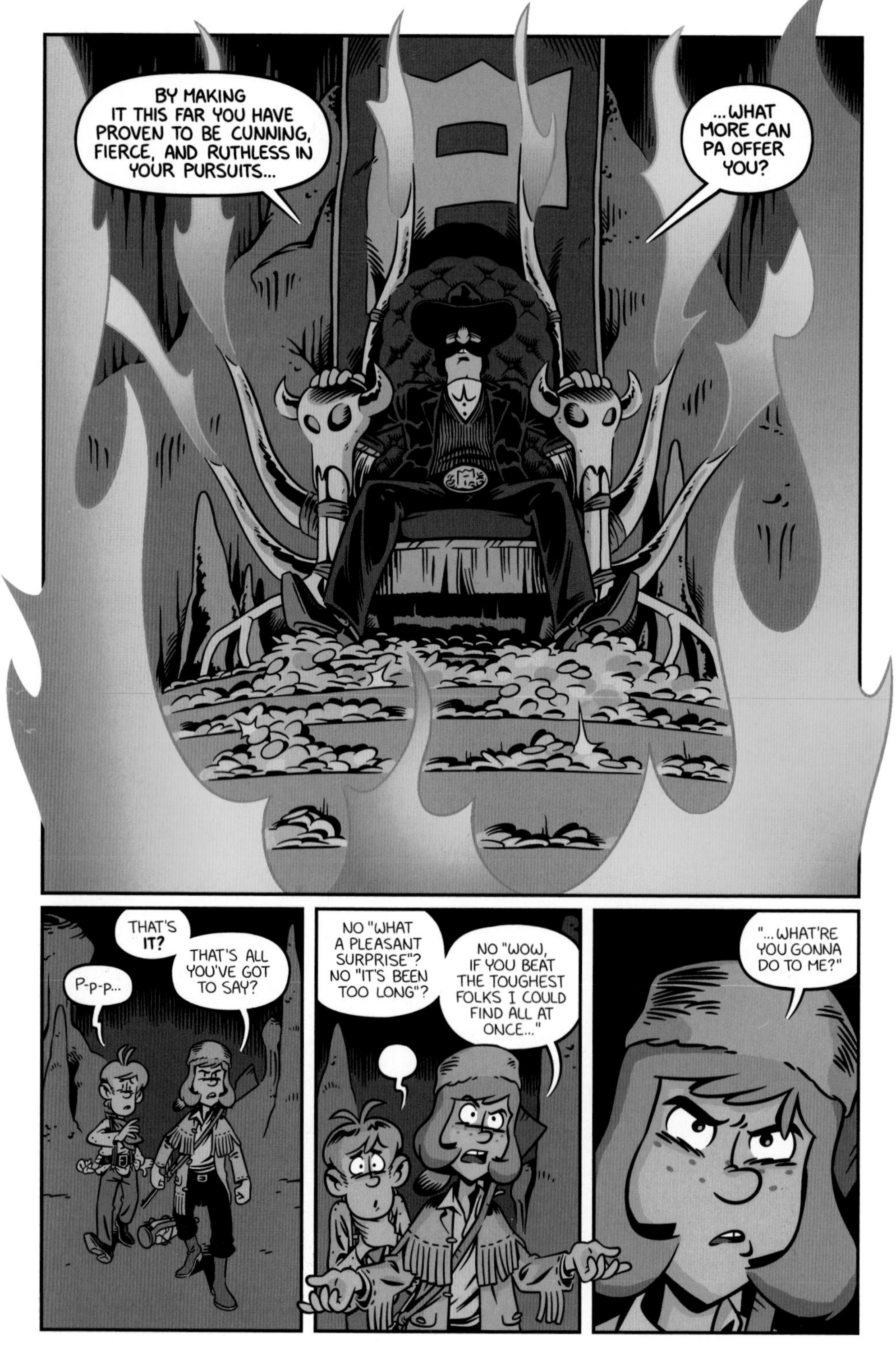
BY MAKING IT THIS FAR YOU HAVE PROVEN TO BE CUNNING, FIERCE, AND RUTHLESS IN YOUR PURSUITS...
...WHAT MORE CAN PA OFFER YOU?
THAT'S **IT?**
P-p-p...
THAT'S ALL YOU'VE GOT TO SAY?
NO "WHAT A PLEASANT SURPRISE"? NO "IT'S BEEN TOO LONG"?
NO "WOW, IF YOU BEAT THE TOUGHEST FOLKS I COULD FIND ALL AT ONCE..."
"...WHAT'RE YOU GONNA DO TO ME?"

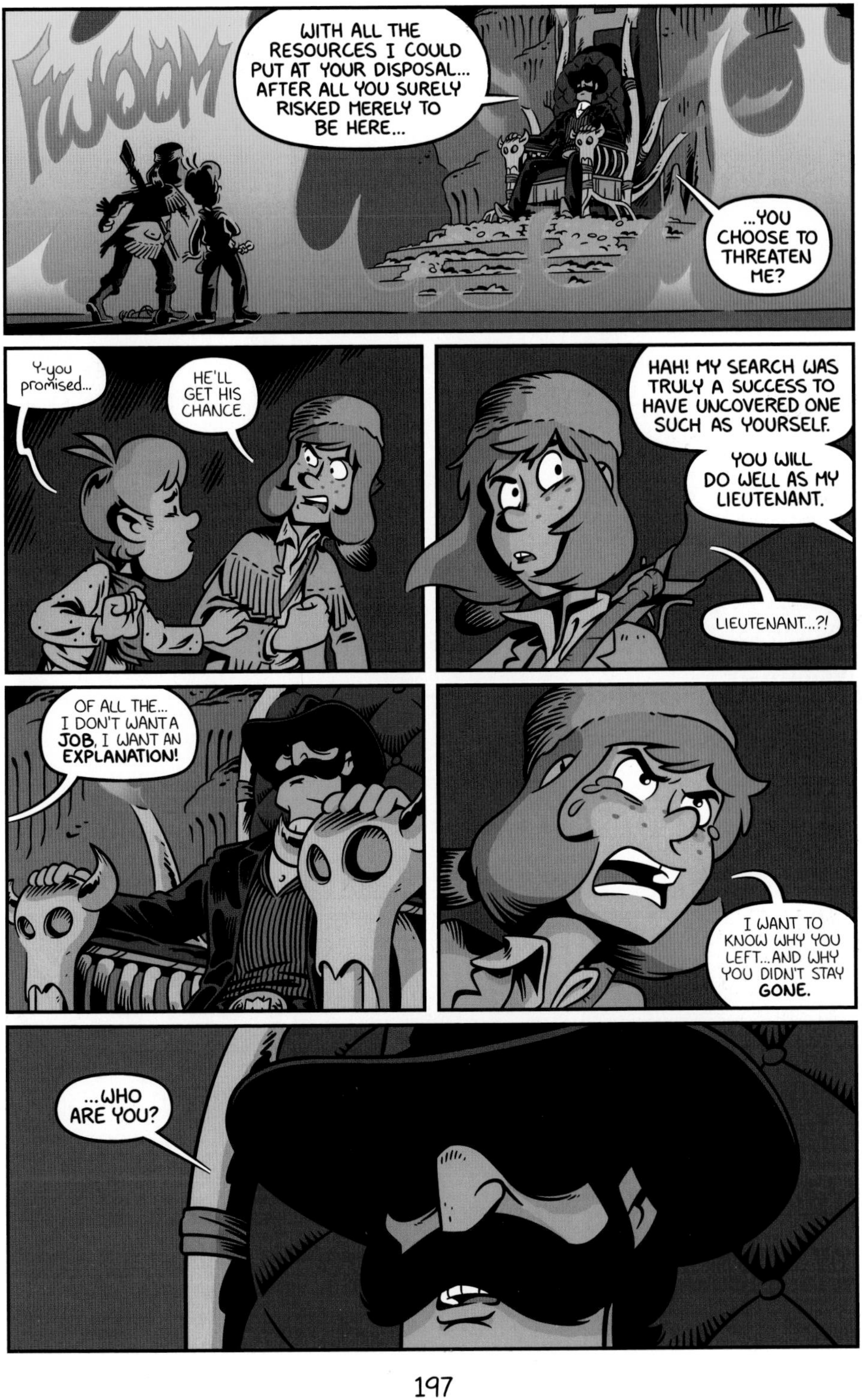
FWOOM
WITH ALL THE RESOURCES I COULD PUT AT YOUR DISPOSAL... AFTER ALL YOU SURELY RISKED MERELY TO BE HERE...
...YOU CHOOSE TO THREATEN ME?
Y-you promised...
HE'LL GET HIS CHANCE.
HAH! MY SEARCH WAS TRULY A SUCCESS TO HAVE UNCOVERED ONE SUCH AS YOURSELF.
YOU WILL DO WELL AS MY LIEUTENANT.
LIEUTENANT...?!
OF ALL THE... I DON'T WANT A JOB, I WANT AN EXPLANATION!
I WANT TO KNOW WHY YOU LEFT...AND WHY YOU DIDN'T STAY GONE.
...WHO ARE YOU?

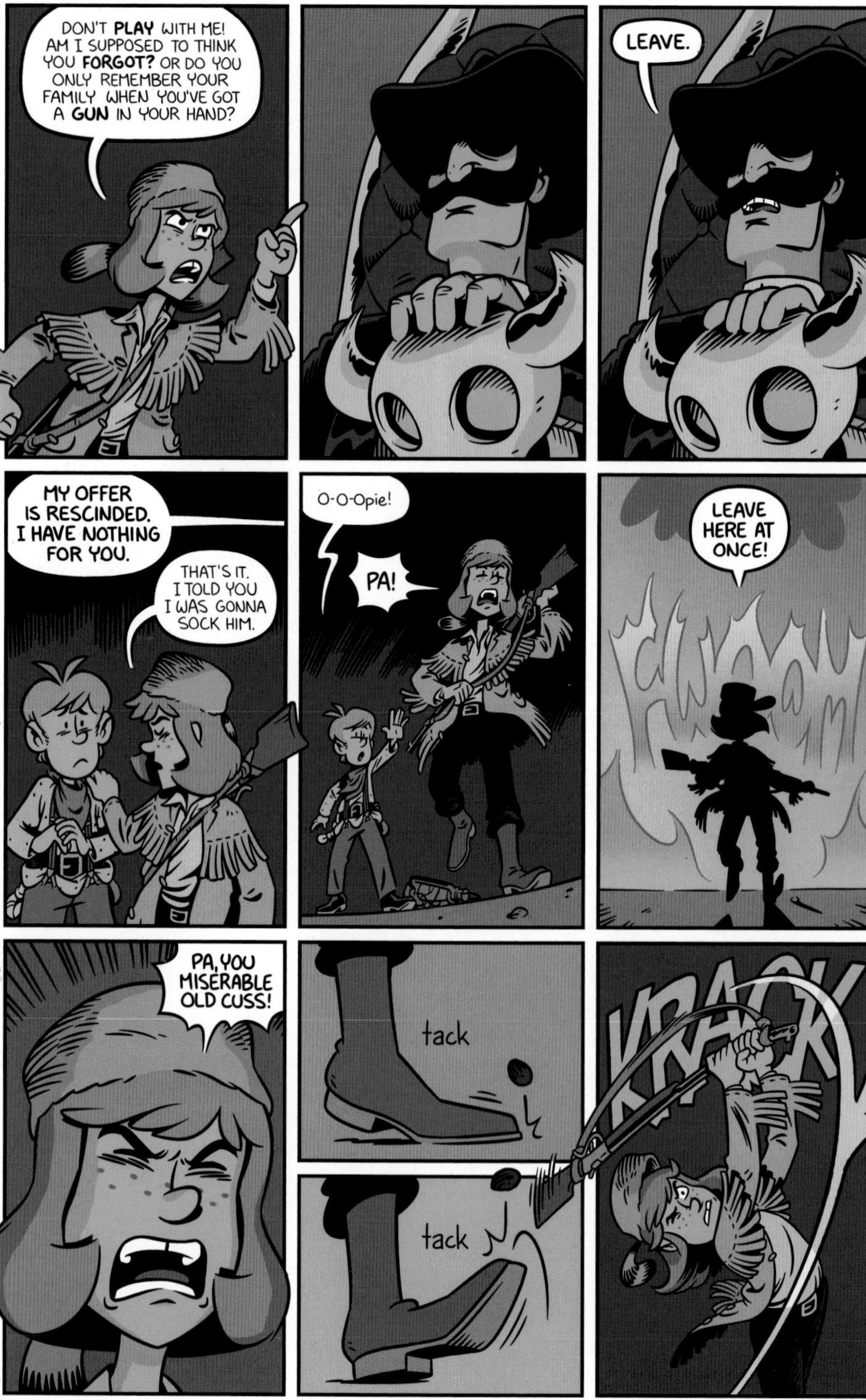
DON'T PLAY WITH ME! AM I SUPPOSED TO THINK YOU FORGOT? OR DO YOU ONLY REMEMBER YOUR FAMILY WHEN YOU'VE GOT A GUN IN YOUR HAND?
LEAVE.
MY OFFER IS RESCINDED. I HAVE NOTHING FOR YOU.
THAT'S IT. I TOLD YOU I WAS GONNA SOCK HIM.
O-O-Opie!
PA!
LEAVE HERE AT ONCE!
PA, YOU MISERABLE OLD CUSS!
tack
tack
KRACK

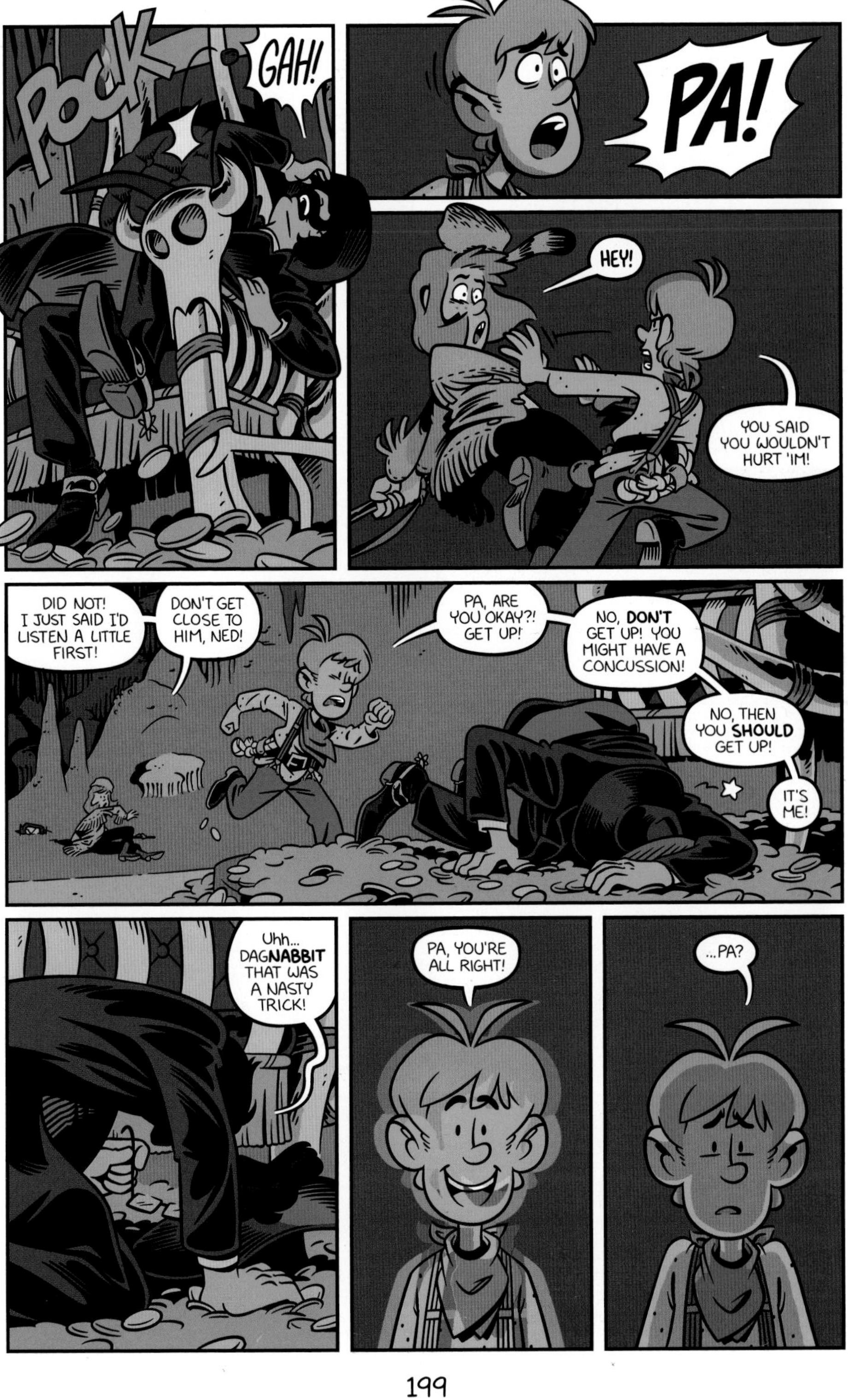
POCK
GAH!
PA!
HEY!
YOU SAID YOU WOULDN'T HURT 'IM!
DID NOT! I JUST SAID I'D LISTEN A LITTLE FIRST!
DON'T GET CLOSE TO HIM, NED!
PA, ARE YOU OKAY?! GET UP!
NO, **DON'T** GET UP! YOU MIGHT HAVE A CONCUSSION!
NO, THEN YOU **SHOULD** GET UP!
IT'S ME!
Uhh... DAG**NABBIT** THAT WAS A NASTY TRICK!
PA, YOU'RE ALL RIGHT!
...PA?

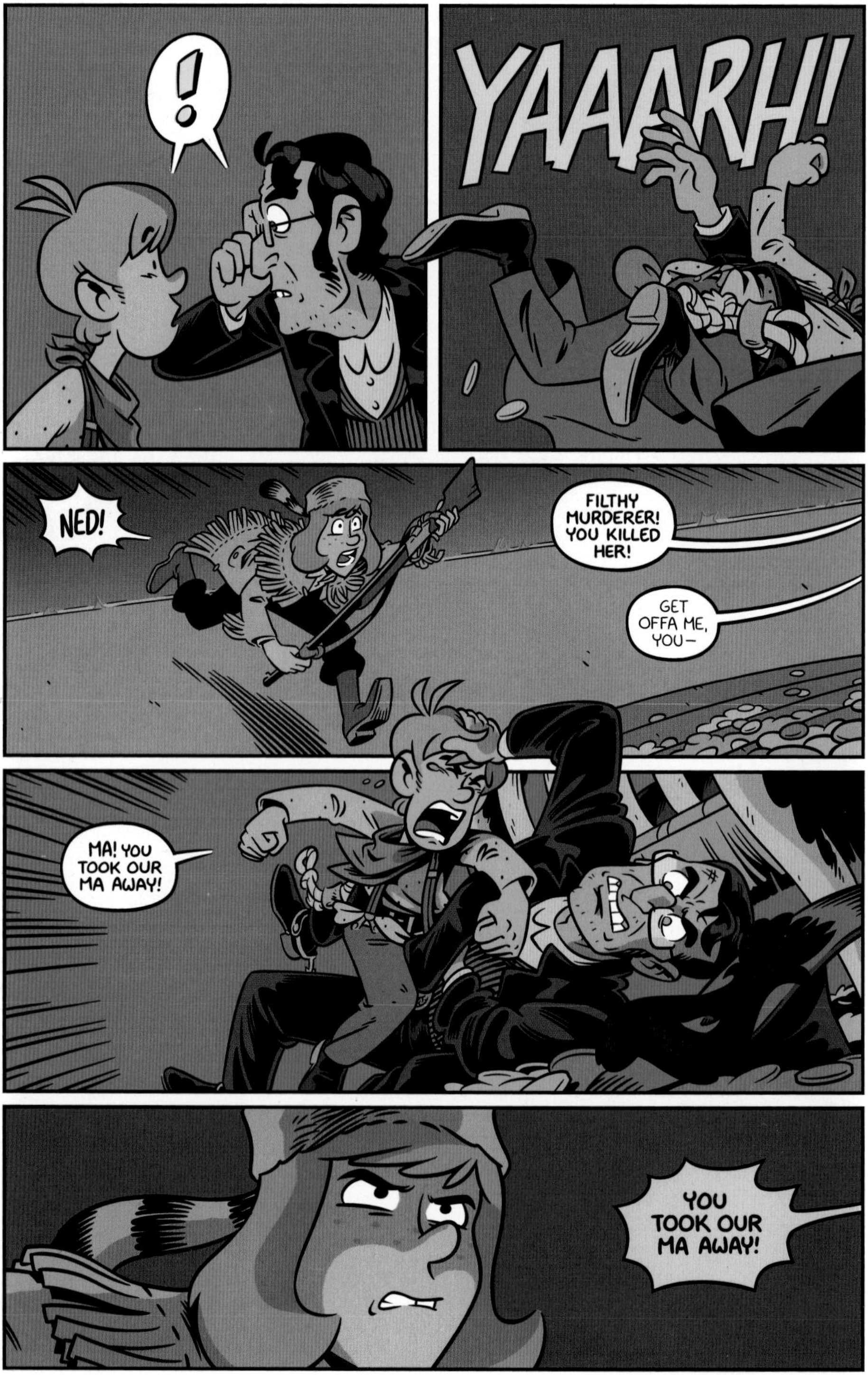
!
YAAARH!
NED!
FILTHY MURDERER! YOU KILLED HER!
GET OFFA ME, YOU—
MA! YOU TOOK OUR MA AWAY!
YOU TOOK OUR MA AWAY!

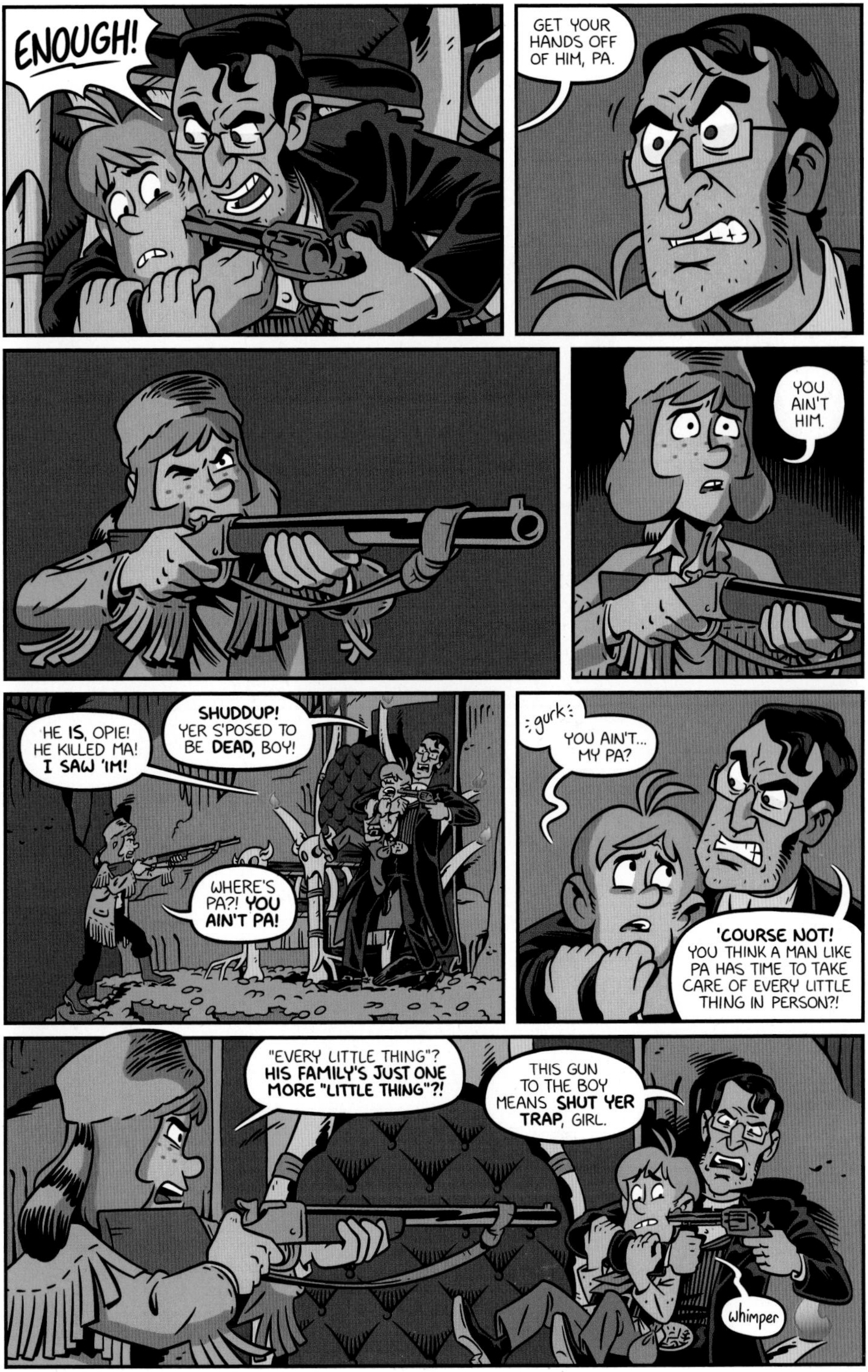
ENOUGH!
GET YOUR HANDS OFF OF HIM, PA.
YOU AIN'T HIM.
HE IS, OPIE! HE KILLED MA! I SAW 'IM!
SHUDDUP! YER S'POSED TO BE DEAD, BOY!
WHERE'S PA?! YOU AIN'T PA!
gurk
YOU AIN'T... MY PA?
'COURSE NOT! YOU THINK A MAN LIKE PA HAS TIME TO TAKE CARE OF EVERY LITTLE THING IN PERSON?!
"EVERY LITTLE THING"? HIS FAMILY'S JUST ONE MORE "LITTLE THING"?!
THIS GUN TO THE BOY MEANS SHUT YER TRAP, GIRL.
whimper

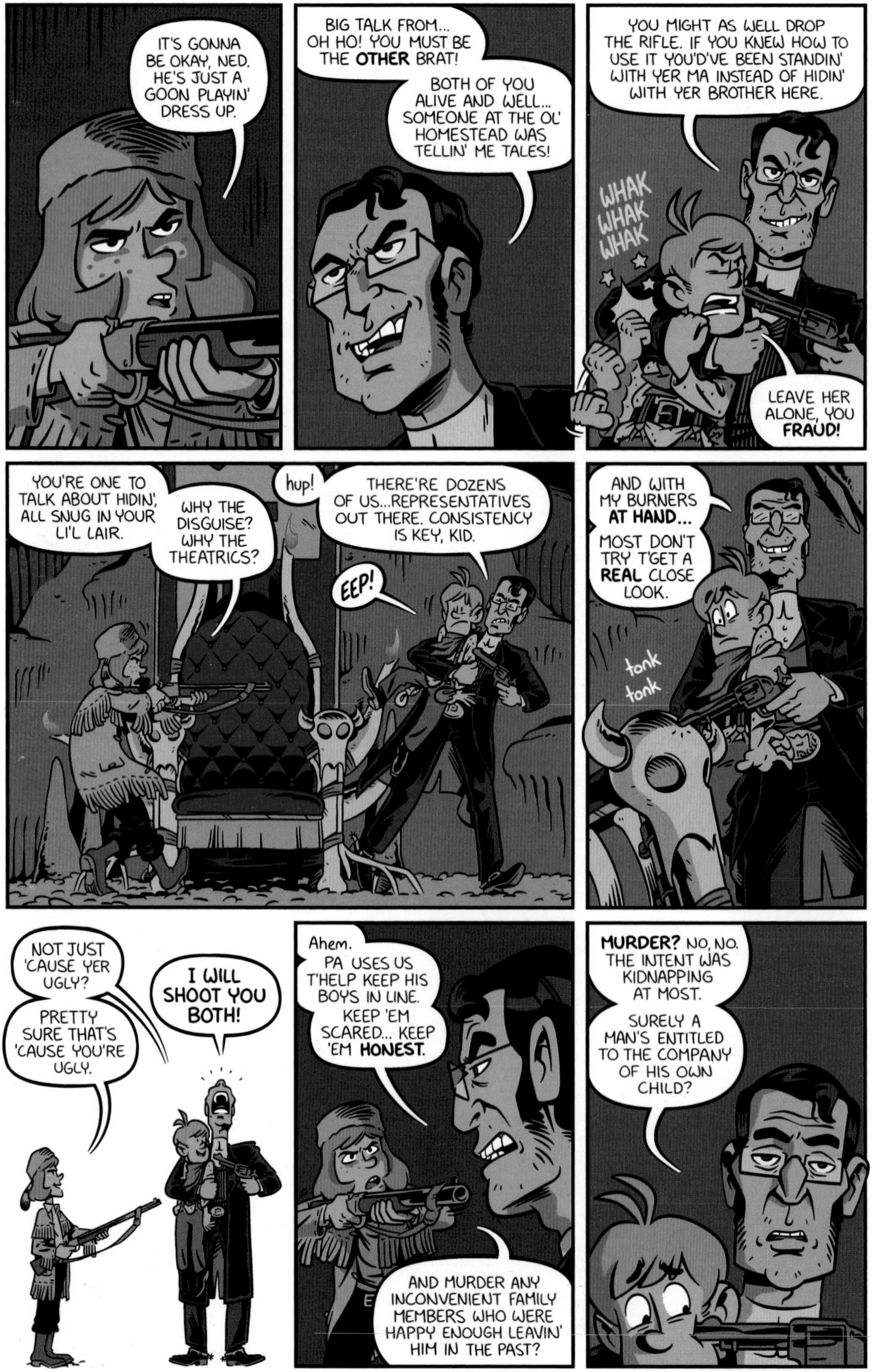

IT'S GONNA BE OKAY, NED. HE'S JUST A GOON PLAYIN' DRESS UP.
BIG TALK FROM... OH HO! YOU MUST BE THE **OTHER** BRAT!
BOTH OF YOU ALIVE AND WELL... SOMEONE AT THE OL' HOMESTEAD WAS TELLIN' ME TALES!
YOU MIGHT AS WELL DROP THE RIFLE. IF YOU KNEW HOW TO USE IT YOU'D'VE BEEN STANDIN' WITH YER MA INSTEAD OF HIDIN' WITH YER BROTHER HERE.
WHAK WHAK WHAK
LEAVE HER ALONE, YOU **FRAUD!**
YOU'RE ONE TO TALK ABOUT HIDIN', ALL SNUG IN YOUR LI'L LAIR.
WHY THE DISGUISE? WHY THE THEATRICS?
hup!
THERE'RE DOZENS OF US...REPRESENTATIVES OUT THERE. CONSISTENCY IS KEY, KID.
EEP!
AND WITH MY BURNERS **AT HAND...**
MOST DON'T TRY T'GET A **REAL** CLOSE LOOK.
tonk tonk
NOT JUST 'CAUSE YER UGLY?
PRETTY SURE THAT'S 'CAUSE YOU'RE UGLY.
I WILL SHOOT YOU BOTH!
Ahem.
PA USES US T'HELP KEEP HIS BOYS IN LINE.
KEEP 'EM SCARED... KEEP 'EM **HONEST**.
AND MURDER ANY INCONVENIENT FAMILY MEMBERS WHO WERE HAPPY ENOUGH LEAVIN' HIM IN THE PAST?
MURDER? NO, NO. THE INTENT WAS KIDNAPPING AT MOST.
SURELY A MAN'S ENTITLED TO THE COMPANY OF HIS OWN CHILD?

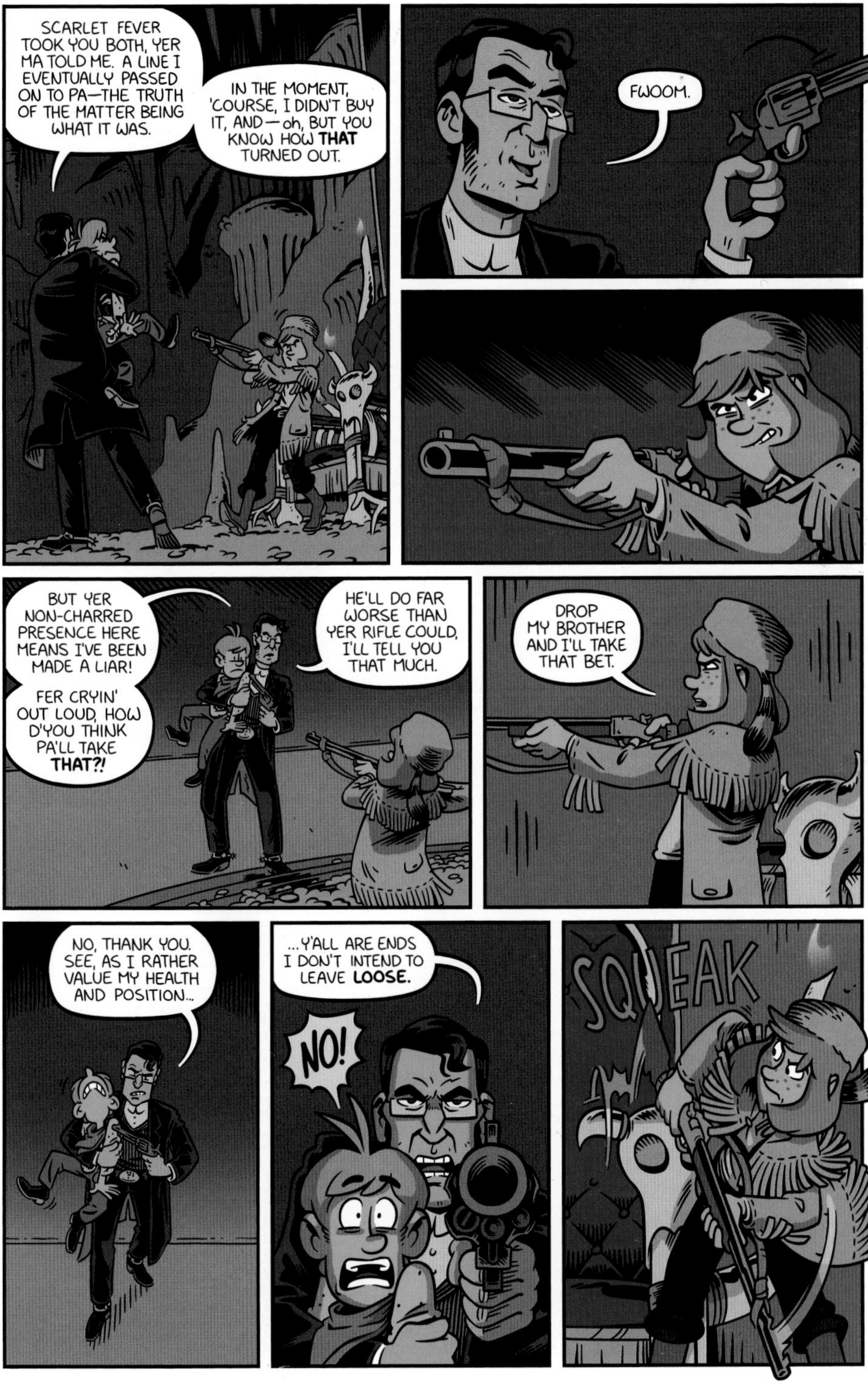
SCARLET FEVER TOOK YOU BOTH, YER MA TOLD ME. A LINE I EVENTUALLY PASSED ON TO PA—THE TRUTH OF THE MATTER BEING WHAT IT WAS.
IN THE MOMENT, 'COURSE, I DIDN'T BUY IT, AND—oh, BUT YOU KNOW HOW **THAT** TURNED OUT.
FWOOM.
BUT YER NON-CHARRED PRESENCE HERE MEANS I'VE BEEN MADE A LIAR!
FER CRYIN' OUT LOUD, HOW D'YOU THINK PA'LL TAKE **THAT?!**
HE'LL DO FAR WORSE THAN YER RIFLE COULD, I'LL TELL YOU THAT MUCH.
DROP MY BROTHER AND I'LL TAKE THAT BET.
NO, THANK YOU. SEE, AS I RATHER VALUE MY HEALTH AND POSITION...
...Y'ALL ARE ENDS I DON'T INTEND TO LEAVE **LOOSE.**
NO!
SQUEAK

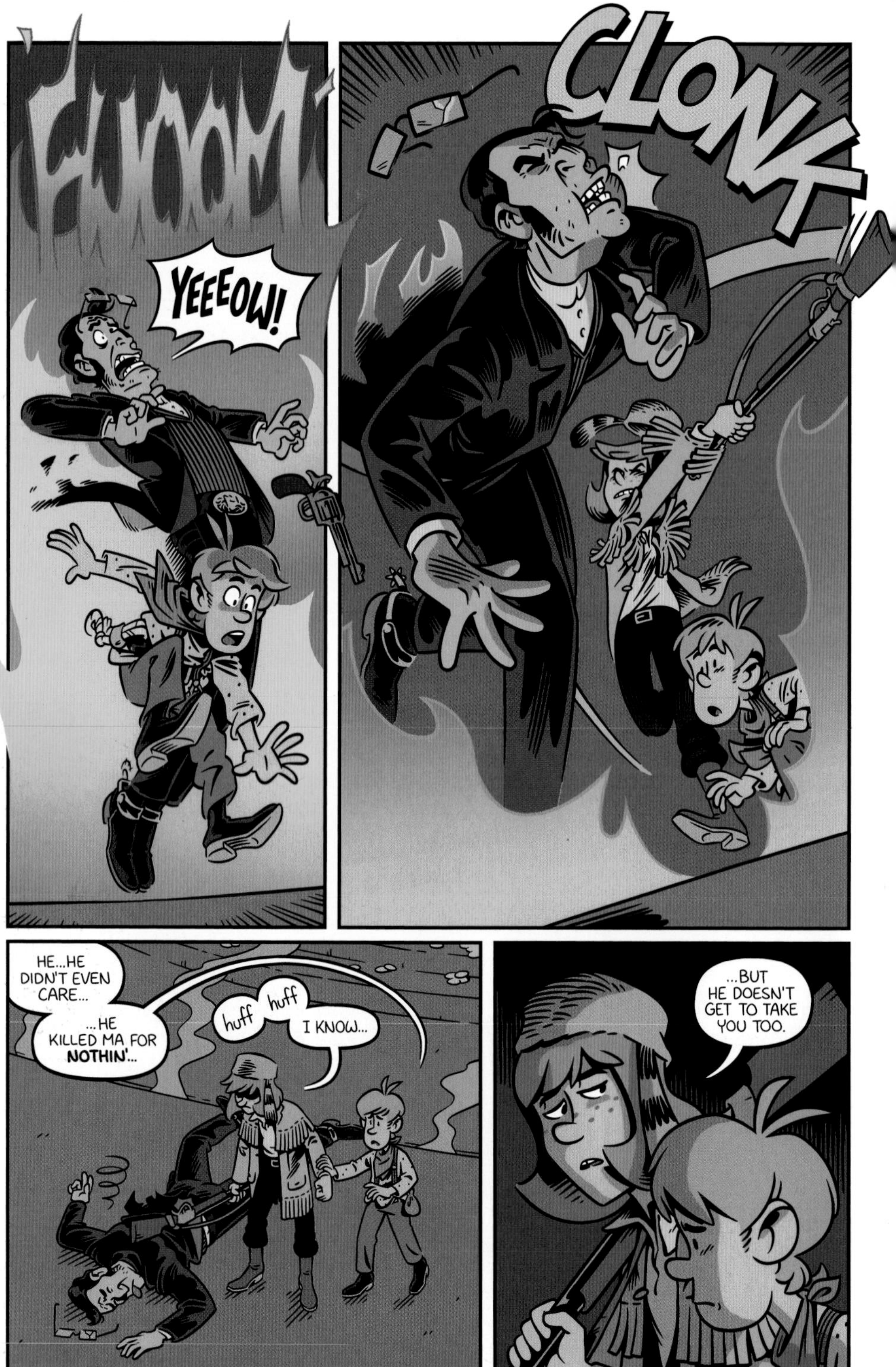
FWOOM
YEEEOW!
CLONK
HE...HE DIDN'T EVEN CARE...
...HE KILLED MA FOR **NOTHIN'**...
huff huff
I KNOW...
...BUT HE DOESN'T GET TO TAKE YOU TOO.

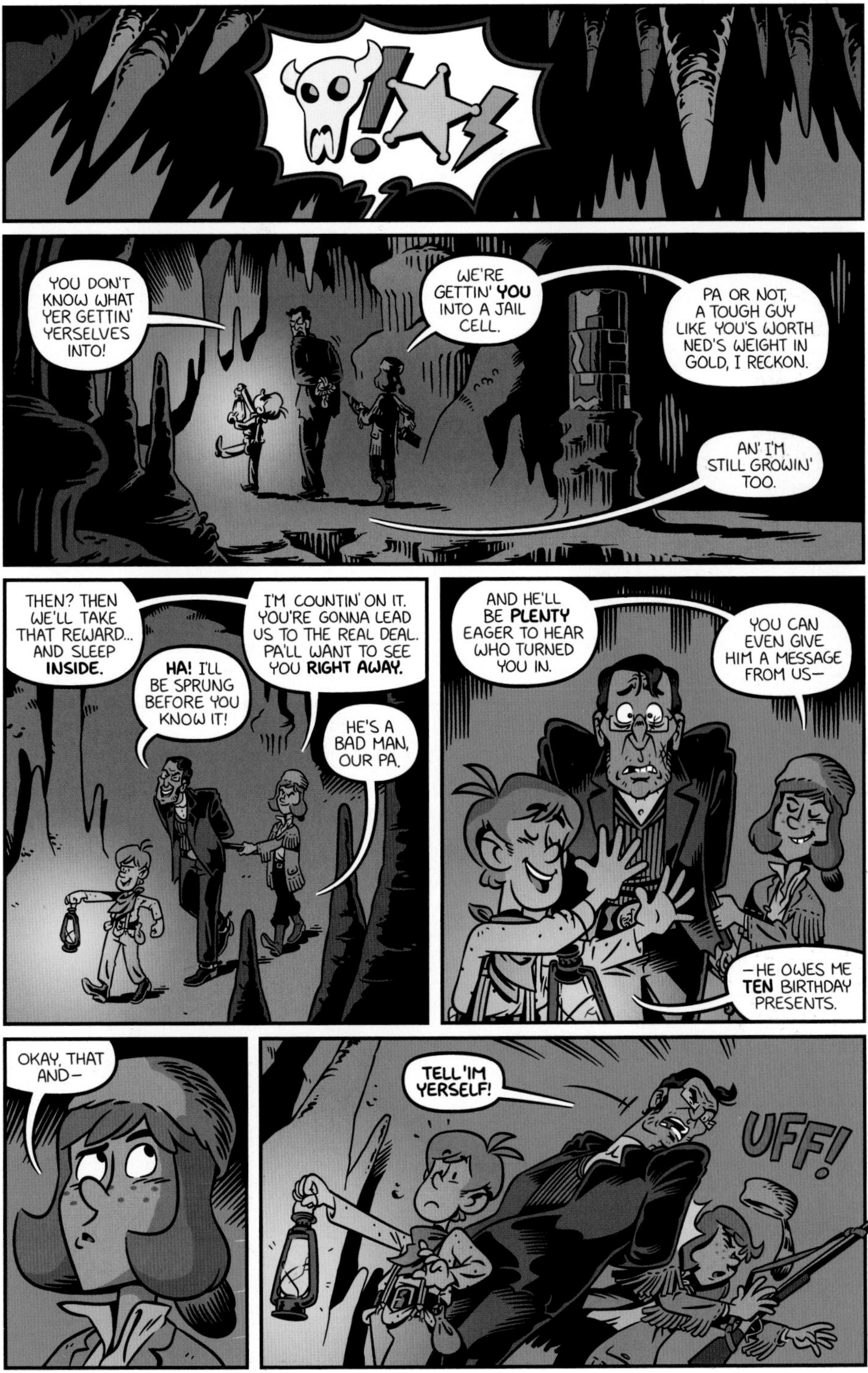
YOU DON'T KNOW WHAT YER GETTIN' YERSELVES INTO!
WE'RE GETTIN' **YOU** INTO A JAIL CELL.
PA OR NOT, A TOUGH GUY LIKE YOU'S WORTH NED'S WEIGHT IN GOLD, I RECKON.
AN' I'M STILL GROWIN' TOO.
THEN? THEN WE'LL TAKE THAT REWARD... AND SLEEP **INSIDE.**
HA! I'LL BE SPRUNG BEFORE YOU KNOW IT!
I'M COUNTIN' ON IT. YOU'RE GONNA LEAD US TO THE REAL DEAL. PA'LL WANT TO SEE YOU **RIGHT AWAY.**
HE'S A BAD MAN, OUR PA.
AND HE'LL BE **PLENTY** EAGER TO HEAR WHO TURNED YOU IN.
YOU CAN EVEN GIVE HIM A MESSAGE FROM US—
—HE OWES ME **TEN** BIRTHDAY PRESENTS.
OKAY, THAT AND—
TELL'IM YERSELF!
UFF!

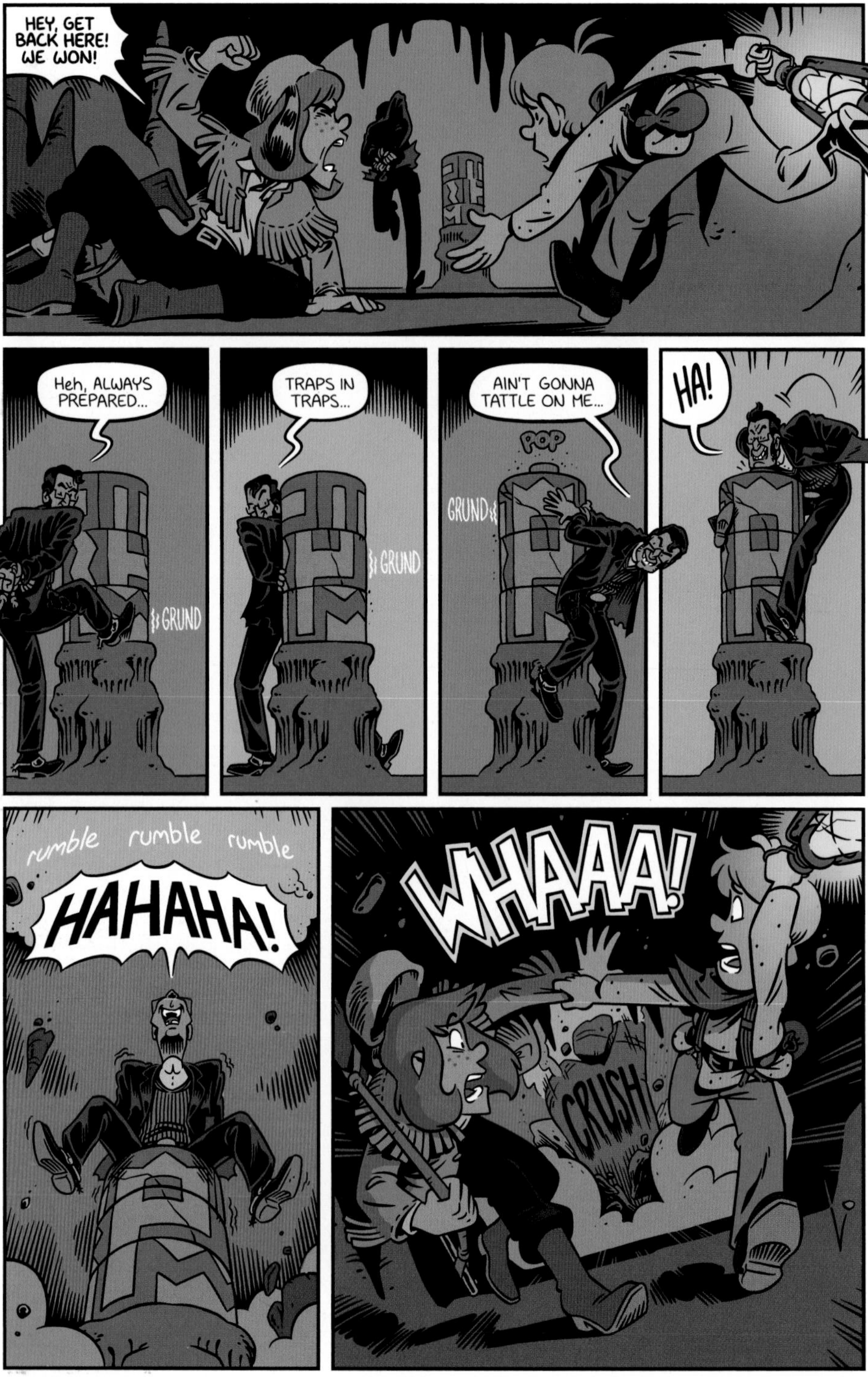

HEY, GET BACK HERE! WE WON!
Heh, ALWAYS PREPARED...
GRUND
TRAPS IN TRAPS...
GRUND
AIN'T GONNA TATTLE ON ME...
POP
GRUND
HA!
rumble rumble rumble
HAHAHA!
WHAAAA!
CRUSH

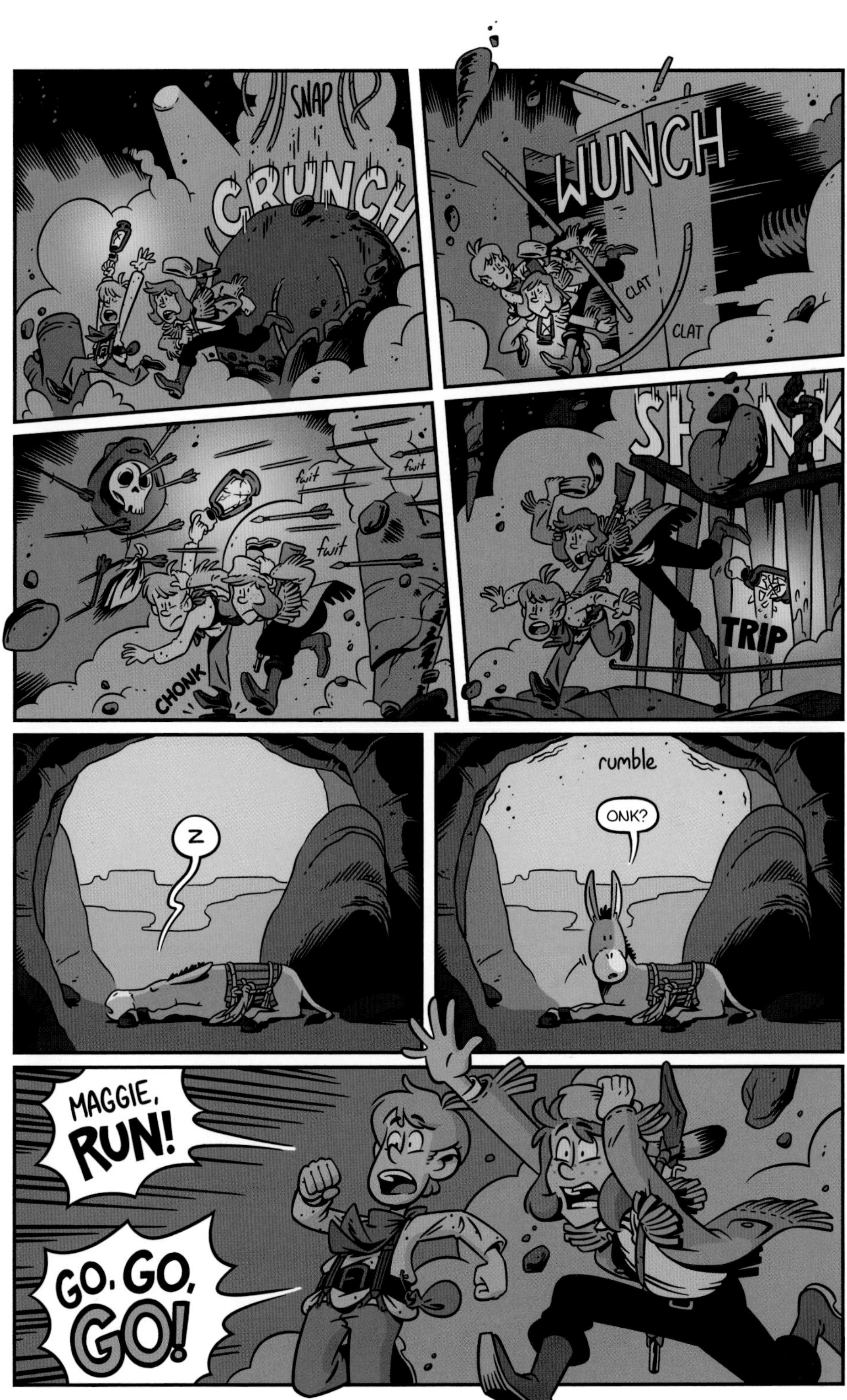
SNAP
CRUNCH
WUNCH
CLAT
CLAT
fwit
fwit
fwit
CHONK
TRIP
Z
rumble
ONK?
MAGGIE, RUN!
GO, GO, GO!

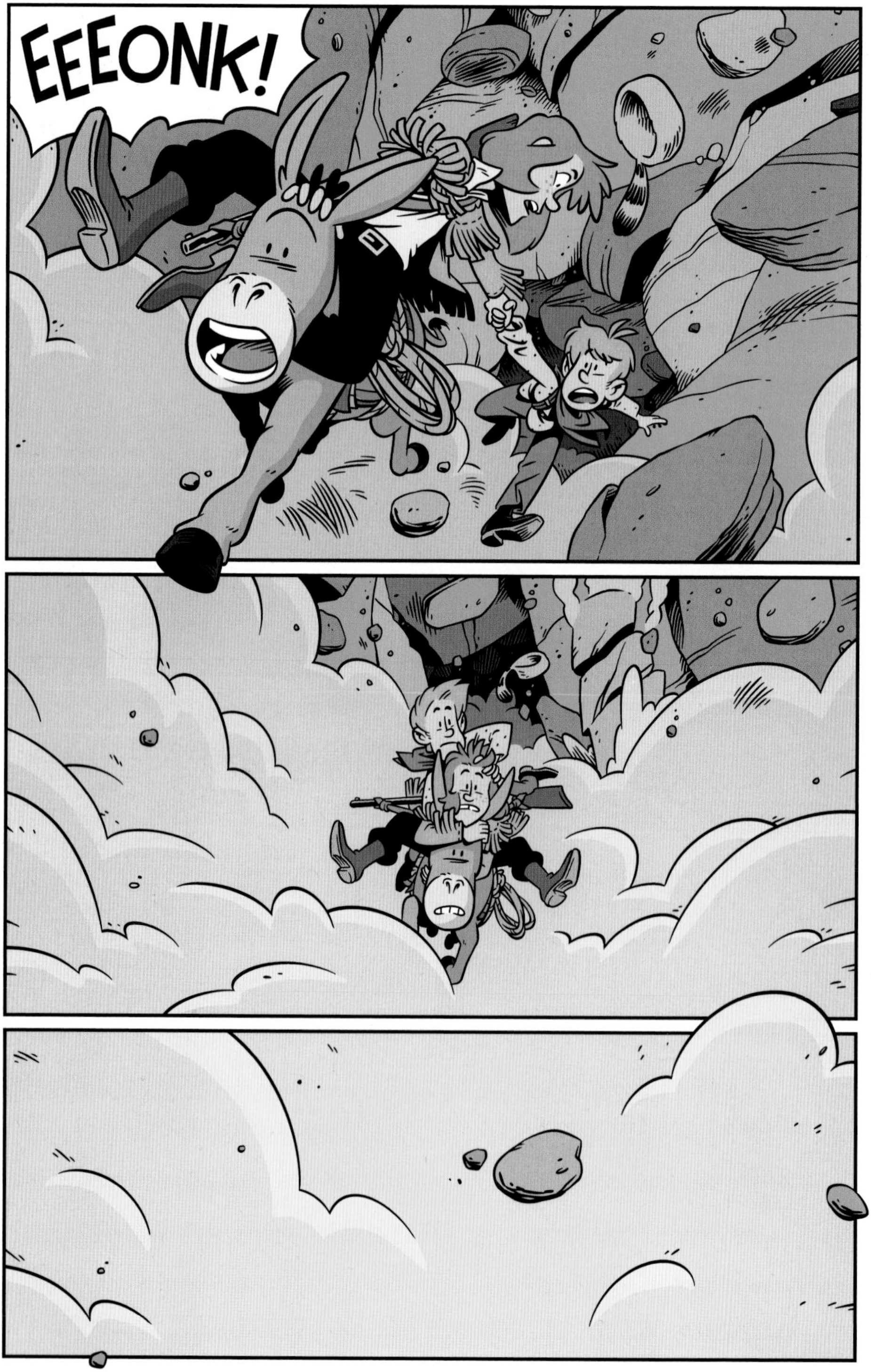
EEEONK!

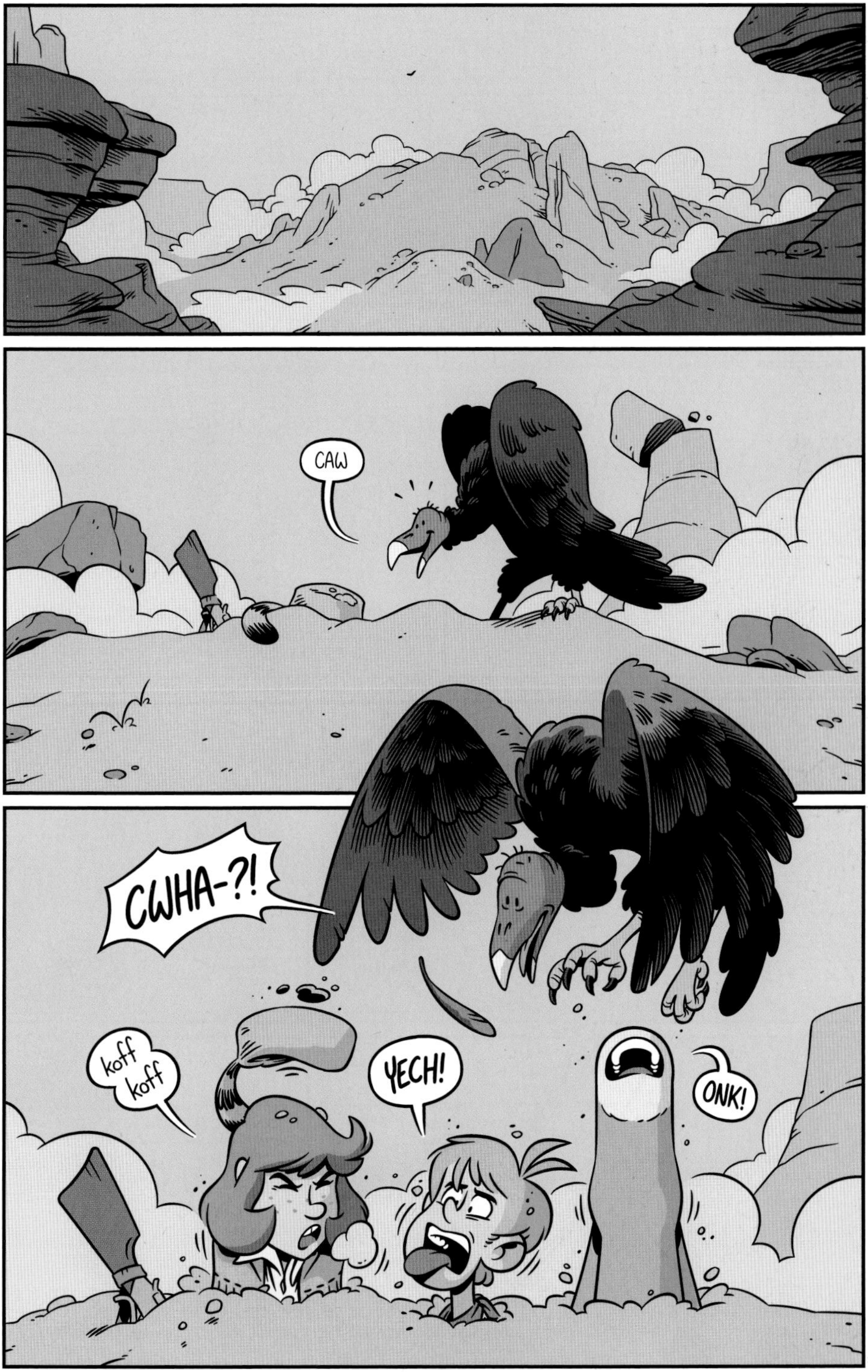
CAW
CWHA-?!
koff koff
YECH!
ONK!

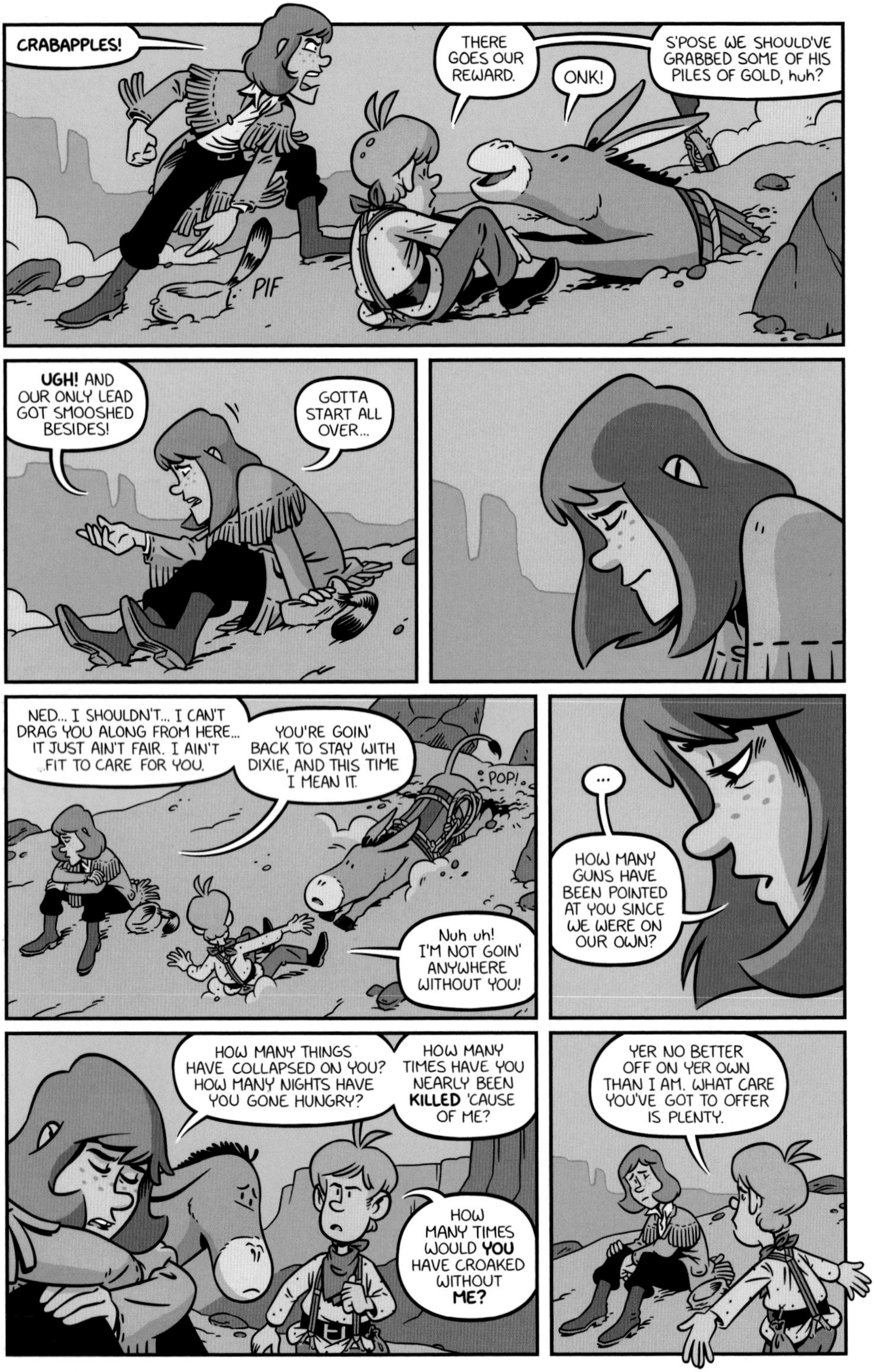
CRABAPPLES!
THERE GOES OUR REWARD.
ONK!
S'POSE WE SHOULD'VE GRABBED SOME OF HIS PILES OF GOLD, huh?
PIF
UGH! AND OUR ONLY LEAD GOT SMOOSHED BESIDES!
GOTTA START ALL OVER...
NED... I SHOULDN'T... I CAN'T DRAG YOU ALONG FROM HERE... IT JUST AIN'T FAIR. I AIN'T FIT TO CARE FOR YOU.
YOU'RE GOIN' BACK TO STAY WITH DIXIE, AND THIS TIME I MEAN IT.
POP!
Nuh uh! I'M NOT GOIN' ANYWHERE WITHOUT YOU!
...
HOW MANY GUNS HAVE BEEN POINTED AT YOU SINCE WE WERE ON OUR OWN?
HOW MANY THINGS HAVE COLLAPSED ON YOU? HOW MANY NIGHTS HAVE YOU GONE HUNGRY?
HOW MANY TIMES HAVE YOU NEARLY BEEN KILLED 'CAUSE OF ME?
HOW MANY TIMES WOULD YOU HAVE CROAKED WITHOUT ME?
YER NO BETTER OFF ON YER OWN THAN I AM. WHAT CARE YOU'VE GOT TO OFFER IS PLENTY.

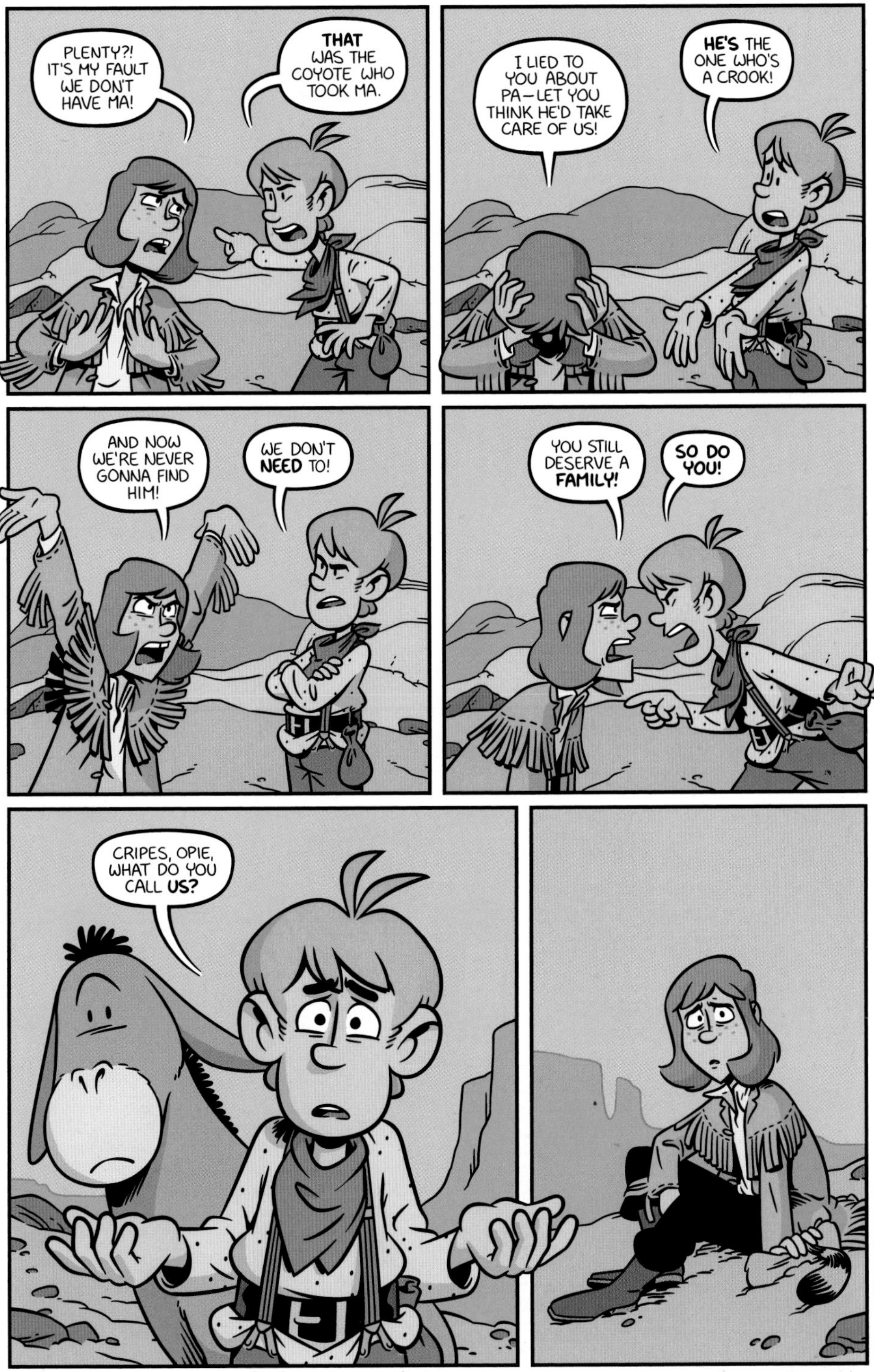
PLENTY?! IT'S MY FAULT WE DON'T HAVE MA!
THAT WAS THE COYOTE WHO TOOK MA.
I LIED TO YOU ABOUT PA—LET YOU THINK HE'D TAKE CARE OF US!
HE'S THE ONE WHO'S A CROOK!
AND NOW WE'RE NEVER GONNA FIND HIM!
WE DON'T NEED TO!
YOU STILL DESERVE A FAMILY!
SO DO YOU!
CRIPES, OPIE, WHAT DO YOU CALL US?

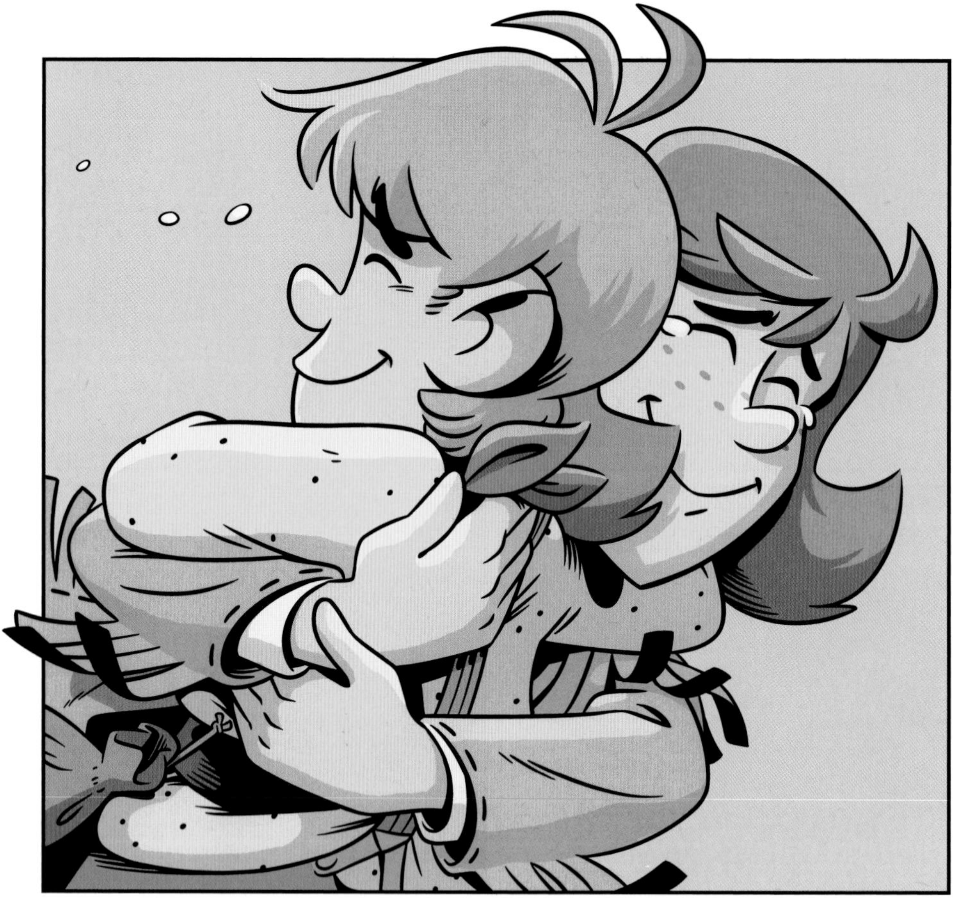

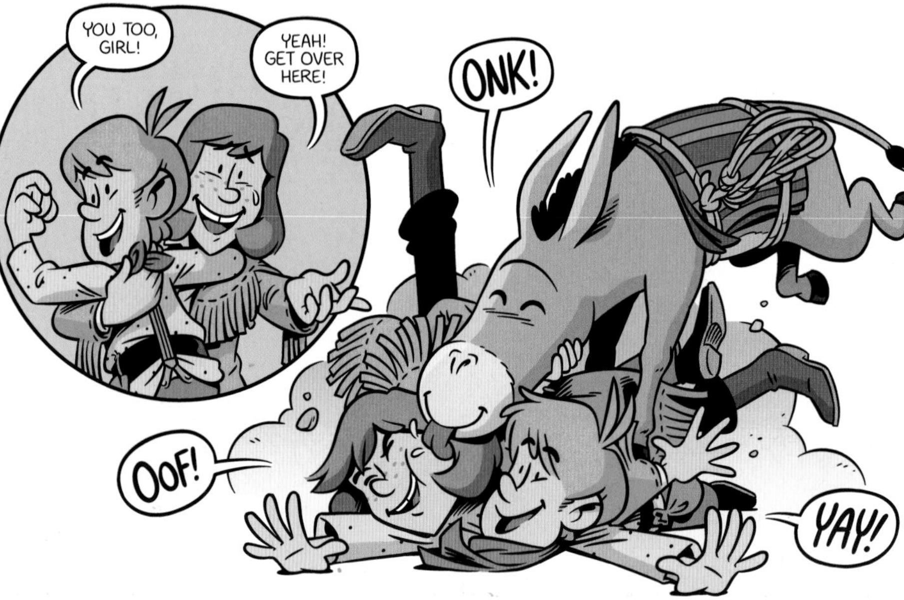

YOU TOO, GIRL!
YEAH! GET OVER HERE!
ONK!
OOF!
YAY!

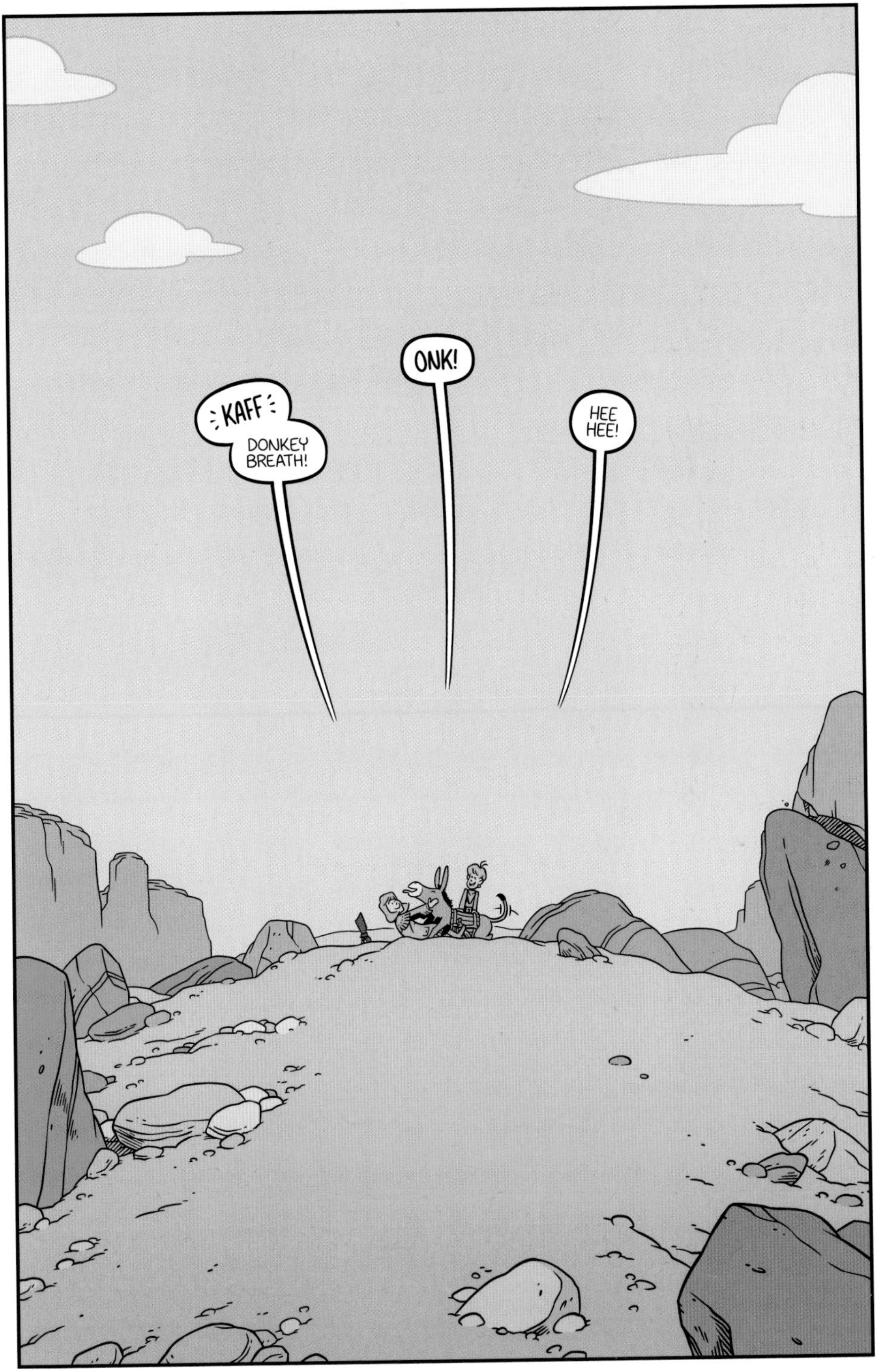
KAFF
DONKEY BREATH!
ONK!
HEE HEE!

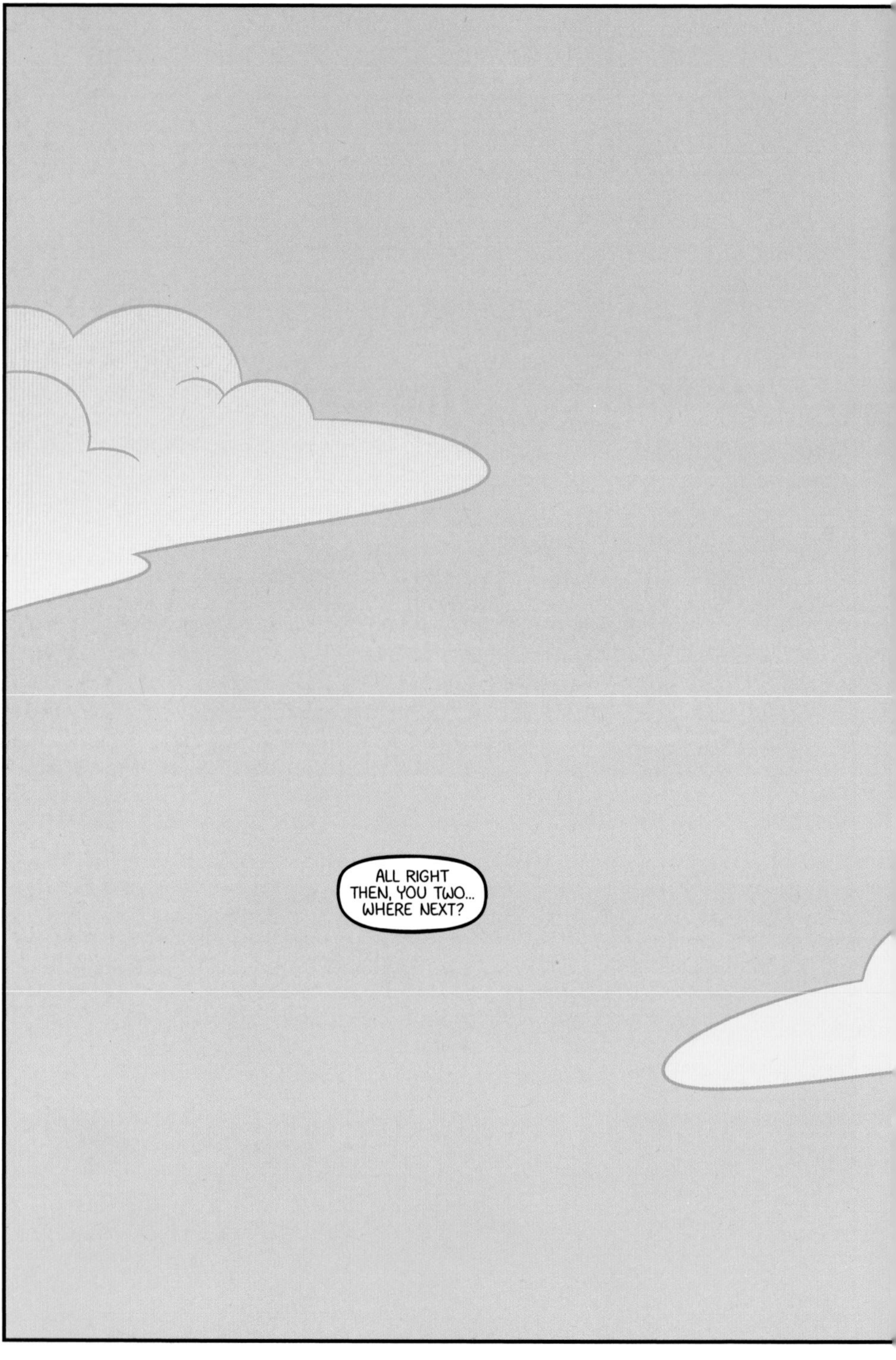
ALL RIGHT THEN, YOU TWO... WHERE NEXT?

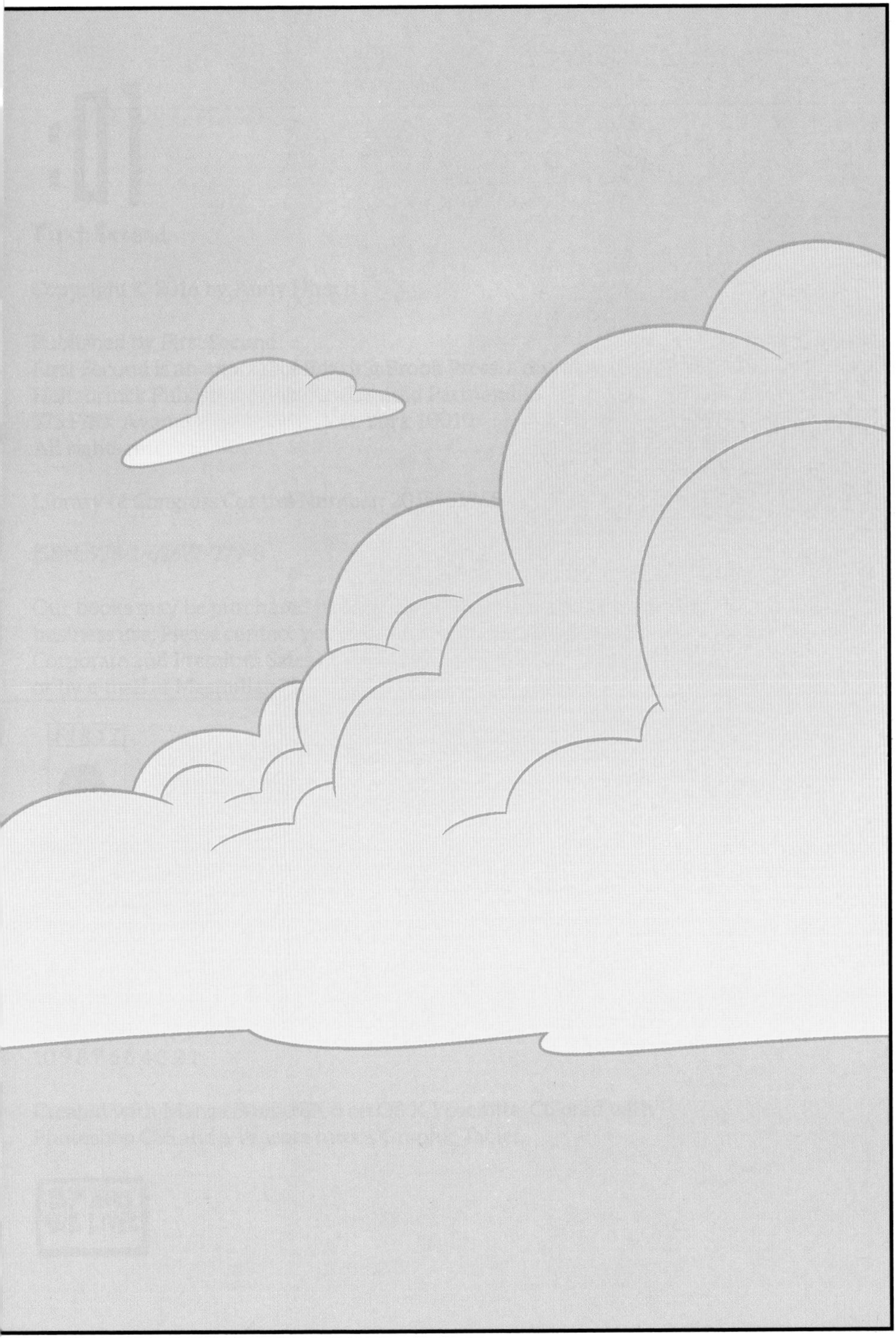